MW01129431

Tropical Quests

A Key West Novel

Wesley Sizemore

TO:

Angela and Wayson who believed in it;
In memory of Thomas, Charles and Diana who lived it;
& to Jason, my son by choice

That's all that life has to give in the way of perfection . . . the warm and complete understanding of two or three in a close-walled room with the windows blind to the world.

Tennessee Williams

One

Shortly after I turned thirty, I moved to a tiny tropical island far out to sea.

It began with a phone call one December morning in Toronto. It was Sunday and I had been sleeping in. When I awoke, I had to gyroscope to remember I was in Toronto now, not Paris, so no bakery downstairs with hot croissants or architecturally confused Ste. Eustache across the way.

Outside sound, muffled, announced snow again.

I crawled out of bed, made my trip to the bathroom, then made coffee. Wrapped in two layers of clothing, I walked out on the balcony and sat, watching snow suck all light and sound away, piling itself up on the black tracery of trees dead for another four months.

Years before, after my first refugee arrival in Toronto, I had visited an exhibition on the top floor of its tallest office building: soapstone and ivory Eskimo sculptures mixed with geological history. In the last glacial age, ten thousand years previous, an exhibit informed me, an ice sheet nearly three thousand feet high had crushed the earth where I now stood, and the earth even today was slowly springing back from that weight. I had stepped back in shock, trying to imagine standing at the edge of that whiteness, looking up at a tongue of ice a half-mile higher than the building I was in. The exhibit made me think the earth had memory, and we humans did not belong on this spot. The ice wanted the land back, the carpet of buildings below me as temporary as a picnic blanket.

Now I drank my coffee and watched the snow and descended into unwelcome self-pity as it fell heavier and faster.

In less than twenty-four hours, I would get up while it was still dark, walk through frozen streets to a subway station, ride for fifty-five minutes in a metal tube with fluorescent lighting to get to the community college where I taught mostly bored and boring middle class students, with fellow teachers who included some of the most neurotic people I had ever met. It was a way of life more alien to my needs, even, than working for the French oil company had been, and I had done this to myself.

All my experience and all my education up to that point, and a life spent in self-examination, had led me to the perfect, enlightened vision of: I didn't exactly know yet, except that I wanted no ordinary life—no children, no barbecues in suburbia, no twenty or thirty years at any job to get the pension. I wanted as much as possible . . .What? Something. A harmonic resonance of thought and action? Vision of what *is* into which I subsumed my somehow-enlightened self?

I had studied intensely for three years with hours of mandatory silence every week in a seminary, had seen the tail-end of the Summer of Love in San Francisco, chosen exile over blind obedience during the war in Vietnam, and had lived in and been completely transformed by three years in Paris. The experiences had changed me, but I had yet to find a place and vocation that said, "This is home;" and had only once found a partner who seemed like a soul mate. She had left me without explanation and married someone else.

The snow fell heavier and heavier.

Encapsulated in my self-pity was the strong and irrational expectation that life owed me more than this. To pay for my education I'd worked twenty and, once, thirty hours a week for nine years, carrying full course loads, and had come out of it without a burning desire to make money and claw further up the economic ladder. I wanted "it" whatever "it" was. I wanted victory, somehow a confirmation that intellectual honesty and effort earned reward, even if only extended times of perfect clarity. I had had a few, too short—unsolicited and unexpected, like Catholic grace—but so powerful when they happened that I could not give up hope that there was a place or vocation that would bathe me in the constant warmth of . . . what?

Then the phone rang. Answer/don't answer. I walked inside. It was Vera, asking me to dinner.

Vera taught at a different community college, and we'd met at the orientation week all new teachers had been subjected to. At the last of several stultifying seminars, the man in charge of our orientation had passed out napkins, twigs, paper clips, and twine to each table of four, telling us to be as creative as possible with what we could jointly make of it.

The table next to mine constructed a trireme. My table, as fed up as I, had me stand on the table and do a pretend hanging from the frame of the acoustical tiles. The instructor had not been amused nor had most of the other teachers-to-be, for whom these jobs meant security and upward mobility. I caught a hot smile from one of my tablemates, Vera, and we started an affair that night. She was second-generation Ukrainian, with model-beautiful cheekbones and skin, and a lovely body. Only a somewhat too prominent nose and small-ish breasts kept her from being a world-class beauty.

I had caught her on the rebound from a bad affair, and she had caught me on the rebound from Paris. We enjoyed each other's company, and the sex was good, but those other stories going on in our lives kept the relationship light.

"It's snowing," I complained when I answered the phone.

"I know, John, and I know how much you hate it. I have the car. Let's go to Florida over Christmas break. You still have your false ID, don't you?"

It was snowing again the night we left. I drove from Toronto to within a few miles of the border and pulled into a gas station to use the bathroom. When I came back out, Vera looked at me and asked if I was OK.

"I had to throw up, but, yeah, I'm OK."

"Are you sick?" she asked, concerned.

"No, it's my weird stomach. Bad fear or violent emotion and I'm off to the toilet. Once I throw up, I'm alright. I know, I know, it's strange. I used to have to puke before every jump when I was skydiving."

"Look, we don't have to do this. We can just turn around and drive back."

"No, I'll be alright once we cross the border. You should drive, though, because the agent will be on the driver's side of the car and might pick up on my nervousness. Make a joke when he asks you the purpose of the visit. Say something like 'going to Florida to thaw my ass out.' They don't expect someone with something to hide to make jokes."

I had crossed many times, sending my draft board and the FBI postcards daring them to catch me. Their reaction was not pretty, and I was nervous.

We reached the border, and my papers identifying me as a French Canadian from Sudbury, Ontario, worked again. The immigration agent waved us through the crossing, and I was back in the U.S. of A., my treacherous motherland. Vera laughed, enjoying my outlaw status as an exciting adventure. I was on full alert.

The next two days were tedious as we drove long hours on mostly boring highways. It did give us time to learn more of each other's histories, and winter's slow release of the land was a pleasure. As a second-generation immigrant and only child, Vera was dealing with the conflicting cultural expectations of traditional parents and her new, more liberal, home. I sensed that a part of her wanted to rebel, but she was having a hard time breaking away from parents who wanted her to behave in expected ways: the stereotypical and difficult immigrant voyage. This trip—unmarried woman traveling with a man—kicked sand in her parents' eyes, and she had mixed feelings about it.

She kept asking, in different ways, why I'd chosen to leave Paris, which obviously seemed to her a life in paradise. I'd already told her about my job and the benefits I'd had.

"If I could have that instead of teaching at a community college, I'd be there, I think."

"Vera, I did love it. But I can't spend my life working for a corporation. And you have to understand how and where I lived. I was right across the street from the central market. I was two blocks from the Louvre. My personal café was the one the prostitutes who serviced the market workers hung out in. I went there because it had heating and my apartment didn't, and it had the best and cheapest onion soup and *steack-frites*. The prostitutes got used to me being there, preparing lessons or writing in my journal, and started calling me Monsieur le Professeur. They'd ask me to translate things for them, letters sometimes, but usually sex stuff related to their work. I'd translate for them, and they'd thank me and sometimes offer me a freebie, but I told them I was engaged and faithful to my fiancée, and they'd get all soft and sit down and tell me their life stories, always sad. It was real in a way that nothing in my life had been before. I was living Balzac and Zola, not just reading them.

"Then the French government decided to tear it all down and move the market to Rungis in the suburbs to get the traffic out of Paris and, suddenly, the heart of a whole city was being ripped out. My apartment building was going to be torn down along with the market. I realized I'd been privileged to see the tail end of Paris as more of a nineteenth-century city, and it was being demolished right in front of me, right outside my door, and I was next. I didn't see the next step there for me as an improvement in my life, and I sure as hell didn't want to spend the rest of my life teaching Frenchmen how to count barrels of oil in English or how to tell a bunch of Texans where to spud in the next drill stem."

She was quiet for a while, then: "OK, I can understand that. I think you're a little spoiled, maybe, but why did you go back to Toronto? You hate it there."

That pissed me off. "Vera, don't ever, ever call me spoiled. We'd be enemies. To this day, I don't know anyone who worked as many hours a week to put himself through college, inspecting Coke bottles, mopping dorm floors, flipping burgers, washing UPS trucks—whatever it took. Because my dad was in the Navy, we moved every two years, and I didn't get any scholarships. All the awards were sewn up by the time we moved into a new town my senior year of high school. But I did it anyway, working ungodly numbers of hours a week, got three degrees, and when I went to Paris I had no job and four hundred dollars to my name. I lived in a tiny apartment with no heat, washed my clothes in my kitchen sink and dried them on lines above my bed. My toilet was upstairs and down a hall. I lived in a kind of poverty no Canadian is used to. I've never understood how people don't understand what it's like to start out with nothing, and when

I say nothing, I mean *nothing*. My dad took me aside two months before my high school graduation and told me he couldn't help me at all, not a penny. So from seventeen on, I've completely supported myself; no little checks or loans from mom and dad, ever.

"Please," I repeated, "you can call me arrogant, an asshole, or whatever, but *never* call me spoiled."

She was taken aback by my anger and apologized. "I didn't know all that," she said. She was quiet for a minute as we drove through the night. "But I don't understand why you went back to Toronto if it makes you unhappy."

"I thought I'd come back and get my Ph.D., then teach at the university level. I thought I'd enjoy teaching something I love, French literature, at that level. But Canada changed while I was in Paris, you know that. They freaked out when they realized how many Americans were on university faculties in their own country, so there's no chance for me to do that now."

"John . . . sorry, Jacques," and she laughed when she corrected herself, "you have to understand our perspective on it. All those Yanks with Ph.D.'s who couldn't get jobs in the States were flooding up north."

"Vera, I understand completely. If I were Canadian, I'd feel the same way. But it's left me hanging out there, screwed. Can't go back to Paris because they've changed the laws for work cards. Can't come back here because the bastards want to put me in jail, even though now everyone knows the war was wrong and stupid, and we protesters were right. What the hell am I going to do? If I thought I had to spend the next twenty years of my life teaching at that community college, I swear, I'll drink myself to death. I'll be the drunk at parties telling everyone for the tenth time that I lived in Paris once, like those sad high school athletes in their sixties whose peak life experience was that championship game their senior year. I won't let that happen to me."

There was a sudden silence in the car as I realized I'd just misspoken. The woman next to me was planning just that, to spend the next twenty years teaching at a community college. For her, this was the pot of gold at the end of the rainbow, even if she wasn't crazy about it. The rest of the night we made small talk.

We hit the Florida border on a perfect sunshiny day and stopped at the welcome center for free orange juice and tourist brochures. Ft. Lauderdale, we decided.

We arrived as the sun was setting, found a motel, showered, and found an open-air restaurant on the beach with the ocean's sound the only music. The setting and warm air seduced us both, seduced us into being more romantic than we usually were during the sex.

Seeing a woman you're having a casual affair with once or twice a week is very different from spending all day every day together. The first time we'd slept together after the seminar, she'd been as casual as I felt about the sex, acting as if she didn't expect or care if it ever became more than that. Soon into this trip to Florida, I started getting subtle hints that she wanted more, and that the original casualness had been an act or an action without thought.

Ft. Lauderdale, in spite of the great beaches, was boring, white-bread America translated to Florida. The waiter we became friendly with at the ocean-side restaurant told us we should drive down to Key West. "You're not gonna believe the views from the bridges, and Key West is something else, man," he said, though he couldn't describe what the "something else" was. "You just gotta see it for yourselves."

We took the bait and headed south. When we hit the first bridges, our jaws dropped. We were hop-scotching across the ocean . . . the ocean, for god's sake . . . in a car, bridge by bridge, one, seven miles long—all built originally for trains, we read, by Flagler, John D. Rockefeller's partner in Standard Oil. The water in every color of blue, green, and in-between wrote a chapter in planetary beauty. By the time we hit the last island in the chain, Key West, we were tired and eye-candied high.

The entrance to the town was ugly, though, and we wondered if we'd made a mistake driving four hours to now drive past the anywhere-in-America strip malls. Then the four-lane road narrowed to two, and anywhere architecture gave way to beautiful, weathered, wooden houses with over-hanging trees. We drove into a town small enough to remind me of the ones that came with toy trains.

Downtown, we stopped at a tall building, the La Concha Hotel, but found that it had been closed for decades, so we drove on down the street and booked a room in the Southern Cross Hotel. The desk clerk was an obviously stoned drag queen only partway out of drag. The clock behind the check-in desk was an hour off from the time I thought it was, and I asked about it.

"Oh, honey, that thing's still on daylight savings time, and I just can't be bothered to change it. Subtract an hour, honey, and you got it," she said and laughed.

A bare bulb in the ceiling provided the light in our room, and it took a long, very long, time for the toilet to refill after a flush. Water pressure in the shower was minimal. This was Third World stuff I remembered from my childhood in Panama and Trinidad. Vera sniffed disapproval.

It was late afternoon when we walked outside after settling in, and the air was thick, textured and fragrant. People were wearing minimum clothing and smiling. Cuban salsa music came from a bar near the hotel.

At the suggestion of the hotel clerk, we walked a few blocks to Mallory Square for sunset. Thirty or so people were spread around the dock, most with drinks in hand, and there was a small group with a portable grill at one end who seemed to be having more fun than the rest, so I guided us in that direction. As we got closer, it became obvious they were gay men and, as we got even closer, I recognized one.

"That's Tennessee Williams," I told Vera. At that she stopped walking.

"We can't just barge in on them."

"Vera, come on now, this isn't Canada. Loosen up. Besides, I've already met Tennessee. Let's see if he remembers me."

I pulled her along and went up to the five men and introduced ourselves. They were polite, but a little wary.

"Mr. Williams, I'm sure you don't remember me, but you chased me up a tree once at Edward Albee's. A friend of mine from the University of Toronto, who's Albee's secretary now, had invited me. After dinner, you, Edward, and Howard Moss took turns tapping out poetic meters on the table after dinner and had us guess which one it was."

Tennessee looked at me. "Howard always won, didn't he?"

"He did that night, for sure. You got the anapest. I got the alexandrine . . . French Lit. major. After dinner, we walked outside and you chased me around, and I climbed a tree."

"Tom!" the other men said in pretend shock. (Tennessee's friends called him Tom; I remembered that from the dinner party.)

"Well, young man, I vaguely remember the chase but not the outcome. Was I successful?"

"Well, I was a little nervous because I didn't know how well you could climb, but then I started talking literature and that cooled your ardor."

"That would do it," he said, and they all laughed and gave Vera and me a drink (Meyer's rum and orange juice, first time for me.)

The man at the grill (Rex, a Conch Tour Train driver, we learned) apologized for not having enough to feed Vera and me, but by then all attention focused on our very own star, the huge, orange-red sun, lowering itself through a thin layer of clouds to touch the surface of the ocean just as a boat under full sail slid past to silhouette itself; then the star became a half-circle, a flattened reflection of itself on the water, and slid under.

At the moment of disappearance, everyone on the dock began applauding. Tennessee clapped louder and longer than anyone and began yelling: "Author, author."

"Thank you for the drinks, gentlemen," I said. "We'll leave you to your dinner."

"You're welcome," Rex answered, "and if you two beauties ever decide to have kids, can I have pick of the litter?" Everyone laughed again. Vera and I headed back to Duval Street.

On the way back up the street, while I was reveling at the surprise of meeting Tennessee again and the beauty of the sunset, Vera was complaining about how uncomfortable she'd felt.

"Vera, that's crazy, I'm sorry. You just met one of the world's great writers, and you're complaining that you didn't feel comfortable because he's queer/gay/whatever. What cave does that thinking come out of?"

She jerked her hand out of mine.

"Seriously, listen to me. You're teaching English to college kids. That man has written words in English that will last as long as the language itself. Remember 'I have always depended on the kindness of strangers' from *Streetcar*? Now you can tell your students you met the man who wrote them."

She didn't answer, and I gave off on the attack, remembering myself when the larger world I'd wanted yet feared began revealing itself. Molting is painful, old skin peeling off, nerves still attached, to make room for the new, larger self.

The next few days were uncomfortable. I was drawn more and more to the obvious quirkiness of the island and its inhabitants, and that soft, warm, perfumed air, and Vera retreated further into herself, repelled by most of the things that attracted me. How could you not like seeing a man walking down the street with an iguana on his shoulder, followed by two obvious queens holding hands and wearing identical T-shirts that said "AVENGE OSCAR WILDE"? And in what other small town in the country would the marquee of a movie theater on the main street downtown advertise in large letters the showing of *Deep Throat*?

The following morning, Vera and I went to a laundromat for coffee, directed by the morning hotel clerk, a stoned, tattooed young Frenchman I swapped a few sentences with. I bought the local paper and read that, in broad daylight and on the main street, a man wearing coconut shells for a bra and a red thong and hula skirt had attacked a man wearing a shark costume. "MAN BITES SHARK" was the headline.

"Vera, read this," I said and gave her the paper, amused. After three years of working for a corporation in Paris, then the community college, I appreciated uncorseted behavior.

"These people are weird," she said and handed the paper back.

That was the way the rest of our stay went. In retrospect, I know I could have been nicer. Here was a woman one generation away from peasant poverty and I expected her to appreciate people who were ignoring the economic possibilities in the world's biggest capitalist society. Yet I was only one generation away from peasant poverty myself, and I was delighted by what I was seeing.

As we explored the town on our rented bikes, I kept pointing out things: "Have you noticed that most of the fences that go to the corners of intersections have been knocked down by cars? These people don't 'get' right angles."

In the cemetery, where many of the interments were above ground, one of the gravestones was inscribed: "I TOLD YOU I WAS SICK." In a different section, a poignant statue of a swabby holding an upraised oar stood guard over the grave of sailors killed in the explosion of the *U.S.S. Maine*.

The house on the lane just across the street had a fence, maybe three feet high, made out of wine and liquor bottles, mortared together, Gaudí-like, with what looked like the wet-dripped sand children make sand castles out of.

"This whole place is weird," was Vera's response to each thing I pointed out that made me realize the inhabitants of the island were not like those anywhere else I'd been.

I went back our last night to watch the sunset. Vera begged off. A small group of people stood watching this unbelievable spectacle, our star sinking into the ocean, a slow disappearance that made you, a twentieth-century intelligence, understand all the human fear gone before you at the light disappearing. And it was *beautiful*. All the trite sunset paintings in the world could not detract from the power of seeing it here, unclouded and close. A bearded, long-haired man on the pier passed around a joint and turned on a tape player of—I couldn't believe it—the sound track from my favorite bad movie: Antonioni's *Zabriskie Point*, with some of the Dead's and Pink Floyd's best music.

Then when the last sliver of sun had sunk into the sea, everyone applauded, like on our first night. This was nothing I had ever seen or imagined, but seeing, knew was sweeter than any daily ritual I knew of anywhere else. In my apartment in Toronto, I had one of the prints run off from the original copperplates of an Edward Curtis photograph: an American Indian offering corn to the setting sun. After eight years of life under the occluded skies of Paris and Toronto, I understood saying goodbye to the sun and making offerings to get it back.

The next morning, our last in Key West, Vera and I walked across the street to Shorty's Diner, a hole-in-the-wall restaurant with a tall horseshoe-shaped counter with bar stools around. Vera was paying attention to her food when I looked out the windows and saw a man in his Jockey shorts run past on the sidewalk; he was being pursued by a naked woman with a knife. Agitated, I looked around at the other customers and saw that three other men had seen it, too. Should I/ we say/do anything? I looked at one of the men across the horseshoe, and he caught my anxiety.

He laughed. "Don't worry, son. That's just Marion Stevens off her lithium again chasing her husband. She won't hurt him. Give 'em a few minutes and they'll walk back together. That's her gallery next door, the one with the Haitian art. She always gets a little nutsy near a full moon." The other diners laughed recognition and went back to their food and newspapers.

Vera asked me what was going on, and I told her. She put her mouth close to my ear: "I want out of here now."

I paid, and as we climbed off our stools, the couple walked past arm in arm on the sidewalk outside. Some of the diners laughed, but some started yelling and applauding, and the woman smiled and gave us a wave as regal as Elizabeth's.

The car packed and the bill paid, we drove out of downtown. When we hit the bridge between Key West and the next island, headed back to the mainland, I looked back and knew two things with certainty: that there was no future to John and Vera, and that I had found my next place.

Back in Toronto, the break-up with Vera had all the usual elements of break-up ugliness in spite of both of us knowing we didn't make a couple. She said hurtful things to me, but I didn't retaliate because I knew I deserved much of it, and I knew she was hurt as much by my inaccessibility as by the break-up. Only one wildly eccentric woman had ever slipped past all the barriers guarding my heart. It ended one night with Vera screaming at me that I was cold and heartless, then begging me to make love "one last time." We did, but I was not proud of myself, thrusting, emotionless, as she wept and clawed, then yelled at me to get out. I was so lost and unhappy with my own life that I couldn't even feel guilt at the pain I'd caused.

Going back to work in Toronto was hell. I carried in me now the warm vision of a place I thought I might belong to, but I wasn't there. The first two weeks back reinforced that I had to get out. First, one of my female colleagues had found a note from one of her students that said he wanted to beat her up, bend her over and fuck her in the ass till she bled. Shaken, she went to the school's counselor, an ex-priest who forced his remedial students to read Dostoyevsky to make himself feel superior and them worthless. His reaction to the note: "Rachel, why can't you accept this student's love for you?"

Then another colleague, a woman in charge of both ecological and women's studies, came to work one morning wearing a coat with a beautiful fur collar and when someone asked her what kind of fur it was, she answered that it was wolf.

"Sarah, they're endangered. How could you?"

"I know, I know, I shouldn't have, but it was too beautiful to pass up."

A week later, the same woman bragged about how good her Haitian maid was, an illegal immigrant and therefore dirt cheap.

One man in my department complained that he would have liked to have seen war. "Look at all the good writing that comes out of it," he said. "It's got to be a formative experience."

"Unless it kills you," I snapped back. Then I suggested that he should have gone south and joined the U.S. Army and fought in Vietnam. "They take foreigners, you know."

"Oh not that war," he sniffed. "I mean a real war."

One of the other teachers had grotesquely long and misshapen toenails and came to work in boots during the winter, then switched to sandals that forced everyone to see them. When a student asked why he didn't trim them, he answered that he liked the look and feel of them, pieces of yellowed, twisted, dirt-encrusted horn.

I overheard another English teacher, a woman in her early thirties, tell another colleague that she always packed tape when she traveled to seal her pussy shut so things couldn't crawl inside.

These were intelligent and educated but unhappy people whose unhappiness or personally felt disappointments made them behave in strange ways, but lacked the courage to leave a secure job. Confront them, and they fought for their claim to be as normal as anyone.

How could I not compare and contrast the harmless eccentricity I'd seen in Key West with this neurotic behavior? This was a nest the cuckoo had not flown over, and I knew that if I had to spend the next twenty years of life there I would become, as I'd told Vera, an embittered alcoholic.

The daily mole-like commutes, the seemingly perpetual gray shroud over the city, the civilized conformity of Canadian society, and work that made me feel worthless were combining to eat away pieces of me. I hated my self-absorption, but I hated the cowl of unhappiness even more. I started spending whole weekends on my sofa, stoned, watching tree shadows dance across the wall and listening to the classical music I'd become familiar with in Paris. What was I going to do?

There are moments in childhood when the young human despairs in face of what seems an insurmountable source of pain only to have the supermen in his or her life, mom and dad, ride to the rescue. They neutralize the bully or take you under comforting arms to let you know that wetting the bed with all its shame is forgiven.

Ted Kennedy did something more wonderful than that for me. Head of the subcommittee that was studying granting amnesty to the forty thousand men who had deserted or refused induction during the war in Vietnam, he was probably the last politician, along with Clark Clifford, ever to challenge the "military-industrial complex" that was ruining the American experiment and its economy.

Kennedy's committee asked the Attorney General to provide a definitive list of everyone under indictment for desertion or refusing induction during the war in Vietnam. A week later, the Justice Department produced the list. The hearings continued that day; then the next day the Justice Department spokesman begged the committee's forbearance. "The list we gave you two days ago left out one hundred and twenty names. We have the new definitive list with those names."

Ted Kennedy stared at the man with complete disdain. "Sir, when the Senate of the United States of America asks you for a list of the men you've criminalized for objecting to a war, and you give us that list, that is the list. If you've left off names, that means they're not under indictment. Do you understand me?"

A chastened Justice Department dropped the indictments against those left off the original list, and I was one of them. One of my colleagues at the college broke into my class and said there was a phone call for me in the office, and it seemed important. It was my mother giving me the news. "Son, they've dropped the charges. It's over. You can come home, son, it's over," and she started crying.

For the first time in eight years, I used my real name when crossing the border and returned to the island over spring break—flight to Miami and bus to Key West—and everything I'd felt at Christmas was reinforced. I talked to waiters in different restaurants, and they told me that it was a sweet life, though wages were low and jobs scarce, but you could buy a house for one-tenth what they cost in Toronto.

In June, I returned again and found a wooden story-and-a-half house on a tiny lot farther from the main street than I liked, but it was only $18,000 and the owner would hold a mortgage for $8,000 of it. I bought it and gave the woman next door the keys so she could let the movers put the things inside I was shipping down, books mostly, and have the utilities turned on for me when I made the move.

I taught summer school and had planned to teach one more semester after that to build up savings, but by the end of October, after the first blizzard, I'd had it. The head of the department, an American wannabe wearing LaCoste shirts and spouting American advertising homilies like "we're going to maximize output by maximizing input," pushed me beyond the point I'd already reached. I quit. My colleagues, with few exceptions, cut me dead. A sympathetic dean gave me a leave of absence in case I changed my mind, and I was free.

My plane lifted off in the middle of another blizzard. After it had climbed into the blue sky above the snow clouds, I went to the bathroom, looked at my reflection in the mirror and laughed. I had *escaped*!

I was afraid, too. Eight years of living in exile and pursued by the police force of my own country made me nervous, anxious, and curious about returning. But also the unsophisticated, frightened, mono-lingual, half-educated young man who had left in protest of an unnecessary war eight years before was returning educated, multi-lingual, (and, yes, maybe a little arrogant) and worried that a small town might not offer enough to keep his interest.

He was also returning with very little money and had to earn a living.

I'd splurged and paid to fly from Miami to Key West instead of taking the bus, which I'd done before. In the waiting room for the flight, there were only four other passengers, three scruffy men and a drag queen in make-up but out of drag. They were passing something in a brown bag back and forth and bantering, obviously enjoying themselves. I was envious.

The flight was called, and the gate attendant led us out on the tarmac to a moment as frozen in my memory as the night I walked out of the Gare du Nord and saw Paris for the first time. There, sitting proudly nose high, was probably the most beautiful airplane ever built, a DC-3, affectionately called the Gooney Bird in WWII. With its wide delta wings, huge windows, and double props, it was UR-plane and airplane, and suited perfectly the escape monologue streaming through my head. This plane verified I was now going someplace very else.

Inside, grabbing the backs of seats, I climbed my way up the deeply sloped aisle and sat down. The engines fired up one after the other, spitting lots of smoke, then reached an ear-pleasing thrum. Airborne, the drag queen fired up a joint and passed it to her buddies. One of them held it up and gave me a questioning look. I took it, they all laughed, and when the flight attendant smelled it, she just looked away and stayed in her jump seat.

We flew above the water at what I judged from my skydiving days to be 5,000 feet. I looked down on the Rorschach pattern of mangrove islands and undersea dunes, mind and emotions swirling together equal parts pleasure and fear.

An hour later, we turned over a mosaic of tin roofs and trees and landed at an empty, open-air terminal. Our bags were thrown through a hole in the wall, and I took leave of my fellow passengers with a thank you for the hit and made my way to the airport lounge for a drink. This move was a tectonic shift in my life. I wanted to take it slowly and memorize the moments. The bar was nearly pitch black, and when I adjusted to it, I saw that the band, playing bad versions of Beatles songs, was topless. After two watery drinks, lots of jiggly tits and more bad music, I left and grabbed a taxi outside.

On the way into town, I marveled at the color of water on one side of the road and the coconut palms and wilderness of mangroves on the other as the driver tried to sell me a charter boat trip, then weed, then a hooker, all of which I politely declined. He dropped me off at my house and drove away. I walked up to the front door and unlocked it.

I threw my bags into a corner and collapsed on the mattress on the floor. I skipped dinner and stayed awake late into the night thinking about Toronto and Paris, wondering if bad hormones and faulty reasoning could have led me to move here. Why did I always make the biggest decisions in my life based on impulse or emotion, or both? Was I a fool, when all was said and done? I had almost no savings left and no job. Was I one of those sad people who stride through life with arrogant certainty, always making the wrong choices, doomed to wind up the most educated dishwasher in town? A disturbed sleep replaced disturbed consciousness.

Two

I woke up to a luminous and fragrant morning and rode the bike that had come with the house six blocks to the open-air laundromat on White Street with the little sandwich shop in the corner. I ordered a café con leche and *pan con mantequilla* (Cuban bread, lavishly buttered and pressed flat in a sandwich press). Standing there, drinking the best coffee I'd had outside Paris, I watched the varied humanity arriving for their caffeine fix and calmed down. I had moved here for several good reasons. Twenty-four hours before, I would have been on a subway in frozen darkness. It would all work out. It would all work out. It would all work out. . . .

I had a second coffee and watched and listened to a sun-leathered man juggling coconuts near the take-out window. Once I paid attention to him, I made out that he was rhyming:

People come from far and near
To start their day with coffee here
A smile, a laugh, a quick hello
And off to work they have to go

He smiled when I looked over. I learned later that this was Juggling Jim, one of the island's eccentric fixtures. He was there every morning, nearly, and his rhymes often had something relevant to the island's news or gossip and earned him his morning coffee and toast from appreciative onlookers.

I bought the local paper and some groceries from the store across the street and biked back. "At three in the morning," the paper reported, "a naked man had banged on the door of the police station demanding to be let in." When they opened the door, he told them that someone had just stolen his grass and his clothes, and they needed to help him get it all back.

Later that morning my next door neighbor, Bee, knocked and came in. She was a painter, she told me. There was an exhibition that night by a serious Key West artist. Would I like to go? My first impulse was to say no. More than anything, I wanted to hide out, listen to music that was familiar, and read a book that would take me away from what I realized I'd done. But Bee had taken charge of getting the things I'd shipped from Toronto into the house and all the utilities turned on. To be polite and show gratitude, I accepted the invitation and spent the rest of the day unpacking and putting things away. I hooked up my record player and speakers, and soon music and a bottle of cheap wine had calmed me down.

When Bee knocked again that evening, we went off in her car to a place on Eaton Street, just in from Whitehead. We walked into a wooden house with no furniture, dramatic lighting, black floors, white walls covered with the artist's collages and constructions, and the familiar chirm of a gallery opening. There were fifty or so people in attendance, walking, looking, and going to and from the back porch where the open bar was. Bee excused herself to talk with people she knew and left me on my own.

Bearing my arrogance like Parisian armor—don't you know what I've seen?—I had expected some amateurish, weekend painter's work, but was humbled by a series of torn-paper collages in one room that were stunning in color, composition, and originality, and a series of small constructions in the next room that were complex, intricately assembled, and witty. Wildly colored tropical plants: bananas, crotons, and others I didn't recognize, broke forth from the earth in the collages, sophisticated compositions of primeval power and sometimes subtle phallic suggestiveness. In the constructions, what were obviously objets trouvés were put together inside wooden boxes in ways both inventive and associative. In one, buttons and drawer pulls made animals that inhabited spaces defined by pieces of manuscript and wires; in another, four small toy cars made a destructive path through bucolic, antique postcards of the island, like the motorcycle tearing through the village in Fellini's *Amarcord*.

Most of the people made a cursory tour of the work and headed toward the back porch. In the center of the collage room, five or six people surrounded a man I assumed to be the artist. One person in the group stood out: she was a chiseled-featured, tall blonde with long, straight hair. Late twenties, I guessed. In contrast to the rest of the group, dressed in what I later learned was called "Key West casual," she was elegant in a tight, aqua-colored, spaghetti-strap sheath and matching sandals with ankle straps and three-inch heels. Minimal make-up—she didn't need it—and no jewelry, apart from earrings that were small, flat pieces of aqua-and-peach-striped glass and, unfortunately, a wedding ring.

In Paris, I had had affairs with two young American heiresses and had accompanied them as they gleefully spent mummy and daddy's money on clothes. High fashion on a hot woman excites me like a beautifully wrapped present does a child: can't wait to plunder the contents.

Like most world-class beauties, this one feigned indifference to her effect. I went back to the collages.

It took serious talent, I thought, to make pieces of torn and colored construction paper on white canvas sing their way into life as exotic plants, and these sang. I decided to buy one in spite of my limited means, and had started to turn to find out how when a voice behind me asked: "What do you think?"

I found myself looking into the lovely blue eyes of Ms. Haute Couture. "Real talent," I answered.

"Hmm. Can't do better than that?"

The tone of voice and gratuitous insult pissed me off. "Well, sweetheart, how about abiogenetic, or does that have too many syllables for you?" and I started to walk away.

She grabbed my arm. "Where do you think you're going? Get back here. I think I like you. Come meet Thomas."

The man I'd noticed was indeed the artist, and he introduced himself when we walked over.

"Thomas Szuter," and he extended his hand. I noticed a large, strange scar on his forearm. Tall, olive-skinned, handsome, and immediately friendly.

"John Cottrell." We shook hands. "I'd like to buy that collage," and I pointed to what looked like a cactus with a bloom exploding out one side.

"Wonderful." He pulled a sheet with adhesive red dots out of his pocket and handed them to my escort. "Can you mark that one, Lee?" (I learned later it was "Leigh").

She took the dots.

"Are you new to Key West?" Thomas asked. I hesitated for a minute, mesmerized by eyes unlike any I'd ever seen, eyes staring straight from an Etruscan mural: brown, large, all-seeing.

"I moved here yesterday as a matter of fact."

"Well, welcome to the island. If you're not doing anything later, why don't you join Leigh and me for dinner."

"Thank you. I'd like that."

I deliberately ignored Leigh, avoiding even casual eye contact across the room, and spent the next hour and a half back and forth between the bar and the works on the wall. The more I looked at them, the more I liked them. When I ran into Bee in the bar, I told her I'd make it back to my house on my own and thanked her for bringing me.

"He's good, isn't he?"

"Better than good, Bee. Why isn't he known? These collages . . . I've never seen anything like them. I bought one."

She congratulated me, then left.

When the crowd started to thin out, Thomas made arrangements with someone to close the place up, and Leigh came over to me. "We're going to Las Palmas for dinner. Know where it is?"

"No, I don't, and I don't have a ride. I came with Bee and she's left."

"Ride with me." A command, not an offer. She irritated me, but I accepted. We walked out of the house and half a block down the street without speaking. The ride was an old beaten-up Oldsmobile convertible, so big I figured six miles to the gallon. The top was patched with duct tape, and when I tried to open the passenger door the handle was broken, so I had to wait for her to get in and reach across to open it from inside.

"Sorry. The old girl has problems," she said and laughed.

I was intrigued by the contrast between her and the car. She put the top down, started it, put it in gear—loud, disturbing clunk—and off we went down Eaton Street. The lack of a muffler precluded serious conversation.

"I don't usually drive this," she yelled by way of an apology. "I usually ride my bike, but I dressed up for Thomas' opening and had to use the car." She reached under her seat, pulled out a joint and handed it to me. "Light it."

Another command. I pushed in the cigarette lighter and fired up. Good taste, strong weed. I handed it to her. To be this rude, she had to be rich or poor, the two groups with the worst manners. The clothes said rich, the car said poor, the commands said rich bitch.

Las Palmas was a small restaurant on the corner of Southard and Frances Streets with a small dining room inside and several tables outside. Leigh led me to one of the outside tables where Thomas joined us a minute later. As soon as we were all seated, an attractive woman with a welcoming smile came out from the kitchen and gave Leigh and Thomas big kisses and introduced herself.

She turned to me. "Hi, I'm Gail. Is this your first time here?" I told her my name and told her it was not only my first time in her restaurant, but only my second night as a resident of the island.

"We'll try to make it special, then," she said. She took our drink order then went back to the kitchen. A waiter brought our drinks, made some small talk and left.

Thomas and Leigh apologized to me because they had to talk some business about the show: what had sold, to whom, and how long to leave it all hanging. The show, apparently, had not been a big success. While they were doing that, I looked around.

Eating outdoors in November . . . how exotic. We were seated under a large tree whose canopy, lit from somewhere below, covered the outdoor area. Something nearby was blooming with a fragrance that screamed *tropics*. Lights along the fence shone up into palms whose fronds made a rustling sound with each puff of wind. The dislocation of having left Toronto in the middle of a blizzard thirty-six hours earlier and being here now was overloading my ability to take it all in, but it was the kind of sensory overload that said: this is rich, this is wonderful, this is nice . . . pay attention.

When Thomas and Leigh finished their business, they turned back to me and Thomas apologized again.

"Not a problem," I said; then I asked him the name of the tree above us.

"Breadfruit tree. See the big fruit hanging on those limbs over there? There are only three of these on the island. It's the tree the *Bounty* was bringing back from the Pacific when the crew mutinied. The British wanted to grow it to feed the slaves on their Caribbean islands. Cheap starch and calories."

"What's the flower I'm smelling?"

They both laughed. Leigh said: "Night-blooming jasmine. The Spanish name is *La Dama de la Noche*—Lady of the Night. Isn't that wonderful? Some people think it's too strong, but for me it says exotic, erotic Key West."

The waiter returned with menus, and we ordered. Then the chit-chat began.

"Where are you from?" That was Thomas.

"I'm a Navy brat. I grew up in Panama and Trinidad; then we came back to the States and lived all over. Then college in Missouri, graduate school, Paris, and Toronto."

Whenever Thomas asked me a question, I hesitated answering because his eyes fascinated me. I had never seen any like them and kept trying to figure out how they were different. They gave me the not totally pleasant feeling that the entire inside of my skull was being scoured in search of everything interesting.

Whenever Leigh asked me a question, I avoided looking at her for more than a second because I wanted her, and I hate being sexually attracted to someone I don't like.

After I mentioned Paris, though, I noticed she started taking more interest in me when Thomas and I talked. There was also a definite sexual tension at the table. I figured out that Thomas was gay, and they were trying to figure which way I liked to swing. Buzzed as I was,

I was still sharp enough to amuse myself by keeping any answers that might reveal the truth as vague as possible.

When they asked the expected question: "Why did you move to Key West?" I hesitated. How much of myself should I reveal to them? How deeply should I go into it? One of my biggest fears about moving to Key West, a small town after all, was that I wouldn't have anyone interesting to talk to. These two were obviously intelligent and obviously interesting, so I set out to making myself interesting to them.

"I know it sounds pompous, but I feel like one of those statues, partly finished, partly still trapped in a block of stone. The life I was living in Toronto was killing me, so I had to make the choice to surrender the struggle to break out, or continue the search for . . . I don't even know what you would call it, my soul? The meaning of life? . . . And if I didn't know what it was, would I even know victory if I achieved it? I've always known I didn't want to live an ordinary life, so I decided to trust whatever carried me this far. When the FBI dropped all the charges against me"—they shot glances at each other at that—"I came here, liked what I saw, and decided the next step started here."

Before they could comment, Gail brought us flan, a kind of Cuban crème caramel. "Here's some port, too, on the house, to welcome you to the island. Don't be a stranger," she told me and gave me a kiss. I was touched and thanked her. I had forgotten how friendly Americans were.

Leigh picked up the check and started dividing it up into the "you had the vegetarian tacos and you had the bean soup" thing that women love to do to the penny, which drives me insane. I looked at Thomas and he rolled his eyes. I reached over and took the check from her. "Let me get this as a gallery-opening celebration." Leigh shot me a dirty look, and Thomas grinned and thanked me.

When we got up to leave, Leigh turned to Thomas: "The Monster?"

"Why not?" He looked at me: "Want to go dancing?"

"Love to."

Leigh said she had to run home and change clothes and would catch up to us. Thomas offered me a ride.

We walked outside. All the fears of the night before were fading, dissolved by the warmth, the silhouettes of palm trees, the erotic brush of a soft, fragrant breeze and, yes, the alcohol and weed.

Thomas' car was a beat-up Triumph, and his passenger door didn't work either. I climbed over it and off we went. "I overheard you telling Leigh that you only sold three pieces. I'm sorry. I think your things, the collages especially, are brilliant. I like the constructions, too, but the collages spoke to me."

"Selling art in this town is tough, John. People want representational stuff: schlocky sunsets, palm trees, and oceans. My things have never sold well."

"Have you ever tried to do something anywhere else?"

"One of the critics for the *New York Times*—Huxtable? Architecture critic?" he looked at me to see if I recognized the name, and I nodded "reviewed my constructions when I had a show in Cleveland before I moved here, and she said they were as good as Joseph Cornell's. Someone offered me a show in New York because of that, but there were too many strings attached. And to tell the truth, I just didn't want to leave here. I was working through some personal things at the time."

We pulled up in front of a brick building near the waterfront, and I could hear music, good dance music, pouring out. "Welcome to the Monster. It just opened. Remind me to tell you a story about it sometime."

We walked into an open-air room, with slate floor and an open-air bar. Twenty or so people were on the dance floor, another ten at the bar. Pot perfume was everywhere and hot, hot music. We ordered drinks, listened and watched, and waited for Leigh.

She arrived fifteen minutes later, gave a yelp when she saw us and took off and handed me a different pair of sandals. "Hold these." Another command. I was ready to slap her. She grabbed Thomas and led him out to the middle of the floor. Thomas danced OK, a little loose-jointed and goofy, but the princess, of course, danced hot. She was wearing a tight, white Polo shirt that showed off her breasts, and jean shorts. I have never been into S&M. The staginess and artificiality of it makes me laugh, but I was beginning to entertain real bondage fantasies.

I dropped her sandals on the bar, ordered another drink, and began eyeing a twenty-something standing alone at the other end. I nodded at her when she looked my way, she nodded back, and I went over and asked her to dance. The DJ was fantastic. Each piece segued into the next even hotter piece seamlessly. My partner excused herself after three dances, saying she had to go back to her hotel and pack to leave the next day: a subtle invitation I pretended not to catch. I had bigger game in mind, so I wished her bon voyage and went back to watching.

Thomas and Leigh were getting wilder and wilder as the music ratcheted up. I nursed my drink and was truly high when a six foot two young man in a Girl Scout uniform with lots of badges came up to me and asked me to dance. 'What the hell,' I thought, 'it's not like we're slow dancing.' We went on the floor, the music came into me, and I let loose and felt good. The Girl Scout and I wore ourselves out, dancing mostly in our private circles, but every once in a while looking at one another and making a mutual move and laughing.

I looked up at palm trees silhouetted by a crescent moon that was horizontal this far south, and I was dancing with a transvestite Girl

Scout not forty-eight hours after teaching English classes in Toronto. I had escaped! I looked at my Girl Scout and burst out laughing again, and she/he did too. Recognition of our common humanity on opposite sides of the sexual barricades? 'Shut off the brain,' I told myself. 'Just dance and enjoy it.'

She broke first. Gave me a big hug and a kiss on the cheek. "Thank you. That was fun."

"It was, thank you. I've never danced with a Girl Scout before."

"Gets you Brownie points." We laughed.

Back at the bar, I looked over and tried to catch either Leigh's or Thomas' eye. When I finally did, I made the roll-it-up sign to let them know I had to go. Leigh nodded; they danced one more then came over. Leigh put her sandals back on and asked where I lived. The dancing had heated her up, and the smell coming off her would have given a dead man a boner.

"Ride with me," she ordered for the second time.

"You really need a muffler," I yelled when we were roaring down the street.

"No shit. A friend of mine's going to put one on next week."

I didn't say another word. Small talk was obviously not part of her repertoire.

We stopped at a building nowhere near my house, and she started putting the top up. "Get out and come up for a drink." Another command, but the little head was now in charge. I followed her up the stairs of a tall, large wooden building in obvious disrepair. She opened a door and turned on some lights. We were in a small, simply but beautifully furnished apartment with a balcony on the street side. She excused herself to wash her feet off, then returned with two beers and another joint. We sat down on two opposing, comfortable, club chairs. She turned on a lamp that had a scarf thrown over it, then got up to turn off the other lights and put on some music, a solo guitar piece that was an interesting blues/jazz mix. She fired up the joint and passed it to me.

"So you lived in Paris. Tell me about it."

I gave her the short version of my years in Paris. I passed the joint back.

"I lived there, too." I waited for more, but she sat there saying nothing as we listened to the music, passing the joint back and forth. Then suddenly: "OK, let's go." I expected to be led back downstairs to the car. Instead, she led me to the bedroom. Where was the husband? I've jumped under a bed just in time once, clothes in hand, forced to listen to bouncy marital sex just above me, and didn't like it. 'What the hell,' I thought, 'if she's not worried, I'm not.'

Clothes flew off both of us, and sex as competitive sport began. Alpha male meets alpha female. Who would be in control? I was just as determined as she was that I would be. Everything she asked for, and she wasn't shy about asking, I refused to give her until I was ready, or until she did something for me. We worked each other up to a white-hot pitch. When she reached the goal line first, yelling, it sent me off, too.

After a couple of minutes she got up and went to the kitchen and brought back a couple beers. When she lay back down, I moved to the bottom of the bed and began massaging her feet, then her calves. I was after seconds, and experience had taught me this was a good way to get them. While I massaged, I scrutinized every inch of probably the most beautiful flesh I had ever seen: smooth, smooth, soft skin, a lovely, lightly-furred crotch, and a flat, velvety stomach leading up to two perfect, pink-nippled hemispheres. Mother Nature had been generous to this princess.

I like physical flaws on a sex partner because they help me distance myself from them when the relationship turns sour. Her only flaw was big toes that had started their inward turn because of the stupid shoes women love to wear.

Since she didn't volunteer any conversation, I asked her, in French, about her time in France.

She answered, in French, that she had spent a year in Tours studying French, then a year in Paris. Her French was error-free and her accent better than mine. We switched back to English.

"Tours was boring, but I loved Paris. I stayed with friends of my family in their apartment . . ." She stopped because I had reached her thighs, and she was ready for seconds, too. A gentler round, lasting longer, with the same pleasant results.

When I rolled off, spent, she turned to me: "I like a man who makes noise when he comes. The ones who do a little grunt and roll off make you wonder why they bother."

"Maybe it's bad timing, Leigh, but what's the deal with the wedding ring?"

"I married the lover of a friend of mine so he could get a green card. Alex, my friend, fell in love with an Argentinian boy on a trip to Buenos Aires, and there was no way to get Santiago into the country permanently unless he married an American. I married him, he got his green card, and we're divorced now, but I like wearing the ring for protection.

"Would you ever move back to Paris?" she asked next.

"That part of my life is over, I think. Visit, yes, but live there again, I don't think so. But I loved it so much I think the veins and arteries in my body are Parisian streets."

"And which street would this be?" she asked as a finger traced the large vein that stands up on the top of my favorite body part.

"The Champs-Élysées, of course, on its way toward the Arc de Triomphc," I said as I ran a hand up her leg. She laughed and pushed it away.

"So what's the deal about you and the FBI?"

"Leigh, that's a very long story and has to wait for another invitation."

"Swear you didn't break into some building and blow people up."

"I swear. I could never do that."

I started yawning, and she did, too. "Leigh, I need to leave," and I got up.

"You don't want to spend the night?" At last some softness, a hint of vulnerability.

"Never on a first date, and I don't mean to sound flippant. That way if you wake up in the morning and have second thoughts and wish you hadn't, you don't have to face it directly. A little time to digest everything."

"The voice of experience?"

I nodded. After I'd dressed, I gave her my address and invited her to come over the next evening for a drink and asked her to bring Thomas. When I leaned over to kiss her goodbye, I said, "I think I like you, too," giving her back her words at the gallery.

She got up, and in all her lovely nakedness walked me to the door. As she started to open it, she turned to me. "OK, I'll bite . . . abiogenetic?"

"From abiogenesis, the spontaneous production of living organisms from lifeless matter."

"Very good, wise ass, very good."

Orienting myself when I left the apartment building, I began a twelve-block walk to my house down unlit streets bordered with lovely, faded wooden houses, and everywhere the perfume of night-blooming flowers. Lizards skittered across the broken sidewalks, heaved up by the roots of large trees. The moon threw a silver cast over everything. The leaves of one tree left perfect fossilized-fern patterns on the pavement.

An occasional cat made its appearance and, once, a dog barked from a backyard. From one house came a Bach sonata for solo violin; from another, soft voices having a conversation on a front porch. Twice, people rode past on bicycles and, once, a car passed me, Led Zeppelin pouring out. It would all work out . . .

Three

The sound of water dripping woke me the next morning while it was still dark. Bee had warned me how expensive water was on the island, so I went looking for the source. It was coming from somewhere outside. I walked out the back door, naked, and was hit with chilly, very still and very wet air. The dripping was condensation coming off the tin roof into the downspouts.

I was unprepared for what I saw.

A crescent moon, horizontal, held Venus almost in its belly, floating above a stand of bananas in a thick ocean of deepest purple—just short of black—which sat on a lighter band of purple, sitting on top of a thin band of dark gold: the most beautiful prelude to sunrise I'd ever seen, and so close I felt I could touch it. I stood there awestruck. There were no human sounds save a discreet and pleasant deep thrum I learned later was the fishing fleet headed out. I felt I was looking back at the planet before us.

I started to shiver from the chill, so went over to the outside shower and stood beneath a stream of warm water—screw the water bill—until the sun rose enough to rob the scene of its subtlety. Were we still allowed entry to Paradise this late in human history? Rational, educated, I didn't care, I wanted in.

Happier than the morning before, I dressed and biked over to the laundromat/coffee shop for my coffee and Cuban bread. The Latino behind the counter recognized me and put in my order without asking, an endearing detail. Juggling Jim was using baseballs and making rhymes about caffeine junkies.

A quarter in the vending machine got me the *Key West Citizen*, which I read sitting in a chair outside the sandwich shop. On page two, the paper reported that the Highway Patrol had stopped a swerving, speeding car on its way into Key West the night before. The woman in the driver's seat, whose license had already been suspended, had explained to the patrolman that she was in a hurry to get to town to pick up her boyfriend who'd just gotten out of jail, and that her passenger, not her, had been doing the actual steering because she had been shaving her pubic hair. "You see, officer," the woman was reported as saying, "I haven't seen my boyfriend in months, and he likes it shaved."

Toto, I thought, we're not in Toronto anymore.

The Want Ads were depressing: few ads and nothing that grabbed me. I sucked it up and decided I would take whatever I could because I didn't have a choice. I had to earn a living.

Back at my house, I shaved and showered, underlined the ads that seemed promising, and rode off on my bike. It was one of the most humiliating experiences of my life. At each place: restaurant, hotel, gas station, I filled out an application, then spoke with a person who looked at it and without hesitation said: "You got too much education for this." End of interview. It was frustrating, especially because I'd worked a dozen shit jobs putting myself through college and was willing to do anything to pay the bills. I started leaving out college on my applications and still didn't get any bites.

The reality of the situation was that there wasn't much work on the island, and what good jobs there were, the Conchs, (the locals), understandably gave to each other. I was discouraged when I got back to my house and started drinking cheap beer. I was well launched when there was a knock on the door, and I remembered having invited Leigh and Thomas over. Open the door/hide ... open/hide? I went to the door and put on my host face. Leigh had dressed down, hair pulled up under a cap, T-shirt, old jeans, and flip-flops. Thomas was wearing a bleach-spotted Polo shirt, jeans, and flip-flops, and handed me the collage I'd bought.

"Come in."

No acknowledgement from Leigh of the night before.

I thanked Thomas, gave him the money for the collage, then apologized for not having any booze (I'd drunk it all) and asked them what they drank.

"Beer."

"Give me a second. I've been job-hunting all day and didn't have a chance to shop. I'll pop over to the store and get some."

"Wait," Thomas said. "What do you want to do to this place?"

"I need to make a place to rent, most of all, separate from me, upstairs if I can."

"Can I walk through it all?"

"Of course."

"OK, go get the beer."

I raced off on my bike to Gulfstream Grocery on White Street, cater-cornered to the coffee shop/laundromat, and splurged on two six packs of Michelob and raced back. Under stress, I like to be alone, so the idea of having to socialize with these two seemed a burden.

When I got back to the house, there was music playing. They'd figured out my system, and the two of them were sitting on the floor, passing a joint back and forth and looking at Thomas' collage, which they'd leaned up against the cardboard box I was using for a coffee table. I could have kissed them both for the relaxed attitude.

I passed around beer and joined them on the floor. What I didn't know was that I was only seconds away from words that would change the rest of my life.

Leigh passed the joint to Thomas, who took a hit, then passed it to me. "Put the rental upstairs," he said, "and close off the stairway to it. Then knock out this wall and that wall and make this one big space. Your present front door becomes the tenants' entrance, and you cut a door in over there for your entry."

It took a second. *Knock out a wall*!

I had lived in Navy housing most of my youth, then the seminary, then college slums, then rental apartments. In my personal cosmos, walls were a given, as immutable as the sun, the sky, and the earth. *Knock out a wall*? My mind raced, filled with the possibilities of what was to become my life's work, and something I was to discover I had talent for. The reaction had just been awaiting that initiating neutron.

"What walls?"

"Those two. Tear out the ceiling to expose the rafters and put cables and turnbuckles in to replace the ceiling joists."

An entire house had just been brilliantly rearranged. I was in total shock, and it must have shown. I started to get agitated.

"Close your mouth and calm down," Leigh ordered. "He's a genius at this stuff. Get used to it, and please pass that joint."

I passed it and stood up, walking around in a space I now saw in a completely different way. I would never look at shelter, one of life's basic needs, the same way again. It was fluid, not static, and I felt a sense of wonderment and awe for this man who could make torn construction paper come to life as plants, and even simple buildings reveal their better natures.

"Let's go," Leigh said, standing up. "We have to be at Robert's in fifteen minutes. Come with us." Another order.

"I haven't been invited," I countered. In reality, newly fragile, I just wanted to stay in my house and digest too much newness.

"Doesn't matter. You need to meet these people, Mr. Abiogenesis." They both laughed. I was trapped.

We rode across town in Thomas' Triumph, me sitting on the trunk, and Leigh, after climbing over the broken door, in the passenger seat. On the way, Thomas swerved to miss a cat, ran up on a low sidewalk and back down, and that was the first time I heard that wild, maniacal laugh that I was to become so familiar with—and love— and my first glimpse into his belief that chaos and accident, not order, were the norm and humorous. Leigh was laughing. Once I recovered from the shock of almost falling off, I laughed too. It was like being teenagers again. We stopped at a liquor store on the way and chipped in to buy three bottles of wine.

A few minutes later, we pulled up in front of a tall, two-and-a-half story wooden building on Elizabeth Street and walked in the front door without knocking. Inside, there was a group of maybe fourteen people of various ages, male and female, all dressed in Key West casual with the exception of one well-dressed older woman and another middle-aged woman in gypsy costume. Everyone was drinking, and joints were passing around, some partaking, some not.

"Aren't you guys afraid of the police catching you?" I whispered to Thomas about the pot.

"They're the ones who supply us. You just have to be a little discreet."

I grabbed a beer and was introduced to a few people, but mostly drifted around listening to fragments of conversation until the host and owner of the building called us to dinner. We all headed to a small garden out back, where table and chairs were set up on a patio of used brick. I was happy when Leigh sat next to me so she could tell me who everyone was.

The table was set with wonderfully mismatched china and silver, and shot glasses for the wine, Italian peasant style. Bottles of wine passed round the table, then bowls of pasta. While the business of food distribution was going on, I looked around at the garden, perhaps eighteen feet deep by forty feet wide, but a jewel. The perimeter was planted with tall palms lit from below that sheltered under-story palms which, in turn, had abundant and colorful plants under them and, again, that exotic smell: night-blooming jasmine. I was getting excited now with the possibilities for my house, and what I saw was possible to do here with even a tiny garden.

"Wake up," Leigh said and poked me with her elbow so I'd take the bowl of pasta she was holding.

"Sorry, I was studying the garden."

The man at the head of the table, in his late thirties I guessed, stood up. "Welcome once again, my friends, and friends to be. Here's to our island," and with that he lifted his glass, and we all toasted.

"Who's our host?" I asked Leigh after a decent interval.

"Robert? He's a licensed architect, a good one, who won't practice because he hates business. He divorced his wife, moved here, bought this house and has been fixing it up for years with stuff he finds thrown away on construction sites. He lives off the rooms he rents in the house and has the whole downstairs for himself. Thomas pays him to do the structural calculations for some of his jobs. Apart from that, he doesn't work ... doesn't like the whole concept of work for pay, he says."

A few minutes later ... "Who's the gypsy lady?"

"That's Eleanor, the woman who has the little hole-in-the-wall store on Front Street, the Key West Cigar Factory. An old Cuban man who used to do it in Cuba rolls cigars right there in the store-front window. She sells them to tourists and ships them all over the

States. Thomas and she are good friends. He designed the renovation of her house just up the street and stops by her shop every day, and she gives him a free cigar. The short, quiet man to her right is her lover—has been for years. It's a real scandal in the Cuban community because he's married, but he and Eleanor love each other, and his wife doesn't want a divorce so he alternates nights with the two."

I caught a piece of Thomas' conversation with the host talking about a performance art piece in Miami. "My problem with performance art is that it's contemptuous of craft, and I think craft is part of all good art."

I didn't have time to debate that with myself before I focused on a wonderfully blasphemous conversation about religion going on at the other end of the table. "Did you know that there were three churches in the Middle Ages that claimed to have the Holy Foreskin as a relic, and one of the churches—now a mosque—in Istanbul had some of the Virgin Mary's breast milk?" one woman informed us. Much laughter ensued at that. "And they had a piece of bread from the miracle of the loaves and fishes, this in 1200 A.D!" More laughter.

"Who's that?" I asked Leigh.

"Shelley, a friend of Thomas' from high school who moved down here from Cleveland with him. Has a degree in Medieval Studies. Very smart and impatient with people who aren't. Very protective of Thomas because he has no money sense, and people always take advantage of him. She works as a bookkeeper at the Pier House."

More general conversation about religion at that end of the table, and then an older man started to talk. "My parents were very liberal and gave us a vague explanation of what religion was and left it up to us to decide. I know it makes me sound terribly superficial, but it took me only five minutes my freshman year in college.

"First, I eliminated all those inscrutable Oriental ones," . . . a few chuckles at that . . . "with all that cross-legged chanting and stuff—too bizarre—then came Christianity, but there you had to choose: Catholic or Protestant. The Catholic Church says if you take pleasure even in the thought of having sex with anyone other than your wife it's a mortal sin, and you can go to hell. That didn't hold much appeal for a teenage boy in full rut, so I eliminated that.

"Protestantism was next, but there were a dozen varieties. Choosing one would be like going to an ice cream store that had thirty-one different flavors and having to order the same one every time, so that was out.

"The last two were Islam and Judaism, and that was really easy. Why would any man want to belong to a religion that starts off by wanting to cut a piece of his dick off?" The table exploded in laughter. When it died down he continued.

"Seriously, though, I have thought of writing a book about the religious experience. I feel closest to the meaning of it all, the divine if you will, when I'm having sex, so I thought I'd make the title *Sucking Cocks for Christ*."

Another explosion of laughter with a few half-hearted protests.

"That's Bill," Leigh told me when the laughter died down, "big-time interior designer in Palm Beach, but lives here because he hates the people there."

Across from me, a man my own age started telling a story about when he was in the army. "One of my jobs was delivering daily briefing papers to Nixon in the Oval Office. He never even once looked up and acknowledged my presence, the prick, but I loved it that sometimes I'd leave his office, change clothes, and an hour later be part of the anti-war protests going on outside."

I looked at Leigh. "Tony Falcone. He and his lover, Bill, just moved here and opened that new store on Duval Street, Fast Buck Freddie's."

The next person whose story I caught was from the well-coiffed, well-put-together woman I had seen when I arrived. I guessed her to be in her early sixties. She waited for a lull in the conversation, and when she started to talk, everyone else stopped to listen.

"I know it's hard to believe," she began, "but I recently qualified for Social Security."

There were a few polite protests of disbelief from the table.

"Given my history," (a few chuckles around the table), "it was an interesting experience. I made an appointment and presented myself at their office in Miami. A very nice, but not terribly attractive, young woman sat me down and started asking all the usual questions about when and where I was born. Then she asked if I'd ever been married. I felt a little uncomfortable at that and asked her why she needed to know that, and she told me I might qualify for my husband's Social Security if he was deceased and had qualified for more than I had.

"So I told her I had been married, and she asked me his name— that was Bob—and she pulled a form out of a drawer and took down his information and started to go on, and I stopped her.

"'Is there a problem?' she asked, very politely.

"Well, he was my first husband, but he died and I re-married.

"'I'm sorry to hear that,' she said, and pulled another form out of the drawer. 'What was your second husband's name?' I gave her all Frank's information and she scribbled away, then started to go on, and I stopped her again.

"'I'm sorry,' she said. 'Am I rushing you too much?'

"No, dear, not at all, but Frank died and I re-married. Her eyes lifted a little at that, but she got out another sheet of paper.

"'What was your third husband's name?' she asked, and I think she emphasized 'third' a little more than necessary." (More chuckles at the table.) "Anyway, I told her I called him Bob II and gave her all his information. Now I caught her looking at her watch.

"She started to explain how my benefits would be calculated, and I said there might still be a problem. 'What would the problem be?' she asked, a little less polite now but still nice.

"Well, Bob—Bob II, like I said—died . . .

"' . . . and you re-married,' she said, completing my sentence. I thought that was a bit presumptuous, but continued.

"Well, yes, to Tom.

"She took out another piece of paper, a little impatiently I might add, and wrote down the information. 'Alright, it may take a while to calculate your benefits because of the marriages involved . . .' and I had to stop her again. Now she was downright unfriendly. 'There's more?' she almost shouted.

"The only photos on her desk were of her and a dog, and I sensed resentment.

"Yes, dear, I told her, but please don't raise your voice. It hurts my ears.

"She then told me to go on.

"Alright. Tom died, and I married Roger.

"Out came another sheet and her pencil was almost tearing the paper when she took down his information.

"'Is that all?' she asked, this time not politely.

"Well, no," I answered.

"'Let me guess. He died, and you remarried,' and she started to get out another sheet of paper. She was starting to make me feel like a black widow. I can't help it if all the men in my life had bad tickers.

"No, Roger and I divorced, *then* he died, and now I'm alone.

"'Mrs. Thompson, I hope you understand it's going to take us a while to sort all this out,' she said rushing me to the door.

"I understand, dear, I answered, and told her to have a nice day. And you know I still don't have my first check."

A couple people had to jump up to keep from spitting drinks on the table. It was several minutes before everyone calmed down again.

Then Robert and a couple others brought out dishes of ice cream with fruit salad on top, and two more joints started around. I got up to go to the john. When I got back, the woman to my right was well launched on a story in one of those Southern drawls where you think you could nap between the subject and direct object of their sentences.

" . . . and, I was still putting my make-up on when my daughter's sperm donor, Rock—that was his name, Rock, don't you love it?— pulled up in his Trans-Am with the big eagle on the hood to take me out dancing when I heard this terrible commotion and ran to look out the window and Rock was yelling at Kid, the pet goat my mother and her girlfriend Mabel stole from a farm down the road, because Kid had jumped up on the hood of Rock's Trans-Am and was eating the decal.

"Goddammit, Katie, that eagle cost me fifteen hundred dollars," he yelled at me. "Get that goat off my car." Then my mother stuck her head out an upstairs window and started yelling at Kid—she was the only person he'd mind—and Kid jumped off and ran away, but he'd scratched Rock's hood, and it just turned into a terrible evening because later Rock and I got into a fight about me seeing someone else, and I just can't handle jealousy and I knew he was really more pissed off about his damned eagle decal than me seeing someone else . . . typical man."

By this time in the story, the entire table was roaring with laughter again, and I had to get up to keep from spitting out my drink and missed the rest of the story, which I guessed was as funny as the beginning judging by the laughter.

When I sat back down, the Southerner was off on another story.

"My grandmother was a proper Southern lady most of the time, but when she'd had too much sherry—that was her drink of choice, sherry, I don't know why 'cause I think it's altogether way too sweet— but anyway, when she'd had a little too much her vocabulary changed, like telling us girls when we had to hurry up to get ready to go some- where she'd say: 'Girls, all we got time for is to powder our pussies.'"

Another roar of laughter at the table.

"And when she died, may she rest in peace, my mother showed me her powder bowl with the big powder puff that had, you know, that kind of hand-strap thingy on it and said 'Katie, do you want this? It was your grandmother's.' And I said, 'God Lord no, momma, don't you know where that thing's been?'"

I was sick with laughter, and the combination of wine and weed kicked in. I leaned back and looked at the dinner guests in wonder- ment. Like the anthropomorphic animals in *Wind in the Willows*, these people were wonderful! It was like some of the parties I'd been to in the English countryside, where the people had lived in the same place and comfortably for so long that they had developed hilarious eccentricities, and their greatest collective outrage was that there weren't enough signs on the roads marking the spring-time frog crossings.

I had forgotten, too, how wonderful American humor was: peo- ple not afraid to make fun of themselves.

When a quiet moment came, Tony, the man with the Army story, asked me where I was from, and I gave him the same shortened ver- sion I'd given Thomas and Leigh.

"Why are the French such pricks?" he asked when I finished.

"You know, I've spent the last few years of my life trying to explain Americans to the French and the French to Americans. I tell the French to think of the majority of Americans as peasants, but rich peasants, and they love that. And I explain to Americans that the difference between the French and us is best seen in the bumper car rides at the carnival. Americans gleefully smash into as many cars as possible, and the French go out of their way *not* to hit anyone, and snarl and give snotty, superior looks at anyone who hits them."

Tony laughed and Leigh turned to me: "I never knew that."

"It's true. You should have seen the looks I got when I started smashing into all of them. You'd have thought I'd served white wine with cheese. My very embarrassed French girlfriend had to explain the difference to me. But I have another story that shows the difference."

"Let's hear it," Tony said.

"An American woman who worked for me in Paris married a Frenchman. They hit a rough spot in their marriage, and when he was gone for a month on a business trip to Asia, she had a short affair with another man, and they took a weekend trip to Copenhagen. The affair ended before her husband got back, but when he returned, the company wanted to send him to Copenhagen for a week. He told my friend, his wife, that he wanted her to come along. She said she didn't want to go, but he insisted. 'Neither one of us has ever been to Copenhagen," he said, "so it'll be a little adventure, a second honeymoon.'

"She now had a problem: the trip was in a week, and she had a stamp in her passport that showed she'd just been to Copenhagen. She couldn't take the chance of her husband seeing it, or the Danish Immigration agent welcoming her *back* to the city, or something like that. So she took her passport to the American Embassy in Paris and asked if they could give her a new one right away. The woman she spoke to told her it would take at least ten days. My friend then asked if she could speak to the woman privately and told her the story of the affair and the offending stamp. 'That's a personal problem,' she was disapprovingly told, 'and there's nothing we can do. You have a valid passport. Use it.'

"So my friend went to the French passport agency. She was married to a Frenchman and had the documents, so she was entitled to a French passport. She was desperate; it was worth a try. It was this or pretend to have lost her passport, or fake an illness. She stood in line for an hour. When it was her turn, she asked if she could speak to the clerk, a man, privately. She told him her tale and asked if he would help her. The clerk looked at her and said: 'But, of course, madame. These affairs of the heart do sometimes create problems, don't they? Do you have your passport photos?' She did. 'Come back day after tomorrow and ask for me personally. I will see that you have it.' And she did, explaining to her husband later that if she was married to a Frenchman, she wanted a French passport. He was touched by the gesture."

There were equal parts shock, disbelief, and amusement at the table when I finished.

"Yeah, but you still haven't explained why the French are such pricks," Tony insisted.

"It's probably because of their loss of status and power in the world, Tony. Think about it. Before World War II, they were the center of the art world and a major European power, and French was the world's diplomatic language. That's why you have a message from the U.S. Secretary of State in French even today in your American passport. After the war, they were a broke, second-rate military power, because power had transferred to the U.S. and the Soviet Union, and the center of the art world was now New York. It was a hard blow to their national ego."

He seemed satisfied with that as an answer; then came the question I'd dreaded ever since I'd decided to move back to the States.

"What did you do during the war?" Did I answer honestly and risk alienating people, or did I make something up?

"I refused induction and went into exile for eight years." Others at the table turned to look at me when they heard that.

"Are you serious? That must have been tough. Good for you. I'd like to hear about it."

"It's a long story. Let's do it another time, OK?"

He nodded agreement, and as I looked around, I saw no disapproval in the eyes of anyone who'd heard me.

When the party broke up, Thomas dropped Leigh off first, then me. I caught a subtle hint of an invitation from her, but I had learned, painfully, never to let a rich woman take control: make them come to you.

On the way to my house, I asked Thomas who the Southern lady was with the funny stories.

"Isn't she a hoot? That's Katie Fritzlen. She inherited a huge liquor distributorship, moved here, and decided to spend her life having fun. She donates to a lot of charities, always anonymously, and she and Leigh set up a non-profit to help abused women.

"And the woman with all the husbands?"

"Patricia Thompson. She inherited from each of them, bought a house here out on Riviera Canal and spends her time socializing. We like her because she's totally unpretentious—as you saw—and very funny, a lot of times unintentionally."

We pulled up in front of my house, and he turned to me. "I hope you enjoyed yourself and didn't find us too provincial."

"Thomas, that was the most fun I've had in years. You're being very kind to a stranger. Thanks for the invitation and for the help with the house."

"You're welcome. I think we're going to be good friends."

"I hope so."

Four

Each morning I woke up with paranoia fighting euphoria: paranoia because I had no job and was burning through my tiny savings;
euphoria at having found a place I thought I belonged to. The air, the
plants, the sunlight, and the smells on the island gave me a feeling of
return.

Born into tarpaper-shack and outhouse poverty in the boot-heel
of Missouri, I was three when my father had re-enlisted in the Navy to
escape that poverty. My earliest childhood memories were from Panama and Trinidad. Did humans, like birds, imprint on early images?
I believed that must be the connection I felt to the island. Riding
my bike down quiet streets—smelling frangipani, jasmine, night-
blooming cereus, ylang-ylang—and listening to the lovely cadences
of Spanish and seductive music that had nothing to do with the rest
of America, was a return to something personally primal. The first
night of rain on my tin roof, crescendo and decrescendo alternating,
shunted me straight to childhood naps in Trinidad.

Walking or biking past the faded wooden houses in Old Town
with their histories, seeing the ones where men and women—Frost,
Stevens, Hemingway, Dos Passos, Bishop—had lived, people who
had helped give America its voice, gave me the same pleasure I had

felt touching the old stones in Paris where Baudelaire and Rimbaud, Verlaine and Zola, Balzac and Colette had lived.

To conserve money, I baked my own bread, made my own yoghurt and granola, had no TV or car or air conditioning, had turned off the water heater, washed my clothes in the kitchen sink as I'd done in Paris and dried them on a line I strung in the backyard. I allowed myself two indulgences: biking over to M & M Laundromat on White Street for a café con leche and buttered Cuban toast every morning, as I scanned the Want Ads looking for a job, and going out to cheap dinners with Thomas and Leigh.

The three of us established a once-a-week routine of dinner together at a restaurant on White Street, La Habana, where they introduced me to Cuban cuisine: *ropa vieja* (literally translated, "old clothes, shredded beef"), and *picadillo* (a kind of hash made with ground beef, onions, garlic, tomato sauce, and green olives); everything was served with yellow rice, black beans, and plantains. The star was the roast pork, a Cuban specialty superior even to the pork I'd had in Normandy.

At La Habana, under Third-World fluorescent lighting that drove Thomas to wearing sunglasses during dinner, we sent out those first exploratory tendrils of friendship. We'd catch up on each other's news: Thomas' latest commission to re-design a house; my perpetually unsuccessful search for a job; and Leigh telling us about one of the women she was helping and, always, lots of laughter at the stories in the *Key West Citizen*, nicknamed *The Mullet Wrapper*, which confirmed we lived someplace quite different.

At our first dinner there, I asked them if they'd seen the paper that day.

"Let me guess which story you liked," Thomas said. "Man in life vest is found swimming two miles out to sea by pleasure boaters?

54

That story?" I nodded.

A man in a life vest had been found swimming two miles out to sea by pleasure boaters and had refused their help, so they had called the Coast Guard, which sent out a cutter. They plucked the man out of the water against his will and asked him what the hell he was doing. "I'm tired of capitalism," he answered, "so I was swimming to Cuba."

"I can sympathize with the poor bastard," I said. "Right now, I'm tired of it, too."

"I'm with you there, my friend," Thomas said. That earned us a contemptuous look from Leigh.

It was gratifying to realize they were as eager to be my friend as I was to be theirs, and the unspoken stand-off between Leigh and me after that first night gave a zesty undercurrent to some of the conversation. The issue was always there, but I wasn't going to be the first to pursue more sex, and she was determined not to be the first either. This was fun.

When they invited me to Bahia Honda Park up the Keys the first time, I watched as they bagged up trash on the way out, unostentatiously. Leigh explained it to me. "These places are so beautiful that Thomas came up with the idea that we always leave them better for our having visited." I was impressed.

Thomas had an intelligence and intellectual irreverence that left me open-mouthed. He was reading the Durants' *Story of Philosophy* and brought up Bergson's *élan vital* one night at dinner. I was doing my best graduate student's disquisition on it when he broke in and said: "You know, I had a braised *élan vital* once in Rio. It was interesting, but I don't think I'd do it again." They both looked at me, tentatively, to see if I was offended, and then we all burst out laughing.

We learned each other's histories. They got mine in chapters. I got the best of theirs when one or the other was absent. Thomas gave me Leigh's over *picadillo,* El Presidente beer, and flan one night at La Habana when she was in New York.

"She comes from as WASP a family as possible," he told me. Not one, but two ancestors on the Mayflower: Farleigh—her middle name—and Dickinson. Family is rich, from both sides, I think, but the father lost a lot of the money a few years back. Father's an investment banker and alcoholic. Mother does charity work and golfs a lot, you know, the whole Brahmin stereotype: Nob Hill, Nantucket, the works. She has a younger brother the parents devote most of their attention to, which Leigh resents because she's smarter. Leigh and her brother both got the prep school/Ivy League education, he Yale, she Radcliffe. The brother married a cousin, the WASP stereotype again, and he's an investment banker now, too.

"Leigh never plays on the super-WASP background, even makes fun of it. She broke up a dinner party here once explaining that WASPs don't have babies, they have heirs, and then except for taking them to the orthodontist, they don't pay any attention to them until they're old enough to understand ladder strategies for bonds, whatever that is. She's got some kind of trust fund her grandfather set up for her. I think she only gets the income from it until she's thirty-two, and she can't direct it until then, but she'll never, ever, tell you how big it is. She guards that secret better than she ever guarded her virtue. Asking her about how big it is guarantees you a nasty look or comment, or both.

"We tease her about it anyway, and it's become a running joke, us trying to find out just how rich she is, and she hiding it.

"I met the parents and the brother when they came down to visit once. Cool, distant, very WASP. The whole time they were here, all of them, especially the mother, looked like they were smelling something rotten. Key West was definitely not Nantucket. The brother was always putting her down in a passive-aggressive way.

56

"Leigh went out of her way to show them a good time and was angry that they didn't appreciate it. Then something happened. It had to do with money. I think they wanted permission to break her trust to replace the money the father had lost, which was the real reason for the visit. She switched overnight from trying to please them to trying to offend them.

"The next to last night they were here, she took them to dinner at the Pier House and begged me to come with her. A couple her parents knew were in town, so she invited them, too.

"The dinner started out alright. The waiters were all giving us special attention because Leigh used to work there, but the brother made some kind of disparaging remark about her, which the parents laughed at. Leigh didn't react, but I knew something was going to happen. That girl *always* gets even. One thing we all admire and fear in her is that she has no social fear, none, zip, zero, probably because of her background and money. Someone's playing their radio too loud at the beach, she tells them to turn it down; if the president of the United States was smacking his gum in earshot of her, she'd tell him to stop it.

"Anyway, during the dinner at the Pier House, the parents mentioned something about her brother's upcoming marriage, to a cousin, of course, and the wife of the parents' friends—just to make conversation—asked Leigh when she thought she might get married.

"I don't care about marriage, and certainly none of this dynastic coupling of trust funds like my brother's," she said. There was stunned silence at the table but our girl wasn't through yet. "You know, the first week I was here, I met three fisherman in a bar, and they invited me to Bahia Honda for the day. I rode up with them, doing them one by one, and they were perfect gentlemen, none of that leg-humping after my trust fund that those Ivy League boys used to do." And with that, she got up from the table and left, followed by a very embarrassed me.

"I guess they spent the last day trying to convince her to change her mind about breaking the trust, and she continued to refuse. She invited them out for one last drink and took them to the Red Doors, the shrimper bar that used to be on Caroline Street. The bar's nickname was the Bucket of Blood because of all the fights that broke out in it. It was where the shrimpers would get drunk and pass out on the sofas in one corner or, if they passed out in the toilet, the other shrimpers would laugh and piss on them until they woke up.

"The parents were horrified, but our girl wasn't through yet. She called out to one of the shrimpers she knew, and they got up on a table and she started doing a real nasty bump and grind with him. Her parents left the next day and haven't been back since. I don't know if she even speaks to them anymore."

We ordered two more beers.

"She's an original. There's a purity to her, and I think some mystery at her core. She's rich, but the only thing she splurges on is clothes. She does her own laundry, except for the designer stuff; cleans her apartment herself; cooks for herself . . . not well, by the way, typical WASP. Don't jump at a dinner invitation for the food. And she makes a point of always working at something menial. She says it keeps her in touch with reality. She does a lot of volunteer work with women in jail, too, trying to counsel them and get them back on the right track. I think I told you that she and Katie, the funny Southern gal you met at that dinner at Robert's, set up a non-profit for that.

"Once in a while when she works a really sad case out at the jail—sexual abuse, husband abuse—it sets her off on an anti-male tirade and she starts screaming about how horrible all men are, and we should all be shot, and on and on. I was shocked the first time, but she ran out of steam, and apologized.

"She's absolutely determined to live life on her own terms, and fortunate enough to have the money to allow it."

"How did you two meet?"

"She went to one of my openings, and afterwards we had a short fling." I must have looked a little surprised because he quickly added, "back in the days when I still had sex with women, too. I told her I was gay, and we ended it; but we've been best friends since, and she's fiercely loyal and very protective. You should see her go after some of the gallery owners if they don't pay me. They see her coming, and that checkbook they weren't able to find for weeks comes flying out of their pocket.

"We lived together for almost a year, and it was fun, a delight, actually. Leigh never, ever runs out of toilet paper, or toothpaste, or olive oil, or anything, and the bills are always paid on time. She's that organized. It was a very comfortable place to live. Now can I ask you a personal question?"

"Depends on how personal."

"Leigh said the two of you got together the night of my show, and I know she likes you, but it doesn't look like you've gotten together again. Did something happen?"

"No. I like her. I mean look at her. She's beautiful, sexy, educated, speaks French, my wet dream. My problem was—is—her money and her bossiness."

He rolled his eyes and chuckled. "At a party last year, we all started giving each other silly imitation Indian names. Mine was Chief-Sees-It-All. You'll love hers: Princess-Talks-Like-A-Man."

"Thomas, I don't have a problem with strong, independent women, I really don't. I prefer them to some 'yes, dear,' limp noodle. But I do have a problem with bossy, rich women. I had affairs with two super-rich American girls in Paris, and the money *always* got in the way. Sooner or later when it came to a conflict—one person wanted to do one thing, and the other person wanted to do something else—they let it be known that they had the money, and that gave them two votes. I can't live like that.

"The one girl in Paris begged me to marry her, and she must have had over twenty million. But I knew if I did, there'd be a day she'd pull rank because the money was hers. She was already pushing me to quit my job in Paris so we could go traveling together. I wasn't having it. Imagine being some woman's little lapdog, having to ask for more money when the allowance ran out. Screw that. Fortunately, I was still recovering from a broken heart because of another woman, so it wasn't that hard to turn her down, but was she pissed!

"You'll love this story, Thomas. The night I was supposed to give Chris my answer, she took us to dinner at the Jules Verne restaurant in the Eiffel Tower. When we got settled in and had ordered, I told her, nicely, that I'd like to remain friends, but that I'd decided I couldn't do it, couldn't marry her. She jumped up in a fury, threw a bunch of money on the table and told me to keep it. "You need it more than I do, and that's all you're worth anyway."

"That pissed me off, so I told her she had the sloppiest pussy I'd ever fucked. She picked up her glass of wine and threw it in my face and stormed out. I was embarrassed because half the restaurant had seen it, but god bless the French, all the men gave me sympathetic looks, and the waiters were all over me, sponging me off and commiserating, clucking away about 'les femmes' and 'les affaires du coeur'. I had the best service I've ever had in a French restaurant and left a hundred dollar tip, thanks to the bitch."

Thomas looked surprised. "You stayed and finished the meal?"

"Of course. When would I ever get to eat there again?"

He laughed.

"You know, Thomas, I know I sound puffed up sometimes, but I've worked hard all my life, not just 'working for money work,' but work to recover from my childhood, and the Church, and the fucked-up culture in this country. My independence is sacred to me, and no amount of comfort or luxury is worth losing that. From a certain age on, I realized that a human life really is a short voyage, trite as that sounds, and I want to wind up at the end of mine not blaming anyone else for not having lived it my way, in as rich a way as my understanding can make it. I can see myself losing that direction if I got together with Leigh. Great money makes you lose direction, I think. The only way a relationship like that could possibly work for me is if the woman put all that money aside somehow, as if it didn't exist."

"Hard to do," Thomas said, "hard to do, but I understand. One of the things I liked about you when I met you was your answer that night at Las Palmas when I asked you why you'd moved to Key West."

"Thomas, look at what you must have gone through mentally and emotionally to get to where you are. Could you give up the independence you earned from all that?"

"How much money are we talking about, John? I'm a lot more corruptible than you are. Twenty million dollars could assuage my compromised conscience for a very long time."

We laughed. I liked this man.

When the flan came, I asked Thomas what Leigh was doing in New York.

"She goes up for meetings with the managers of her trust fund, which she hates, because she can't direct the investments herself for two more years. She's very serious about that money. You can't get *The Wall Street Journal* or *Barron's* here the same day it's published, so she pays the flight attendants at Air Sunshine to bring them to her on the morning flight from Miami. Don't *ever* bother her on a Saturday morning when she gets *Barron's*. Anyway, she has a portfolio on paper of what she'd do with her money if she directed the investments, and she almost always beats the men managing her fund. It infuriates her.

"The other reason she goes up is to indulge in her main vice, clothes. You've seen the girl loves good clothes. When she's through with them, she gives them to the women she counsels."

"Can I ask you a personal question now?"

He nodded.

"What happened to your arm?"

He was quiet for a minute.

"I'll make you a deal, John. It's a long story, but I'll tell you all about it if you'll tell me about you and the FBI."

"Deal, but mine's a long story, too, so let's plan a tell-all evening."

Dinner over, we biked to the Monster and ordered drinks. Half an hour later, he waved as he left with another man. An hour later, I accompanied an English teacher from Cincinnati back to her room at the Pier House for a night of wonderful, carnal excess.

One reason I hadn't given Thomas for not getting together with Leigh again was the availability of willing sex partners, tourists as sexually excited by being on the island as I was. Ceiling fan turning above you, perfume of night-blooming flowers wafting into the room, moonlight through louvered windows throwing slatted patterns on the happy body moving beneath you . . . it was sex as I'd never had it before. These were some of the happiest couplings on the planet. I wasn't ready for monogamy just yet, not even with someone as beautiful as Leigh.

Island sex was great, magnificent candy, but I needed a job. After six weeks of job-hunting, I was still unemployed.

Riding back from downtown one afternoon, I saw a sign in the window of another Cuban restaurant, Veradero, asking for a dishwasher/

busboy. I went inside and applied for the job: six days a week, five p.m. 'til midnight, a dollar fifty an hour plus 10 percent of the waiters' tips and free dinner. I was desperate enough that I agreed and was hired.

They hired me partly out of amusement that a gringo who spoke Spanish with a funny accent wanted the job, and also because they probably sensed my desperation. Most Cubans, I came to learn, have a soft spot in their heart for the downtrodden or desperate.

The job was brutal, as most restaurant work is. I had to do the work of two people: keeping up with a Niagara of dishes, and clearing tables that turned three times a night because the meals were cheap. Busting through the doors between the dining room and the kitchen was passage between heaven and hell. Outside, diners enjoying an evening out; inside, an inferno of food preparation and plating, mistakes and yelling, all in rapid-fire Cuban Spanish where no final S ("es") was pronounced.

Restaurant work, like construction work, is difficult and stressful but creates a camaraderie that few other occupations do. One of the waiters, Rudolfo, Rudy, a man in his late twenties, set the tone for the shift. Good-looking, muscular, and charming, he made heavy work seem lighter with his jokes and refusal to get too upset when things went wrong, and in restaurants things *always* go wrong. In the middle of the worst kitchen panics—which at the moment seem worse than car crashes—he always laughed. "*Tranquilo, tranquilo,*" he'd say when one of us started freaking out.

Rudy kept up comic banter with Maria, the cook, a lesbian black Cuban in her thirties, constantly making jokes to her about what she was missing by not liking *pingas*, (dicks) and offering to "convert" her. She always had a retort, and the thrust and repartee kept us all laughing on the infernal side of the kitchen doors.

All the pressure of a restaurant in full dinner-rush mode concentrated on Maria. You could see the spring tightening in her as she tried to cope with too many diners arriving all at once, waiters demanding food for their tables, running out of ingredients when too many people ordered the same thing, or a waiter dropping his tray and needing immediate replacements or, God forbid: "the Governor of Florida just walked in with his wife and a party of eight."

One night was memorable. The dining room was completely full. Everyone was ordering the pork. Maria was overwhelmed and couldn't keep up with the orders. Tension mounted as waiters came in looking for their plates. Rudy came in demanding his again, and when Maria turned back to the oven, he whipped out his dick and began banging it on the stainless steel table where she plated the food, chanting: "Where's my food? Where's my food?" When Maria turned around and saw the dick, she shrieked, dropped a plate, and fell to the floor crying.

We all came over and hugged her. Rudy tucked his dick back in his pants and told one of the other waiters to take over his tables. "*Chica*, don't cry, I'm sorry," he told her as he helped her to her feet. "We'll help you catch up," and we did. It was a tiny glance into the nobility that often resides in the people who do society's hard work.

That night, Rudy asked me if I'd like to have a drink afterwards, and I suggested the Monster and asked him to invite Maria.

"That's a *maricon* bar, isn't it? Are you queer?"

"Rudy, it's the best bar and disco on the island, and it's the easiest place to pick up women. Come on. If you don't like it, we'll go somewhere else. And, no, I'm not a *maricon*."

The three of us rode our bikes downtown, and I ordered us drinks. The dance floor was already crowded. We clinked glasses.

"Rudy, this may be weird for you, but think about it. You're in a disco where half the men are gay, and almost all the women are straight. Think about what that does for your chances of getting laid."

He laughed at that, and when Maria got picked up by another woman, I asked Rudy to tell me a little about himself.

He'd been born in Cuba, he told me. His father had abandoned the family. Four years before, with two of his buddies, he'd escaped the island by stealing three truck inner tubes they'd lashed together to float on across the straits. He'd told his mother and brother farewell, knowing he'd never see them again.

"The hardest part, *amigo*, was the farewell to my mother. She clinged to me, doing . . . how you say, heavy crying?"

"Sobbing."

"Sobbing, much sobbing, mother clinging me and *mucho* sobbing." He was quiet for a moment then continued, in Spanish.

The three of them had floated for three days and run out of water. One of the friends slipped away during the third night, delirious. The morning of the fourth day, the inner tubes washed up on the Marquesas, and a pleasure boater found the two survivors, dehydrated and almost dead, and brought them to Key West.

When he finished the story as we stood at the bar watching the dancers, I didn't know what to say. When he started dancing with a tourist, I watched him and tried to process the horror of his story but couldn't. My own nighttime voyage into exile had been an act of courage, I had always thought, but it was champagne and caviar compared to his. His love of life in spite of the tragedy made me realize I was in the presence of a kind of life force I'd never met before.

When I asked Rudy in a break between dances what his long-term plans were, he snorted. "Long-term plans, *amigo*, is a gringo idea. I want to drink, smoke dope, dance, and get lots of sex. I could die tomorrow, and what good would long-term plans be then? Come on, *amigo*, let's have another drink and explain to this *guajiro* (hillbilly) why so many of those men dancing out there want each other when god has made something as beautiful as pussy?"

When we were both out on the dance floor with two tourist women, I worked my way close to him and pinched him on the butt. He turned around, ready to fight, then started laughing when he saw it had been me.

"*Pendejo*! I'll get even with you on tomorrow night's shift."

Rudy got lucky that night, I got lucky that night, and Maria got "engaged" that night, proving the truth of the joke: What do lesbians do on their second date? Answer: They move in together. The three of us became friends, and Rudy became a personal hero, a man with no existential angst, no constant questioning of life's meaning and direction, just a human being seeking to enjoy life. How could I not have a sneaking admiration—in truth, envy—for him.

He also kept me supplied with killer weed.

Apart from the camaraderie in the kitchen and the partying after our shift, I hated the work. It happened at the end of the day, so the entire day was a count-down to the drudgery awaiting you, instead of a day-time job where the count-down ticked toward personal freedom and pleasure. It was as stressful, unbelievably, as any job I'd had and paid a tenth of my last one.

Ashamed, too, I had to admit that the lack of status bothered me, and I hadn't thought that was a part of my character. To have people Thomas and Leigh had taken me to dinner with see me bussing tables made me feel ashamed. Then I felt ashamed that I felt ashamed.

One Sunday while I was still in Paris, the front page of the *New York Times Magazine* had had a photo of one of the Federal Reserve governors working with a garbage collection crew in Manhattan. The man, Jesuit educated, believed that he needed to see work in the society whose economy he helped control. It was also an act of self-abnegation, like the Pope's annual washing of feet. I admired the man and felt a kinship, which is why I felt ashamed at feeling ashamed. But I couldn't give up the job because it paid the bills, barely.

Two months of it, though, with no responses to any of the job applications I'd turned in, I'd had enough. I was drinking too much with the kitchen crew after every shift to decompress and recognized I was sliding into a lifestyle that was self-destructive.

One night on my day off, I biked down to Mallory Square and sat watching the moonlight on the ocean, listening to dolphins breaching and blowing out their breathing holes, and admitted defeat. I would sell my house and move back to Toronto and my old job. My move here had been folly, a wonderful dream, but destined for the slag heap. I biked slowly back to my house through now familiar streets, carrying a tumor of sadness in me, saying goodbye as sadly as I had in my goodbye walk through Paris.

I called Thomas the next morning and told him I was leaving.

"John, don't do that. Give it a little more time."

"Thomas, it's not the time, it's the money. I've only got five hundred dollars left, and I can't be an underpaid dishwasher the rest of my life. I'm barely paying my bills, and I'll lose my house and my pathetic life savings."

"Look, listen to me. It's always hard to get established here, but don't do anything rash. Let me see if I can find something for you. Hey, why don't you join me and Leigh for lunch tomorrow, and we'll talk about it. Meet us at Louie's Backyard. Do you know where it is?" I didn't, so he gave me directions. "Twelve o'clock. Lunch is on us, so don't argue."

Louie's Backyard, Louie's to locals, sits on the water on the Atlantic side of the island at the intersection of Vernon and Waddell Streets. There are tables inside a perfect restoration of a historic two-story wooden building, but the coveted seating is on the outdoor decks and bar behind. From there, beneath the two large sea-grape trees (one with a low branch the waiters bang their heads on), diners are afforded an incomparable view of the ocean, sunlight shimmering on blue water, sailboats on the horizon, a venue the equal of anything in the world.

The food is a worthy match for the view. It was here that Norman Van Aiken went on to national renown experimenting with "fusion" cooking, blending flavors and ingredients from different regional and national cuisines.

I learned all that later.

I rode up on my bike, and Thomas and Leigh were already there, he tanned and dressed Key West casual, she in form-fitting white pants and a sleeveless linen something in the pastel color we used to lick off Creamsicles. She and I did the French both-cheeks-kiss, and Thomas and I did the half-shake-the-hand/half bashful hug that straight men do with gay men.

From the moment we sat down, I knew I had been set up. Our waiter, they warned me, was an outrageous queen known as Marvelous Marvin.

"This the number you're both after?" he asked them after he'd introduced himself and ducked under the sea-grape branch above the table. He looked at me, pushed out a hip, and put a finger to his mouth, pretending contemplation. "Think his ass is cherry?"

"What the fuck did you say!"

"Calm down, girl. These two told me to give you the full treatment." I shot Thomas and Leigh a dirty look when he walked away, laughing.

"We told you he was outrageous."

After we ordered, I told them I was touched they were going out of their way to say goodbye, and that I knew we would stay friends,

They looked at each other. "It's not goodbye yet," Leigh said. "We don't want you to leave. We like you. Hang in there a little bit more. Don't be stupid."

I jerked my head back at "stupid," and she apologized.

Thomas took over. "John, admit it, you're a tiny bit intrigued by both of us and you should be, and you love the island, and we like you. If you left here now, you'd ask yourself the rest of your life what your life would have been had you stayed." He was grinning. This was a team at work.

Somewhere in the meal between the conch fritters with pepper jelly, the eggs Benedict with artisan ham, heirloom tomatoes and perfect Hollandaise . . . as I downed two, maybe three Bloody Mary's at their insistence, but before the crème brûlée, Cuban coffee, and Ten-Year Taylor Fladgate Port, I gave in.

"Alright, I won't leave yet, but I can only hang in for four weeks at the most. I have to give the dean up there some notice I'm coming back."

We left the restaurant and rode together up to South Street, laughing when Thomas ran into a coconut palm overhanging the street, then blew kisses at each other and separated, me carrying a warm alcohol and people-like-me buzz back to my house.

Princess-Talks-Like-A-Man called me the next day and told me to take off the next weekend. We're taking a trip. Pack two days' clothes and a swimsuit."

"Leigh, I have to work."

"Dumb ass, tell them you're sick, whatever. You can't miss this."

I called in sick and met them at the marina on Stock Island early Saturday morning, and they led me to a large sailboat, and we boarded. The husband-and-wife crew and Thomas and Leigh were all brusque and business-like, stowing bags, food, and always abrupt whenever I asked a question. We motored out of the marina and, once outside, the crew killed the engines and unfurled the sails. Thomas passed around a joint, and I saw I had been kidnapped onto one of those voyages that most humans only experience in a TV commercial, or never.

We sailed west, and the first two times I asked them anything, they put their fingers to their mouth to silence me, and I got it. It was something to see, let slide through you, and not spoil by trying to describe. It was as magnificent as anything I had ever experienced, pushed across a blue sea by nothing more than wind. Hours later, we anchored off islands they told me were the Marquesas, which we explored for a while.

We were served dinner on deck as the sun was setting, and given three hammocks above deck for us to sleep in. The husband and wife wished us good night and disappeared below deck. Leigh took the middle hammock and the three of us talked softly together for a while, holding hands, watching the moonrise and stars as brilliant as I'd ever seen them. How could I leave this, and them?

Five days later, Thomas called me. "A friend of mine is doing the renovation I designed for a customer and needs a combination laborer and carpenter's helper. It doesn't pay that much, but it might be a start."

"How much?"

"Nine an hour. Work starts in a week."

I made quick calculations: nine dollars an hour times forty hours was three hundred and sixty dollars a week. I had just won the jackpot.

"Thomas, thank you." I took down the directions to the house and arranged to contact the lead carpenter. I popped the cork on a bottle of wine, put on music, and started dancing around my house. I could stay! I could stay! I could stay! Another human angel had touched my life.

I felt bad giving notice at the restaurant because these people had become friends. When I apologized in the kitchen, Rudy and Maria came over and told me it was OK. "We understand, *amigo*," Rudy said, putting an arm around my shoulder when he saw I was upset. "*Tranquilo, amigo.*"

Rudy and Maria organized a goodbye party for me on the day the restaurant was closed. They took me to the La Concha Hotel, the seven-story building on Duval Street Vera and I had first tried to book a room in and learned it had been closed for decades. The owners, Rudy told me, had kept the bar on the top floor open so they wouldn't lose a valuable liquor license, and that's where we headed. We walked through the strangely empty lobby and rode a creaky elevator to the top.

Apart from a lone bartender, we were the only ones there. We danced, we drank, we got stoned and walked around the outside terraces with the 360-degree views of the island at sunset, golden light bouncing off tin roofs and catching the dancing tops of coconut fronds. At some point every man and woman came up to me and gave me a hug and wished me good luck. "*Somos amigos, gringo*" each man and woman said. "We're friends." Rudy and Maria kept coming over to me and saying in different ways that we would always be close.

Their goodbye gift was a framed piece of cardboard on which Rudy had printed "TRANQUILO, TRANQUILO" with a red magic marker, and they had all signed it.

Five

Thomas and I met at M & M Laundromat for coffee and toast a half hour before I was supposed to show up for work on the new job. "It's on Peacon Lane," he told me. "It was originally Grunt Bone Alley, after the fish, but that was deemed inelegant, so the city changed the name a few years ago. It used to be Henry Faulkner's house where he kept Alice, his pet goat, but I'll tell you about all that tonight at La Habana. The new owners are a real blue-nosed couple from Toronto, and why they moved to the island, I don't have a clue. They got my name from a friend of mine at the building department and hired me to design and supervise the renovation.

"Jeff Hagel's the lead carpenter. He's one of the best . . . Vietnam vet, very disciplined and demanding. Just do what he says and watch, and you'll learn everything you need to know to do the work on your own place."

I thanked Thomas again, and we biked to the jobsite, Vietnam paranoia sprouting in my head again. War resister working for a Vietnam veteran didn't seem like a happy mix.

Thomas introduced me to Jeff, went over a few details with him and left.

Jeff was shorter than I, had what are called rugged good looks, was very compact and muscular, and extremely polite, but I sensed a barely suppressed tension in him. This was going to be like not screwing up in front of the high school football coach and losing your claim to masculinity. He asked how much experience I'd had in construction.

"I was a hod carrier two summers at the University of Missouri, but that's about it. I'm willing to do anything, though, and I should learn pretty fast."

He smiled at that. "OK, Mr. Hod Carrier, first thing is to clean up the jobsite and keep it clean. Keep the floors swept and scrap wood and other trash in the dump pile out front. A clean jobsite is easier to work in and safer. Later this morning, I'll have you do cuts for me on the chop saw."

I picked up the broom, determined to be the best floor sweeper in history, and I think it amused him. When the time came for me to start making cuts, he told me the system and showed me how to make them accurately: scoring the board first, then cutting through it. "I'll call five or six out to you at a time. Write them down on something, make them, mark each one, then bring them to me."

The first day at a new job is stressful, and his kind patience reassured me but ironically made it even more stressful because I wanted to please him as a thank-you for that patience.

At the end of the day, Jeff gave me a list of tools I'd need for the job. "If you don't have the money for them, charge them to my account at the lumberyard. You can pay me back on payday."

I was beat by the time I got home at the end of the day, but I hadn't screwed up, and I had a job that would pay the bills!

Leigh and Thomas were already at La Habana when I showed up. "How'd it go?"

"OK, I think. Jeff's intense. Scares me but he's good, just like you said."

"OK, now you get to learn things about the island because of us, but we have to know you'll keep your mouth shut. It's a small town. Agreed?"

"Discretion is *de rigueur*, my little abiogenetic friend," Leigh added. "Understand?"

"OK, agreed, understood. Lips sealed 'til death."

Thomas started the story he'd promised me that morning. "I told you that the house you're working on used to belong to Henry Faulkner. He was a recognized painter and a friend of Tennessee's. He showed in New York and Palm Beach and made a ton of money. Everyone here knew Henry, mostly because of Alice, the goat that lived in his backyard. Henry wore dresses sometimes when he went out, and he always took Alice with him. Alice loved bourbon, and bartenders would automatically pour a little into a dish for Alice when Henry showed up. The only time there was trouble was when they gave her too much, and she started stumbling around and butting the furniture and other customers.

"One Sunday afternoon during the weekly hermit crab races at the Midget Bar"—Leigh started laughing at the memory—"the hippies kept giving Alice more bourbon, and she went crazy and started charging everyone. John, it was utter, wonderful chaos: Henry, with his skirts lifted, screaming and trying to catch her; the hippies grabbing their crabs and jumping up on the bar, the pool table, out windows, trying to escape; and the bartender yelling at all of them. One kid started using his shirt like a bullfighter's cape, and Alice nailed him good, took the breath out of him. Alice and Henry were eighty-sixed from the Midget Bar."

Leigh took over the story. "Henry liked 'seafood.' That's what gay men call sailors. Enlisted men didn't make much money in those days, so they ran out of money before payday. Henry would give them a beer and five dollars if they'd let him blow them. Word spread, so there'd be a line of them on the lane outside Henry's the night before payday, joking, talking about some sports game, tossing a ball back and forth, whatever.

"Dorothy Raymer, a reporter for the *Key West Citizen* and also a friend of Tennessee's, lived across the lane. Dorothy liked to drink, and she also liked 'seafood.' When the line outside got too long and too noisy, she'd come boiling out of her house, screaming across the lane at Henry. 'Goddammit, Henry, keep those boys quiet. Why do you have to have so many anyway? Send one of them over here,' and one man would lose his place in line and have to service Dorothy."

Our food arrived and another round of El Presidentes.

"Do you know who Marie Cosindas is?" Thomas asked.

I shook my head no.

"Marie was one of Edward Land's official photographers, the man who invented Polaroid. The Boston Museum collects a lot of her work. She lived here, too, back then, and was one of Henry's friends. One morning she went over to Henry's and found him in bed with two sailors—didn't bother her—this was Henry, and this was Key West. He flung the covers off his boys. 'Pretty, aren't they, Marie? Why don't you take their picture?'

"She had them put their bell bottoms on, tops off, and posed them in front of one of Henry's paintings. Look in the Time-Life book on color photography, and you'll see the photo."

"You can't tell the blue noses any of that, though," Thomas cautioned. "They're too tight-assed to appreciate the story."

"Or the art," Leigh added.

"You got more stories like that?"

They looked at one another, then me. "Where do you think you've moved to? This is an open-air asylum. Have you seen the movie, *King of Hearts*?"

"Are you kidding? It's one of my favorites."

"Well, Key West is like that little town in France. The inmates have escaped the asylum and are running the town. That's one of the reasons this place is so much fun."

After dinner, I raced home and found my copy of the Time-Life book on color photography, and there it was, on page twenty-eight: "Sailors, Key West." Two shirtless sailors looked calmly into the camera, one lying on an oriental carpet, head resting on his hand, the other squatting behind him. Behind them both, leaning against the wall, was one of Henry Faulkner's paintings, a beautiful still life of flowers in a pitcher set on a chair.

When the owners showed up on the job site two days later, noses in the air, acting like the mere presence of sweaty workers was an affront to their sensibilities, it killed me not to lead them into the bedroom and tell them how much 'seafood' had been eaten there.

Slowly I learned the skills of the trade and about my fellow workers. All three were Vietnam vets. Jeff had had the most combat experience, which probably explained the tightly-wound-spring vibes he gave off. The other two deferred to him completely. I suspected it had to do with what he'd done in Vietnam compared to what they'd done.

Always nervous about the question of what I'd done during the war, I was relieved that I wasn't asked about it.

One of the carpenters, Colin, looked like an Irish elf and was notorious for his corny jokes, always told in pairs, rapid fire. On my second day as we were setting up, he stopped me. "What'd the elephant say to the naked man?"

"I give. What?"

"How do you breathe through that thing?"

Before I could react: "Red-neck goes up to a parrot at the zoo and says: "Hey, dummy, can you talk?" Parrot answers: "Yeah, dumb-ass. Can you fly?" We all laughed, then went to work.

The men I'd done construction work with in Missouri had been dumb, brutal, and cruel. These men were their opposite. Jeff was intelligent, funny, and well-read. The intelligence showed in his work. It was obvious that Thomas and Jeff respected each other's skills, and there was never a joke about Thomas' sexuality behind his back after he left.

This was a difficult renovation because it was a very old house and nothing was square, level, or plumb. Thomas told us the house had been moved to this site and was actually older than the one on Duval Street that advertised itself as the 'Oldest House'.

One day, I was witness to Thomas' design genius again after the owners presented him with a real problem. What we were working on was actually three small houses joined together, one behind the other, each with its own gable roof, what was called a saw-tooth design because of the figure made as one gable dipped down to a valley and the next rose from that valley to its peak before it dipped down to a valley to meet the next one, three triangles in a row. The owners wanted to remove the wall supporting the valley where the first two gable roofs met in order to make the space more open, but they didn't want an I-beam or tripled wooden beam to transfer the weight to the exterior walls because the ceiling was already low and "it would look too heavy." This presented a serious structural problem, which Jeff and Thomas both recognized. That wall supported half of two different roofs.

"Let me think about it," Thomas told the owners and Jeff. "I'll get back to you tomorrow."

At the end of the day, I asked Jeff what he thought Thomas would come up with. "I don't have a clue," he said, "but I'll bet it's original, good-looking, and structurally sound." Can't get a better compliment than that from a man who actually builds the stuff.

There was a little bit of anticipation the next morning as we set up and waited for Thomas to show up. When he did, we all gathered around as he looked at the wall that the owners wanted to disappear.

"OK, we have two issues here. The first is obviously structural: we have to support the valley where the two roofs intersect. The second is esthetic: the owners want this space to feel more open. So let's do this: let's build a structural bookcase."

We all looked puzzled. I didn't know enough about construction to understand it, but Jeff got it immediately. "Brilliant."

Thomas went on. "Studs are on sixteen-inch centers, but if we use two-by-twelves for studs instead of two-by-fours, we can go to thirty-six-inch centers. Double them so they don't twist. Triple the ones on either side of the opening. Then we do a triple two-by-twelve top plate, crown molding on the face with cove lighting behind, and have only very low shelves so you can see through when you're sitting down. They can display stuff on top of the low shelves and light it with display light strips behind a valence. We'll make the walkthrough opening between the two buildings sixteen inches in from the left exterior wall."

"Brilliant," Jeff repeated. "We just have to be careful re-supporting the valley when we take out the wall, but I'll figure that part out, probably two-by-sixes at an angle from the floor to near the end of each rafter. I'll check underneath the house, too, to see if what's there can take the re-distribution of the weight or if we need to add piers."

We all congratulated Thomas, who took a small bow, grinning, and gave me a wink. This was fun.

When the structural bookcase had been built and wired, Thomas staged it for the owners to approve, but invited us over to look at it the night before they got to see it. Music was playing, Pink Floyd's "Dark Side of the Moon," and he handed us beers as we walked in. There it was: where a solid wall with a single opening had separated the two buildings, there was now a beautiful architectural element, with an opening to one side large enough to walk between the two buildings, which now seemed to flow together. He had placed what looked like American Indian pots and baskets on top of two low shelves, and hidden lights illuminated them. Others glowed from somewhere behind the crown molding above. With the other lights off, it had become the focal point of two-thirds of the house. Seeing what it had been before and now seeing this, I was in awe of both of them: Jeff and Thomas.

Late one afternoon, I was sweeping up after everyone else had left when Jeff showed up after a meeting he'd had with the owners.

"How'd it go with Mr. and Mrs. Tight-Ass?"

"Usual bullshit: why's it taking so long and costing so much?" and he started venting. "I don't understand why people don't understand that building or renovating a house is the last hand-made thing in industrialized countries, and the most expensive thing a person does unless you're rich enough for yachts and private planes—of course it's expensive. Every board in this renovation will have been touched seven or eight times before the place is finished. Do they bitch when Sears or the phone company charges them twice as much an hour as we get? Hell no. They just pay it and think that's normal. Sorry, it gets to me sometimes."

He was quiet for a few minutes, and I was getting ready to take out the trash cans when he started declaiming in a mock-serious voice: "Everything was for tomorrow, but tomorrow never came. The present was only a bridge and on this bridge they are still groaning . . . and not one idiot ever thinks of blowing it up."

I looked at him in total disbelief. "Jeff, that's Henry Miller. I forget which book, but definitely Henry Miller. I know that's Henry Miller."

It was his turn to look in disbelief.

"Jeff, Henry Miller kept me sane all those years of subway riding in Toronto and Paris. I've read everything he wrote. I visited and touched every place he lived in Paris I could find."

That started a game of dueling quotes between the two of us. Every so often, out of the blue, one of us would quote something. If the other didn't know it, he'd get the name of something wonderful to read.

"Sterility is the only 'decadence' I recognize." I couldn't guess, so he gave it to me: "Hart Crane. He died just offshore here. Drowned himself."

"If the doors of perception were cleansed, everything would appear to Man as it is, infinite."

"Piece of cake, Mr. Hod Carrier, William Blake. That's where Huxley got the title for his book."

"Alright: "Ecstasy does not answer the bidding of the will.""

"I like that one. Who?"

"Rolland's *Jean-Christophe.*"

"Alright, get to work. We're building soffits today."

I groaned. "The mortal enemy of the soul is the daily wear and tear. *Jean-Christophe* again."

Through my work with Jeff, I got to know an expanding circle of people in the construction trades. Some were intelligent and educated, and some were dumb as rocks. Shared guild membership trumped the differences, and the guild became my tribe, modern man's greatest unmet need. The camaraderie they provided was the equal of what I'd had with my musician friends in Paris. It surprised me, but gave me great pleasure, too, to be sitting in a bar after work, sharing our stories of what the day and the customers had put us through and to realize that with all my education, this work gave me more satisfaction than anything I'd ever done, and these fellow workers more a sense of belonging than any I'd ever had. At the end of each day, you could look at the evidence your eight hours of work had accomplished.

I began to develop great pride in my new profession. Once, in the middle of flying the roof trusses for a house, once again while helping pull the half ton of copper wire into an underground conduit run to a convenience store, I caught myself and thought: Look what little old French major can do, and my chest swelled. Leigh teased me that I was developing a swagger.

Jeff and Thomas, together, taught me deep respect for these old buildings, most built by New England ship builders, which explained the quality of the construction. To open a wall and find the penciled dimensions of a board cut, put there over a hundred years ago by men doing what we were doing, but with primitive tools, was humbling. To cut into some of the old Dade County Pine beams, a dense, resinous wood now on the brink of extinction, provoked reverence. One afternoon after work, on that first job with Jeff, we took a piece of beam he'd had to replace from the hundred and twenty-year-old house and started counting rings of varying thickness.

"I count a hundred and thirty-six," I said. "What'd you get?"

"One thirty-four. OK, let's say a hundred and thirty-five." We both started counting backwards. One hundred and thirty-five rings in a house one hundred and twenty years old: the tree the beam had come from had started growing at least fifty years before the Declaration of Independence.

Six months later, with Jeff's help, the upstairs apartment at my house was finished and had been rented. I knew, consciously, that the financial pressure was off me now, but the subconscious dread didn't lift until one Sunday afternoon at the Monster.

Few of us had money, so the Monster had started Dollar Dinner Tea Dance on Sundays: passable spaghetti and a piece of garlic bread cost you one buck. Friends discreetly shared joints and stood each other to drinks while checking out the day's sexual provender.

I walked in one Sunday and got big hugs from Rudy, Maria, and her partner, Dolores. Then the two Cubans who served me coffee and toast every morning showed up with waves and *"Hola, que tal?"* Then Bill and Tony, who had started Fast Buck Freddie's department store on Duval Street; Tennessee Williams with Gore Vidal; and Jeff and Colin, who hit me with the usual two quick jokes. When Thomas and Leigh came in, I introduced them to Rudy, who in turn got me, them, Jeff, and Colin seriously stoned before picking up a tourist and dancing.

When Thomas, Leigh, and I worked our way into the middle of the crowd and started dancing, I looked around and realized I knew at least twenty people there. All the dread and fear that I might have made a mistake moving here just lifted from me, like air bubbles on a scuba dive. I could go home that night with no fear of being broke and having to leave. I was happy—strange man was happy—dancing and bumping against Thomas and Leigh, getting my butt pinched back by Rudy who gave me a laugh and a thumbs up.

Six

The island I had moved to was forgotten, poor, and near the bottom of one of its many boom-and-bust cycles. When you told people in the rest of the country where you lived, you almost always had to explain where Key West was.

The infrastructure kept the town barely above Third-World level, and we jokingly referred to ourselves as inhabitants of a banana republic. The electricity went out all the time, and one year someone at the Stock Island plant pumped seawater into the turbine there, one of only two generating stations, and an entire summer of rotating blackouts began. They were hours long and never scheduled, making life hell for businesses and for people trying to cook, especially people like me who baked a lot.

Water for the island came out of the Biscayne Aquifer a hundred and thirty miles away on the mainland, through a WWII Navy-built pipeline that snaked its way out to sea along the highways and bridges, and from a small desalination plant on Stock Island that left enough salt in the water that doctors warned their hypertensive patients not to drink it. A quarter of all the water produced was lost out of the distribution pipes. Ice cubes dumped out of trays had a film of salt on the bottom. Water pressure on the island was so low that when someone downstairs flushed a toilet, people upstairs lost water, always fun in the middle of a shower. It took five full minutes for a second-floor toilet tank to refill and the shower to come back on. Leigh, who had a second-floor apartment, had worked out a deal with the tenants downstairs where they agreed not to use water for a half hour the same time each evening so she could shower uninterrupted. It worked unless they had house guests, or got stoned and forgot.

The sidewalks, where there were sidewalks, were heaved up and broken by the roots of the large trees that lined the streets. Walking on them sober was challenge enough; drunk was fun or dangerous. The curbs were weathered and broken pieces of granite or slate that had been ballast in the days of sail. Outside Old Town, there were few sidewalks and, in a few places, not even paved streets.

Street signs were ground-level, slim, tapered concrete stelae, two-and-a-half feet tall, painted white with faded black lettering.

Driving or biking down the streets was a teeth-shattering ride over tarmac chopped up so many times by the Aqueduct Authority that the slit trenches they cut and badly re-paved, in combination with the intrusion from tree roots, turned the surface into asphalt copies of a drunkard's nose.

The banks were turn-of-the-century. The tellers in the main downtown bank worked in brass cages. A regular out-of-town check took three weeks to clear; a cashier's check, two; and if you deposited cash, it took two days to get even that credited to your account.

The paper money in circulation on the island was the rattiest I had seen outside Latin America: dollar bills almost worn through and often in pieces, taped together because they circulated so many times around the island before landing back at a bank to be sent off and destroyed.

The wooden houses of Old Town, the largest collection of historical wooden houses in the country, hadn't been bulldozed only because no one had had the money to do it. They sat there with their beautiful lines and gingerbread details, weathered, sagging, like old people on a park bench waiting for someone to tell their wonderful stories to. The plumbing hung on the outside of the houses, having been added long after their original construction. Most of the houses in Old Town still had some or all of the original knob-and-tube wiring from the very first years of residential electricity.

The sewage system, like the rest of the infrastructure, was minimal. The town pumped everything, untreated, directly into the ocean. When tourist season cranked up in the winter, the clot of visitors overwhelmed the pumping stations, and a cloacal smell surrounded them.

TV was three channels provided by a cable company whose lines had been tapped into illegally by so many people that the signal was perpetually fuzzy.

Local phone calls required dialing only five numbers. Long distance worked OK except for international calls, which still had to go through an operator, but neither worked at all when a builder or a highway crew or the Aqueduct Authority cut through the 120-mile-long cable that joined us to the mainland. That happened about every six weeks and created heart-stopping moments for those few on the island who played the stock market.

Most of the locals, called Conchs (pronounced "Konks") had abandoned Old Town for the modern, slab-on-grade concrete block houses of New Town, mostly built in the '50s and early '60s, or the island's tonier but tacky suburb, Key Haven, two islands up the road. A few eccentric relatives and eccentric refugees from elsewhere were just about the only people left downtown, where a one-bedroom apartment, like Leigh's, cost a hundred and ninety dollars a month, utilities included.

Downtown Key West was divided into two parts: Lower Duval and Upper Duval Street, both with several boarded-up storefronts.

A few stores survived on Duval Street: a hippie leather-goods store, Tsew Yek (Key West spelled backwards); a head store, Environmental Circus, where we bought our rolling papers; another Cuban restaurant, El Cacique, with great *picadillo* and mediocre *paella*; Shorty's, the diner I'd eaten breakfast in with Vera; and a few bars: Delmonico's, the Bull and Whistle, both open to the street, and the Monster, where we all met and danced together.

Lower Duval also had the beaten-up, rundown hotel Vera and I had stayed in, the Southern Cross Hotel, with ratty rooms and bad water pressure. Up the street was the La Concha Hotel, a seven-story building from the pre-Depression rich days. It was closed except for the seedy bar at the top, named The Top, where Rudy and Maria had given me the goodbye party. Kress and McCrory's, two second-rank, down-at-the heels five-and-dime stores, stayed open, barely, selling cheap beach towels, suntan oil, and souvenirs to the few tourists, and serving lunch and the best Key Lime pie on the island, baked daily by a wonderfully friendly black woman.

Farther up the street was the Monroe Theatre, with a big, classical marquee hanging over the sidewalk announcing in big letters the only movie it ever screened: *Deep Throat*. Enough tourists from religion-bound America needed a "dirty sex" fix that it kept the theatre afloat, and nary a local protested. Money was too tight.

At night the town was dark. Only a few streets had streetlights and not many of them. Riding a bike through town at night was a child's trip through fantasyland: bright moon and stars, night-blooming flower perfumes, no traffic, and quiet. It was possible on many of the backstreets in town to stop your bike and not hear a human sound.

There were three flights a day off the island to Miami. The plane was a DC-3, the beautiful WWII relic I had flown in on my first flight onto the island. The island was small enough that if you were expecting someone to fly in, you could wait until you heard that ear-pleasing thrum overhead, then drive to the airport and meet them just as their bags were getting thrown through a hole in the wall into the terminal.

The terminal was pure tropics: a single story building open to the elements with an airport lounge, The Conch Flyer, that featured the topless band I'd seen on my first arrival.

There were two sad shopping centers in New Town with tired stores whose names I'd never heard of: American capitalism worn out by dragging itself down all those miles of bridges.

The *Wall Street Journal* was available, sometimes a day late, or maybe two, which was why Leigh paid the Air Sunshine flight attendants to get her copy on the day it and *Barron's* was published. To get the Sunday *New York Times* required a reservation at a small newspaper and magazine store on Upper Duval called Valladares, run by the family of that name. It was in there, or the Pier House, or Louie's Backyard that you were most likely to run into the pods of prize-winning writers who lived on the island, Williams and Merrill, Lurie and Hersey, Kirkwood and White. It was there one Sunday that I got to thank David Halberstam in person for *The Best and the Brightest*, his brilliant dissection of the arrogance and stupidity that had led up to the war in Vietnam, and then its prosecution.

The town dump, on Stock Island, the last key before Key West and the highest point in the entire island chain, was unimaginatively nicknamed Mt. Trashmore. It regularly caught fire, giving it a somewhat volcanic look when viewed from in town.

The Mosquito Control's DC-3 overflew the island, and its trucks droned through the streets in spring and summer spraying god-knows-what behind them, followed a few minutes later by the sound of dead dragonflies (called mosquito hawks by the Conchs) raining down from the trees.

Transportation for us newcomers was mostly on Conch cruiser bicycles (high handlebars, big seat, coaster brakes) with a stolen MacArthur Dairy milk crate for a basket. The milk crate was a constant thorn in the side of the milk company who always threatened prosecution for theft of property, until someone in marketing figured out that we represented several thousand free, rolling advertisements and backed off.

The few of us who did have cars, drove wrecks, also called Conch cruisers, like Leigh's clunky Oldsmobile convertible that wouldn't have been allowed on the road anywhere else. But where did we have to go but across the island or a few miles up the Keys to Bahia Honda State Park? Cars with missing doors, or windows, or fenders were common. Thomas' gypsy magic fed his passion for strange cars: one month he'd be driving an Austin-Mini, the next a Lincoln land yacht with suicide doors, and once a London cab complete with meter and roof light.

If you did own a car, there was a learning process, a certain cooperative ballet necessary to negotiate the narrow streets of Old Town, which had been built for horses. Two cars approaching from opposite directions on streets where they couldn't pass each other would recognize the situation, and one would give way, pulling into an empty parking space, then giving a wave of the hand as the other passed. Cars and bicycles co-existed. A car pulling up behind a bicycle on Olivia Street, for example, a narrow one-way street next to the cemetery, slowed down and crawled along behind the bike until the bicyclist found an empty parking place where he could pull closer to the curb and let the car pass, waves obligatory.

There were events that allowed all car traffic to stop, and anyone honking in impatience earned them asshole status. A great white heron landing on the roadway, then making its royal, slow, long-legged procession across the street, brought traffic in both directions to a halt. When his plumed majesty had safely traversed the street, cars moved again, the drivers smiling and waving at fellow witnesses to a tiny piece of island magic.

It was allowable to stop for planetary beauty, too. Imagine driving into town up over Garrison Bight Bridge and there, larger than you have ever seen it, is the setting sun, sinking through a thin line of dark clouds, out of which a small, dark-gray finger tries to reach downward and finally does: a waterspout, silhouette-twirling across the sun's huge orange face. Cars begin to stop, and people get out . . . but wait . . . this is Key West. What's dessert without a topping? As the waterspout dances across the face of the sun, the flight from Miami, the beautiful, delta-winged DC-3, turns out over the harbor and banks, silhouetting its pretty wings in front of the waterspout and the setting sun. Plane passes, waterspout pulls back up into the clouds, and people look at each other, smiling, shaking their heads, get back in their cars and drive home for dinner.

Clothing for men in Key West was loose, short, cut-off jeans, no underwear, T-shirt, and flip-flops. Women were equally casual with no panties, no bras, cut-off shorts, and loose shirts. Dicks and balls were always falling out of shorts, tits out of shirts; and beaver shots, those quick, sweet glimpses of coozes that drive men wild, were plentiful.

When the style for men changed with the arrival of Ocean Pacific shorts, one gay man wrote a letter to the editor of the independent newspaper complaining about the testicle deficit. "No more," he wrote, "the casual eye candy of a man on his bike stopped at an intersection with his equipment hanging out, cooling itself, putting a smile on women's and gay men's faces. Not fair, guys." The newspaper printed the letter.

With all its differences from "up there," the island also had some of the sweetest parts of small-town America, including my favorite American institution, the small-town diner, where a town knits together a voluntarily communal life. Key West had three: Shorty's Diner on Duval Street, Fisherman's Café on the corner of Caroline and Margaret, and the Deli Restaurant on the corner of Truman and Simonton: bacon and eggs, real coffee, and constant back-and-forth with the waitresses, who obviously enjoyed their work. It was in there that your plumber or bank teller roped you into buying their kid's Girl Scout cookies or you got to ask the mayor face to face to put up a stop sign at a dangerous intersection.

What had drawn us here, several thousand strong, at more or less the same time, straight and gay, young and old, rich and poor? We had thrown careers and past lives in trash cans; shucked our Northern clothes and donned T-shirts, cut-off's, and flip-flops in a mass molting; and swapped our cars for bicycles. No one wore a watch, and it was always amusing when one Key Wester asked another one what time it was. The answer was usually something like: "I don't know, about 10:30, I think," or they'd both look at the sun and guess it within fifteen minutes. On an island where anything we wanted was no more than a five-minute bike ride away, that was close enough.

Why had we done it?

Individual answers were individual, but the communal answer was simple: pursuit of pleasure, a very un-American goal, in a place that accepted and celebrated eccentricity.

At one dinner party, Tony Falcone, one of the founders of the Fast Buck Freddie's department store, repeated Leigh's and Thomas' comparison of our lives to the movie *The King of Hearts*, when the Germans and the locals retreat from a small French town leaving the gates of the asylum open. The inmates are free and the town is empty. They leave the asylum and race through the town, each assuming the role and dress he or she likes best. One becomes bishop, another gay hairdresser, another madam of the brothel. And then, that out of the way, they all start having fun. This was us landing in Key West.

A Ph.D. in Astronomy opened an ice cream store and shared his knowledge and telescope many nights at Smathers Beach. Several teachers became carpenters, general contractors, and electricians; a nurse became a gallery owner; a friend with a degree in medieval studies became a bookkeeper; another with a degree in psychology became a seamstress.

Many of the arrivals started out the hard way, heading shrimp at the local fish-house or bussing or waiting tables. Many of the gay men made waiting tables a permanent occupation because it allowed them to party late, sleep in, then catch some afternoon sun.

The Conch accent was also an island, a linguistic island in a country becoming linguistically homogeneous, New England strained through a Bahamian sieve. Though many Conchs would admit to a Bahamian heritage, they wouldn't admit to the historical fact that some of their ancestors had gone to the Bahamas originally as United Empire Loyalists, American colonists on the wrong side of the War of Independence. When the Bahamas had proved to be an economic disaster, their descendants trickled over to the Keys.

They were a tight, tight community of survivors, the Conchs, on an island where financial survival had usually been difficult, interspersed with times of great wealth. The island had gone in a few decades from being the richest city per capita in the United States in the late 1800s—one year exporting 100,000,000 cigars to the rest of the country—to being bankrupt during the Depression, when it had had to surrender its city charter to the State. Any municipal jobs now—schools, public works, aqueduct authority, electric utility, building department, police department, fire department—belonged to the Conchs as they took care of each other.

Conchs ran the town, but sometimes with a Keystone Kops incompetence that was hilarious and wonderful. Right after I moved to the island there was a story in the *Mullet Wrapper* about a man who'd lost control of the city's street sweeper, taking out a fire hydrant, three parked cars, and thirty feet of fence on someone's property. It turned out they'd checked his record and it was clean, but had never asked if he had a driver's license. He was the Cuban refugee relative of someone on the city commission and had never even driven a car before.

Thomas called me one day and said we should go to the dedication of the new two-story parking garage that the city had built with federal money. "Thomas, I'm beat. Do I really need to see this?"

"John, this is one of the ways you get to understand the island. It might be pure corn, but it might be fun, you never know."

I biked down to the corner of Angela and Simonton Streets, locked up my bike, and found Thomas and Leigh already there.

There was a small clot of local dignitaries Thomas identified for me: the mayor, the commissioners, the police chief—who, it was rumored, along with his top men, guaranteed our pot consumption—and a few men in suits that had to be Feds. Thomas had already explained to me that people being transferred to a branch bank from anywhere else were instructed never to show up for work in a suit when they moved to the island because only Feds out to catch smugglers or corrupt politicians wore suits.

There was also a reporter from the *Mullet Wrapper* that Thomas and Leigh waved to: "Dorothy Raymer," Thomas told me, "the woman who lived across from Henry Faulkner."

There was a screech from the feedback in the mike they'd set up, then one of the suits stepped up and mouthed platitudes about the wonderful connection between the island and the federal government, a mutually helpful connection, and that he was pleased the federal government had given this gift to the island.

The mayor stepped to the mike and matched platitude for platitude. "We are happy, indeed, that we can be a home for the American military," (and their payrolls, but he didn't say that) "and we thank you for helping us relieve the parking problem in our fair city with this garage."

The mayor and the number one Fed walked over to the ribbon stretched across the ramp leading to the second-story parking entrance and together cut the ribbon, followed by applause. A car drove toward us from Simonton Street, a huge land yacht, a 1960 Cadillac convertible with its top down. "That's Ismelda, the police chief's wife," Leigh whispered. Ismelda was enormous, fatter even than her very fat husband.

People waved, and there was a small amount of cheering as she approached the up-ramp. What no one knew was that the ramp had been built to the Fed's specs for today's slightly smaller cars. At the first turn in the ramp, there was a horrible scraping noise as the car became stuck, with its engine racing, its tires burning rubber. We didn't understand what had happened at first, and there was hysterical screaming from Ismelda, who for sure didn't understand what was happening and kept trying to accelerate. The police chief ordered one of his men to the rescue, and he climbed over the trunk and back seat, reached over and shut off the ignition, then ran back to his boss for further orders.

There was a hurried, whispered consultation, and this time two police officers climbed back over the trunk and back seat to pull and push a now hysterical woman, weighing half a hippopotamus, up over the back seat, then over the trunk, giving us all a view of red lace underwear and thighs that could feed sub-Saharan Africa for a week.

Everyone in the crowd who didn't depend on city government for their livelihood was laughing themselves sick.

When we left, Thomas looked at me: "Aren't you glad you came now?"

The *Mullet Wrapper* the next day mentioned only the successful opening of the garage.

Black Conchs formed a tight community within a tight community. When a black Conch recognized or greeted anyone, it was with a single word "Alright," and a wave of the hand. Black funerals were as elaborate as those in New Orleans, with a band and a parade.

For all Conchs, the rest of the world was "up there." You could tell one you'd been to Mexico, Paris, or Morocco, and most would ask: "What are things like up there?" It took a long time before any Conch trusted any "outsider," as anyone from anywhere else was called.

Every party included joints passing around, and one either did or did not partake. In a town where it was possible for a man to get a ticket for being bare-chested more than three blocks from the beach, it was difficult to get arrested for marijuana possession unless you were especially flagrant, because the police were the suppliers. Some of the Key West cops wore T-shirts that said "SAVE THE BALES" when they were off-duty, a reference to the bales of pot that boaters kept finding. One cop started calling the bales "square grouper" (grouper was a local fish), and the name caught on and soon several restaurants had a square grouper sandwich on the menu.

The local politics were corrupt: the fire chief with the improbable name of Bum Farto, known for wearing all red, was busted for dealing out of his chief's car and then disappeared forever before he could testify, leading to the best-selling T-shirt that said "WHERE IS BUM FARTO?" The city attorney, the deputy police chief, and several of the street cops were drug-busted next—the police chief was an un-indicted co-conspirator, we'd heard—leaving the town for a short while with only five cops to patrol all three shifts and a serious shortage of pot.

When the Feds got really annoyed, they made even bigger busts, one getting the name "Big Pine 29" after the number of men indicted. Big Pine Key was an island thirty miles up the Keys where many of the smugglers brought in their loads. At the trial, un-busted men sat next to each other in the courtroom audience wearing T-shirts: "Big Pine 30," "Big Pine 31," "Big Pine 32" . . . to tweak the Feds' nose.

The star witness in one of the big drug busts had gone missing the week of the trial, and the Feds had had to go looking for him. They found him in a local motel, passed out, with a vibrator up his butt, battery run down, the newspaper informed an amused and un-shocked town.

Conchs referring to the prison time of one of their own would refer to it as "college" when outsiders were in earshot, as in "That was when Bubba Joe was away to college." When Bubba Joe graduated from college, there was almost always a job waiting for him in the city government.

The Feds hated trying a Conch in Key West because it was impossible to get an impartial jury. This led to legal disconnects, like one case where a lawyer, an outsider who had been arrested for bribing the mayor, was convicted, got time, and was disbarred. The man who took the bribe was a Conch, and at every appearance in the Federal Court on Simonton Street he was given a hero's welcome by other Conchs lining his path into court. He was acquitted.

Those of us who were new to the island shrugged off the corruption in the local politics because we were busy settling in, and the Conchs had all the power anyway. This was proven to me beyond any possible doubt when I went to dinner with a friend of mine from New York one night at a restaurant on Margaret Street in Old Town. While I was there, the mayor and his wife came in and sat across the room from us. Ten minutes after their arrival, the lights went out . . . another island blackout. The waiters started distributing candles.

The mayor snapped his fingers at one of the waiters and told the man to take him to a phone and bring a flashlight. The phone was on the bar, right next to my table. The mayor dialed a number. "Ray, this is Tom, the mayor, dammit. What the hell's going on? The wife and I are in Compass Rose trying to have dinner and the lights went out." A few seconds of silence as he listened to the person on the other end. "Look, I don't give a good goddamn about that, get the lights on here." Another pause as he listened again. "Screw the airport. Shut 'em off. They got generators for the runway lights. Get the lights back on here."

Only God and a Conch mayor could say: "Let there be light, and light was." The lights came back on in the restaurant, and the paper the next day reported that the power to the airport had been off for four hours in spite of being tied to a preferential grid. My New York friend shook his head in disbelief.

The arrival of the two thousand or so of us in the '70s into a town of only twenty-eight thousand caused major changes. The old wooden houses of Old Town became occupied again, the boarded-up storefronts on Duval Street started losing their boards, and a whole new community whose woof was pleasure and whose warp was, well, more pleasure started weaving itself together.

The funkiness of the infrastructure acted like a natural filter, shunting white bread America to places like Naples, Sarasota, or

Palm Beach, and if that wasn't enough to keep them out, there was the old Seven-Mile Bridge. No one, not even us, liked driving it, the very narrow roadway the Feds had thrown up on the original train bridge after the hurricane of '35 had destroyed the railroad. It was so narrow that a van and a semi coming from opposite directions had six inches, maximum, of clearance, and many people lost their mirrors, and a few their lives.

If our daily life on the island was the melody, the physical beauty was the basso continuo: the trees, the flowers, the birds, the skies, the famous ocean sunrises and sunsets, the stunningly colored water, the underwater forest of coral and sea life . . . and each other, people whose lives were their own property, not deformed by disappearing into the great metastasizing maw of corporate America.

Food, shelter, clothing . . . we all made enough to eat, we all had someplace to stay because houses and rents were dirt cheap, and clothing, enough said.

What we had in abundance was time. Commuting was a five-minute bike ride to work unless you stopped to talk to all your friends on their porches, which could extend it to forty minutes. Time expanded ever outward, joining with the incomparable sunlight to give us . . . what? The alluring feeling that time was not passing? That we were immortal? The best lies are always the most seductive.

Seven

Summer heat returns to the island in May, Thomas and Leigh had warned me, and when it slammed me that first May, I was shocked, but not alone. Everyone around me kept saying: "I don't remember it ever being this hot before," which Thomas and Leigh told me everyone said every year when the heat came back.

"Just slow down and accept it," Thomas advised. "Once you get used to it, you'll like some of the things that come with it. Floating in the languor of a Key West summer afternoon can trick you into believing that immortality is possible." He actually said that at dinner one night, and I had to write it in my journal: May 26, 1977, Key West.

My friend was right. The skies turned from blue to bluish white from all the water evaporating into the air, and sunlight flooded the island, palpable, filling every space, illuminating everything, transforming everything, turning the ordinary scene of a person walking down the street into a tableau vivant of a human moving through liquid amber.

Only seven months from the prison of exile and teaching in Toronto, I peeked through my fingers, not trusting the road sign that said: "Caution, Happiness Ahead," and tiptoed toward the little glimpses of paradise behind it. Wouldn't those flowers and exploding vegetation conceal vipers?

Useless to resist. Multi-colored bougainvillea crawled over fences; the Royal Poinciana trees exploded into gigantic umbrellas of outrageous red; and the perfume of tamarind and frangipani trees, ylang-ylang and jasmine, night-blooming cereus, and joe-wood took over from the sun at night to seduce and inebriate you.

One afternoon in my Paris life, I had been trying to get the eight executives in front of me to actually speak English, one of my jobs: *animer la conversation.* These were some of the most intelligent and best-educated humans on the planet, but French culture required they not make mistakes in front of each other, impossible if you're going to learn another language. Frustrated, I tried getting them to speak by asking where they went on vacation. The most blocked student, a woman who controlled the investment of billions of dollars in oil revenues, opened up. "I go to ze South of France."

"Why?" I asked.

"Because of ze light." Then she switched back to French. "*Je ne suis pas artiste, mais je comprends la lumière.*" (I'm not an artist, but I understand light.) It gave me goose bumps and went into the journal. I wasn't an artist either, but I understood that the island's summer light was benediction.

These were our "very rich hours," my friends and I: you wake up and bike to the open-air laundromat where you get your morning coffee and a copy of the *Mullet Wrapper* with its hilarious crime reports that reinforced you lived someplace quite different.

After reading the paper, you bike to work, sweat through eight hours of it with friends, then bike down to Simonton Beach. Crossing the intersection at Eaton Street, through a tunnel of overhanging mahogany trees with their new, impossibly green leaves, you see the blue water of the harbor at the end of the street and, if you're lucky, a sailboat crosses and you sigh, maybe begin to trust the road sign.

Three or four of your friends are already there, and you knit together your individual day stories and laugh at the newspaper's latest tale of human folly. The water off Simonton Beach, the harbor, is quickly deep, clear, and wonderfully cool. We dive in and swim towards Sylvia, the channel marker sixty feet off the beach named after a local cocktail bar singer. The current is strong, so the last few feet leave you gasping. Leigh, a powerful swimmer, is always the first to arrive. We pull ourselves up the steel beams on a rope someone had attached to the platform where the beacon rests.

When we're all on top, like over-sized seabirds, someone pulls out a joint from a Zip-loc bag and fires it up. We smoke and have complicated conversations about what's going on in the rest of the country, quick reviews of a new author discovered, and then silence as the star slips underwater. After one sunset that summer, with under-lit clouds off to the east pouring rain, we were all gushing superlatives when Thomas said: "Yes, but I thought the magenta was a bit wanting," and we all laughed and recognized that he was telling us in his own way not to try to describe or define it, just watch. We dived back in and joined up for dinner later, fortunate, happy tribe.

I peeked through the fingers again: "Caution, More Happiness Ahead" the next sign read, and I still didn't trust that all this could be happening, really happening, happening to *me*. After a gothic childhood, years of struggle and poverty, there was reward, and what reward! Do all Americans have this mistrust of pleasure? How many people on this many-peopled continent were channeling this simple love of life and place?

At least once a weekend, I would bike to the Green Parrot bar at the corner of Southard and Whitehead downtown to hang out with the guys, my construction worker buddies. The Green Parrot, always called "the Parrot," is a true locals' bar. Its signs reflect Key West humor: "SORRY, WE'RE OPEN" is one; "ADJUSTING ATTI-TUDES SINCE 1890" is another; and my favorite: "NO SNIVEL-LING." The two street sides of the bar have huge openings to the street with drop-down wooden shutters and no glass, so sidewalk traffic is right there next to you. It always amuses us who frequent the bar to watch the reaction of tourists passing by who look in. They've heard Key West is "colorful;" this place looks colorful, should they go in? There are construction workers inside, so most walk on by.

One Sunday afternoon, a yuppie couple stopped to look in, and the husband started to enter. His wife pulled him back and said: "Honey, don't go in there. They look dirty and dangerous." The bar exploded with laughter, whistles, and applause, and the couple scur-ried off. The Parrot's owner had T-shirts made up with the slogan "DIRTY AND DANGEROUS," and we all bought one. One of the guys inside that day had just gotten his contractor's license and named his company D & D Construction.

In the Parrot, the dumbest, butt-cracked plumber was as welcome as the best-educated contractor. In the Parrot, it was possible to dis-cuss literature with the man on your left and joist sizes with the man on your right, a kind of democratic meritocracy that didn't exist any-where else in the world I'd visited.

Jeff was there for one of my favorite Parrot afternoons. We were on stools next to one another talking about the best book ever written about war, Michael Herr's *Dispatches*, when a late-forties woman with short hair curled tight to her head, smallish breasts, and strong features tip-toed in and sat at the one empty barstool and ordered a beer.

Jeff interrupted me. "Look at what just came in." I looked over.

The bartender delivered her a beer. She pulled out her compact and powdered her face, took a dainty sip, and looked around. Conversation around the horseshoe slowed. This was late Saturday afternoon in a working-class local bar, where the only sane women who wanted entry were the tough, wise-cracking bartenders.

Two or three "not just quite right" gestures, and Jeff and I figured out this was a transvestite.

"Jeff, I'm leaving. I don't want to see what happens next. I hate violence."

"No, wait. This is Key West. It'll probably be fun. If they try to hurt her, I'll stop them."

Watching the other guys watching "her" was like watching a cat examine something new. Some of the other guys figured it out and told their buddies. She kept drinking her beer, then started swaying to the music on the jukebox.

Conversation built up again, and then Arturo, an A/C journeyman with an IQ somewhere south of the Equator, yelled across the horseshoe. "Are you one of those drag queen bitches?"

All talk stopped as suddenly as on a plane struck by lightning. The target of the question set her beer down and ran her hand over the back of her head. She looked at him, and then in an accent that would do the royals proud, answered: "I am Mary, sir, a cross-dresser, but not a bitch. A bitch is a female dog, which you would know if you weren't an uneducated dolt."

Yelps of laughter and applause, then two men had to restrain Arturo.

Mary called the bartender over. "Drinks for everyone on me, honey."

More applause. You can always win over the crowd in a construction-worker bar by buying the drinks. Then people started buying

Mary drinks, and when she was drunk, she got up and started dancing. When she got too drunk, and it was discovered she also didn't have any money, everyone chipped in to cover her tab. The bartenders called her a cab, and everyone chipped in to pay for that, too. Helped out by the bartenders, she turned and gave a royal wave: "Love you, boys. Lovely time. More fun than the last Ascot."

On another Saturday afternoon at the Parrot, Jeff told me about the softball games they'd organized at Peary Court, the vacant Navy property where the city had put in a ball-field with a ratty concession stand and some rickety bleachers. One of the scenes in the Goldie Hawn movie, *Crisscross*, takes place there.

"Come out and join us. It's a good way to meet people, have some fun, and let off some steam."

"Jeff, I don't like competitive sports. Competition pulls something ugly out of me, so I try to avoid it."

"Lighten up, John. We play for real, but the fun's more important than the competition. You're too much of a wonk. Crack out of the old routine."

I agreed to show up for the next game for two reasons: I was in serious awe of this man's conquest of what he had done and seen in Vietnam, and deferred. The other reason was personal. In my childhood, the Navy had moved us every two years from one unknown place to another. We would be driving through small unfamiliar towns at night because my father liked to drive after dark, and every time I saw those brightly lit, small-town ball-fields, I ached to be there, strange boy wanting to belong somewhere.

Peary Court was a forty-three acre, open, green space just off White Street near Garrison Bight, where the charter boats docked. It had once been the site of Army barracks and a parade ground. It was from there that the Union troops on the island had marched out and taken control of every strategic installation on the island when the Civil War started. Key West, with all its slave owners, as far south of the Mason-Dixon line as possible, had remained in the Union under a boot-heel during the entire war. It was the genesis of Conch disrespect for the federal government, a disrespect alive over a hundred years later.

I started playing softball once a week with a ragtag group of construction workers. We played seriously, even though few of us would have passed a breathalyzer or piss test those nights, and it wasn't unknown for a runner and a baseman to share a hit off a joint waiting for the next batter to do something.

Doug Arnold, a Conch electrician I knew slightly from jobs, was always there on the opposing team. Though he was short and got teased for being gay, he was a real athlete. Conch baseball, which he'd played in high school, was a force to be reckoned with in the State, and Key West High School had sent several hometown boys to the majors.

Because he was short—five foot, six inches—pitchers had a harder time hitting the strike zone, so he walked a lot. When he was at bat, the catcher would try and break his concentration by teasing him about how cute his ass was and what he'd like to do to it, but Doug was wiry, strong, and focused. When he connected with the ball, it was usually a double. He was also fast, and he and I shared a passion for base-stealing.

Doug was playing second base one night when I got lucky with a sweet pitch and hit a double. When I reached second and was waiting to be sent home, I looked across the street at two weathered, abandoned-looking, two-story wooden houses. They were joined together on the first floor a few feet back from the front facades, and the one on the right, the shorter of the two, leaned slightly towards the larger one. The original windows had been replaced with aluminum louvers, as gray as the siding, and something about the buildings grabbed me.

Doug saw me staring at the houses. "Beautiful, aren't they? Look at how they're joined. Makes me think of a man and his wife with their kid between them, and she's about to rest her head on her husband's shoulder."

I was surprised by the lyricism, but took advantage of his distraction to steal third base. When I stood up from my slide, I doffed my cap and made a slight bow in his direction. He flipped me the bird, but grinned.

After the game—my team lost—some of us made our separate ways to the Parrot. I stopped to say hello to Leigh, so by the time I locked my bike up outside, several of the other players were already seated at the bar. Doug was inside, and there was an empty stool next to him. I sat down and poked him in the ribs: "Thanks for the steal."

He laughed. "Prick. Not fair, but we won anyway."

He bought me a beer, and we started talking and joking about the game. Then he asked me where I was from. I'd seen him doing electrical work on jobs, and he and I had played ball a few times together. I knew he was a Conch and gay, but not much else. I didn't know how much, if anything, he knew about me or how much I wanted to reveal, so I explained that I was a Navy brat and had grown up in several different places, but had lived in Canada and France after college.

He turned on his stool. "Where in France?"

"Paris. Why?"

"I lived in Paris, too."

"Are you serious? When?

"1972 to 1973. I was at the American University."

"That's when I was there...'72 to '75. Where did you live?"

"In a tiny room in the First Arrondissement near the PTT (the telephone exchange) on the Rue du Louvre."

"Doug, you're making this up. I lived right around the corner on the Rue Berger, right across from the Pavillon Baltard and the Bourse de Commerce. I used to walk through the Pavillon over to Au Pied de Cochon for *steack-frites* and a glass of red wine."

"I ate there all the time, too. *Steack-frites* and red wine: a dollar seventy-five. It was one of my favorite places, especially late at night... all the butchers in their bloody aprons at the counter, because it was cheap, and all the high society folks at the tables having their onion soup after the opera or theater. It was wonderful."

"Damn, Doug, I can't believe this. We were probably eating there at the same time and here we are. Unreal. Must be fate." I raised my beer and proposed a toast: "To Paris, Key West, and to second acts in American lives." He recognized the quote and toasted.

Then he looked over to the entrance and swore. "Damn, there's Pete." A mountain of a man, a mason with the reputation of being a real street brawler, came in with a friend and sat down opposite. They were talking and didn't seem to notice anyone else at the bar.

"What's wrong?"

"Pete never passes up a chance to mess with me in public about being gay. Watch this."

Doug called the bartender over and ordered drinks for Pete and his friend. She told them who'd bought them and nodded over toward Doug.

Pete looked over. "Doug," he roared in a voice that could clear cut forests, "if you think you get to blow me by buying me a drink, you got your head up your ass, you little pickle sniffer." The insult sucked all the air out of the place, and everyone turned to look at its target.

"Worked last night, didn't it?" Doug yelled back. The entire bar yelped with laughter, and banged on the bar-top, then stopped as Pete got off his stool and lumbered over to us, pissed-off look on his face. The bartender started to come out from behind the bar to head him off but was too late. Pete banged into Doug, grabbed him, lifted him completely off the stool, swung him sideways a couple of times like a rag doll, then dropped him.

"How you been, you little dick smoker?" and Pete extended his hand.

"OK, you gorilla," Doug answered and extended his. "But why do you have to embarrass me every time you see me?"

"'Cause I love you, you little runt—not that way, you homo—but I love you. You're good people. You fixed my old lady's bathroom light for free. And if I ever caught anyone else messing with you, I'd tear 'em apart." They gave each other a big, backslapping hug, went back to their stools, and it made the whole bar laugh again and feel good about themselves and Key West.

When everyone calmed down, I turned to Doug again. "Can I ask you a personal question?"

"Shoot."

"Does the teasing ever bother you about being gay?"

"You want the long answer or the short answer?'

"Whatever you feel comfortable with."

He turned to face me. "This kind of teasing by these men is as good as it gets for a gay man. They even feel comfortable enough around me they tell me gay jokes. Imagine being an openly gay construction worker anywhere else in the country, let alone getting plastered in one of their bars. When they tease me, they're including me, not excluding me, and that makes me feel good. I think it makes them feel good about themselves, too.

"Look at Pete, for example. You just know he was brought up to hate gay people. He probably bullied all the class sissies all through school. But I think most people like the feeling they get when they rise above the prejudices they grew up with. Look at how everybody clapped when Pete and I hugged each other."

He stopped for a minute and ordered two more beers. When the bartender took the order, she smiled at Doug. "Honey, do you know how surprised I was to find out you were gay?"

Doug laughed. "Sweetheart, think how surprised *I* was to find out. I'm *what*? Wait. Do I get a say in this?"

She laughed and went to get our drinks. Doug turned back towards me.

"I had to earn this kind of respect from these people, John. I did it slowly, buying the coffee at break time on jobs, going by their places after work when they needed electrical work done, and doing the small stuff for free or a couple beers. Then I'd meet the wives, who I always charmed, maybe stay for dinner. That way the guys saw me as a person, not a taboo. And they respect me for my work when they see me crawling out from under a house pulling wires, getting dirty just like them." He laughed. "It helps, too, that most of them are scared to death of electricity, and they see me elbow deep in live electrical panels.

"And then there're the Conchs." He shook his head. "Only a few guys I went to school with speak to me at all. I don't know if you've noticed me on any of the jobs, but the Conchs will barely even nod to me even though my family's been here three generations. For Conchs, it's alright for outsiders to be gay, but not one of their own. Someone as outrageous as Henry Faulkner with his goat—do you know about him?"

I nodded.

"Well, someone as outrageous as him is fine with the Conchs.

"What's really strange is that a Conch can sort of get away with being gay if he's over-the-top outrageous, too. There was a guy in my dad's generation, Johnny Knight, who ran that little store on the corner of William St. and Windsor Lane, and he was a real flamer. There's a story about his famous chicken dance at a place out on Stock Island called Nebo's. Johnny hard-boiled some eggs and stuck them up his butt one night, then got naked and jumped up on the bar squawking and flapping his arms like a chicken, stopping every few seconds to pop out an egg."

"I don't know whether to laugh or throw up."

"The guys at Nebo's probably didn't either. Johnny was OK, but the Conchs treat someone like me who's just an ordinary Joe like a traitor."

"What about your family?"

"My mother's a Cuban Conch, and she's sort of OK with it, but my dad doesn't speak to me much anymore, and my brother has become real distant. It hurts."

"I'm sorry, Doug, that's not right."

"Hey, it could be worse. I got these guys."

We were quiet for a minute and then he started asking me questions about Paris. "Did you ever go to …? What did you think of…?" and off we ran, two Yanks on a nostalgic ramble through the City of Light.

When I was ready to leave, we shook hands, and I promised to steal another base next game. He laughed. "Fat chance. I know what a sneak you are now."

The next game was a mirror image of the last. I was third baseman and Doug reached there with a triple. When he touched base, he nodded toward the two houses across the street. "Did you notice the 'For Sale' sign on them?"

"You think I'm going to fall for the same trick? I'm not looking over there."

"I'm serious. They're for sale. I'm going to walk over after the game and get the realtor's number. Want to come with me?"

"Ask me after the game."

My team lost again. Doug sought me out, and we walked across the street. The houses were obviously empty. I tried one of the front doors, but it was locked. There was a large yard—large for Key West— on the side of the larger building and a garage in the far corner, with its entrance off the side street.

"Do you think the yard's part of it?" I asked him.

"Must be. The steps off the side doors go down into it."

We walked the two accessible sides of the property. "I don't know what it is, but something about the place intrigues me," he said, and I agreed. "I'm going to call the realtor tomorrow. I want to see inside. Want to come with me?"

"If you can set it up for after work."

The realtor let us in at a little past five the next day. We entered through the front door of the larger house. There were scurrying noises and an acrid smell, a combination of dust, mold, and rodent scat. This house, though tall, was only two rooms deep, with beaverboard-covered walls and ceiling, sagging floors, and a minimal nasty bathroom in a corner of the rear room.

A rickety staircase led upstairs to one large room with the same wall and ceiling finish, all painted a god-awful pink. Back downstairs, we walked through a small passageway, the join we could see from the street, into the smaller house. The ground floor was a single large space with a broken stove and, upstairs, by another bad staircase, another, single, open room.

Doug pointed out a strange feature: there was no inside covering on the walls of this smaller building. "That's the backside of the tongue-and-groove siding on the outside, and look: it's vertical. I've never seen that before."

Back downstairs, the realtor led us out the back door of the first house into a sixty-foot-long, single-story shed built out of what looked like mostly scrap lumber. At the very end of it was a big surprise: an enormous, igloo-shaped, brick oven.

"This was a bakery?" I asked the realtor. He shrugged. "It must have been. Look at the machine up there." I pointed to a large, rusted piece of equipment with two wheels mounted on the collar ties. "I'll bet that had belts that kneaded the dough."

"That would explain the buildings," Doug said. "The house without finished walls was the store, with storage upstairs. The owners lived in the big house, up and down, and this is where the work was done."

"You're from here. Do you know anything about it?" I asked him.

He shook his head no. "I'll ask some of the old Conchs and go see the historian at the library."

We walked outside into the yard, which the realtor said did go with the houses. There were two mango trees, a papaya, an avocado (the Conchs called them "alligator pears"), and one fruit tree with large, green, heart-shaped fruit. "Guanabana," Doug said when he saw me puzzled. "Makes great ice cream but you have to catch the fruit before it falls," and he pointed to the ground where several lay splattered, covered with fruit flies.

We went over to the garage and peeled back a piece of the loose tin siding. Inside, floor to ceiling, were automobile parts: head gaskets, crankshafts, and also some beautiful steering wheels from old Studebakers and Hudsons.

The realtor asked if we'd seen enough. "We need to look at the foundations," Doug told him and checked under the smaller house. I found a place to look under the large one and saw what I had expected: the foundation beams of the house were rotten and sitting on pieces of stone quarried from the big cistern we'd seen behind the small house.

I met Doug back on the street out front. We thanked the realtor and compared notes. The foundation of the other house was in equally bad shape. Both suffered from having been built low to the ground. Years of leaf litter and the city paving and re-paving the street had put the foundation beams partly below grade, which caused them to rot.

We stood there looking at the facades. $150,000 was cheap for this much square footage and a yard in Old Town.

"No one's bought them because they have to have everything," Doug said. "New plumbing, new electrical, new foundations, *everything*." He shook his head. "I want them."

"I do, too. They *are* beautiful. I like that it was a bakery once. Think of all those poor people working back there with all that heat and smoke and no fans and no AC. But think of the work, not to mention the money to fix them up."

"I know." He turned away, then turned back. "Hey, if you're not doing anything for dinner, come over to my place and let's talk about it."

"I'm supposed to have dinner with a friend ."

"Bring your friend. I made moussaka yesterday, and there's more than enough for all of us." Moussaka sounded way better than another over-cooked and under-flavored WASP meal, so I biked over to White Street and a pay phone and called Leigh and extended the invitation.

She accepted. I turned to Doug: "What's the address?" He gave me an address on Fleming. "Upstairs apartment." Leigh agreed to meet us there in an hour. I went home to shower and change clothes.

It started raining on my way to Doug's, so I was soaked when I got there. Leigh's bike was already locked up on the sidewalk, so I headed up and heard familiar laughter behind Doug's door. I knocked and Leigh opened it in mid-laugh, toweling off her hair, wearing what was obviously Doug's bathrobe.

Quick kiss. "I'll get you a towel, too," she said and headed off somewhere inside.

Doug said hello and handed me a glass of wine, then continued the story he'd been telling Leigh when she got back with my towel.

". . . So, Mildred"—Doug turned to me and told me that Mildred was a hostess everyone hated at the Pier House so I could follow the story he'd been telling Leigh—"so Mildred went looking for the waiters. She turned into the waiters' station, and there was Alice on her knees blowing Daniel. Mildred screamed, then Alice screamed when she slammed her head into a shelf getting up, breaking glasses."

Doug and Leigh started laughing themselves sick before he could continue.

"Everyone in the dining room was now looking towards the waiters' station. Mildred yelled: "What were you doing?" even though it was obvious. Alice said: "I woke up dick hungry," and walked out to take care of her tables. Daniel swept past her and went back to his tables, too."

I interrupted the story. "So, you two know each other already?"

"I've known Sally for years. We used to work together at the Pier House."

"Sally?"

"Sally Snatch. That's my nickname for her."

"One which he can and you *cannot* use," Leigh quickly interjected.

"I gave her that nickname because she used to screw up orders so much. I told her she was thinking with her snatch instead of her head." They both laughed and kissed. "We haven't seen each other in a while, so this is fun."

"So, go back to your story," Leigh said. "I heard about it, but it was right after I quit."

"Well, Mildred, in high dudgeon, went looking for David" (the eccentric, cheap, and gay proprietor of the Pier House). "David was living in that construction trailer in the parking lot at the time, so off she went and knocked on the door of the trailer to complain about Alice and Daniel and also that Terry, the dishwasher, hadn't shown up.

"David opened the door and invited Mildred in. Her first shock was when Terry stumbled naked out of David's bedroom asking for breakfast. Then, when she'd recovered from that sight, she told David what Alice and Daniel had been up to and demanded that he fire them both. David looked at her for a minute then said: "Why?"

"End of Mildred," Doug gargled out, and the two of them screamed with laughter.

I was envious of the shared history and obvious camaraderie. Once they calmed down, Paris talk brought us together. Doug had a framed map of the Paris Metro on his wall, and we all went over to it and pointed out the stops we'd lived near and swapped stories.

Doug served the moussaka and a salad, and they told me some of their other Key West stories, which always made me wish I'd been able to move here earlier. While they talked, I looked around at Doug's apartment, which resembled Leigh's: comfortable, second-hand furniture with several original touches. A couple silk screen prints of old Conch houses I now recognized as Thomas Szuter's work—Doug knew Thomas, too— hung on the walls along with framed photos of old Parisian storefronts.

One entire wall, nearly floor to ceiling, was a bottle collection on narrow shelves. Doug explained, when I asked, that his family and he had collected them over the years, mostly from Rest Beach, where the town had dumped all the debris from the Great Fire of 1886 that had destroyed most of what was now Old Town. He showed us their different characteristics: how perfume bottles differed from medicine bottles and how color was important. He picked up a cobalt blue bottle. "This is an old poison bottle. They're the most valuable. Funny, huh?"

Over a piece of homemade pineapple upside-down cake and glasses of port, the 'Bakery' came up. Leigh, who hadn't seen it yet, played devil's advocate. "Are you sure you guys want to do this? Combining business and friendship is dangerous, you know that, and if it's in as bad shape as you say, where are you going to get the money to fix it up? Also one of you is gay and one's straight. Could that be a problem, living and working together? Plus, you've only known each other a short while. Sure you want to do it? I'm not trying to talk you out of it, but there are issues you both need to think about."

Leigh and Doug hugged and kissed and promised not to lose touch again. Leigh and I kissed goodnight outside, where it had stopped raining. I headed over to Angela Street and stopped in front of the dark and empty buildings. They still spoke to me. Every transformational thing in my life had come from a leap into the unknown. Why not another?

Doug found out that the buildings had indeed been a bakery, La Yndia Bakery, with the nineteenth-century orthography where today's "Ingles" was once "Yngles." They had been built, Tom Hambright, the city historian, discovered for us, over one hundred years ago, only the second buildings put up in that part of town. He directed us to an amateur historian in town who found a photo of a canvas-covered, mule-drawn delivery wagon with La Yndia Bakery painted on the side. Two very short, rough-looking Cubans stood next to the wagon, looking directly into the camera. We paid to get a large copy of the photo made.

The day before we put in an offer, Doug invited me to lunch at the Sands, where we sat on the beach at a table with umbrella, toes digging into the sand. Tennessee and another man were at another table. Doug waved to them.

"Herlihy," Doug told me when I asked if he knew who Tennessee's companion was. "He used to live here on Baker's Lane and wrote *Midnight Cowboy* there. It was a real hippie hangout, men and women walking around naked, smoking dope in the trees. He left when he got famous and lost his privacy, and also because the cops hassled him for harboring hippies. Has a huge wiener, and he's a lot of fun in the sack, but I guess you don't want to know that."

"I'm no prude, but I think I'd rather focus on his literary accomplishments."

We ordered. I had assumed the topic Doug wanted to talk about was the property we were about to buy. It wasn't.

"John, you know I'm gay, but does it bother you in any way?"

"Doug, that's kind of a strange question to be asking now, isn't it?"

"A lot of my friends—the gay ones—are telling me I'm making a mistake doing a deal like this with a straight man. I don't think so, but to be fair to both of us, I thought we ought to bring it out in the open."

"To tell you the truth, Doug. I don't think about you being gay very much. When I think of you, I think of your intelligence and education, your honest work on the jobs, your sports ability, the shared history with Paris. The gay business, I guess it doesn't mean more to me than an individual quirk" and I caught myself, "and don't take that the wrong way. For me, it's like finding out you're left-handed, not right. Anyway, how someone else gets their nut isn't something that interests me very much. Remember, too, I have a master's degree in French. A lot of the other men in my classes and almost all the profs were gay. Some I liked, some I didn't. It just isn't a big deal to me. My mental eye doesn't vet people that way. I respect the difference just like I expect you to respect that I'm not gay."

He smiled. "You mean that I won't hit on you, even though you're hot?"

"Well, I assume that as basic respect. And I've heard you're pretty successful, sexually. Good for you, but I don't want to see a bunch of guys' swinging tackle all over the place, and you probably don't want to see a bunch of tits and coozes either. There has to be a little privacy. The place is big enough we can work all that out."

"So no hanging tackle?"

"Right, and no exposed pussies."

"No throbbing rods?"

"And no glorious gashes." We both started laughing.

"No magnificent members?"

"And no clamorous clits."

"No wagon wheel coffee tables."

"And no statues of David."

"Agreed." I extended my hand. "Partners?"

"Partners," and we shook. I liked this man.

On our way out, he introduced me to Herlihy, whom I complimented. He accepted the compliments graciously, and then I introduced myself to Tennessee for the third time because he never remembered me.

We put in an offer of $140,000.

We were hooked on the houses now, so when the owners countered with full price, $150,000, we agreed. I found a buyer for my house right away, we lined up a mortgage from the bank, and six weeks after the dinner at Doug's apartment, we walked out of the lawyer's office with the keys to 1216 Angela Street: La Yndia Bakery.

We biked over to the property, stood across the street in the ballfield, and admired our wrecks. After a couple minutes of quiet contemplation of our folly, Doug said: "Let's go!"

We walked across the street, and he unlocked the door. On a whim, I lifted him up and carried him across the threshold. "Put me down, you asshole." He opened a bottle of wine he had in his backpack and produced two glasses and, drinking and planning, we explored our property. After we'd done a tour, we walked out into the yard, sat down under one of the mango trees, and finished the wine.

"You know we're completely nuts," I said.

"Got that right. At least we know what we're going to be doing the next few years."

"Yeah, and just think what we're going to have when it's finished."

Eight

Thomas and Leigh were the first people invited to see the Bakery, as we all came to call it. Keeping Thomas out would have been like barring a horny sailor from a whorehouse. They showed up on a Saturday afternoon, Thomas on a penny-farthing that he slammed against the porch railing so he could dismount.

Doug had never seen one before, but I knew the ridiculous bicycle from cartoons.

"A penny-farthing, Thomas? How in god's name did you find that?"

"A guy in a bar downtown sold it to me last night."

"Can I take a spin on it?'

"Sure. We'll hold it for you. Climb up on the porch railing to get on." I rode it down the street, falling into the bushes in the right of way when I tried to turn. That huge front wheel forced hugely wide turns. The three of them were laughing when I walked it back.

Doug and I took the two of them inside and walked them through all three buildings. Everything went fine until Leigh saw the bathroom and screamed: "That's disgusting."

"Come on, Sally, it's not as bad as it looks," Doug said. "We've scrubbed and disinfected everything in there."

"I don't care. It's only one step above an outhouse."

"Sally, get serious. What would you know about outhouses?"

"Summer camp, smart ass. That's why I only went one summer."

"Well, one of our first jobs will be to build a bathroom fit for your royal butt."

Doug and I had named the buildings to make discussion easier: the smaller two-story building was "mom"; the taller two-story building was "dad". We hadn't named the long single story building in back yet. We told Thomas what we'd already decided we wanted: in "mom", a master bedroom and bathroom upstairs, and two guest bedrooms and a shared bathroom downstairs. Doug and I both thought the idea of a parlor, a large, formal living room, would be great for the downstairs of "dad," with another large master bedroom and bathroom upstairs. We wanted the sixty-foot-long, single-story room attached to the rear of "dad" to be the great room: a combination informal living room, dining room, and kitchen.

One problem we hadn't solved was access to the second story of the two buildings. Stairways use up a lot of space and create privacy problems. Another unsolved problem was what to do with the huge brick oven in the rear building.

When we were all standing in front of the oven, I explained to Thomas the reverence I had for the work that had been done here, especially under the conditions of a hundred years ago.

"I understand," Thomas agreed, as he tapped on the oven walls and looked at the chimney where it penetrated the roof. When he was finished, we all went back to the front room and sat in the cheap director's chairs we were using for furniture. Doug poured us all some wine. Thomas went into deep thought, and we three talked softly so as not to break his concentration. Leigh told us she had to pee but was not going to sit on *that* toilet, so I got her some toilet paper and directed her to a private spot in the yard. Doug poured Thomas a second glass of wine, which he carried with him on another solitary walk-through of the buildings. When he came back, he was ready. His audience was more than ready.

"Extend the join between the two buildings all the way to the rear of both and up another story. The join is only three feet wide, so it won't detract visually from what's here as long as it remains "stepped in" from the facades, like it is now. Make the downstairs porch railing of "mom" continuous with no opening, to block access to that building from the street. The entrance to the whole property will be the door right here that we came through into what you're calling "dad." Eliminate the stairway in the other building and keep the one in this building. With the join extended to the second floor, this stairway gives you access to the second story of both buildings; extending the join back and up also gives you room for all your bedroom closets.

"Tear down the oven—it's sad, I know—but it's in bad shape and won't ever be used again. One good hurricane and the chimney's coming down anyway. Memorialize it by re-using the bricks somewhere on the property. Display all the artifacts from the bakery, the oven door, the kneading machine, the bread paddles, and hooks somewhere in the great room, where they were used."

I was as open-mouthed as I'd been when he'd told me to knock out a wall in my first house, and once again Leigh told me to close my mouth and pass the joint. In less than an hour this man had looked at and solved every problem in a complicated renovation.

"Thomas, you're a frigging genius," Doug said, and I repeated it.

"Thank you. Oh, also, you should put gable-end windows in the upstairs bedrooms so you can watch the sky from in bed."

Except for adding an additional bedroom and bathroom off the kitchen, what Thomas recommended was exactly what we did.

He refused any compensation for his design advice, even though that was how he earned most of his living, so Doug and I invited him and Leigh for a bang-up Sunday brunch at Louie's.

Every day after work that whole week, Doug and I moved our things in and set up temporary living arrangements. I took the upstairs of "mom" and he took the upstairs of "dad" as our bedrooms. We set up a temporary kitchen—two-by-four legs, plywood countertop—in the downstairs rear of "dad" and hooked up coffeepot, microwave, toaster, toaster oven, and crockpot. Instead of having to use the two-foot-square cracked fiberglass shower in the bathroom, we had a plumber buddy install an outdoor shower hidden from the street by a grove of bananas. By the end of the week, we were in and ready to start work.

That Sunday's brunch at Louie's was the first for all four of us--Leigh, Thomas, Doug and I--together. I warned Doug about Marvin, the waiter, ahead of time, but he told me he already knew him. "He and his partner used to come to the Pier House and torture all the waiters. Now it's my turn to have fun."

That fun began when the four of us walked in, and Marvin caught sight of us. "Oh my god," he screamed and faked a near fainting spell, "so many men and so little time." He seated us, then looked at Leigh. "Girl, you show up first with one hot one," and he pointed at Thomas. "Then you show up with a second hot one," and he pointed at me. "Now you add insult to injury by showing up with a *third* hottie. Tell me, bitch. What you got I don't have?"

"A pussy," she shot back without a second's hesitation. It was the only time in Louie's history that Marvin was rendered speechless. He took our order in pretend huff.

"Why do they serve *five* conch fritters," I complained when they arrived. People usually come as a couple, or two couples, so there's one left over and everyone has to do their Alphonse and Gaston routine: You have it; no, please, you have it."

Leigh speared the fifth fritter, cut it in two, put half in her mouth and gave the other half to Thomas. "Problem solved. You and Doug make it up on the calamari." I flipped her the bird. Of such silliness are traditions started.

The conversation at lunch—two Bloody Mary's each, followed by two bottles of wine—was wide-ranging: books (Thomas had just discovered Tom Sharpe's *Wilt* for us), building in general, and the renovation ahead of Doug and me. When there was a lull in the conversation, genuinely curious and feeling protected enough by the presence of the other two to enter dangerous territory, I asked Leigh why she liked managing money.

She gave me a suspicious look. "Those two put you up to this, haven't they? They're using you to try to find out how much money I have."

"No, I swear and cross my heart. I'm just curious. Studying financial pages and balance sheets seems boring, but you obviously love it."

"If you really want to know, I'll tell you. There are two reasons I enjoy it. The first is because it's pure, clean."

"That's a funny way to describe anything to do with money."

"OK, let me give you a comparison. Look at real estate, which I hate—sorry, John and Doug—because look at how complicated the transaction is. Real estate agents on both sides of every transaction, a survey, a home inspection report, an appraisal, with each part taking a bite out of you, then the closing where they all line up to stick it to you: closing costs, doc stamps, a fee to mail you the documents, etc., etc., etc. And you go through all that buying *and* selling. Then you have property insurance and taxes every year.

"Now look at buying stocks: you put in an order to buy, and it happens in minutes, with a single commission. You sell, same thing."

Marvin interrupted her when he delivered our entrées, bumping his head on the sea-grape branch, sending us all into sick laughter.

"You bitches. I'll spit on your crème brûlée."

"We won't leave a tip," Doug threatened in return.

"Alright, but if you feel pain tonight it's because I've stuck needles in voodoo dolls for every one of you."

When we settled back down, I asked Leigh about the second reason.

"Because it's a game, the biggest game on the planet, and I love competition if I get to choose the game, and I chose this game. I'll be damned if I'll let someone else, especially a man, beat me financially. They might do it short-term, but never overall."

"Have you ever lost big?" Thomas almost choked on his eggs Benedict when I asked that, and she gave him a filthy look.

"OK, Chief-Sees-It-All, go ahead and tell them the story if you think it's so god-damned funny."

"Alright, I will, Princess-Talks-Like-A-Man."

"Imagine the morning," Thomas started out, "a lovely morning in late July. Her Majesty, my exceedingly lovely friend here"—Leigh stuck her tongue out at him—"Her Majesty and I are on a boat, headed out to spend the day on Ballast Key, David Wolkowsky's private island. One of David's not-very-bright employees is piloting the boat. He has his radio on, which I'm not paying much attention to other than being annoyed by it. The news comes on, and the announcer mentions that rain has fallen in Iowa, which had been suffering from a drought, the kind of story that no one pays attention to.

"This one, Her Majesty, suddenly screams, and I mean screams: 'Turn this boat around *now*. I have to get back to Key West, *now, dammit*. I'm long corn.' Long corn . . . what the hell does that mean? Sounds like a foot problem to me. The pilot and I looked at one another in total incomprehension as he turned back towards Key West.

"Her Majesty then tried to explain commodity futures—did I get the term right?" (she nodded)—"to probably the two human beings least likely to understand what they were. We docked, she went to a pay phone and made a call, then came back, very unhappy. When I asked her if her corn was OK, she gave me the 'village idiot' look and was not great company that day."

"Village idiot! If you're long corn, the minute it starts raining, you've already lost money."

"You must've lost a lot of money," Doug asked.

"Almost . . ." and then she caught herself before the figure came out. "Very good, my sneaky friend, very good; you almost got me, but not good enough. How much money I have or lost is none of your business, but I'll tell you one thing, I never played commodity futures again. Rain in Iowa and I lose money. Christ! What a stupid game."

We took a break, looking out at three sailboats and a lone shrimp boat, its outriggers extended like butterfly wings.

"OK guys, help me here," Doug said. "I have a semi-serious question I need to ask advice on. Someone invited me to an orgy this weekend. I've never been to one. Should I go? Have any of you ever done it?"

Thomas and Leigh shook their heads no. When I didn't, all three turned to look at me. "Have you been to one?"

"Pour me another glass of wine, and I'll tell you." He poured.

"Well, the quick answer, my friend, is 'don't do it.' It's one of those things that's more exciting in the imagining than the realization. Mine happened when I was dating a rich American girl in Paris. She and some of her rich friends were doing the 'Cordon Bleu' experience and decided they wanted to 'try' an orgy. Chris asked me if I'd ever been in one. I told her I had, even though I hadn't, because I was curious, too. So, twelve men and women, some English but most American, showed up at an apartment on the Place Dauphine, where the Cordon Bleu students had spread out a true feast. Do you really want to hear this?"

Thomas looked at me: "Stop now and I'll never give you design advice again."

"OK. I was a few years older than everyone else, and everyone was nervous, knowing what they were there for, but didn't know how to start it. I told the host to put on some hot music and for everyone to get naked, grab a glass of wine, then make a toast to youth and fun. They thought that was great. Then I told everyone to pull together in a tight circle, and dance together to the music. People started rubbing against other people, women started that lovely moaning, people dropped to the floor and . . ." I paused, deliberately.

"And what?"

"OK, so soon there's this writhing mass of twelve people on the floor, heavy breathing. I'm slithering as best I can towards my goal, but people keep trying to put fingers, tongues, or worse in my fundament, which I'm not liking—sorry, guys, no offense to present company—and just as I'm inches away from my intended target, an English beauty with a beautiful ass, an American girl in the pile starts screaming: 'Plunge me, plunge me.' We all tried to ignore it, but one of the English guys in a *very* tony accent piped up: 'Plunge me? Did the lass really say plunge me?' Everyone burst out laughing, and that was that. Laughter is the enemy of an orgy. It was a good party, though, and the only time I ever got into one of the buildings on the Place Dauphine. So that's my orgy story, buddy. Sorry, it's probably no help."

Marvin, head wrapped like a mummy's, returned bearing port and our crème brûlée.

"What a drama queen," Doug told him, first time I'd heard the expression. "You're just faking to get a bigger tip."

Marvin laughed and stripped the towel off his head. "Love you guys. Tip big. I need a new boa. Rats made a nest out of the last one. Pink boa, pink nest . . . must be gay rats," and he cackled as he walked off.

With the last of the port, Leigh proposed the toast that became our tradition: "To our magical island and our family"—she was the first one to call us that—"and I'll bet we had the most interesting conversation here today."

Because we had invited them, Doug and I picked up the check, so we were all spared Leigh's breaking down the bill into each person's share to the penny, which always drove me right to the edge. Had New England's stony soil been so poor that generations later the rich descendants of its first tillers were still pinching pennies?

The party we gave to celebrate buying the Bakery went beyond fun. We put in food and alcohol enough for almost fifty people, and more than that came. Our construction buddies were in serious awe of the project. The women reacted to the place, especially the bathroom, the same way Leigh had. What made the party legendary was something Thomas had suggested at Louie's. "Make it a demolition party. Tell everyone to bring a photo or letter of someone they hate. Duct tape them to the wall and hand them a sledgehammer to bash away."

I pasted photos of my Vietnam War enemies—MacNamara, Rostow, the Bundys, Westmoreland, Johnson, and Nixon—in a circle on the wall downstairs in "dad" that was coming out. When Doug gave the signal, I smashed those arrogant authors of the war with glee and hoped they felt a twinge of pain.

Next up was a friend of Thomas' who taped a photo of her ex on the wall. "Leave me with a kid and no money, asshole," she said, then blasted away, destroying the photo, everyone cheering. "Damn, that felt real good," she said, passing the sledgehammer to the next in line.

Next was a plumber Doug and I both knew. Up went a high school photo of him with a girl. "You want to fuck my best friend and dump me, you bitch, take this," and two powerful, wall-smashing swings of the sledge destroyed that photo and another piece of wall.

Leigh put up a photo of her trust fund manager and nailed him good with a single blow.

The sweetest swing came from the asthmatic eight-year-old son of a carpenter. The parents had him write the word asthma on the wall, and they taped an old inhaler to it. Then the father helped him swing the hammer twice, smashing the word and inhaler into oblivion with everyone cheering again and high-fiving the kid.

Great party, lots of dancing, and Doug seemed especially happy because several of his construction worker Key West High School buddies were there, slapping him on the back.

I asked Leigh to spend the night but she declined because of the bathroom and lack of privacy.

Three weeks later, the *Citizen* informed us that the Navy had decided to take back Peary Court right across the street from us and build housing on it, claiming a need. The entire town was angry because the military had taken over most of the best land on the island already and had plenty other places to build on. We were going to lose one of the last big, open, green spaces and our softball field. Doug and I were angrier than most people because having the park right across the street was part of the Bakery's charm.

A month after the town got the news, the bleachers and concession stand were gone, and construction fencing and construction trailers were installed with lots of "No Trespassing" signs. No more magical ballgames.

What the Feds hadn't counted on was this not being a "normal" community.

Harry Powell, a semi-hippie who'd been voted onto the city commission mostly by outsiders, lobbied the federal government not to build on Peary Court, giving them several cogent reasons why they shouldn't. Every reason fell on deaf ears. A few days after the trucks started drilling auger holes for foundations, Harry walked into the main construction trailer with what he said was a dynamite belt strapped to his waist, switch in hand, and a simple request: "Stop construction."

The entire town came to a halt as crowds showed up on White Street to watch federal, state, and local S.W.A.T. teams do their stuff, setting up command posts and strutting around in bulletproof vests. A bomb demolition truck drove up, and more cops poured out. People we assumed were negotiators went in the trailer, shaking their heads in frustration when they came back out.

Thomas and Leigh came over to the Bakery because we had ring-side seats from the upstairs balconies, and it was Thomas who came up with the idea. We grabbed a sheet, spray-painted our message, and hung it off the balcony railing: "GIVE 'EM HELL, HARRY." There was applause from the people who could see it, and then the Feds saw it, and four of them headed our way.

When Leigh saw them coming with their shotguns and vests, all she could say was "Oh, shit!"

Doug and I raced downstairs to lock the front doors; then went back upstairs.

The four men stopped right in front of the downstairs porch and one yelled up: "Remove that sign NOW."

"No way," I yelled back down. "First Amendment right to free expression."

"I could arrest all of you."

"The ACLU would get you laughed out of court, and you know it."

Suddenly, there was lots of cheering, and we could see Harry, in shackles, being led out of the trailer to a police van.

"Look," you got your guy. "Leave us alone."

The leader looked up at us and spit, then led his men away.

"Damn, that trumps your demolition party!" Leigh said.

Bad juju comes from destroying green spaces. On their fifth day of drilling holes, the machines started pulling up human bones, and all work had to stop, mandated by federal and state archeological site protection laws. Scientists flew in from Washington and Tallahassee to examine the bones, but it was Tom Hambright, the city historian, who solved the mystery first. One big section of where they wanted to put houses was where the Army had buried the soldiers who'd died during the yellow fever epidemic of 1887. The Feds were desecrating one of their own burial grounds, and fifteen houses had to be cut from the project. The site was fenced off and honored with a plaque. Two tall mahogany trees stand in the middle of the space, weeping their red tears.

Nine

Doug and I agreed to renovate "mom" first to give each of us a clean bedroom and bathroom. The main problem with all the buildings was that the foundation beams supporting them were rotten because of age and exposure to water from the rise in the ground—grade—around them. They sat, unfastened, on chunks of soft stone which themselves sat unanchored to the ground. A hurricane's storm surge or wind could float or blow the buildings off their foundations.

We needed to jack the buildings up and support them in the air, dig new piers three feet into the rock (which was already two feet below grade), pour the new piers, then build new beams and attach them to the piers. Then the buildings would be lowered back down onto the new foundation and fastened to it. This was the new building code, and I agreed with it, given the island's exposure to those buzz saws that roared across the Atlantic and up from the Caribbean.

We couldn't afford steel I-beams and a crane at a hundred dollars an hour, the standard way to lift buildings, so I devised a system of two-by-twelves bolted to each side of every stud down the two long sides of "mom," then four sets of double two-by-twelves running perpendicular and under the first set, with two-foot legs sticking out each side to place jacks under.

We cut the join completely off the buildings, and then it was here that Doug's Conch connections paid off. An old Conch, Red Beccaise, who used to move whole houses for a living (it happened more often on the island than one imagined), was out of business, but loaned us his old railway jacks and all the dunnage lumber to support the houses once they were lifted.

One Saturday, shortly after we moved in, we started. It's the only thing I've ever done in construction that depended on sound, which Red had explained to Doug. We placed jacks under the first two-by-twelve 'legs' and started lifting, stopping when we heard the first cracking sounds. Then we placed lumber under those legs to support that height and moved to the next set. Placing the lumber was the most time-consuming part of the job, crisscrossing pieces of chopped-up railroad ties under the legs after each lift.

By the end of the day, after three trips around the building, lifting it higher each trip, "mom" was two feet higher in the air than at the beginning of the day. We knocked off, exhausted, but exhilarated. The next day we cut out the old beams and stacked them to use the good parts somewhere later in the house, pulled out the old foundation stones to use somewhere in the garden, and began digging.

"Mom" needed twelve, sixteen-by-sixteen-inch holes four to five feet deep. We had to squat under what we hoped was a stabilized house sitting up on dunnage, digging with trenching tools and a jackhammer. It was agonizing work because of having to squat, and it took over two hours per hole. It was the first time we thought maybe we'd taken on something bigger than we could handle. How were we ever going to find the time to do it all, given that we were both working full-time? The answer was: work every night and every Saturday and Sunday.

My respect for Doug grew each week. He was the anti-thesis of the stereotype of a gay man. He out-worked me, and I worked hard.

There was no task involved in the renovation beneath him, and he was fun as a fellow worker, cracking jokes, making light of what was heavy, heavy lifting, doing silly boogie moves with the jackhammer when a good song came on the radio.

Digging the holes for the new piers was such mindless work that we had a lot of time to talk. The topics were wide-ranging: favorite books (we both read a lot), favorite movies, more talk of Paris, and sometimes things much more personal.

One day he asked me about my relationship with Leigh. "You don't have to talk about it if you don't want to, but I'm curious."

"No, I don't mind, as long as we have an agreement that when we talk about personal stuff it stays here."

"Agreed."

"I think she's a remarkable woman. In her own way, she's brave, too, bucking most of that WASP tradition to live life here on her own terms."

"Helps that she's rich."

"Of course that helps, but I've never seen her play 'entitled rich bitch' or fail to get her hands dirty if she believes in something, and that's hard to do when you could easily either not do it or just pay someone else to do it. Look at the work she does with the women in jail and at the shelter. I like the way she joins in on the fun with us, too. Her sense of play is more like a man's, and I like that.

"She can be bossy, and it's annoying. I thought at first it was because she's rich, but the more I get to know her, the more I think it's partly a style she's adopted to force people to keep their distance. Being that beautiful it's like she said: every horny male thinks he has a right to address her, mentally undress her, and it gets old. I care for her a lot, I may even love her, but I don't think I could ever marry a woman that rich. It's like I told Thomas one night: rich people think they get an extra vote when there's a conflict because they have the money. Story to be continued."

I began to jackhammer loose some more of the stone in the hole we were working on. When I'd loosened enough, he took the trenching tool and started removing it, throwing it out from under the house. While he was doing that, I looked up again at the two-story house sitting above us in the air. I was pretty confident we'd supported it OK, but it still made me nervous. One good squall with rogue winds and it would come down.

Next door, Rose Gonzalez, a seventy-year-old Conch who'd worked in the cafeteria at Key West High when Doug was there, started playing Frank Sinatra. It was Saturday, laundry day for her, and she always put on Sinatra or Tony Bennett and sang along. When 'Ol' Blue Eyes started in on "Summer Wind," Doug and I joined in, and Rose came out of her house laughing and stuck her head under the house to find us.

"You boys like my music?"

"Yes, ma'am, nothing better. Is our working bothering you?"

"Not at all. I'm glad to have neighbors here again. I'm making some guava duff today. I'll bring some over."

"Don't spoil us, now."

"My pleasure."

We cut and placed the re-bar cages in the holes and poured the piers one Saturday, then had to wait a week for the concrete to cure.

While we were working on the first building, Doug and I slowly worked out the living arrangements that were to serve us so well that we continued them after the house was finished. He came up with the idea of one week on, one week off with cooking. At first, I was skeptical, because a whole week's grocery shopping, cooking, and clean-up for both of us seemed onerous, but it wasn't. The person who was on that week provided the groceries for breakfast and lunch but only had to cook dinner, though we learned eventually to cook enough in the evening to have lunch from the leftovers. The week off was vacation.

Crockpot, toaster oven, grill, and microwave constituted our kitchen, so the meals got monotonous sometimes, but the companionship and shared hardship of the work compensated. I had never been made happier by work. Dirty and repetitive as so much of it was, it gave me—both of us—real satisfaction to shower at the end of the day, fix a drink, and tour the job site and inspect our progress.

Doug's sense of humor added spice to the experience.

He started the scorecard that became famous. From the beginning, we were plagued with rats. The buildings had been abandoned so long and there were so many fruit trees in the yard that the rats were everywhere: in the walls, under the house, in the ceilings, hidden in the tops of the trees. They ate through canisters to get at flour or rice and left droppings on what passed for our kitchen counter. We set traps everywhere and every night we could hear them going off. On one wall, Doug began recording the kills, like fighter pilots on the fuselage of their planes. For each dead rat, he drew a figure of one on the kitchen wall. Leigh called it creepy, but we celebrated after ten, then again after twenty had been dispatched.

Doug was the first one to play redneck when we were sitting drinking beer one day in what passed for a living room. He finished one, belched, and tossed the empty can into a corner, beginning a tradition that I, and every visiting construction buddy, loved. It satisfied the pig gene that resides in every male. We lived in a dump, so we'd bag the empties when we felt like it.

He was as conscientious as I was about paying bills on time, so any concern I'd had about that issue was laid to rest early on. Any worries I'd had about sharing a living space with a gay man had also been for naught. Our shower was outdoors, surrounded by bananas. It was hidden from the street, but visible from the house and yard, but Doug never stared when I was naked. Eventually I became comfortable enough that I didn't even think about walking out to the shower when he was outside.

Leigh never spent the night at La Yndia because of the infamous bathroom, and I rarely brought any other woman over, so there were no accidental encounters Doug had to deal with. Doug, however, had a parade of young males over, late enough that I rarely ran into one except coming out of his room in the morning. Usually they were strangers, but occasionally there'd be someone I knew, a carpenter or a laborer from one of the jobs. They'd look like a deer caught in headlights, horrified at being caught with a gay man, mumbling excuses and sometimes pleading: "Man, please don't say anything to anybody, please."

I always reassured them that whatever happened there stayed there and did my best to calm them down by fixing them a cup of coffee while Doug and I got ready for work. I asked Doug one day how he managed to get so many partners that I assumed were straight. "Whatever it takes," he answered, smiling, "money, a joint, work on one of my jobs, charm, just whatever it takes."

I was shocked only once, one Saturday afternoon when my job up the Keys had been canceled because the concrete batching plant broke down. I drove back to Key West, came in through the garage and the great room, which is why no one heard me, and walked into the parlor to find four women practicing blow jobs on zucchinis, Doug giving pointers. They shrieked in embarrassment and I bolted.

I apologized to Doug that night. He shrugged it off. "I should have warned you, but I knew you were working up the Keys today."

"Do you mind me asking why you were doing it?"

"Almost every straight woman with a gay friend gets around to asking him how to give good head. Enough women asked me that I thought I'd teach them all at once."

"Zucchinis?"

"About the right size and shape, and the skin lets them know if their teeth are scratching it, number one no-no. One woman did say she needed a cucumber instead of a zucchini and got dirty looks from the other women. Anyway, it's good they weren't working on the real thing when you walked in," and he laughed. "I promise I'll give you warning next time."

One day while we were working on the first new bathroom, Doug told me a little more about himself.

"It's probably hard for someone like you to imagine a childhood like mine," he told me the day after we'd lowered the building back down and were installing floor joists. "Cuban mothers do everything for their sons, and I mean everything. My second year at the University of Florida, a friend of mine and I rented a room off campus, with kitchen privileges. The first week there, he was going to make tuna salad for us for lunch and handed me the can and can opener while he chopped up some onion and celery. He turned around when he was ready for the tuna and caught me staring at the can and the opener and asked me what was wrong. I had to tell him I didn't know how to open a can. I'd never done it before."

"Doug, you can't be serious."

"No, I swear it's true. Then the first time he asked me if I wanted to ride along with him to the laundromat, I told him I didn't use one. I mailed my dirty clothes to my mother every week, and she mailed them back washed and ironed. He looked at me like he'd just encountered an alien species and told me I had to come along and learn how to do my own laundry. I'm glad I learned those things now, but it hurt my mother's feelings when I stopped sending her my laundry."

Doug was my opposite in that he had a sunny disposition and woke up every day with high expectations for pleasure in contrast to my control-freak awakenings, alert to where the day's disasters were coming from. He also had an enviable self-confidence, so much so that, fascinated, I asked him one day if he'd ever had any great self-doubts or emotional crises. By then, the house was on its new foundation, and we were well into the finish work. That day, we were tiling the upstairs bathroom in "mom," he setting the tiles and I making cuts and mixing the mortar, so we had lots of time in between cuts or mixing mud to talk.

He thought about it a minute. "Not really, I guess. I was knocked back when I realized I was gay because I knew the social consequences of it, especially in this town, but I guess I've always been comfortable with who I am. I did have a really hard time the first time I fell in love, though. That almost drove me to suicide."

That surprised me. "Can you talk about it?"

"Sure, just give me a minute to get these two tiles in." He was tiling the inside of the shower niche, and every tile had to be custom cut. He handed the two back to me. "Shave a sixteenth off both."

I took them outside, cut a sixteenth of an inch off and brought them back. "Smooth as a Patsy Cline glissando," he said as they slid into place. "OK, let's start the back wall."

Once the bottom row was in, he took up his story again. "The roommate who taught me how to use a can opener was straight and just an all around good guy, no complicated nature, no dark side or anything. We had fun together, double-dating and partying. I just liked him as a friend. Near the end of the school year, my sophomore year, he found out about construction jobs in the Colorado Rockies and asked me to come along with him.

"I'd gone back home the summer after my freshman year and realized I needed to see a bigger world than Key West, so I agreed to join him. When summer came, we packed up his car and headed out West. Now remember, at this point in my life, I had never seen mountains or snow and never been out of Florida." He stopped his story and handed me the empty mud bucket. I took it outside and mixed another batch, then went to get us a couple beers while we waited for the mortar to slake. When I came back, I gave him the mud, and he continued his story.

"It felt strange going through all those different states, but Jim was a great traveling companion, making a game out of everything. Remember the old Burma Shave signs? We'd make up obscene versions of the ones we saw and laugh ourselves sick. Nothing upset him, not even getting two flats in a row out in bum-fuck Kansas. Back then the Interstates weren't finished, so we were driving across Kansas and Eastern Colorado on a two-lane highway that sort of undulated across the Plains 'cause they're not really flat.

"I'm a big fan of Kerouac's *On the Road*, like you, and I kept imagining him and Cassady and Ginsburg on those very same highways. It seemed mythological to be traveling across those great empty spaces. Jim was just as excited by it all as I was. Anyway, we were East of Denver a ways when I caught sight of the Rockies the first time. John, I don't know what it was, but something about them grabbed at me like nothing else ever had. I was spellbound looking at those snowtopped peaks getting closer and closer.

"Jim wanted to check out Denver, so we spent a night and a day there. I liked it, but I wanted up *there*. I could feel their presence, and I wanted to see them, be in them. Have you been there?" I nodded.

"The next day when we started climbing and climbing, and I saw those beauties with their forests and streams and old mining towns,

I felt a kinship no other place but here has ever given me, sort of like what you said you felt the first night you arrived in Paris. When we got to the top of Loveland Pass, I felt exhilarated like never before in my life, and so did Jim. I couldn't believe I was there, little Conch boy on top of the Rocky Mountains. It was fantastic.

"So in my mind, the actual first time I fell in love was with a place, that place. I got a job working on the section of I-70 coming out of the west end of the tunnel they were digging under the Continental Divide. I was working at nearly ten thousand feet. Often, once in July even, storm clouds would roll up the valley, hit the divide, and dump snow—snow!—on everything. I'd never seen snow before. Some of the other laborers and I had snowball fights in July! From where I was working, I could see elk grazing above the tree line on the mountain they were tunneling through. There were beaver in the stream running down the valley below us. Every day was pure magic.

"Jim got a job at a concrete batching plant. We rented a dumpy apartment in Breckenridge and spent our nights drinking 3.2 beer— Coors—dating local girls, unsuccessfully, and playing pool in all the funky bars. Sunday was our only day off, so we used it to go exploring all over the place: Estes Park, Leadville, Royal Gorge.

"You know that John Denver song, "Rocky Mountain High"? Corny as it is, that's how I felt all summer, high. I loved it all, even the hard work. For the first time in my life, I felt free somehow, that somehow I'd gotten out of myself. I was sad when the summer ended, and we had to leave. We both agreed we'd come back the next summer. I felt like a balloon slowly deflating on the drive back to Florida, and Jim said he felt the same way.

"Now we come to the tragic part, violins in the background," and he laughed, then stopped for a minute. "I can joke about it now, but it was no joke back then. The tragic part for me was that I was completely unaware I'd fallen in love with Jim, didn't know it was happening. We were just buddies having a great time together. It was only when we got back to Gainesville and the school year had started that I realized it. If I'd known it was happening, I would have tried to stop it. I wanted the friendship, not the other.

"I fell hard. The fun we'd had together, the whole summer of being high on the Rockies, the whole thing combined. I was in love, capital L. I sank into the only dark depression of my life, and I was bitter. Why did I have to have these feelings that I knew were going to spoil the best friendship of my life?" Then he looked at me. "Until now."

He paused for a minute and measured the cuts where the side shower wall met the rear wall. "I'm going to need twenty-four of these," and he handed me one marked for the cut, "but cut only six at a time in case one of the walls creeps in a little." I went to the front porch, made the cuts, and returned. He fitted the first two, then continued the story.

"Jim and I still hung around together, but he saw something was wrong. The first time he asked me about it, I put him off. The next time he asked me, a couple of weeks later, in some redneck bar outside Gainesville with those gut-wrenching country-western songs on the jukebox, I told him.

"I told him I'd fallen in love with him. I told him I didn't know it had happened. I told him I hadn't even known for sure that I was 'like that,' meaning gay. He listened, but he was obviously shocked and tried to convince me that I was just confused. He tried to talk me out of it, and I wished he'd been able to, but no dice.

"Jim was a really decent guy, and we were friends, so we danced around it as much as we could, but the more he was decent and tried to re-establish the relationship the way it had been, the more I fell. He was my friend, he was un-self-consciously good-looking, we'd shared a great experience, and I wanted more, and I hated myself and felt dirty for wanting it.

"Everything changed. Before, I could see him walking naked out of the bathroom and just feel a twinge of curiosity more than anything. Now when I saw him naked, I wanted him, and he must have sensed the difference because he started to wrap a towel around his waist. And you know something, John? He was doing it as much to make it easier for me as it was to make himself more comfortable. That's how good a person he was.

"The end came near Christmas time. We'd gotten drunk together, and he'd pulled out the photos of our summer together. I was leaning over him looking at them, and I couldn't help myself, I kissed him on his cheek. He didn't pull away or say anything; he just fell silent. Then he stood up, and I was afraid he was going to punch me. What he did was worse, much worse," and Doug paused, memory's thorns pressing in.

"Jim looked at me and said: 'Doug, you know I'm not like that, but you're the best friend I've ever had. If you need it that bad, I'll try to help you out' and he stripped naked, lay down on the couch, and closed his eyes. I couldn't believe it. I knelt next to him and touched his stomach, my first time with a man. When I moved my hand down to touch him lower, he tensed, then jumped up. "I'm sorry, man, I'm sorry," he kept saying as he pulled his clothes on. "I just can't do it."

"He ran out of the room, and I didn't see him for two days. I hated myself for spoiling something that had been pure. I mostly just wanted to die. When he showed back up, he told me I was still his friend but that he had to move out.

"We still saw one another once in a while. We even went drinking together a few times. The next summer, we both went back to Colorado, in separate cars, and he took his girlfriend with him. She and I got along fine, but my heart was breaking. One night when she and I were out together without him, she told me that Jim had told her the story. Then she asked me if I still loved him. I told her the truth, and that nothing had happened between us. She was great about it. She put her hand on mine there in the bar and said she was sorry, that she knew what it was like to be in love with him, and what it would do to her if she lost him. Great woman.

"Late that summer, I met another construction worker in one of the bars. Turned out he was gay, too. We got together a few times and slowly, very slowly, I started to feel like there was a way out of all I was suffering. We took a trip together one weekend to Aspen. We stopped once on the way where there was this great view and got out of the car. While I was standing there, he came up behind me and put his arms around me and pulled me to him. For a moment I felt pure joy, looking at that view and being held by another man. The pain was gone.

"Johnny—that was his name—had gonorrhea and didn't know it, at least I hope he didn't know it. Anyway, when he saw he'd infected me, he left town without a word, and I never heard from him again. Now I felt even dirtier and had to invent a fictitious female partner when I went to the doctor."

He put in the last tile of the top row, tapped it into place, and dropped the trowel in the bucket. "Done. If you'll clean up here, I'll make us some mango-guanabana daiquiris. The mangoes are ripe, and I caught a guanabana right before it fell. I can finish my sad tale then."

"Sounds good to me." I picked up the bucket and sponges and went outside to wash everything off. It always amazed me how much water was involved in laying tile, and how much pain love could cause, whatever side of the fence you were on.

Doug served us the daiquiris in the side yard. They were two-thirds guanabana and one-third mango with lots of Meyer's rum. The guanabana gave it a little vanilla-and-something-else flavor. They were outrageously good, best I'd ever had.

"It's nice having your own fruit trees," Doug said, "but if you ever make these, make sure you purée the guanabana first, because it's got a lot of fiber in it." We sat there for a few minutes, taking in the yard and the beauty of the day, waning sunlight coming through palm fronds.

"You ready for the rest of the tale?"

"Sure."

"I dropped out the next semester. There was no way I could study anymore, and I wanted to get away from seeing Jim. I went to Miami Beach and got a job waiting tables. One night when I was walking home, a customer from the restaurant pulled up next to me in his car and offered me fifty bucks to blow me and I thought, Why not? I didn't have any moral objections to it. It didn't seem any different from providing any other service, like waiting tables, and the pay was better. So I started hustling and did it for a few months. Most of the time I just felt sorry for the customers, mostly lonely old men, clinging to me as they sucked, trying to get some emotional contact with the sex. In them I thought I was seeing my future. Some of them asked to see me again and again, but when I saw them getting attached, I dropped them.

"Then one night back in my room, drunk, after being serviced by a particularly sad case, I heard Warwick singing "Walk on By" from that first summer in Colorado, and all the pain came back with it, and I decided I'd had enough. I fixed myself a couple strong drinks and knocked them back. I went out on the balcony and climbed up on the railing. I put my hands behind me so I'd hit head first when I jumped. I just wanted all the pain to end."

He stopped talking for a minute, and I went over to him and put my hand on his shoulder. "I'm glad you didn't, my friend."

He patted my hand. "Thank you."

I sat back down.

"What stopped me was seeing a woman walking down the street with her young son. I knew how much my mother loved me, and I couldn't do that to her. I went back inside my room, packed up, and went back to Gainesville and re-enrolled. I changed my major from business to psychology, hoping it would give me some great insights."

"Did you ever get together with anyone else?"

"I met a man when I did the studies at the University of Paris, and moved in with him for a couple months. He was French and taught me a whole new way of loving: fun, not desperate, where souls have to merge. We had great times together, and I slowly realized that I really didn't want to be married to another man, that these friendly couplings that went no further served my needs best. Sure, every once in a while I have what I call an affairette and get infatuated. It passes. I like keeping friendship and sex apart now, and you've seen I prefer sex with straight men. More of a challenge." He looked over and saw my glass was empty. "Ready for another one?"

"Sure."

He brought out two more and sat back down. "I was more or less resigned to the fact that I was going to live alone the rest of my life until we got together and did this. And you know something, John, this suits me perfectly. I love you, you're a great friend, you really are, and you, me, Thomas, and Leigh together is something I never dreamed of having. I'm happy."

"Did you ever hear from Jim again?"

"Oh, yeah. We'd go drinking together sometimes when I went back to school. That first summer in Colorado was a part of his personal mythology as much as it was mine, and he loved to talk about it. Every once in a while he'd shyly mention that he'd heard there were bars for people like me, meaning gay. Once he even offered to go to one with me if it would help me—that's how decent he was. How could I not love the guy?

"He married Carol, the girl he took out to Colorado the second summer, and I was best man. I was genuinely happy for both of them. They've been down here a couple times, and I always show them a good time. They have two kids now—I'm godfather—so it's harder for them to get away. They keep inviting me to visit them.

"Anyway, end of Doug's sad story. Alright, I've bared my soul to you. Fair's fair. Next tile work has to be accompanied by the story of your first heartbreak, deal?"

"Deal."

A couple minutes later, he looked over. "You're not afraid I'm going to fall in love with you, are you? After my story? I love you, John, but not that way. I know now. I do love you, but because you're a friend, a soul-mate."

"Doug, you're as close to me now as any friend I've ever had, but I'm straight and you're gay, and our friendship is probably better for the difference. I'm not afraid, and I'm not afraid to tell you I love you. I went to eleven different schools by the time I graduated from high school, always the outsider, always lonely. When I got here, I was desperate, Doug, lost. Do you know how lucky I feel to have you and Thomas and Leigh in my life now? I'm honored that you feel comfortable enough with me to tell me what you did. And it's a deal. I'll tell you my heartbreak story. And I want another daiquiri. These suckers are over-the-top good."

Doug was very much a Conch in one respect: this was his town, and we were all outsiders. It never showed with our family, but it was obvious when he didn't like someone else from outside. The only thing I feared about him was his tongue. Like other gay people I knew, he could insult in a way that cut your throat and left your head hanging on your chest.

I was carpenter and Doug electrician for a couple who'd bought and were renovating a house near the cemetery. A chubby, older, gay man and newcomer to the island had started a landscaping business and had been hired to do their garden. The man rubbed everyone on the job the wrong way immediately by acting as if he were boss of the entire project instead of observing the custom of the trades, respecting and working around each other. It was: "Get out of our way" or "Move this" or "Help my guys get these plants in here," and never once a please or thank you. He was notorious, too, for staring at the good-looking workers on the job, but treating them the worst.

He made the mistake one morning of ordering, not asking, Doug to move all his electrical materials from a porch so he could store his own things there. Doug looked right at him: "I can't help it that you're a bitter old woman trapped in a fat man's body, but don't *ever* order me to do anything, understood?"

The man looked stricken and walked away speechless. The other workers whooped and whistled and clapped Doug on the back: "Right on, my man. Beer is on us tonight."

I went up to Doug. "You know you've made an enemy for life."

"I don't care. It's my home, not his, and nobody talks to me like that. Anyway, I think your enemies define you as much as your friends do. It tells the world what you're not. He's a rude, arrogant asshole, and I'm not."

That night at dinner, I brought the topic up again. "Promise me you'll never say anything that devastating to me, not even if you're really mad at me."

"John, you know I never would. I love you. You're family."

Then I repeated it: "Bitter old woman trapped in a fat man's body," and looked at him, and we both started laughing.

The downstairs bathroom was next. We started tiling it early on a Saturday morning, Tony Bennett's "I Left My Heart in San Francisco" coming from next door. We were tired, but completion of "mom" was now within reach.

I mixed mortar again as he spaced out the tiles on the walls. When the mud was ready, I brought it in. "Doug, I'm barely standing. I'm going over to M & M to get another con leche. Want one?" He nodded.

When I got back, he'd already started laying the long back wall, leaving out the last vertical row where two walls met. "I need eighteen cuts," and he gave me the measurement, "but only do four at first in case one of the walls creeps in again."

They fit, he re-measured and gave me a slightly smaller measurement for the next eight. When I brought those back, he did a test fit, then placed them. "OK, keep me awake. Tell me your heartbreak story."

"Sure you want to hear this?"

"Absolutely. I told you mine. Fair's fair."

"OK. You know I refused induction and went into exile in Canada. That first winter in Toronto I was lonely, scared, and depressed, desperate. I don't want to be too dramatic but walking those cold, dark streets, I thought my life would never recover. After I got my work papers, I signed up for a master's in French at the University of Toronto. I thought being back in college would cheer me up, and maybe I'd meet people.

"Canadians aren't as open as Americans, and most of the kids at the U of T were from Toronto, so they already had their little groups. I didn't make a single friend the first semester. The next semester, I took a seminar in French symbolist poetry: Baudelaire, Rimbaud,

Verlaine, de Nérval. I loved it, you know, you studied some of them. Those words spoke to me like nothing had before and made the same connection that the Beats had.

"There were only eight of us, and we each had to do an oral presentation of a single poem. I chose Baudelaire's 'Le Cygne.' You know that one?" Doug shook his head. "One of the lines is: '*Et mes chers souvenirs sont plus lourds que des rocs.*' (And my precious memories are heavier than rocks). I guess I must have shown some emotion reading it, because the class applauded at the end. At the end of class, one of the other students, Jacqueline Besson, half French and half English Canadian, stopped me and asked if she could buy me a cup of coffee.

"Jacqueline was a chameleon and pretty, not stunning, but pretty: black hair and hazel eyes, the kind of eyes the women in Paris have . . . brilliant, alive. Sometimes she came to class dressed like a prep school girl, sometimes in outlandish hippie garb, and she always wanted to talk about the emotions the poems evoked, which drove the prof crazy. He was French, from France, *French*, and you studied literature '*l'homme et l'oeuvre*' (the man and his work). Those poets came out of the chute down the assembly line, and we were supposed to chop and dice them all the same way.

"Over coffee, Jacqueline—Jackie—and I talked about how wrong it seemed to study French poetry dispassionately. Then, out of the blue, she asked me why I always looked sad, and it all came tumbling out, the loneliness, the cold, the never-ending snow, and I couldn't help myself, I started crying. She came over and sat next to me in the booth and put her arm around me, whispering '*mon pauvre petit, mon pauvre petit*' until I gained control of myself."

"'We can't have this, *mon pauvre petit*,' she said. 'There's a big snowstorm coming Sunday, and I don't want you to be *triste*. Will you be my guest for something?'

"For what?" I had asked.

"'It will be a surprise to cheer up my sad American friend whose memories are heavier than rocks,' she said."

I had to stop and make the cuts around the mixer valve on the next wall. When Doug placed those and they worked, I continued.

"Sunday came and, indeed, there was a snowstorm, the millionth that winter. Jackie picked me up outside my apartment a little before noon and wouldn't tell me where we were going or what we were going to do.

"We headed north out of the city, and the snow got heavier and heavier. We talked about the course we were taking and which poets were our favorites and which poems. Then she pulled out a joint and lit it, and we were quiet for a while, listening to the radio where a French-Canadian chanteuese was singing the Gilles Vigneault song: '*Mon pays n'est pas un pays, c'est l'hiver.*' (My country isn't a country, it's winter), and we both laughed.

"Then she turned off the highway onto a country road, and a few minutes later pulled into a wooded area, trees all heavy with snow and more snow falling. She turned off the engine. 'I have to do a little preparation,' she told me. 'You have to stay in the car until I say you can come out. And keep your eyes closed, too, until I say open them.' I was intrigued and did as told.

"A few minutes later, she knocked on my window and said I could get out, but still had to keep my eyes closed. She led me a few steps into the woods, then told me I could look. There, spread on the snow, was a blanket with lunch, a bottle of wine, and a lantern on each corner with lighted candles. 'It's a snow picnic,' she said, 'so my sad friend will always have another memory of snow.'

"Doug, I don't think any gesture has ever moved me as much as that. She kissed me, and we sat down and ate and drank and laughed, and the candles defined a small, happy space that enclosed us and defied the snow that was coming down faster and faster. *'T'es content, mon cher?'* she asked as we finished the wine.

"Yes, happy, and touched."

"Now for the dessert, *mon petit*. Close your eyes again," and I did as told. When she told me to open them again, she was standing in front of me, completely naked, with a string of little battery-operated lights wrapped around her neck blinking on and off. 'Now you have to get naked, too, *mon cher*, and try to catch me.'

"We'll freeze to death."

"'Oh, I think I know a way to warm us up,' and she ran off laughing.

"I stripped naked, and it was *cold*, especially on the feet, but off I went chasing her through the woods, snow falling heavier and heavier, taking all color and sound from the world but for those twinkling lights and her laughter. When I caught her, when she let me catch her, she pulled me to her and gave me a kiss, a passionate kiss, then led me back to the picnic site and pulled out a big sleeping bag she'd stashed behind a tree.

"We were both freezing now. She stripped the lights off her and hung them, still blinking, from a branch of the tree we were under. Shivering, we crawled into the sleeping bag for one of the best and most interesting fucks of my life, starting off wild and crazy then becoming intensely emotional, with lots of kissing and intense eye contact. Then we fell asleep.

"She woke up first, then woke me, and in that tender mood with a new partner, we got dressed and packed everything back up.

"Doug, I'd been the ugly duckling in high school but hit my stride in college and had sex with a lot of women there. But apart from a couple of sexual infatuations, I mostly just wanted to hit and run to make up for those lean years from puberty on. With Jackie, I fell in love. I'm a sucker for the grand, romantic gesture. I was hooked, smitten, and she seemed to be, too, though there was a mercurial side to her personality that always made me feel insecure, which, of course, made me want her even more. You've been there, haven't you?" Doug nodded.

"I don't know how to describe it exactly, but from a certain moment on in my life, I knew I didn't want to waste it. I didn't care much about money or things, I wanted the real heartbeat of it all." He nodded again.

Time for the cuts around the showerhead. It took three tries this time before I got them right—cutting a circle in a square tile is a challenge—and then it was easy sailing again.

"Jackie gave her presentation on Baudelaire's poem, *'L'Ennemi,'* about time, with that chilling final stanza where 'time is the enemy that gnaws on your heart,' and she was emoting left and right, amusing all of us but distressing the prof who could barely contain himself. When she'd finished her presentation and the professor was ready to jump on her, she looked at the class and said: 'If great poetry can inform our lives, what should we learn from it? I think that at the end of life one should be able to say this,' and she burst into singing Piaf's classic, *'Je ne regrette rien,'* and, Doug, she had a fantastic voice. We were stunned. When she finished, we all looked at the teacher, nervous.

"He began applauding. *'Extraordinaire, madamoiselle, extraordinaire.* What else can I say?' and we all stood and gave her a standing ovation. We loved her for it, and then we turned and applauded the professor for his Frenchman's surrender to the grand gesture, and he was obviously touched. I'm sure that's the warmest memory of his teaching career, poor Frenchman living in gray Toronto.

"That night I took her to a cheap restaurant on Bloor Street to celebrate her performance and asked her why she'd done it. 'Baudelaire was right, *mon petit*. Time is the enemy and it *will* eat our hearts. I intend to enjoy my life.'

"That summer, I borrowed money and went to Europe for the first time. I've told you the effect Paris had on me when I saw it that first night. Jackie came over and we spent ten days together. We'd drink late into the night—we closed Café Flore twice, once with Baldwin at the table next to us—and we talked and talked and talked, my years of loneliness ended.

"We heard the Fauré *Requiem* in Notre Dame cathedral and the *Fourth Brandenburg* in one of the vaulted chambers of the Conciergerie, saw a spectacular production of Molière's *Le Bourgeois Gentil'homme* at the Comédie Francaise.

"One day we went to Chartres, and I told her how I'd learned about it in my undergrad humanities class one morning after washing UPS trucks all night and couldn't figure out why we were supposed to care. We both laughed at youthful ignorance.

"We toured the cathedral, saw the famous Chartres blue, puddles of fascinating color on the floor, then climbed the north spire. Alone up there, she said: 'Let's do it right here,' and pulled me back away from anyone looking up from below. I unzipped and was just getting ready when a calliope a block away played the opening notes from the 'March of the Toreadors' in *Carmen*. We looked at one another and burst out laughing. I got ready a second time, and the damned calliope did it again, and now we couldn't stop laughing and had to give it up. A waiter in the restaurant where we had lunch told us the calliope was practicing for a festival in town later that week.

"Jackie's last night in Paris, she called a gay French friend of hers, Daniel Chassard, who worked at the Club Sept disco just off the Avenue de l'Opéra, and set up something. We showed up at four in the morning, after it had closed, and knocked on the door. Jackie introduced me to Daniel, and Daniel introduced us to Guy, his boy-friend. We were the only ones there. Daniel served us drinks, then turned on the music. The three of them stripped naked and got up on the bar and started dancing.

"'Come on, *mon petit*,' Jackie yelled at me above the music. 'Paris is too sweet and life too short for *complexes*.' Daniel fed me another strong drink, and I stripped and got up on the bar and danced my naked ass off, all four of us laughing and dancing . . . dancing and laughing. The night ended with Jackie and I having sex on one end of the bar and the two of them on the other, and then we all fell asleep right there on the bar-top.

"When we woke up, hung-over, we stumbled over to a nearby café for coffee and croissants. When I looked up the boulevard and saw the Garnier opera house, I had to keep telling myself that this was real, that life could be this sweet. Daniel gave me an indulgent smile and said: '*C'est beau tout ça, n'est-ce pas?*' And his 'everything' meant everything: Paris, our wanton night, life, *everything*. *Oui, c'est beau*, I answered.

"Doug, that morning, drinking coffee at that café, I felt for the first time that my life not only hadn't been destroyed by going into exile, but might actually explode into something more wonderful than I could ever have imagined. And something else: All those years of my life up until then I'd always suspected that I had it in me to live a life that wasn't ordinary, and I wanted that, but I didn't have the knowledge of what that life might be or how to go about getting there. Then there it was. I almost cried from the happiness of it. Jackie must have sensed what I was feeling or was feeling the same thing because she looked at me and smiled and put her hand on mine.

"Jackie and I both decided that we wanted to live in Paris, so I moved there first, got the place to live and a job at Total, the French oil company. She came over a month after my move, but I could tell something was wrong from the minute I picked her up at the Gare du Nord.

"'Nothing's wrong, *mon petit*, nothing's wrong,' she'd tell me whenever I asked her if something was bothering her. And there were moments as wonderful as before. I remember listening to Roberta Flack's 'First Time I Ever Saw Your Face' on the radio late one Saturday afternoon in bed with her, in each other's arms, watching the sun setting on Ste. Eustache across from my apartment. I was in love, I was in Paris, and I felt complete in a way I had never felt before in my life. I think she felt the same right then because she turned to me during the song and said: 'Life is moments, *mon petit,* and this is one,' and stroked my head and kissed me.

"That moment, Doug, is burned into my brain, like yours with that guy on the trip to Aspen. My loneliness, curse of my strange life, had ended, I thought, on a loft bed in a ratty apartment in the First Arrondissement in Paris.

"Two months after she arrived, Total sent me out for two weeks to the drilling rig they were running in the North Sea. My apartment didn't have a phone—it took four years back then to get one in that neighborhood—so I couldn't call her. When I got back, she was gone. The note she left said only: 'Have a good life, *mon petit*, and never let snow sadden you again.'

"This quixotic women who said she hated all that was ordinary, went back and married a rich Canadian insurance executive. I felt all the usual bullshit: anger, heartbreak, rejection, frustration. I was as devastated as you say you were with Jim. One of the things that tortured me was the loss of that shared history: our poetry class, the snow picnic, Paris, Chartres, the night at the disco. I didn't want all that to be some fossilized memory. I wanted it to be a shared mem-ory, a living thing.

"It messes with all the past joy you shared when it ends like that. Was she just pretending all the time when we shared things together? Was she holding back her real self and just performing with me? I've been with a lot of women, and I know that what we had was real, at least for the time we had it. I have to believe that when she gave me the snow picnic, when we were in bed in Paris listening to Roberta Flack, that she was feeling what I was or I'd go crazy. So why did she leave me?

"My whole new identity, the man who'd escaped middle-class America for this wildly romantic life in Paris, had depended a lot on being with her. I was destroyed.

"To keep from going crazy or killing myself, I decided to make the best of my time there and went out to something—a play, an opera, a concert, an old movie—every single night, and lots of afternoons, for three years. I went to the Louvre every weekend and toured it section by section, then started touring the other museums. In place of love, I got a great cultural education and saturated myself with Paris.

"I had a couple affairs with the women I call the heiresses. I've told you about those. Then my last few months in Paris, I fell in with a group of classical musicians through a Danish woman I met at Total, and life gained some flavor again. One of the musicians was the American harpsichordist, Bill Christie, who went on to found the chamber group, Les Arts Florissants, that performs early French music. Bill and my friend, Sophie, were both friends with the man who managed the Dowd studio, and we'd go there every time for the first concert when they 'voiced' a harpsichord. Don't you love that expression? It means when they put the strings in. Pieces of unfinished harpsichords hung from the walls, and there was sawdust all over the floors. We would hear the first public performance of a new harpsichord.

"Those musicians were wonderful and saved me. They were intelligent, wild, bawdy, outrageously talented, and fun. We'd have meals together after a concert and get seriously drunk. Our conversations would swirl around the table in two or three languages and covered everything: music, of course, art, food, sex, and the combined sex lives of all the people at that table would have made for a very funny novel.

"One night after one of the group, Nöel Lee, gave a Schubert concert at the Salle Pleyel, we all went to Au Pied de Cochon for onion soup. Then, drunk as lords, we went singing through the streets, making up obscene lyrics to our respective national anthems. I was laughing and almost happy again, one of those moments you know with certainty, even as it's sliding through you, will define you and your time alive. I couldn't help but think of the person who should've been beside me, the one woman I knew who would have reveled in it as much as I did. That could've been the life I'd been looking for."

"Did you ever see or hear from her again?"

"Never. I found out when I got back to Toronto that she'd moved to Vancouver with her husband. Later, I ran into one of the men who'd been in the seminar with us, and he asked me if I'd heard. She'd died in a car crash. I knew, I thought I knew, that I would never be in love like that again, and maybe that's for the best.

"And what if we had stayed together? Would we have wound up hating one another years later because I squeezed the toothpaste tube one way and she another? That intensity can't last, I know, but dammit, I wanted it to.

"So that's my story," and we were both quiet for a couple minutes. He slapped in the last two tiles we had mud for.

"John, we can't leave this shower with the karma from that intense a broken-heart story in it. Think of something to cheer it up."

Two weeks later at the house-warming party for the completion of "mom," we filled the tub with ice and stashed beer and wine in it. I stuck little red party hearts, torn in two, on the shower walls and sprinkled small ones on top of the ice. He and I were in there re-stocking the tub during the party when one of our construction worker buddies came in for another beer and said: "Hey, what's the deal with all the hearts?"

Doug and I looked at one another and laughed: "Private joke."

When I took Leigh upstairs to see a bathroom fit for a royal butt, I was expecting lots of hand kissing instead of the shriek when she saw the urinal. "What is that?"

"You know what it is, it's a urinal. It's the guarantee there'll never be splatter on the toilet seat, and that the toilet seat will always be down. That's what women always complain about, isn't it?"

"It makes it look like a public bathroom."

I was not happy. "You know something, Princess, Freud was right when he said: 'What do women want?' There's a soaking tub in there, which you said you liked having, two bathroom sinks so you don't have to share, a shower big enough you don't need shower curtains, and a toilet whose seat will always be dry and always down." I walked out and went back downstairs to the party. She followed me and apologized, but it took some of the sweetness out of the party for me.

Lifting up "dad" and renovating it was next. That seemed more oner-ous than doing "mom" because the novelty of it was gone, and we knew ahead of time how much work was involved. It was the same story: working seventy and sometimes eighty hours a week, but we did it.

After the building was lowered onto its new foundation, we built Thomas' two-story join, which gave us easy access to "mom," instead of the sloping, open-air gangplanks between buildings we'd been using. Then we hired a couple of laborers to help us on weekends and divided the tasks: Doug put in floor joists and flooring on both floors, while I took down the original tongue-and-groove pine interior wall sheathing, numbering each one-by-four board on the back. Every day after work and all weekend, I threw boards up on sawhorses and sanded off two layers of wallpaper and three layers of paint to get down to the beautiful, honey-colored, original surface. Then I put the boards back up. The finished product was beautiful and worth the hours of being covered with paint chips and wallpaper dust.

We laid mahogany flooring upstairs and down, used salvaged lumber for the risers and treads of the staircase, put in the bathroom upstairs and installed central air units for both buildings with the compressors on the roof of the join, so they'd be invisible from the street or anywhere on the property.

We finished the last week in May, exhausted and broke, but happy. I had the master suite upstairs in "mom," and Doug had the master suite upstairs in "dad." We took one of the bedrooms downstairs in "mom" for a joint office and general storage, the other for a guest bedroom. The downstairs of "dad" was now a proper living room. We were living in high cotton.

One night over dinner and copious amounts of wine, we agreed to hold off on working on the single-story building with the oven, though we were both desperate for a real kitchen. "I don't know about you, John, but I need a rest, and I need to build up some cash again, too. I don't like living this close to the edge financially."

"With you there, partner."

If you want to hear God laugh, tell Her your plans.

They start off early in the season, the Cape Verde storms, as disturbances coming off the tropical belt of Africa. Then the vagaries of atmospherics take over: they remain just big storms or, off the Cape

Verde islands, the Coriolis effect from the Earth's rotation cause them to wrap around the center of the low pressure. Once a storm completes the circle, it feeds on itself, spinning slowly counter-clockwise and tightening, creating an even lower pressure eye that sucks in moisture from the air and heat from the water. Near the end of the season, the Cape Verde storms abate and the Caribbean births them. They are one of Nature's most beautiful and powerful phenomena, hurricanes; and their function is very simple: to re-distribute heat across the planet.

After only a year or two of residence on the island, the new inhabitant has become familiar with all the vocabulary: Category One to Five (Five is worst), how many inches of mercury (the lower the pressure, the deadlier the storm), the three- and five-day cone of possible path, feeder bands, steering currents, and the dates June 1 to December 1, hurricane season, though they have even been known to form outside that time.

Each resident makes his own calculations to answer the ultimate question: evacuate or not, because the Florida Keys are the most dangerous place to live through a hurricane, and one of the most difficult to leave. Evacuation, at its worst, means a 120-mile trip up a low-lying, two-lane highway to the mainland. One accident, more likely with panicky, hysterical drivers, traps you with the real possibility of a horrible death bearing down on you.

The storms were once unnamed, then were given women's names and then, with the advent of the women's rights movement, had male and female names alternate.

They are monsters and very efficient killers, releasing the equivalent in energy of several A-bombs an hour. The winds can drive a two-by-four one foot into a living tree, and the storm surge, the bubble of water the storm drags along with it, can reach more than twenty feet above normal sea level. The big ones have tornadoes embedded in them as a garnish.

The Labor Day hurricane of 1935, the most powerful in history, washed Flagler's Overseas Railroad out to sea and left the bodies of WWI veterans working on it up in trees, trapped in sunken dormitory boats, or simply gone. Hemingway, a Key West resident at the time, wrote a report full of outrage over what he saw when he rode up to the Middle Keys where the eye had passed. The few survivors who had clung to the very tops of the few coconut palms that hadn't snapped in two, described the roar of a hundred locomotives, the eerie glow caused by the friction of grains of sand hitting one another at two hundred miles an hour, and a black horizon, a twenty-five-foot high wall of water coming at them.

That hurricane had rendered Key West accessible again only by boat or plane until the federal government built the Overseas Highway on the foundations of the old railroad bridges.

Thomas took it as his duty to inform every newcomer to the island he met of the possible danger from these storms. One day when I was visiting him and he was showing me beautiful sepia-toned silkscreens he'd done of some of the old Conch houses, I asked him if I should be afraid of David, which was spinning towards us.

"Come outside for a minute." I followed him.

"Now imagine this," he said, "the perfect combination of circumstances: a Cat Five storm whose eye comes over the island at high tide when there's a full moon." I nodded that I was following.

"Now look up," and he pointed to a tall power pole. "The storm surge would be as high as the top of that pole. The entire island would be underwater."

I stepped back in as much shock as when I'd read about the glacier where Toronto now sits. "You can't be serious."

"That's what hit up the Keys in 1935. If it had hit here, or if one hit now, 98 percent or more of the population would die. Take them seriously."

David missed the island but came close. Then I noticed dozens of small, colorful birds I'd never seen before. "Finches and warblers blown over from Cuba," Leigh explained. "They'll all be gone in a week. Cats get them all."

As they form, then buzz-saw their way across the Atlantic or up the Gulf, everyone on the island stays close to a TV or radio and becomes an amateur meteorologist: "It's only a Cat One;" or "it's another Emily, it'll turn away;" or "it's gonna hit the mountains in Haiti, that'll tear her apart" . . . and we all catch ourselves doing bowling alley body language, trying to direct the ball of fury one way or another, but *away*.

But they have a mind of their own, and the best computers and best meteorological minds and all the hurricane hunter planes flying in with all their sophisticated instrumentation still come up with only educated guesses. Once, a single hurricane crossed the Florida peninsula then crossed back, hitting some towns twice.

The real fun begins when the five-day cone showing the storm's projected path first includes the island, and you realize how loosely hinged most people are. Panic!

The supermarkets are stripped bare of bottled water in a matter of hours, and trucks start coming down from the mainland to re-stock that and the canned goods that are also disappearing rapidly.

Ten days after the dinner where Doug and I agreed to stop construction on the Bakery for a while, a strong Category Three hurricane, Albert, came roaring toward South Florida, and we spent two days boarding up the Bakery, Rose's house, and the neighbor's behind us. Key West was in the cone, (the projected path).

Thomas told me that Marion Stevens, the naked woman I had seen chasing her semi-naked husband on my first visit to the island, was considered a good indicator of whether the island would be hit or not. "If the barometric pressure starts dropping dramatically, you'll see her walking up and down Duval Street shrieking, and you should consider evacuating." Albert didn't drive her to that, so we felt safer.

The devout and truly scared go to St. Mary Star of the Sea Church on Truman Avenue to pray at the grotto on the church grounds that a nun had built after the devastating hurricanes in the first decade of the century. Local lore had it that the grotto protected the island from being hit again. When I drove past, I saw eight or nine people on their knees in front of a miniature version of the Lourdes shrine.

Albert wobbled at the last minute and hit the towns south of Miami, causing war-zone destruction. We'd been spared . . . we thought.

A week later, the bank called and asked us to come in.

"What do you think they want?" I asked Doug.

He shrugged. "Don't have a clue. We've never been late with a payment."

We had to wait half an hour beyond the meeting time we'd been given before the bank officer called us into his office.

He opened our file. "The insurance company wants to cancel your policy."

Doug and I looked at each other. "Why?"

"Part of the property is in such bad shape, they don't want the risk. The bank's problem is that you have to have insurance to have the mortgage. Otherwise, you have to pay it off in full and immediately."

"Can't we get insurance from someone else?" Doug asked.

"After the hurricane's damage to the mainland, it'll be the same story with any company."

"What are we supposed to do?"

"We've spoken to the insurance company, and they've agreed to keep the policy in force for a year, but you have to have the entire project finished by then."

"How are we supposed to do that?"

"Give us an estimate of the cost to complete, and we'll give you a construction loan for 80 percent of that. That's the best we can do."

We left the bank shocked and depressed and went back to work. That night, we treated ourselves to a night off: we ordered pizza and had a bottle of wine each.

"I can't believe the bastards did this to us." I was furious. "Why didn't they inspect it before we closed on the property? What pisses me off even more is the stuff coming out in the paper about *why* there was so much damage up there." (An after-storm investigation of the damage to the mainland showed that 70 percent of it was due to shoddy construction, and a building department that looked the other way or just didn't look.) "What are we going to do?"

"It doesn't look like we have a choice. We borrow the money and finish the house in a year instead of our original plan of doing it slowly out of earnings."

"Can we afford the payments on the loan?"

"We'll have to find a way. We've both got all our savings in this already. I know I can't afford to lose mine by having the bank take it back. We can't sell it half-finished. We'd never get our money back out of it."

When Leigh heard what had happened, she offered to loan us enough to finish the renovation, interest-free.

I thanked her. "Leigh, that's wonderful, and I love you for it. But I can't take money from you, even a loan. I explained that to you before. Whatever our relationship is, it works even with the difference in wealth, in spite of the difference, because I maintain my independence."

"The offer stands, Mr. Bull-head, if you change your mind."

Then Thomas, the gypsy angel in our lives, took some of the sting out of the setback.

Ten

On walls in London, Paris, Istanbul, Buenos Aires, and Mérida, there hang similar photographs: a person facing the camera and smiling is sitting in a rowboat in the middle of a swimming pool with the ocean, coconut palms, and a huge sky behind them. Ask about the photo, and the owners smile and say: "Thomas' birthday party, Southernmost House."

Arden Catlin, a vulgar woman who made a fortune by getting in early on Fire Island real estate, owned the Southernmost House in Key West at the intersection of South and Whitehead Streets. The phone-booth-sized concrete building adjacent had once been the terminus for the Key West–Havana undersea cable. On the same corner, hanging on the chain-link fence that stopped at the ocean and separated the Navy's Truman Annex from the rest of town, was a small, hand-painted sign with an arrow pointing seaward that said, simply: "HAVANA—90 MILES."

Bishop Kee, friendly patriarch of a Chinese-African-Cuban family, set up tables every day on the sidewalks where the two streets met and displayed seashells and seashell jewelry to the few tourists who passed, and blew on his conch shell each time a Conch Tour Train drove by. At sunset, the family packed up their tables and wares and left, leaving that corner of the town quiet and deserted.

Arden's house, a single-story, concrete block structure painted pink, had been built and lived in by Thelma Strabel, writer of a not good novel about the wrecking (ship-salvaging) industry in Key West, made into an even worse movie by Cecil B. de Mille, one of his first. Released in 1942, it starred John Wayne, Paulette Goddard, Susan Hayward, Ray Milland, Robert Preston, and Charles Bickford. One of the scenes featured a giant squid, which says it all.

The tour guides of the Conch Train included the information that Mrs. Strabel, author of *Reap the Wild Wind*, had lived in the house, and one guide, an obvious queen, always added in a phony English accent: "And I had the pleasure of meeting Mrs. Strabel in her lovely home. She was a delightful woman." Pure lie—the dear Mrs. Strabel was pushing up daisies before that one had sniffed his first pickle.

Arden had married, for convenience, a gay fashion photographer from New York with dyed hair and a vicious tongue he used on anyone who dared question he was straight. I had met them once, briefly, at a cocktail party where Arden, picking her teeth with a fingernail, yelled across a room of fifty people: "Em,"—short for Emmerick—"suck up some of these shrimp before they're gone." Em did as he was told, little lap dog, and the two of them nearly cleaned out a pile of 15/20's (the big local shrimp) meant for an entire party.

Thomas had designed a renovation of their kitchen. In a rare bit of opportunism, he held his nose and schmoozed the vulgarians. In recompense, he received an invitation to be caretaker of Southernmost House for the summer. When Arden and Emmerick departed for their place on Fire Island, leaving the house a pigsty, Thomas moved in, cleaned up, and invited Leigh, Doug, and me to dinner.

Thomas—typical Thomas—had arranged a visual treat. A table was set up with white tablecloth and candles on the concrete deck between the pool and the seawall, and we sat drinking and watching a setting sun color continents of cumulus clouds floating over us, then he lit the candles and we had dinner. Someone photographing us with the ocean in the background would have taken us for the privileged rich on the Mediterranean.

I lifted my glass and proposed a toast: "To Thomas, the magician." Everyone clinked glasses. "Thomas, how do you always wind up living in magical places?

He put his chin on his hand, pretending to think, then answered: "I don't have a clue! It just happens."

"It's that Hungarian gypsy blood," Leigh hypothesized.

"Whatever it is," Doug added, "it's a talent."

When it was completely dark, Thomas pointed out Sand Key Lighthouse five miles to the southwest, with its rotating light. Doug poured more wine, and we sat there drinking, and drinking in the beauty of it all.

Thomas cleared his throat. "I have a proposition to make. I have this place for five months. My only obligation is to pay the utilities and take care of the place. Why don't you all move in with me? There are enough bedrooms for everyone."

I was surprised by the offer and stoned, so I didn't answer right away. Leigh said she didn't want the displacement of moving. Doug said he'd love to, but had to talk it over with me when we weren't stoned.

"Think about it. There's no rush." He went inside to fetch another bottle of wine.

While he was gone Leigh looked at Doug and me. "You two ought to do it. You'll have a real kitchen and evenings away from the struggle." I started to protest that I didn't want to talk about it right then, but she raised her hand to stop me.

"Shut up and listen to me. Take the loan from the bank. Drop all your other work and work only on the Bakery. Summer's almost here so you can work late every day. That way you can finish it by the time you have to move out of here. Hire other people if you have to. Give yourselves weekends off. Use the loan money to make the monthly payments. If you run short near the end, trust me, they'll give you more because they don't want the house, and the loan-to-value will work because of the renovations. But if you take Thomas up on his offer, I think you should offer to pay all the utilities. You know how he is with money. It would help him. Dammit, listen to me. Do it. I'm better at this money stuff than you are, and it will give us all a wonderful summer."

I looked at Doug, Doug looked at me. It seemed to make sense so I nodded yes, and we shook hands. When Thomas came back, we told him we'd be honored to accept the offer, but only if we paid all the utilities.

"She made you offer that, didn't she?"

Doug and I grinned and made the "lips zipped shut" gesture.

So Doug and I moved toiletries, books, records, and clothes to Southernmost House and settled in.

Thomas drew detailed sketches of the location of every painting or wall hanging, every piece of furniture, every carpet, every knick-knack, and we moved every bit of it into the unused bedroom and shut the door. Then he moved his minimalist furniture in, and what he didn't have, we pulled out of the Bakery.

"Now we don't have to worry about damaging anything of theirs," Thomas said. "Besides, they have horrible taste. Did you see the fabric on those sofas!"

The walls soon sported his collages, constructions, and prints, and he was very careful to use existing holes in the walls to hang them.

The stage was set for what we all came to call Southernmost Summer. Fantasies of life as a winning lottery ticket for me had always included certain elements: satisfying work, an intellectual round table—a place to talk about ideas, books, politics, and life with friends—and lots of fun and sex in a beautiful setting. A few parts I got right in Toronto, more parts in Paris, but I got it all right that summer.

All three of us were good cooks, so Doug and I persuaded Thomas to join in our deal: each person was responsible for all three meals for a week. The arrangement didn't work well this time because Doug and I worked late to take advantage of the summer light. By the time we finished, we were too tired to fix dinner. Thomas suggested a different arrangement: Doug and I would buy all the groceries, and he would fix dinner every night but weekends. That worked perfectly.

Though the three of us all knew each other (the four, if you included Leigh), the first two weeks were an exercise in excessive politeness, as we made sure not to annoy or intrude. We quickly got comfortable with each other until we no longer felt like visitors. It helped that we had similar tastes in music (whatever sounds good no matter what it is or where it comes from) and books (whatever gives pleasure of any kind, no matter what it's about or who wrote it).

The fun started with the bad southernmost jokes. After all, we were living in the southernmost house in the continental U.S. In a town that advertised itself to be the "End of the Road," we were at the end of the road at the end of the road. The United States ended here at the seawall.

Doug started the jokes: "Thomas, would you care for a southernmost beer?"

Then it was southernmost quiche, southernmost joint, southernmost . . . fill in the blank.

Leigh became the southernmost lay when she came over, or southernmost snatch (from Doug only), and she came over often.

Every night after watching the sunset, followed by the dinners/drinks/weed on the seawall, I went to bed with a feeling of such privilege that Baudelaire's '*luxe, calme et volupté*' kept coursing through my brain.

Conversations on the seawall, as complex as any I'd had anywhere in the world, took place here on a tiny piece of the planet that had no subterranean transport dues, nor seasonally occluded light. This was special, and I tip-toe-whispered through it, afraid I'd break the spell, get caught in an expensive seat I'd snuck into at intermission and be thrown out.

At the end of each workday, Doug and I would survey our day's accomplishments on the Bakery—work grants no greater pleasure—then bike to Southernmost House and jump in the pool.

Our dinner conversations ranged from the silly to the most serious, from hilarious descriptions of the worst sex partner we'd ever had or detailed discussions of our place in Nature or our obligation to the society at large, given that three of us—two homos and one draft dodger—were outside the pale. Mostly there was talk of writing, writing, and more writing. With the exception of Thomas, the most educated/uneducated of us all, we all had at least one graduate degree, but he was the beating heart of the summer, and he fascinated me.

One night after work I came "home" and saw Thomas removing the alligator emblem from his Polo shirts and asked him why he was going to the trouble.

"Because I want a shirt to be just a shirt, not an advertisement."

Then one day shortly after moving into Southernmost House, I came "home" and noticed the microwave, the fridge, even the bottles of vinegar and olive oil, all had pieces of tape covering the brand names. I had to ask.

Thomas seemed apologetic, but explained: "I can't *not* look at the letters, like KENMORE, and can't then stop analyzing why they chose that font, that size, that shape, that placement on the machine. It wears me out. I want a fridge to be just a big white box, a TV set to be an empty box until it's turned on—without advertising the brand with pretentious lettering. I know it's crazy but I can't help it. It's more restful for me this way. Come look in my bathroom."

I followed him down the hall and looked inside. The labels were soaked off everything he could, and the other toiletries, like the toothpaste tube, had cozies over them. "Crazy, huh?"

"No, I don't think it's crazy. It makes sense if you're that visual a person. But how do you stand going out?"

"I try to choose what I look at. What's toughest is to be inside someplace ugly, like in a restaurant where the door openings don't line up across the top, or the crown molding isn't proportioned to the room and the like. I can't stop looking at what's wrong, like running your tongue over a cracked filling."

He urged us all to always "look up," not some New Age precept, but a real command, because the sky above the island always held something interesting: Navy SEALS parachuting outside the Bight, a flock of curved-beak ibises flying in classic V-formation under-lit by a setting sun, frigates flying impossibly high without a single wing flap, and those clouds, clouds that thirsted for a Turner.

Thomas was usually the last to bed, refusing to come inside until the heavens had rewarded him with a shooting star, however small. If you stayed with him, you saw that there was at least one every night.

One day as we were standing on the seawall together, looking out at an empty ocean, I exclaimed how beautiful it was. "It is," he agreed, "but I think that some landscapes or seascapes aren't as beautiful as the same scenes with the hand of Man well or lightly placed on them.

Look now." A beautiful sailboat had just rounded the point. "I think the ocean is prettier with that sailboat on it, like a wide mountain view is made richer by seeing a little cabin off in the distance. I know it's not logical, but for me that helps justify Man's existence on the planet."

No professor had ever said anything that changed the way I looked at the world as much as those words: "the hand of Man well or lightly placed". Until then, I had held the '60s unexamined belief that everything Man did was, at the least, a small desecration of the planet.

Thomas was the first person I'd ever met that I knew with certainty saw the world and processed its information in a way not known to me. I was fascinated even more than I had been by the musicians I'd known in Paris. There, they had been brilliant interpreters of music already composed. Here was a man who created the music, visual music.

I began to understand that he *saw* everything around him, *always*, while I *glimpsed* everything around me, *sometimes*, the fee I'd paid to work my way out of poverty and ignorance. I had been rushing through life, tagging and filing things—pretty tree, beautiful view, interesting architecture—then speeding on. "Sorry, gotta rush .... gotta get to work .... got a paper to write." Yet born into similar poverty and ignorance, he had not done that, not sacrificed a quiet, thorough examination of all he saw. My 'eye' was a dictionary; his, an encyclopedia.

One afternoon that summer, he and I were walking out to the seawall, and he stopped at one of the palms in the yard that had just recently dropped one of its fronds. He pulled off a piece of the fiber still clinging to the trunk and looked at it as we continued walking.

On the seawall, we looked down at a couple of horseshoe crabs crawling slowly along the seafloor. Then, with those Etruscan eyes, he looked at the fiber again, something I wouldn't have given a second look to before throwing it in the garbage. He passed it to me.

"Look at this."

I looked, and handed it back.

"Look, John, it's *woven*. Isn't that wonderful? I'll bet something like this gave humans the idea for weaving cloth."

"Thomas, when did you start noticing things this way?"

"I honestly don't know. I do remember my first fascination with color. I must have been four or five. My aunt and uncle lived outside Cleveland and had a nursery with two greenhouses they heated during the winter. We were out there for Sunday dinner one weekend after a heavy snowstorm. While we were eating, the heater in one of the greenhouses exploded, blowing plants all over the place. Everyone rushed outside to grab as many plants as they could to put them in the other greenhouse. I stood there, frozen, fascinated by the orchids' color against that white, white snow."

I learned more about him as the summer progressed. He had grown up in a large, second-generation Hungarian family in Cleveland, mother and father both factory workers. He was interested only in art, which perplexed the parents. He dropped out of school in the tenth grade, moved out on his own and went to work at a bookstore. By the time I met him in Key West he was, along with Jeff Hagel, the best-read person I'd met on the island.

When he realized he was gay with its cultural consequences, he started drinking. Then one night, staring down at the Cuyahoga River, it caught fire. It triggered a suicidal depression in him for some reason, which he satisfied by pouring gasoline on himself and lighting it, which explained the scar on the forearm. A passerby jumped on him and put out the fire, and he was taken to the hospital.

A mental hospital was next. Then a girlfriend from high school who'd always admired him talked him into a trip south. When they'd hit Key West, he knew he'd found a home. He found a gay partner and a patron in a man living quietly on the island, and began to hit his stride. The island made it OK for him to be gay, to be different—appreciated his difference—and develop his talent. He began designing renovations early on and designed and built a house for him and his partner right on Front Street, and another on Roatan, one of the Bay Islands off Honduras, where he spent as much time as he could afford.

When his partner, like Hemingway, couldn't take the increasing number of tourists coming to Key West anymore, he sold the Key West house and moved to England, settling some money on Thomas (who pissed it all away). The house he'd sold was now the Monster disco, the slate dance floor their original bedroom floor. I loved the Monster, but when Thomas told me that, I couldn't believe that he could still bear to go there.

"It's tough, sometimes," he admitted when I asked him that. "But things evolve, and when I'm there with good friends, it's OK. It helps, too, to be fucked up."

Thomas was the stage designer who had to have constant eye candy. We would come home from work, and a huge Bismarkia Nobilis palm frond would be hanging from a ceiling, the table on the seawall would have four just-sprouted coconuts lined up perfectly down the center, and a piece of driftwood with candles in its limbs would light the way down the steps from the house.

The next day, it would be something different: a series of lanterns with candles burning would line the seawall, and a beautiful piece of fabric would be perfectly hung from a tree, sensuously wafting in the sea breeze, or a large, urn-like black vase filled with three papyrus stalks would be sitting in the corner of the living room, their delicate, feathery heads backlit. For him, this was as easy and necessary as making coffee in the morning was for Doug and me.

That summer I saw the truth, too, of what Leigh had already told me, and Thomas freely admitted to: he was an alcoholic. His addiction took a strange form. Every night, Thomas, Doug, and I would have three beers apiece and share a joint after dinner and that would usually be enough for him. But every fifteen days or so, some unknown and unknowable impulse started him binge drinking. He was never mean when drunk; in fact, the maniacal laughter and the desire to have fun increased, and he would push closer to the edge of danger. More than once he came home bruised and bloody from a bike accident when he'd been drinking, or from trying to pick up the wrong man.

There was no stopping him when he started a binge, and we could only be worried and silent observers, trying to protect him as best we could. The aftermath was also always the same: great shame on his part and withdrawal. He would lie on the seawall listening to music, always something instrumental—the *Gymnopédies* or *Brandenburg Concertos*, or Shankar—and make no contact, walk into the house, eyes cast down. Leigh was the only one who could reach him when he was like that, and we would see them out there together, his head in her lap. We learned to let him be and slowly wend his way back. Then in a day or two, he would apologize and be his normal self again.

Having an ironically stern view of pleasure, I didn't understand, beyond a certain point, the need for "artificial paradises." We were so rich, those of us who lived in these modern, industrialized societies, that we had little right to complain about much. But I had to admit that a demon lived inside Thomas completely outside my ken, and I had to accept its existence if I wanted to be his friend, and I wanted that very much.

Fascinated, I watched once that summer as he created a piece over several evenings after dinner. He started with several small pieces of wire, perhaps one-eighth an inch in diameter, and began shaping and pulling them. He talked to Doug and me the whole time he was manipulating the wire, and even answered a question of mine, which was, did he ever do sculpture.

"I can't do anything that requires subtraction, like cutting something out of a piece of stone or carving wood. I don't know why. I just don't see it. I can only do things that add, like collages, constructions, or a sculpture that builds, like this," and he looked down at what he was working on.

"Do you know what it's going to be?" I asked.

"Not yet. It's vague so far. I have a feeling more than anything," and he continued to twist little pieces of wire into shapes that he abandoned, then re-formed.

The next night, a recognizable shape began to emerge, a human form, but just barely.

Two nights later, it became a piece of art. A figure, recognizable as a man from the waist up, was straining terribly forward. His arms, extended painfully behind him, morphed into something like a long cloak that dragged the ground. I was open-mouthed at the simplicity and complexity of it. Finished, one saw in the partial abstraction of tiny pieces of wire a man being born out of the ground, pulling himself into existence or, alternatively, a man struggling against a weight behind him that was pulling him back into the earth . . . or both. It was brilliant.

I had known or been acquainted with great writers and great musicians, but never this. This was a kind of human consciousness and talent that I could not categorize and define, and I was hooked. When I saw the finished piece, I asked Thomas, for the second time, why he didn't try to get his stuff known in a bigger venue like New York, and he answered that he did these things for himself. "I really have no ambition," he said. "I'm satisfied if I make enough to let me live here as peacefully as I can. If I became ambitious, the pressure would make me kill myself."

There was only one hindrance to our pleasure in life in the Southernmost House. The man the owners had hired to service the swimming pool was also a Baptist minister, and there was a real clash of cultures from the start of our stay because he knew Thomas was gay. His first tattletale call to the owners was about the pot plants growing next to the laundry shed. What he didn't know was that Emmerick, not us, had planted them. When Emmerick called, he apologized, but insisted we take the blame for him and just pull them up, which we did.

The next complaint to the owners, relayed to us, was that the things we left in the pool—floats, drink floats, etc.—made it difficult for him to vacuum. Thomas apologized to the man and suggested that he come at the same time on the same day each week and we would make sure the pool was empty.

"I can't do that," he said in response. "God's ministry doesn't allow me to schedule."

In a futile attempt to placate him, if one of us was at home when he showed up, we would jump in the pool and remove the offending objects. But there was no satisfying him. He wanted to discover and punish sin, so a passive-aggressive struggle began that mirrored the religious-secular conflict in society at large.

Finally, we matched his refusal to cooperate. If we heard the gate opening at least one of us stripped naked and plopped into a lawn chair, pretending to sunbathe. It was the only thing that stopped him from trying to preach to us. One Saturday he came in to find Thomas and Doug skinny-dipping, and Leigh sunbathing topless. He stopped dead in his tracks when he turned the corner. "I'll come back later when you cover yourselves up."

"No, please stay, we have to leave for lunch now anyway," Leigh shouted, making a point of giving him a good view of everything as she headed towards the steps to the house, then rubbed salt in the wound by yelling over to him: "There's some mustard algae growing around the pool light you need to scrub off." Sure enough, that rated us another phone call from the owners asking us to be more discreet. It also caused him to start leaving religious literature behind, heavy on Sodom and Gomorrah references, which we made into paper airplanes and left in conspicuous places.

Again Thomas requested that he come at a scheduled time so there'd be no conflicts, and again the man refused, referring to the demands his ministry placed on him. "God doesn't work like that." We knew, of course, that he enjoyed surprising us and had probably gone home and had a good wank the day he saw Leigh in her unclothed beauty.

Victory in that war would come later.

I surrendered to Thomas in a way foreign to my control-freak personality, an intellectual surrender I had never made to another human being. He had things to teach me and ways to make me see differently, and I wanted them. When he suggested we do something, I never questioned it because, even if it went terribly wrong, that wild, chaos-loving laugh rose above the experience and made it wonderful.

An example of the gone wrong: one Sunday morning before the summer began, Thomas called us all and begged us to go to Bahia Honda, the state park forty miles up the Keys with the world-class beach. He picked each of us up in a Citroën, a rolling advertisement for why the French should have stayed in the nineteenth century. This Citroën, a convertible, had the adjustable hydraulics that lift and lower the chassis. It also had holes in the floor. Top down, we headed up the Keys, talking about the usual stuff: the latest *Crime Report*, the latest country the United States had invaded, and Leigh's discovery of Tanizaki's *The Makioka Sisters*. As we hit Big Pine Key, a squall line passed over the island, and it started pouring. Thomas punched the button to raise the top, but nothing happened. The tires started throwing dirty water up on us through the holes in the floor. Then the adjustable hydraulic system started lifting and dropping the chassis, and Thomas couldn't stop it.

We were getting soaked by rain from above and dirty water from the holes in the floor, and were hopping up and down the road like a demented rabbit. Leigh, the princess, who I would have expected to scream in outrage, was laughing as hard as the rest of us. Thomas's laugh, which I will carry with me to the grave, rose above all ours, laughter that defied human frailty and folly, laughter that celebrated wonderful chaos.

An example of the gone right: Two months before Southernmost Summer had begun, Thomas had bought a Beetle Cat after Las Palmas Gail's new boyfriend, Jeff, bought one.

Beetle Cats are beautiful: twelve feet long, broad-beamed, gaff-rigged, and easy to sail. New Englanders teach their children on them because they're so stable. Leigh and her brother had cut their teeth on a Beetle Cat, and she and Jeff taught Thomas how to sail his. Jeff's parents let them both dock their boats behind their house on Key Haven, Key West's suburb.

One Sunday, we provisioned the boat with weed, wine, and food, unfurled the sails and tacked our way out past a spit of land attached to Key Haven and headed east. Some experiences demand whispers or silence, and this was one.

Thomas called out: "Coming about" to warn us as the boom swung over our heads when he tacked, and we made our way to a large mangrove island. When we got close, he and Leigh furled the sail, and Thomas gave Doug and me oars and directed the rowing to a barely visible opening in the mangroves. This was Channel Key, Thomas told us. "Pull us into the channel using the mangrove branches." Ten minutes later, the channel opened up into a twenty-foot-wide pool of perfectly clear water, surrounded by mangroves on all sides. Two Great White Herons lifted off as we entered the pool.

There was nothing human visible apart from us, and we sat there, silent. Leigh opened a bottle of wine and handed out sandwiches. At a certain point, I could feel the gentle tugs from the nature around me, pulling me further into the scene, and I tried to relax into it, but the naked ape's brain had evolved too far, too differently, to be subsumed, but how wonderful to be a guest.

When Thomas gave the signal for us to leave, Doug and I pulled us back out to open water. Thomas and Leigh unfurled the sail, and a following wind pushed us easily across the water. We sailed around for a while on open water. When we got back to the dock, we unloaded and lashed the boat and went back into town, regenerated.

With few exceptions, Doug and I took every weekend off. Sunday brunch on the seawall under a patio umbrella became an obligatory event, a sacrament, attendance required, Leigh included. Our conversations were hours long, like dinner parties in France. All of us loved to read, and it was most often at brunch that one of us would share something newly discovered, which the others would then read. This was what I had thirsted for and only partially gotten in graduate school.

Thomas introduced us to Erskine Lane's *Game Texts* that he'd discovered on a trip to Guatemala where he'd met the writer. Spare, dense prose, as deliberately simple and beautiful as haiku.

Doug gave us another gay writer, Edmund White, a sometimes visitor to the island, who created awesome metaphors and similes, seemingly without effort.

I discovered Jorge Amado and introduced him around. We all then read everything he'd written, in admiration and surprise that we didn't know him, probably because he wrote in Portuguese. Part of each Sunday we talked about another Amado book, until finally we agreed that his not having won the Nobel Prize was a crime and collectively wrote a letter of protest to the Swedish Academy, signing ourselves The Southernmost Literary Society. In the letter, we begged them to consider Amado for the prize for the "life-affirming bawdiness in *Tieta*" and referred to the scene in *Jubiabá* where the rich girl, now destitute and turned to prostitution, is climbing the stairs of one of the lowest rungs in Salvador's slums, and her tears at her fate were dissolving the filth on the stairway.

"If Puccini were alive," we concluded, "there would be an opera called *Jubiabá*."

Leigh gave us Edward Abbey's *The Monkey Wrench Gang* and *Desert Solitaire*.

One day that summer, scouring the racks of the local library, I chanced upon *Conversation in the Cathedral* by Vargas Llosa, a writer none of us had heard of. I read it first, in disbelief that a talent this Olympian was not yet known. I raced home every day to get back to it. When I finished it, sadly, I gave it to them. They each read it slowly, mouths open at a skill so great he could even play with the form, and we wrote our second letter to the Swedish Academy.

To be doing all this against a backdrop of planetary beauty made us all feel that this was exactly what life was supposed to be.

Every weekend that summer, I spent at least two hours in one of the hammocks slung between the palms at one end of the swimming pool with a shaded and privileged view of sea and sky. The three of them easily accepted the explanation of my real psychological need for time alone, time where my mind just wandered, little synapse maids tidying up whatever needed it, or knitting tiny insights into new being.

One late Saturday afternoon, lying in the hammock, watching the three of them talking and laughing on the seawall, a feeling hit me as intense as what parents must feel when the product of their love makes its bloody, wonderful entrance into the world. Not only had I found a home, I was in love with these three people whose existence I could never have posited, people who cared for me and sought my company. I climbed out of the hammock and joined them for sunset on the seawall, but felt something different . . . a kind of fragility . . . and grace bestowed.

Thomas' birthday was near the end of July. Two days before the party we'd planned, I was standing on the seawall and noticed a small, empty rowboat adrift a short ways out. I yelled "Wreck Ashore" in the best Key West wrecking tradition, then yelled to Thomas and Doug to come outside and help me. I dropped a ladder off the seawall into the water and swam out to the boat and dragged it to the base of the ladder. With Thomas and Doug pulling from above and me pushing from below, we got the boat up on the deck, and that's when we noticed it had a glass bottom.

"This is way too cool," Thomas said. "I wonder who owned it and what they used it for?"

"Could have been a lot of things," Doug said. "Sponging, looking for conchs, or just recreation."

"Whatever it was, I, John Cottrell, found it and claim it. Salvage rights. But what are we going to do with it?"

"Put it in the pool, what else?" Thomas said. "But we have to wait until the party or preacher man will call the owners again. Let's hide it on the other side of the garage for now."

The day before the party, Thomas went to the neighbor's house and told him that we were going to have a party the next night and set off some fireworks right after dark. "I just wanted to warn you, but also in case your kids wanted to come out and watch." The neighbor thanked him and said he'd tell his kids.

Birthday day arrived. Leigh came by after lunch and helped us set up tables outside, and get things ready. Doug, Thomas, and I dragged the rowboat from behind the garage and put it in the pool. Thomas got out his camera, and we took turns having our picture taken sitting in the rowboat.

Two hours before sunset, people started arriving. Thomas had set up speakers outside so we had music, food, and alcohol. The party started off slowly, and the presence of the older, A-list group kept things restrained. Thomas kept his camera at the ready, and we took turns taking pictures of everyone who ventured into the rowboat.

Slowly, as people got an alcohol buzz and the older guests left, you could sense an increase in energy. Thomas turned the music up, people started dancing on the deck by the seawall, and joints started passing around. By the time the sun set, there were still about twenty-five people there, not counting us.

Thomas on his way back south from buying his Beetle Cat had stopped at the border fireworks store in the Carolinas and bought four hundred dollars' worth to use on his birthday. When it got dark, he dragged the large box out to the seawall along with a lighter and some sparklers to light fuses. People were standing around waiting for the show to start. A young married couple, friends of Doug's who'd hit a rough patch in their marriage, were sitting in the rowboat having what looked like a deep conversation.

Leigh came over to me and asked me to help Thomas light the fireworks. "It'll be too slow with only one person doing it."

I joined him on the seawall and took a sparkler and lit it.

"Ready?" he asked.

"Ready."

He grabbed a Roman candle, and I grabbed two screaming meemies and lit the fuses and aimed them out over the water. The candle described its arc and exploded at the same time my two went off screaming and tracing wild, erratic and noisy paths. Then we did two candles at once. From next door, we could hear the neighbor's kids clapping and yelling.

As we hit our stride, the pace picked up, and we got a rhythm going, making a good combination of noise, color, and booms. Five minutes into it, we'd barely made a dent in the box's contents.

There is disagreement about what happened next. However it happened, it did, and it was what made every guest smile years later when you mentioned Southernmost birthday party. I think Thomas, in perpetual search for *more*, deliberately dropped the sparkler into the box. He always swore it was an accident. About the outcome, there could be no disagreement.

Fireworks started exploding out of the box with huge roars and in all directions. As people started running and screaming, Roman candles roared across the deck and pool and arced up into the air, hitting the house, the roof, and even the neighbor's roof. The neighbor's kids, thinking it was all still under adult control, kept yelling for more even as they dodged the screaming meemies headed their way.

People cowered under the buffet tables, behind trees, and around the corners of the house. The couple in the rowboat tipped it over and sank it trying to escape to the safety of the pool. There was a short lull, and people came out to see if it was safe, then a spark would light more fuses, and there'd be more fire and explosions, and everyone would go shrieking for cover again and, above it all, Thomas' familiar maniacal laughter.

The entire episode lasted only five or six minutes, but it seemed much longer before there was silence.

Everyone came out from their hiding places. When they realized no one had been hurt, they started laughing and congratulated Thomas, and it took the party to a whole new level. The rowboat couple dragged a lawn chair out of the light and started seriously making out. Clothes came off other people who went skinny-dipping, and the drinking and smoking began in earnest. Then there was one last burst from the fireworks box, which caused everyone to scream and duck again, but that was the last gasp.

By the time I was ready for bed, so was Leigh. Thomas and Doug were nowhere to be seen, so we went inside to my room and collapsed, leaving whatever revelers were left to their own devices.

The brain's little guard dog that lets a person sleep through some noises but bolt awake at a tiny one that signals possible danger popped me out of a sound sleep around seven the next morning. I had heard the noisy hinges of the gate.

I looked out the bedroom window. The Baptist preacher was walking alongside the house towards the pool. I raced to another window to watch.

God's reward to me for being an atheist was what I saw next.

When the preacher turned the corner, he stepped back in shock, a look of fascinated horror on his face. He took it in slowly: the beer cans and liquor bottles all over the decks and yard, men and women's underwear around the pool, the buffet table with fly-covered food. Then another head jerk when he saw the naked couple asleep in adjacent lawn chairs, and the *coup de grâce*: a rowboat at the bottom of the pool.

He dropped his equipment, turned around, and walked away. I heard the gate shut behind him a minute later but knew what was coming next. I pulled clothes on and woke Leigh up. ("Leave me alone. It's too early.") I shook her and told her the problem. She jumped out of bed, and while she was dressing, I ran and banged on Thomas' and Doug's doors.

From Doug's room, nothing. From Thomas' room a "Go away, leave me alone." I yelled through the door what had happened. "Alright, alright, I'll get up." A few minutes later, he stumbled out of his room followed by Doug, who looked at me and winked.

We shot out of the house, all with massive hangovers. Thomas woke up the sleeping couple on the lawn chairs and sent them on their embarrassed way, then assigned the tasks. Leigh brought a whole box of garbage bags from the kitchen, and we started furiously bagging everything, underwear, bottles, cans, food, firework debris, everything. "Tie up the bags and put them in one of the bedrooms," Thomas told us. "He might look in the garbage cans."

Doug and I got in the pool and raised the boat. We dragged it to the seawall and dropped it into the water. When it stayed against the seawall, I climbed in the water and took it out far enough that the currents took it away, and I wished it god-speed.

While Thomas and Doug put the tables back inside the house, Leigh made coffee for us. I used muriatic acid that Thomas got out of the garage on all the stains the fireworks had left on the concrete decks, then poured water from the pool on them to dilute the acid.

We did a superficial clean-up in the house, then collapsed into the chairs around the patio table and started drinking our coffee.

"Won't be long now," Thomas predicted, and it wasn't. We heard the gate open, and a minute later the man the owners used to check on the house occasionally turned the corner with the pool guy and saw four people having a quiet cup of coffee. Thomas offered the two of them some, but they declined. The pool man looked around in disbelief, then walked around the decks and yard, then over to the seawall and looked down.

"We heard that there was an out-of-control party here last night with lots of damage," the spy said.

The pool guy headed for the area next to the garage where the garbage cans were kept. Thomas had been right.

"I had some friends over," Thomas answered and named some of the A-list people, "but I don't understand what you mean by out of control. Are you sure you wouldn't like some coffee."

"No, thanks. I'm sorry but . . ." and he gestured towards where the pool guy had gone, "he had some wild story. I had to check it out."

Both men left, the pool guy with a murderous glance in our direction. An hour later, the phone call came from the owners.

"What the fuck is going on, Thomas?" It was Arden. "The pool man called me with this wild story about a party and a sunken boat in the pool, yet our friend tells us everything is fine."

"Arden, the pool guy hates me because he's religious, and I'm gay. I think he's on drugs, because he's acting strange. A friend of mine does pool maintenance, charges less and does a better job. Why don't you let me hire him?"

"Do it. I'm tired of these goddamn phone calls."

Christians–0, Lions–1.

Thomas had the photos developed and blown up of everyone sitting in the rowboat in the pool, framed them, and gave each person a copy.

One night in late August, we were all standing on the seawall watching the moon's reflection on the ocean when Thomas asked what the date was. None of us knew, so he went inside to find out. When he came back out to the seawall, he asked us to be available the next few nights for a surprise. "I'm not sure what night it will be, but be sure to keep every night open, OK?"

"Can't you give us a hint?" Leigh asked.

"Nope. Has to be a real surprise. You'll love it, so be available."

Every night, Thomas stationed himself on the seawall after sunset with a walkie-talkie nearby. We were used to his habit of never turning in for the night until he'd seen a shooting star, but he seemed more focused those nights, looking out toward Sand Key Lighthouse.

The third night after he'd made the request, Doug and I were on the seawall with him when he said, "I have a feeling it's tonight."

A few minutes later, there was a squawk on the walkie-talkie and Thomas picked it up and listened for a minute, then thanked the person on the other end.

"Let's go," Thomas said, "and hurry. Put on your swimsuits. I'll call Leigh."

We met by the front door, and Thomas handed us two duffel bags and rushed us to his latest car, a '55 Chevy whose previous owner had installed rumble seats where the trunk used to be. "We're meeting Leigh at Garrison Bight Marina." He wouldn't volunteer any other information.

Leigh was at the marina when we pulled in. Thomas told us to bring the duffel bags, and we headed to the docking area where he directed us to a twenty-five-foot Boston Whaler.

"A friend loaned it to me," he explained as we headed out the bight. He piloted us past Trumbo Point and Fleming Key, through the harbor, and then headed out over open water toward Sand Key Lighthouse. Now I was scared as well as intrigued. I am in awe of the ocean, and the ocean at night is a mystery I wasn't keen on exploring.

We raced across the water, and thirty minutes later slowed as we approached the lighthouse, where two other boats were moored. I noticed a strange glow coming from underwater as Thomas stopped the boat and dropped anchor. After he'd secured the line, he turned to us.

"Two years ago in Australia, researchers discovered the phenomenon of the mass spawning of coral then found out that corals all around the world do it. They pump out bundles containing both sperm and eggs that break apart and disperse in the currents where they mix and create genetic diversity. The researchers think they do it this way to overwhelm all the fish that eat the bundles. There's just too much for the fish to be able to eat all of it, so enough survives to carry on. Here it happens within eight days of the August full moon. That's why I asked you to keep all the nights free. Friends of mine are down there now, photographing it," and he pointed to the underwater glow. "One of them gave me the signal that it's started. This mass spawning has probably been going on longer than Man has existed, and it's supposed to be spectacular. Let's go see it."

He, Doug, and Leigh pulled masks, fins, and snorkels out of the duffel bags and put them on, then looked at me.

"What's wrong?"

"I'm scared, dammit. Look at all those shadows down there," and I pointed to the dark shapes of very large fish darting around the circle of light. "I don't like not being at the top of the food chain."

"Suit yourself," Thomas said and handed Leigh an underwater light, and the three jumped overboard. They adjusted their masks and rubbed spit on the inside, then swam toward the circle of light and dived down together.

I cursed myself, called myself a coward . . . argued with myself. "Well, John," I said to myself, "you've always said you didn't want an ordinary life and here you are face to face with a great experience and what do you do but chicken out. Why don't you just go back to being a teacher in Toronto, you big, sissy *coward*." But my fear was overwhelming. Those darting shadows were real and very large.

I saw the three of them surface for air inside the circle of light. Thomas and Doug went back down, but Leigh swam back to the boat. In those comforting, soft tones that mothers use with frightened children, she looked up at me and yelled: "Get your ass in the water *now*, you wimp. You can't miss this. Two queers and a woman in the water and Mr. Macho Man is quivering in the boat! Give me a break. You have to see this."

'Oh hell,' I thought, 'what's the worst that can happen to me? Get eaten by a shark? Oh hell, as long as it's quick.' I went to the other side of the boat and threw up, then grabbed mask, fins, and snorkel and flung my fear out ahead of me like I'd done when I was sky-diving. By the time the fear boomeranged back to catch me, it was too late, I was already committed: I was in the surprisingly warm water.

I swam towards the circle of light and when I reached it, got hit by the strongest déjà vu of my life: for the second time in my life I was following a woman with a light into a forest during a snowstorm, but this time it was all upside down. The forest was below me, the spectacular coral heads and sea fans, and the snowstorm I was passing through was rising not falling.

Four divers with tanks were on the bottom with powerful underwater lights illuminating something not to be believed. Pieces of what looked like colorful but inanimate stone—the coral heads—were pulsing out billions and billions of tiny white and peach-colored bundles we were swimming in and through as they slowly rose to the surface. Small tropical fish in the hundreds, if not thousands, were everywhere, gobbling them down in a feeding frenzy, but there was so much, swirling and rising, that they were overwhelmed. Larger fish darted quickly in and out of the lighted space, too intimidated by the even larger swimmers—us—to come closer.

The divers on the seabed gave us a thumbs up, and their underwater lights created a space I stayed inside as I tried to suppress my fear of what lay outside. I went up for air, then back down, up and down, through this 'snowstorm' and finally calmed down and focused and became comfortable enough that I joined my three friends in turning and rolling in this primordial storm of gametes, paying homage. How tiny one-celled animals knew it was a full moon in August was just one of the wonders I contemplated.

When we were all tired and back in the boat, I started babbling. "That was spectacular, I don't know . . . primeval . . . primordial soup . . . stupendous," and they all laughed at me.

"Oh, so you're glad you jumped in?" Leigh teased.

When we'd docked the boat back at the marina and made our way back to Southernmost House, we rinsed off in the pool, then grabbed drinks and went out on the seawall and looked out towards the lighthouse standing guard over the mystery we'd just witnessed.

"You know, as wonderful as that was, I can't shake the feeling we were intruding on something private," Thomas said. "What happens next? Thousands of tourists down there every time they spawn?"

Near the end of our stay in Southernmost House, Thomas found himself a place to live in as caretaker again, but told us we couldn't see it until he was ready.

We removed all our belongings from Southernmost House, then used Thomas' sketches to place all the owners' belongings back exactly as they'd been. We gave the house a final cleaning, made easy because Thomas' parents had visited in late September and his eighty-year-old mother, a cleaning machine, had gone around, in spite of our protests, cleaning everything, including using a toothbrush on the tops of the baseboards and the mullions of the windows.

Arden and Emmerick had called Thomas to tell him they would arrive on the 25th of the month. "I know them, though," he warned us, "and they'll be here before then hoping to catch us unprepared."

A month before we had to leave the house, a hippie couple had sailed up in a makeshift thirty-foot boat and anchored and stayed a hundred yards off the seawall. Watching them had been interesting: the forays to shore for provisions in their minimal rowboat dinghy, the maintenance on the boat, and the obvious pleasure they took in each other's company. Occasionally they waved to us as we all watched the sun set, and they danced on their deck as we danced on the seawall to the music we were playing.

Doug and Thomas came out to join Leigh and me our last night there, and as we were all sitting on the seawall together, the couple weighed anchor for the first time since their arrival, raised canvas, waved to us, bowed farewell, and sailed off into another spectacular sunset. We watched, pulled forward into the diminishing sail and the freedom it represented, then looked at each other and laughed again at the beauty and improbable timing of it.

"Our last night here; you scripted that," Leigh said to Thomas. "Too perfect, you gypsy."

"The sailboat part was easy. Getting the sunset right was tough."

"Stop while you're ahead."

We were completely out of the house by the 20th, but Thomas and I would spend an hour or so there at the end of every day just to check on things, pick up any fallen palm fronds and rearrange the lights to be left on at night.

Around six in the evening on the 22nd, we heard the gate open, then a key in the door, and Emmerick burst in without looking at us or saying hello, scanned the room, and said: "But it's all exactly like we left it," as if that disappointed him. Thomas and I looked at each other and grinned. Arden came in and said exactly the same thing.

Thomas introduced me, handed them the keys to the house, told them we'd stocked the fridge with some beer and wine for them, thanked them for letting us stay there, and we left.

When we walked outside the gate to the street, Thomas looked over at me. "Sad?"

"How could I not be?"

He got on his bike and rode off down Whitehead, and I rode off down South Street.

Eleven

Thomas' next place was an empty, wooden, three-story building on the corner of Fleming and William Streets that had once been a furniture store and warehouse. He was caretaker now for as long as it was on the market. A month after we'd dispersed from Southernmost House, he invited us all for dinner.

Doug and I walked in together. Thomas and Leigh were waiting for us in director's chairs at the end of an allée of trees in pots, typical Thomas staging. We joined them in an open area, about eight feet by eight feet, enclosed, strangely, by a two-foot-high spindled railing. Thomas poured some wine, then went over to a corner behind us as we chatted with Leigh.

Suddenly, we started rising slowly and smoothly into the air. When he saw our shock, Thomas burst out in manic laughter. "It's a counter-weighted freight elevator," he explained as he pulled on the rope that controlled it. We stopped at the second floor, where he tied us off and opened the little railed gate.

We were now in a nearly two thousand square foot space with huge windows on all four sides and no interior walls. Two sofas with a floor lamp for each was the living area; a hollow-core door slab on sawhorses was the dining area; and a small kitchen and curtained bathroom hugged one corner. I had never seen a place I envied more; it was more magical, even, than the Bakery, a luxury of unbelievable and uncluttered space.

After we'd gotten over our wonder at that, Thomas herded us back on the elevator and pulled us up to the top floor where he had his monastic bedroom: bed, reading lamp, and bookstand, with the same huge windows as on the floor below. In one corner of the space, he'd set up more doors on sawhorses for his studio.

In between courses at dinner, Doug and I took turns playing with the elevator. It was a kid's dream, like tree houses, rope bridges, and makeshift forts. After dinner, Thomas led us back onto the platform and lowered us to the ground floor. We said goodbye and watched him slowly ascend, with that wild laughter.

We rang in the New Year at the Bakery, but Thomas gave a party at his place ten days later. Doug and I heard the party above us as we pulled ourselves up in the elevator, but smelled the surprise before we were high enough to see it. Thomas had collected over a hundred thrown-away Christmas trees. We walked off the elevator platform into a beautifully lit forest of evergreens, a real forest with narrow pathways, on the second floor of a wooden building, on a tiny, tropical island a hundred and twenty miles out to sea. The children at the party were thrilled, hiding and chasing each other through the 'forest' with gales of pure laughter.

That ushered in the year after which it was no longer necessary to explain where Key West was when people asked you where you lived.

When Kresge's dime store on Duval Street closed, Tony Falcone and his partner, Bill Conkle, had moved Fast Buck Freddie's, the department store they'd started, into the much larger space. One of its advantages was the eight huge storefront windows, six on Duval Street and two more around the corner on Fleming, which Tony and

Bill exploited to the point of genius. The entire town started antici-pating the unveiling of the new windows on the first of every month, creating traffic jams as people went out of their way to drive by. One month, against plain white backdrops, a flock of pink flamingos flew from window to window all the way around the corner.

The most famous windows were in February of that year, celebrat-ing Valentine's Day. On February 1st, the curtains dropped. In each window a bright red "LOVE IS ETERNAL" banner hung above a five-foot-high photograph of Liz Taylor with one of her six hus-bands: Hilton, Wilding, Todd, Fisher, Burton, and Burton again. The town roared with laughter.

One afternoon that month, when Leigh and I were walking past the store, she said, "Don't look now, but that's Liz across the street checking out the windows. She and Richard must be in town to visit Philip."

Philip was Philip Burton, Richard's adoptive father, who lived in a small house on Angela Street in the heart of Old Town.

People disbelieved us that Taylor had been in town until Tony Falcone confirmed it. A lavender envelope had arrived at the store a month later. Inside, on monogrammed stationery, was a gracious letter from the actress herself, thanking them for a good laugh and ending with: "You have two unused windows. Does that mean I can have two more marriages?"

Mel Fisher was a retired chicken farmer from Indiana turned treasure hunter. He'd moved to Key West to search for the *Atocha*, a Spanish treasure ship that had sunk somewhere off Key West during a hur-ricane in 1622. What was known about the *Atocha* was that it had been carrying hundreds of emeralds from the Muzo mine in Colom-bia, tons of gold bullion, and silver, plus hundreds of gold and silver artifacts: gold chains, chalices, and belts. What wasn't known was where the wreck was. People had sought the treasure for years with no luck.

Mel searched for years, too. He'd become a local fixture, picking his teeth with a solid gold combination toothpick/ear scoop they'd found on the seafloor, selling more and more shares in his company, Treasure Salvors, and annoying every waitress in town with his traditional under-the-plate ten-cent tip. He and his crew ran up bills all over town, so he was often short at payroll time and had to promise even more shares if they ever found the treasure. He'd finally become a laughingstock with his unrelenting 'Today's the Day' motto, but then an object of pity when one of his sons and the son's wife drowned when their ship capsized in the search.

The location where the *Atocha* was driven onto the reef and presumed to have sunk was in the archives in Seville. Mel sent a researcher back to those archives to read everything again. The researcher found a small but significant ambiguity in the geographical description of the presumed wreck site, and Mel moved the search. One afternoon that year, the salvage ship anchored above a new section of the seafloor and aimed its prop-wash deflectors downward and blasted. When the silt cleared, Kane, one of Mel's sons, radioed to shore: "Put away the charts. We've found the mother lode." A wall of bullion sat staring at the amazed divers.

The word of the discovery swept across the island faster than a hurricane's wind. I was in the Deli Restaurant having a late breakfast when someone ran in the door, yelling: "Mel's found the *Atocha*!" and we all stood and applauded.

Camera crews arrived from several countries to film the story. Celebrities like Johnny Carson flew in to dive the site and look in wonder at the tons of gold and jewels that had been sitting there for nearly three hundred years. The prince of Spain flew in to look at the treasure that had been destined to help his ancestors pay for their part in the Thirty Years War.

Leigh's remark when she saw the treasure put on display was: "Look at the color of those emeralds! God! They are my favorite stone. Did you know those Muzo emeralds are still the standard all other emeralds are judged by?"

National Geographic came to town and made a film about the wreck and its discovery.

The year before, Frank and Joe from the Key West Aloe company and Bill and Tony from Fast Buck Freddie's had started what they called Fantasy Fest as a way to draw tourists to the island during a normally dead time. They got permits from the city to close Duval Street for a parade and scheduled it for Halloween weekend to enhance the fantasy and costume aspect.

After the four of them had pitched it successfully to the city, the Chamber of Commerce begged all the locals to join in the party to make it a success. When Thomas read that he hooted. "Begging Key Westers to party is like asking an alcoholic to drink."

What none of us could have imagined is that we were about to begin what would become one of the largest parties in the country, and that a few years later one of the biggest problems would be at the airport, finding parking space for all the private jets.

That first Fantasy Fest had been a great hit, with thousands of visitors coming mostly from other parts of Florida to enjoy the kind of party everyone wishes they could throw, and to watch the locals make fools of themselves; and we made glorious, happy fools of ourselves. There was a parade of hilariously amateur floats and one great one: Fast Buck Freddie's float had King Kong's hand opening and closing in suggestive ways around his sexy captive whose legs went up in the air.

The chunky Cuban woman who ran one of the laundromats where we all got our morning coffee wore a breastplate that gave her mammoth-sized breasts and did a solo salsa so hot that it got her a rolling ovation as she made her way down Duval Street.

Guys with black dog collars and little else were led by their 'masters' down the street. The local population of drag queens outdid each other: there was Marie Antoinette; a beautifully dressed geisha who lifted her kimono to flash an oversized plastic phallus; and TWO Barbra Streisands who hissed and spit whenever they came too close to each other. Enough breasts were exposed by real women to nurse the baby population of a major city and satisfy the imagination of every straight male for months.

Fantasy Fest was such a hit—and a financial boon to the island's economy—that it was decided to make it an annual event.

There were voices of dissent. Letters to the *Key West Citizen* complained about the nudity, and one man, who had been hired by the city to provide additional security, railed in a letter to the editor against all the exposed breasts that his sixteen-year-old son and helper had been forced to look at. That generated more laughter than anything else. Firstly, what sixteen-year-old boy would not like to look at lots of breasts; secondly, the father in question had just gotten out of "college" for importing and dealing large amounts of grass. Most of the town welcomed the party and its economic boost, as accepting of the lewder parts as they were of the main street movie theater advertising *Deep Throat*.

Now, this second year, with the decision to throw the party again, a certain institutionalization of the event began. The tourist council and the city commission voted funds for providing security, Porta

Potties and cleaning the streets afterwards. Waivers were given to allow alcohol to be sold on the street. A king and queen of Fantasy Fest were to be chosen. As a sop to those who found the nudity offensive, it was stated clearly that Fantasy Fest was to be an adult party, but the city commission, in return for any funding it provided, maintained the right to regulate what could and could not be done.

The king and queen of Fantasy Fest were elected at a party at the Pier House and were suitably Key West choices. The king, Steve, was a gay construction worker, and the queen, a transvestite named Bob—who called himself Alice—was Steve's partner and a maid at a gay guesthouse. Steve referred to Alice as his old lady, and both were saving up for Alice to have a sex change operation. Steve, the local rumor mill had it, had a dick big enough to chin yourself on and turned tricks to help save for the operation. Why a gay man would want his gay partner to become a female eluded most of us, but what the hell! This was Key West, after all, where T-shirts that said: "KEY WEST—WHERE THE WEIRD GO PROFESSIONAL" were thought by most of us to be in bad taste, not because of the statement, but because it stated something too obvious to need print.

Where else in the country—the world—would you see the following all walking on the same block downtown at the same time: an entire extended Mennonite family—grandparents down to newborns, all rosy-cheeks and innocent eyes—being passed by two very tall drag queens discussing some transvestite point of ethics, followed by a man with an iguana on his shoulder, two sport-dressed lesbians holding hands, a man so pierced an MRI would tear him apart, and two Pulitzer-Prize-winning authors discussing narrative voice? All this in a small American town of twenty-eight thousand people.

The city took Steve and Alice's election in stride, we thought, but before the now famous battle that brought news cameras to the island, the cameras arrived first for a human epic no one could have imagined.

In April, four Cubans drove a bus through the fence of the Peruvian embassy in Havana and asked for and were granted political asylum. Castro demanded that the men be turned over to his government, or he would remove all the guards at the embassy. The embassy refused his request, and the guards were removed and the guard shacks bulldozed. What happened next surprised everyone, especially Castro: Ten thousand Cubans stormed the fences of the Peruvian and other embassies and requested asylum, which was again given. The eyes of the world were now focused on the Cuban government, which couldn't stand close scrutiny.

Castro, always a brilliant adversary, decreed that all ten thousand asylum seekers were free to leave the country, as well as anyone else in the country, as long as they had someone come pick them up. Mariel was designated the exit port.

Miami, home to hundreds of thousands of Cubans, many with relatives still trapped in Cuba, nearly came to a halt as thousands drove to Key West, the nearest point to Cuba, hundreds with boats, the rest with money in hand looking for a boat to charter.

Key West was overwhelmed. One lane of Roosevelt Boulevard, all three miles of it, was filled trailer hitch to trailer hitch with boats waiting to launch or waiting for its owner to find a captain. Every downtown bar in Key West became standing room only as desperate exiles tried to find transportation across the straits to pick up relatives and meet and negotiate with local boat captains.

Doug and I had to use alternate routes around the island to get to our jobs, swamped as it was now with cars, trailers, and boats. Every night when we got home we compared notes. "I've never seen anything like it since the Cuban missile crisis in '62 when we had anti-aircraft missiles on the beach," he told us.

Boats dropped into the water as fast as the person in front pulled his trailer off the ramp. To Castro's surprise, again, over one hundred thousand people made their way to Mariel, and the largest armada since Dunkirk began transporting them from Mariel to Key West, where the U.S. government set up the reception center. The Miami and the national networks spent half of each broadcast on the most amazing exodus since Moses.

In our free moments, Leigh, Thomas, Doug, and I joined crowds of people on the docks to watch the arrival of the horribly over-crowded boats. You could hear the cheers of the refugees from far out as they started chanting, boat after boat, "*Libertad, Libertad, Libertad*" when they caught sight of our island. To watch old grand-mothers hobble to shore and kiss free earth was a humbling political science lesson no professor could ever equal.

"I want to go up to some of them and hug them," Leigh said when we saw one boat disgorge people in their sixties and seventies arriving with nothing but the clothes on their backs, falling to the ground to kiss it.

One night during the boatlift, the intercom at the Bakery buzzed, and it was Rudy, my friend from my first job at Veradero.

"*Amigo,* I need a big favor. I need to get my mother and brother out of Cuba. They're ready to go, but I need to pay the boat captain from Miami six thousand dollars. Can you help me, *amigo*? I have only four thousand. Maria and Dolores loaned me a thousand, but I'm still a thousand short."

Rudy called me the day his mother and brother were supposed to arrive, and we went down to Mallory Square together. He paced as first one boat, then a second arrived, always with the chants of "*Lib-ertad, Libertad, Libertad*" starting from the boat's first glimpse of the island.   *209*

As the third boat approached, the entire upper deck overloaded with escaping humanity, Rudy jerked alert. "I see them," and ran up to the cordon of federal immigration officers who told him he couldn't pass through. One of the officers was Hispanic and convinced his buddies to make an exception. When his mother and brother walked down the gangway, Rudy ran over to them, and there was much hugging and "how you say, *amigo*, heavy crying."

When the officers took him back outside the cordon, Rudy came up to me, wiping his eyes, and walked back towards Duval Street with his arm around me. "They're taking them to Miami to be processed. I'll go up there to get them." He gave me another hug. "You are a real *amigo*, Juan. *Ahora somos hermanos para siempre* (We are brothers forever now). I will never forget your help. If you ever need anything—anything—let me know."

There was an ugly side to this mass jail break, as anyone who has seen the Pacino version of *Scarface* is aware of. Castro, ever the evil genius, took advantage of this embarrassment to his government to empty the mental institutions and jails of his country and forced the captains of every arriving boat to take some of them along with the refugees they had come for. When President Carter discovered this, he declared the open door closed and ordered the confiscation of every boat still arriving. Dozens of innocent people, including many Key Westers, lost their boats and livelihoods.

In the end, over 125,000 Cubans landed in Key West and were processed. Bus after green bus, windows wire-caged, roared through town taking all the refugees to detention camps around the country. The unsuccessful late arrivals from Miami packed up their boats and returned to that city where the dregs from Castro's prisons joined the cocaine cowboys from Colombia already there to start a crime wave of unbelievable proportions. By the end of September, the Mariel boatlift was history.

Key West's fragile tourist economy was as devastated by the events and national publicity as if a killer plague had broken out. The national media, with the repetitive camera shots of the arrival of thousands, then tens of thousands of desperate Cubans had left the entire country with the mistaken impression that our island was overrun, definitely not a place to visit. Not one network bothered to mention that all the refugees had been taken off the island.

I had work, Doug had work, but the hotels and bars started laying people off.

Then Mother Nature delivered a second punch to the island. A wet front moved down the Florida peninsula and ran into another system over Cuba, causing it to stall right over Key West. It began to rain, and rain, and rain. The front sucked in more moisture from the Gulf, and it rained and rained, a torrential, tropical rain. Slowly, all commerce on the island came to a halt as it continued to rain, and rain, and rain.

It was a work day, but Doug and I were both rained out and went home, watching the water rise in the yard. Leigh called. "What the hell is going on?" We called Thomas who said he'd never seen anything like it.

The Miami news stations heard about it and sent camera crews down who filmed people water skiing on Duval Street, pulled by high-rise trucks, and people rowing small boats up and down the street, and it continued to rain and rain and rain. The T-shirts that came out of it said: "I SURVIVED TWENTY-FOUR INCHES." When it ended, thirty inches of rain—two-and-a-half feet of it—had fallen on the island in thirty-six hours. All three national networks carried the story with different pictures of a flooded island.

In reality, the actual damage was minor because we were, after all, an island, and the rain ran off into the ocean almost as fast as it fell. But negative national exposure, twice in a short time span, did its work. The streets were empty, the hotels and restaurants had no customers, and people were desperate. The town was on the ropes *again*. The tourist council ramped up its campaign to let the country know that Key West was back in business, and the publicity for Fantasy Fest became even more important. Colorful flyers were included in newspapers across the country with pictures of the previous Fantasy Fest and statements such as: "COME TO OUR PARTY," and "FIND OUT WHAT YOUR LIFE HAS BEEN MISSING."

The *Miami Herald* chose the last week of September, a dead time in that city, to do a story about Key West's upcoming party and, in its usually spiteful way, led with the headline: "GENDER CONFUSION MARKS ISLAND PARTY." Of course, it made fun of the king of Fantasy Fest for being a "queen," and the queen being a male about to become a female. What we thought was charming and showed off the town's tolerance was made to sound dirty.

City leaders panicked; the town needed tourists. A tough, matronly Conch on the city commission, Mrs. Elizabeth Thompson, requested that a new king and queen be elected, and that the city commission meet specially to authorize a new vote. The commission, in a four-to-one vote agreed, and all hell broke loose. Religious leaders and some business leaders welcomed the commission's decision. The rest of the town was outraged.

Normal civil discourse turned into shouting matches as one side argued for the preservation of a quirky way of life and the other for presenting a more Christian and normal (and hopefully more lucrative) face to the world. The usual morning civility at the laundromats where we had our café con leches was injured. I got into an argument with an AC subcontractor I'd worked with on several jobs.

"God made Adam and Eve, not Adam and Steve," was his closing argument, one I'd heard before. How do you argue with people
whose brains are closer to Eve than to Plato?

Gay organizations, which provided a lot of the floats, threatened
to boycott the parade. Religious organizations threatened to protest
during the parade. The chamber of commerce and the tourist council
tiptoed around, trying to find a middle ground where none existed.
Both sides dug in, and business leaders wrung their hands.

What everyone had forgotten was that this bit of rock at the tail
end of the country was not an ordinary place, that we were not ordinary people, and that magic was always at hand when needed.

The city commission meeting to force a new king and queen vote
was to take place on the first Thursday evening in October. The usual
venue, the decrepit municipal building on Angela Street, was too
small given the interest in the meeting, so it was scheduled to take
place at the old City Hall building on Greene Street.

Living quietly as he had for decades in a small, unpretentious
house on Duncan Street was what the *New York Times* routinely
referred to as "The World's Greatest Living Playwright," Mr. Tennessee Williams, a man most of my friends and I had met several times
and danced with at the Monster. He was frequently sighted around
Key West, which left him alone—no groupies asking for autographs.

Mr. Williams told Wendy Tucker, his friend at the *Key West Citizen*, that he would like to address the commission meeting. The *Citizen* mentioned it, the *Miami Herald* picked it up, then the *New York
Times*. Suddenly, what was a local issue became an object of national
attention. The commission decided again to move the meeting, this
time to the high school auditorium.

The tension on the island by the night of the meeting was unbear-
able. TV trucks had arrived from the mainland with reporters outside

the high school doing lead-ins. Leigh, Doug, Thomas, and I headed for the high school an hour early and barely made it inside and had to stand in the back. By the time of the meeting, not only was the auditorium full but hundreds of people waited outside. Right before the meeting began, a group walked in together and went to the front where seats had been held for them: I recognized Jimmy Merrill, John Hersey, John Ciardi, Jerry Herman, and Jimmy Kirkwood, a who's who of American arts and letters come to listen to a fellow wordsmith. Across the aisle from them were Steve and Alice holding hands, she looking chaste in a simple, white, summer dress, and both looking stunned by what they'd gotten into.

A *Miami Herald* reporter was standing next to me taking notes, so I told him who the artists were and what they'd written. "No shit, no shit," he kept saying as he scribbled excitedly, then raced outside.

The four commissioners and the mayor filed onto the stage, Mrs. Thompson last. Doug whispered to us that she was personal friends with Tennessee from way back. "He comes over for 'tea and conversation,' as he calls it. She helped him find the house on VonPhister that his sister, Rose, lived in for a while. This puts her in a tough spot."

The auditorium fell silent as a preacher went to the dais and intoned a prayer asking God to help the commission in its business and its all-important vote. Then the mayor, looking uncomfortable at all the attention, asked everyone to stand and recite the Pledge of Allegiance. That over, everyone who had seats sat down, and the mayor gaveled the meeting to order.

"This evening's special meeting is being held to consider whether to require a new vote for king and queen of Fantasy Fest. Will all speakers please address themselves to that issue and no other. Each speaker will have five minutes. First speaker on the list is Rev. Willett of the First Baptist Church."

Rev. Willett opined that the types of persons chosen for king and queen "though they might be good people, had transgressed God's laws where only man and woman might cleave together." There were a few murmurs of agreement in the crowd, but mostly groans. He ended by saying: "Let us not give our children an example that God would not sanctify."

"Thank you, Reverend Willett," the mayor said. "Next speaker, please."

The next man introduced himself as president of the Business Guild (gay chamber of commerce-type organization) and spoke to the importance of gay tourist dollars to the town's economy and the importance of preserving the town's reputation for tolerance. Overall, it was a good speech, but we were here to hear Tennessee Williams.

Two more speakers, one for, then one long-winded one against. The mayor had to gavel the latter into silence, reminding him that there was a five-minute restriction on the speeches.

Then from outside, working its way in, there was a loud, rolling buzz: "He's here, he's here," and in walked Mr. Williams, dressed in slacks, tie, and sports jacket. The crowd parted like the Red Sea, and people started standing up, cheering and applauding, and the noise was deafening. We were an island who loved its writers, and especially this one.

The cameras started turning as he made his way to the front, stopping to shake the hands of Wendy Tucker, Steve and Alice, and his fellow geniuses in the artists' row.

He climbed the steps to the stage and shook the hands of each commissioner, stopping last in front of Mrs. Thompson whom he hugged, then whispered something to. After what Doug had told me, now I recognized him, too, as a master politician. "Ladies and gentlemen," the mayor said, "Mr. Williams has requested permission to speak before the commission, and we have agreed that as a special friend of Key West, he will not be held to the five-minute limit. The room applauded.

Tennessee went to the dais, and a room that only a minute before had been deafeningly loud, fell silent. Tennessee adjusted his notes, and one fell to the floor. The mayor raced to pick it up for him. Tennessee started to speak, then coughed—what a ham; he knew how to play an audience. He went over to Mrs. Thompson and asked for a glass of water, which she poured and gave him. Now she was anointed for all the world to see as a special friend of a world-famous writer. You could almost see her preening her feathers.

Tennessee returned to the dais. The room was about to piss its collective pants waiting for him to start. Leigh, Doug, Thomas, and I were holding hands, squeezing hands.

"Mr. Mayor, (his Southern voice redeemed the accent), Honorable Commissioners, Friends, Ladies, and Gentlemen, I am honored to be allowed to speak before the leaders and citizens of this town, which has been my beloved home for so many years and a refuge for me and so many other artists." He nodded toward them, and the row of Pulitzer-Prize winners waved back.

"This evening, Mr. Mayor and Honorable Commissioners, I am understood to believe that you have before you a decision on whether to require a vote for a different king and queen of Fantasy Fest," (he emphasized the alliteration of the last two words) "thereby nullifying the vote which has already elected one king and queen." All heads turned to look at Steve and Alice.

"I am a simple scrivener" (self-deprecating shake of the head) "with neither the talent nor the wisdom you possess to make the decisions required to run this wonderful island town, so I humbly defer to whatever decision you feel obliged to make," and he turned to look at them, then turned back. "Let me speak, then, only to what I understand.

"Two human beings, citizens of this island as you and I are, have been chosen to represent us at an event which people from all around the country see fit to attend. Should not the issue be decided based on the suitability of these two individuals to stand as our representatives?"

The cadence and intonations were delightful, pure music. "Suitability" rolled off his tongue like a confection.

"Some among us, friends and neighbors, hold to a belief that the special nature of these two young people should disqualify them to stand in for us." His voice conveyed surprise. "I humbly believe, however, that those very differences will show those visitors who might visit our island for this festival of fantasy," (heavy alliteration again) "a larger and kinder sense of what it means to be human, and that our humanity is not narrowly defined.

"Is not one head lying on the chest of another, listening to the beloved's heartbeat, justification enough for that love, whatever form it may take?"

"Think back, too, to our childhood when we were so much closer to the divine hand, however defined, that placed us on this Earth. Remember what play we had! What wonder in trying on so many different roles: today Superman, tomorrow fireman, today princess, tomorrow doctor. What cruel displacements and constraints life then uses to form—no, *deform*—that divine putty! Were not those our purest dreams?" He paused a second.

"That these two people have made choices dissimilar to ours, might it not be because they were brave enough to remain true to those dreams? I think that choosing them to represent us shows this large and many-peopled country that love and tolerance of a divine quality exists here . . . on this rock . . . on this island . . . at the end of the road . . . my home. Thank you."

The room exploded with applause and a standing ovation as he made his way past the commissioners, shaking hands again with each, with a kiss for Mrs. Thompson, and down the stairs to the artists' row, where someone gave up a seat for him.

The applause roared on, and when it started to slow down, it built up again and stopped only when someone started the chant "VOTE, VOTE," which the entire room took up. The mayor huddled with the commissioners, then came back and motioned for the crowd to be seated and be quiet.

"The commissioners and I have decided to vote now on whether to require a new election. A "no" vote means we keep the existing candidates; a "yes" vote means there will be a new election. The clerk will call the roll."

The city clerk, seated off to the side, began the roll call. "No."

Cheers erupted and the mayor banged his gavel. "Please be quiet while the vote is taken."

"No . . . No . . . No . . ."

When the clerk got to Mrs. Thompson, she said: "I would like to thank my good friend, Mr. Williams, for clarifying in his usual wonderful way an issue of great import. I vote no."

The room exploded again, with people yelling, "We won, we won!" Tennessee went over and shook hands with Steve and Alice again, and a phalanx of friends escorted him and the other artists out of the auditorium.

Outside, reporters were telling the story to cameramen from the Miami TV stations.

My little family retired to the Parrot to have drinks and savor the victory and ran into half the people we knew in town. Soon dancing started that spread out into the street.

Who knows what elements create the perfect party? If we knew, they would all be perfect. The second Fantasy Fest was a perfect party, and the last one uniquely ours, no corporate sponsors, no bead tossing.

After the Mariel boatlift, the biblical rain, and the threat to our public and communal love of a kind of human diversity not celebrated elsewhere, we were ready to cut loose.

Little pieces of magic began stitching themselves together on the lead-up to the night of the parade.

Fast Buck Freddie's windows were an explosion of wild Halloween paraphernalia and a master mask maker from New Orleans' Mardi Gras, who sat in one of the windows making custom masks out of feathers, beads, glitter, and other exotic materials.

Dick Pischke, a carpenter friend, and I had been working together that month on Margaritaville, the store and restaurant that Jimmy Buffett was opening on Duval Street next door to Fast Buck Freddie's. Dick was staying after normal working hours every day to build his costume, a perfect reproduction of a Rancilio espresso machine, like the ones in all the Cuban coffee shops we all went to every morning. He had a body-length plywood box painted dark green with the word "Rancilio" prominent on the sides. The box sat on his shoulders and his head stuck out the top. Bags of Bustelo coffee were stacked on the top and glued down so they wouldn't fall off. Styrofoam cups also sat stacked on the top. Two of the cups sat alone: one had coffee incense in it, and another had a hole next to it that Dick could stick his finger through to make fall over. Then, with a hidden string, he pulled the cup upright again. To complete the machine, pipes stuck out of it, and a fire extinguisher he activated from inside the box shot out realistic steam.

One night when he was working on his costume after hours, Jimmy Buffett showed up with his sound engineer and manager to check on our progress on his project and asked Dick what he was doing. Dick showed him the costume and explained how it all worked. Jimmy, a true lover of the eccentric and wonderful, was intrigued.

"I've got a little rap song that goes with it, Jimmy. You want to hear it?"

"Sure."

Dick put on his costume, bounced up and down, shot steam out the pipes, and sang his little song. When he'd finished, he looked at Jimmy and asked him what he thought.

"Dick, it's a great costume, but you've got the worst sense of rhythm of anyone I've ever heard. Look, come over to my studio in an hour, and I'll record the song for you."

Dick raced home to tell Julie, his wife, and to call a couple of his buddies, and they all showed up at Buffett's studio, where he arranged them as a back-up group singing "Buchi, Buchi" (Key West Cuban slang for a tiny shot of sweetened coffee). Jimmy read the lyrics, had his sound man turn on the equipment, practiced the lyrics with his back-up talent, and then recorded it.

And there on Duval Street on Fantasy Fest night, Dick bounced along in his espresso machine, steam pouring out, with a rap song blaring out to the astonishment of people who looked at one another and said: "Hey, that's Jimmy Buffett singing!" Dick won second prize for individual costumes, and a week later was the opening act for Steve Winwood and Buffett, himself, at the Margaritaville restaurant.

First prize went to a man who shimmied down the street in the middle of a ten-foot-high explosion of feathers, sequins, and lights that would have given peacocks an erection.

Diana Verlain, a short, stunningly beautiful woman who wrote plays, acted, and mentored other writers, stood, an almost naked Cleopatra, covered in gold paint and gold lamé, cracking a whip over the heads of sixty-five nearly naked men pulling her barge slowly down the street. Diana, who had a good eye for male flesh, told us later it was like "Water, water everywhere." They were all gay. Her compensation was to be born on the shoulders of two of the men into Delmonicos after the parade for the contest of Real Queen, and the competition, all drag queens, gave it to her; that's how wonderful she was.

Fast Buck Freddie's float had a volcano that actually shot fire out the top with some very stoned natives and a sacrificial virgin. The virgin was, well, not quite.

Then a roar of applause as the king and queen of Fantasy Fest, Steve and Alice, crowns on their heads from Goldsmith Jewelers, rolled down the street on top of a wedding cake float that Fast Buck Freddie's and the Key West Business Guild had provided them. Steve's muscular body was naked except for his crown and a leather codpiece, and he and Alice, in a white wedding dress, danced, along with ten nearly naked men and women on a lower level of the cake, to some hot reggae coming from somewhere in the float.

Two human beings who would have been ostracized (at the least), or beaten and murdered (at the worst), in the rest of the world, had been given undeniable proof of their place at the table in this little town. Tennessee had seen to the heart of it and said it well.

"God, I love this town," Leigh said as their float went past. Doug was open-mouthed. "I never thought I'd see anything like this in my hometown in my lifetime."

In the middle of the parade was a young man, a local preacher, dressed in a loin cloth, fake crown of thorns, carrying a full-sized cross with wheels on the base and a sign that read "REPENT" where "INRI" should have been. A man near us yelled out: "Great abs, Jesus." Jesus rolled onward, bearing our sins.

Someone had had the brilliant idea of putting a band with huge speakers on a flatbed truck. When the parade was over, the truck rolled slowly up Duval Street with thousands of dancers trailing it, dancing with wild abandon. Leigh, Thomas, Doug and I jumped into the middle of the crowd. Dancing in the middle of a street we usually drove on, surrounded by what seemed like our entire community was magical, one of the only moments of pure joy in my life: laughing and dancing and bumping against my friends, my family, my tribe. I recognized Rudy, Maria, and Dolores just ahead of us and slipped up behind Rudy and pinched him on the butt. He whirled around, laughed when I lifted my mask, then pointed to an older woman and a man his own age, dancing with them: a family reunited.

Five minutes later, I looked over to the sidewalk and saw one of the teachers I'd hated in Toronto, standing alone with a fascinated, wistful look on his face. I danced on up the street and laughed at him and the fear and self-doubt of my first night on the island.

Leigh and I wound up at her place where I gleefully tore into the Pan Am stewardess, circa 1960 costume. Sex while wearing masks is exciting. Who knew?

Twelve

The Civil Rights Movement and the war in Vietnam were the defining experiences of my generation. Whenever anyone on the island asked me what I'd done during the war, I deflected the question because I didn't want to offend those men and women who'd fought it; they'd suffered enough. I deferred, too, because my reasons for choosing exile over accepting induction were too complicated and nuanced to explain in a couple of sentences. Leigh, Thomas, and Doug knew some of the story, as did my friend, Jeff Hagel.

I respected Jeff for multiple reasons. He was a superb craftsman in the building trade, highly intelligent and well-read (only carpenter I knew who'd read Proust), and had a kind of visible, earned, core integrity. He was also a combat veteran of the war. Telling him the first time that I'd refused induction was an existentially frightening moment. When he looked at me after I'd told him and he said: "Good for you." I felt the same relief a person must get after a life-defining medical test comes back on your side.

As the fifth anniversary of the Fall of Saigon approached, there was mostly silence in the media. We'd lost the war, so it wasn't going to get much attention. A few letters to the editors of the *Key West Citizen* and the *Miami Herald* on the lead-up to the anniversary replayed all the old fights: "We could have won it except for the peaceniks," or "We should never have taken over from the French," and all the others. I was annoyed.

In one of those coincidences that only real life or poor fiction offers up, I'd just finished a kitchen repair job in Key West By The Sea, the condo complex out by the airport. The owner was Floyd Thompson, the longest-held POW from the war in Vietnam. The man had obviously been physically and psychologically traumatized by the experience. I wanted to go up to him and apologize for the whole country, but war resister and warrior was potentially too explosive a mix. I did the work and charged him only for the materials, but it stoked my anger over the war.

One of Thomas' friends came up with the idea of a reconciliation day: speeches from all sides of the war to be given one afternoon in the library auditorium. Jeff and I were both invited to speak. I wanted to decline. Thomas had said once that his preference was always to observe, not be observed, a strange thing for a visual artist to say, but it struck a chord in me. I preferred passing through life watching, not being watched, and I had a serious phobia about public speaking. Jeff convinced me to speak.

On the afternoon of April 30, 1980, the fifth anniversary of Saigon's fall, forty or so people, including five men wearing vests with combat medals, assembled in the library auditorium, a small hall with acoustical tile ceiling, ugly carpet on the floor, fluorescent lighting, and a plaque on the wall: "Tennessee Williams Center For The Literary Arts." Rows of chairs and a podium had been set up. Five people were to speak, me last.

The first was a retired historian who narrated the historical facts of the conflict, from the beginning of French colonialism to the American departure from Vietnam. He was thorough, intelligent, and non-judgmental, and he provided a good context for what came next.

The second speaker was a veteran who said that he had fought for his country, that it had been his patriotic duty, and that Jane Fonda and the war protesters had caused us to lose the war. He complained about the treatment returning veterans had received when they returned home, and there was polite applause when he ended with "God Bless America."

The next speaker was an ex-SDS anti-war organizer, a man who'd been beaten at the Chicago convention. His description of the beating he and his friends had suffered, which we'd watched on TV, brought back the forgotten horror of that night. Listening to the man I knew only as a painter, I marveled at how courageous some people were, and also at the wonderful complexity of so many people on the island.

Jeff spoke next.

"I am a combat veteran of the war," he started, then he gave the dates and names of some of the engagements he'd been in. "No one I served with over there," he stated emphatically, "believed in what we were doing. We all believed it was a useless war, fought stupidly, and we grunts were completely expendable, pawns in a game being played out in Washington by men who didn't care at all for our lives except as how that loss affected public opinion. In return, we avoided combat whenever possible, going out on patrol and finding a place to hide until time to return, firing our weapons from time to time so base would think we'd made contact with the enemy."

Then he described, graphically what he'd seen next to him: men getting "stitched" across the chest by automatic weapons fire, men being blown apart, men "wasted" by "friendly" fire, the effects of napalm on humans . . . I felt sick all over again, and disgusted again by the vocabulary the war had created.

"There was no way I could function in civil society after what I'd seen and done. After my tour of duty was up, I went to Kauai and lived in a cave for a year before I was ready for so-called normal life. It changed me forever. It was a stupid, unnecessary war, and I've earned the right to say that."

He finished to great applause. Then it was my turn to speak, and I could barely suppress the need to throw up. I went to the podium.

"Before I start, I need to say for everyone, pro-or anti-war, that the way returning soldiers were treated, both by the government and civilians, was unforgiveable. I was anti-war, never anti- the men and women who fought it." There was applause at that, and then I began.

"In 1962, I was putting myself through college at the University of Missouri. I was staying in a real dump off campus because it was cheap, and all I could afford. My roommate was a 45-year-old Vietnamese man studying for a business degree, getting a tiny check drawn every month on a Swiss bank. The war back then was minor, a few hundred American 'advisors.'

"I didn't like having an 'exotic' roommate, but out of politeness I asked him questions about Vietnam and learned about the Catholic Diems, propped up by us, suppressing the Buddhist majority. From him I learned about the U.S. supporting France's post-war determination to keep Vietnam as a colony, even though we had forced Britain to give up its colonies. France blackmailed us with the real threat that France, itself, would go communist because it had a strong, powerful communist party. Ho Chi Minh, the United States' new enemy, had begged us to make the French leave after the war, and we had ignored his plea.

"I learned all this in 1962 because of my Vietnamese roommate, so when the monks started setting themselves on fire and Americans were so shocked, and sarcastic articles started coming out about

Madame Nhu ('What's Nhu This Week?') because of her obvious greed and unconcern about anything but money and power, I could understand what was going on because of my roommate.

"My roommate was Catholic, like the Diems, and his family had fled North Vietnam to escape the persecution of Catholics there. But when I told him that everything should be better in Vietnam because we were there, he laughed in my face.

"You don't have a chance in hell," he told me, "because you don't have a clue. The French used to round up the dissident Vietnamese," he told me, "and hold them in underground cages until they had enough to fill a boat. Then they'd drill holes through the right hand of each man, or woman, and run a rope through them all, load them on a boat, take them out to sea, and drop them overboard."

"I didn't call him a liar but thought he was because I couldn't believe that any civilized country, apart from Germany, could do something that barbaric. When I saw the French film, *The Battle for Algiers*, years later, and saw what the French had done there, I wanted to cry for how stupid I'd been.

"You're supporting the French," my roommate said. "When we finally defeated the French at Dien Bien Phu, you took over from them," he shouted. "All of Vietnam celebrated after Dien Bien Phu because we'd kicked the monsters out, and you came in to carry on after them. Don't you know that we hate you?"

"I was offended at that and didn't speak to him for days and finally got switched to a different room. No one had a right to say that to me. My father was a career Navy man, I was as American as it was possible to be, and we were the good guys.

"Kennedy was assassinated, Johnson escalated the war, and I was confused. I'm flipping burgers and washing trucks twenty hours a week and taking a full course load. I didn't have time for this.

"Then the teach-ins started, with what was advertised as the real truth about the war, and the first big protests had started, and I really, really didn't want the information. Funny enough, my dad pushed me to go. A twenty-year Navy veteran, he had complete contempt for the military. On one of my trips home, the subject of the war came up and he said: 'After Korea, the Commandant of the Marine Corps said we should never again engage in a land war in Asia. These assholes didn't listen.'

There was some laughter from the audience.

"So I went to the teach-ins. The professors, mostly men who had never had a callous on their hands, talked about the oppression of the masses, American imperialism, et cetera, and it rolled off my back. But when the veterans from my class of people came on stage and talked about the lies, and the things they'd done that had then been lied about, I added that information to what my Vietnamese room-mate had told me and saw that my government, that body that owed its existence to brilliant minds and two sacred documents, had lied to me, repeatedly, and I hate being lied to.

"I slowly became anti-war, but I was student-exempt (2-S, I think it was) and then they changed that to where we all had to take an exam and I hit 99th percentile so I was still exempt. And then they changed it again. You were exempt for your bachelor's degree but nothing more.

"Around me I saw men marrying women they didn't love and getting them pregnant so they wouldn't have to go, men faking homosexuality or mental illness to exempt themselves. I felt great dread from the tidal pull towards a decision I did not want to have to make.

"I was now working on a master's degree in American history, and the summer before what I call 'that night,' we had visiting professors from NYU, brilliant, articulate men who taught graduate seminars and tortured our Midwestern brains. From the perspective of years later, I realize they must have looked at us, compared to their NY students, as though we were on another planet, but they never once showed an ounce of condescension.

"Now we read the primary sources: George Kennan's paper on containment, a policy paper on MAD (mutually assured destruction), and they picked, picked, picked. It was exciting to be made to think and question everything, but it is never easy to be forced out of your accepted mindset. Sometimes in that summer's seminars, I lashed out. But they were brilliant men, mentors and teachers of the highest order, and they gently led me to the truth: the history of my country, the country I loved, was darker, bloodier, and uglier than I had ever wanted to admit; yet, those brilliant words at the beginning gave hope, allowed change and transformation.

"That same summer, I had to face that I was going to be drafted, and an intense inner struggle began. Go, or not. The one thing I knew I had to answer was that I would not make the decision because I was afraid, though any normal person would be.

"I saw an ad in the *Student Union* in June for people to come out and watch skydivers and maybe join the club. I knew that I had just found the test to absolutely make sure that what I was probably going to do was not based on fear. I made ninety-eight jumps that summer. Unlike some of my fellow jumpers that I got to know and like and get drunk with, let me tell you, I was scared every single time I jumped out of that plane. In the bars we went to after jump day to share our jump stories, they always teased me about what I looked like on exit, flailing my arms like a non-swimmer trying to stay afloat."

More laughter from the audience.

"The greeting came in November, November '68, 'Greetings from the President.' I had been ordered to report for induction.

"I was being drafted six weeks before finishing my MA in American history. Two of my professors, the decent ones, gave me an incomplete. Three gave me F's for not completing the course, even though they knew why I couldn't. I called them, and continue to call them even today, assholes.

"I met the bus at five in the morning near the courthouse in Columbia, Missouri, that day, along with the other students pulled from their studies, and rode to the induction center in St. Louis.

"We arrived and entered an ugly industrial building with lots of men in uniform telling us what to do, where to form lines, when to expose our genitals and butts and which line to form next. We filled out forms and were given a folder to carry with us. In one line, a low-ranking man in an Army uniform examined each folder and separated us, one group Army, one group Marines. The Marines affected a cachet that they didn't need to draft, but now we saw that lie. One man, twenty or so, tall, powerfully built and probably a farm boy, was shunted to the Marines when the man looked at his folder. The man protested: 'But I don't want to be a Marine.'

"'Shut the fuck up and get over there,' the man yelled.

"The guy started crying. 'I don't want to be a Marine,' he repeated. The uniform slapped him across the face and told him again to shut up.

"Then there was a commotion down the hall where I saw a hippie being dragged along by his hair. A few minutes later, we heard two men in uniform bragging about how they'd dragged the man to the oath-taking ceremony and forcibly held his arm up. 'That mother is Nam-bound,' and they laughed.

"I had already written my draft board that I would perform four years of alternate duty in a veterans' hospital. I wrote the Supreme Court, reminding them of the precedent we had ourselves helped establish at the Nuremberg trials: that an individual not only had the right but the duty to refuse an unjust, illegal, or immoral order. The answer from my draft board was that I had to be part of a recognized group like the Quakers or Jehovah Witnesses to qualify for alternative duty. The answer from the Supreme Court was that I couldn't object to a single war, but all war, to be considered a conscientious objector.

"When we lined up at the final checkpoint before taking the oath, I told the man there that I wanted to perform alternative service, not be drafted." He laughed and told me to shut up and join the others. It was time to decide.

"Was I defending my country if I accepted induction? If my country were attacked, I would be one of the first picking up a gun, a spear, a stick. But this wasn't defending my country; this was something that my intelligence, my education, and all the information I'd gotten from the returning veterans told me was not only a mistake but wrong, as wrong as the war that Abraham Lincoln and Thoreau had protested.

"There were only two options left for me: refuse induction and spend four years in prison; or go into exile, and I only had a few minutes left to decide. I refused to let a government that was waging an unjust and unnecessary war punish me for refusing to join in the fight.

"I pretended to head to the bathroom, walked downstairs, caught a bus to the airport, and landed in Toronto in the middle of the night, in the middle of winter, December 10th, 1968, with a dollar seventy-five in my pocket and no contacts. I know that compared to what the men in this room suffered in Vietnam, it counts for little, but it remains the most difficult and traumatic experience of my life, leaving the country I loved for what I assumed would be forever.

"I slowly got established in Toronto, but I was angry, very angry; and I began to nourish a great hatred for what the government had done and was doing. It was wrong, stupid, and enormously destructive to the United States as well as to Vietnam, and the arrogance of the men in power—Johnson, then Nixon, McNamara, the Bundy brothers, Rostow, Rusk, Kissinger—infuriated me. They lied, often and continuously. When a reporter challenged McNamara's report on the war's progress and he answered: 'We have information you don't even know about, and it tells us you're wrong,' then refused to share that information, I was pushed over the edge.

"For eight years, using false papers, I began crossing the border back into the States, sending the FBI and my draft board postcards daring them to catch me. I sent them a photo of me at the Statue of Liberty, another of me in front of the Capitol Building, and once, at a farewell party for a general at the U.S. Army Headquarters in Heidelberg, Germany. The FBI was not amused, and tapped my parents' phone, my sister's phone, and my grandparents' phone, visiting each in turn, asking where I was. My grandfather, a World War I veteran who'd been gassed in that war, told the two men to 'go fuck themselves.' My father, veteran of WWII and Korea, told them the same.

"People have asked me why I felt compelled to taunt the government. The simple answer, again, is that they were lying to me, the nation, the world—and on many different levels. My little pinpricks were my way of getting even.

"Charges against me were dropped in 1976 through a Justice Department clerical error shortly before Carter granted amnesty."

The men in vests in the back of the room booed at that. This was what I'd feared. Jeff stood up and quieted them.

"I debated a long time before deciding to move back here. Every year on December 10th, I stop to re-live that day and night, and I make a point of re-reading Eisenhower's warning against the military-industrial complex.

"Would I do it again? I hope I never have to, and I hope I still have the courage to do it if I think it's the right thing.

"I was sitting in a good restaurant in Paris once during my exile—someone else was paying—" (that got a few chuckles) "when a short, Asian man and his elegantly dressed wife, dripping jewels, came in and were seated. I asked our waiter who they were. It was a South Vietnamese general, and I wanted to strangle the man and his wife. How many American dollars had he stolen at the expense of how many American lives to afford Paris and that jewelry?

"I was lucky enough to see Janis Joplin and the Grateful Dead in the summer of 1968 in San Francisco. But the greatest concert I have ever been to was given by Mikis Theodorakis in Paris. He was probably the best Greek musician of his time and was living in exile in Paris after the Greek military junta. The concert hall held two thousand people, exiles from Argentina and Chile and Uruguay, the United States and Greece, all the countries of Eastern Europe, Turkey and Vietnam, all people fleeing a military out of control. It was the only time in my life I felt kinship to the entire human race. There were fourteen encores.

"The war in Vietnam, in my opinion, was a mistake, and continued long past when that was known by the men in our country who directed it, men who valued the life of those fighting it less than their own reputations and power. They should be in prison for that and, of course, never will be.

"I believe that there are times when love of country demands that you NOT do what the government tells you. I still believe that that was one of those times. I always remind myself that we Americans are only 5 percent of the world's population, and no one made us God. In my opinion, we would be better off taking better care of our own people instead of wasting our wealth on being the world's policemen.

"To those men in the audience who fought the war, please don't hate me. I was against the war, never against you. It is, let me repeat it, inexcusable to treat veterans shabbily. Your sacrifice must be recognized. Thank you."

Most of the audience applauded, though some didn't. The organizer of the event thanked the speakers and the audience, and then it was over. Leigh, Doug, and Thomas came up and hugged me, and then I sought out Jeff Hagel. We gave each other a hug and a slap on the back, and the war in Vietnam ended for me at that moment. I doubted that it could ever end for him.

Thirteen

The move back to the Bakery after Southernmost Summer had been bittersweet. Forced by the bank and insurance company to borrow money to complete the renovation, instead of doing it slowly as we earned money, had left us with a three thousand dollar a month mortgage payment. I also missed the more communal life of Southernmost Summer.

Walking around the renovated buildings still gave me great pleasure. Having a kitchen now, a great kitchen, was reward, but the financial pressure generated familiar feelings of dread. Our dinner conversations were often about money, and even the possibility of selling the place.

I had finally done something I had sworn never to do: become so attached to a *thing* that it warped the rest of my life. But how could I not be attached to these buildings that from foundation to roof we'd restored to life, and still looked from the street like the same weathered beauties we'd first noticed while playing softball.

For the first time in my life, a building felt like home.

What we jointly arrived at was that we both needed to earn more money and to do that, we needed licenses, so we started studying.

Doug already had a Journeyman Electrician's license, so he took and passed the Master Electrician's exam, which allowed him to start his own electrical business. I took and passed both the Journeyman Electrician's and General Contractor's exams and we started our own construction company: AC/DC BUILDERS, which earned us appreciative laughter from the town and our construction buddies. Doug ran the electrical side of the business and I did the building, but we could switch over if one part of the business got busier than the other.

One of my main concerns about going into business was that it put me in competition with Jeff Hagel who had taught me most of my skills. He told me not to worry. "There's enough work out there for both of us, and if a job comes along that's bigger than either one of us can handle, we can always do it jointly."

Doug's and Thomas' connections got us work from the very beginning, and we started earning more than double what we'd been making before. It sometimes seemed a Pyrrhic victory. Dealing with federal, state, and local government paperwork and taxes was onerous. Then I had to buy a work truck, which meant truck payments and insurance. Thomas said once that he judged the quality of his life by the number of keys he had to have. It was an inverse relationship: the more keys, the lower the quality of life. I now carried house key, bike key, two truck keys, and keys for the padlocks on the table saw and compressor I used in my work. He was right.

I had never imagined myself in the role of employer and wouldn't have chosen it except under duress. In a small business, I learned quickly, you're married to everyone who works for you and a participant in every crisis, real or imagined, in their lives. One carpenter who worked for me in the beginning drove me especially crazy. Peter was a good, even brilliant, carpenter. No one could figure miter cuts faster or do them more accurately, but he somehow never put in a five-day week. One day a week I'd get a call from him that he was sick. I was sympathetic about the "food poisoning" the first week, the "asthma attack" the following week, and the "migraine" the week later, until I realized he was just lazy.

When he ran out of familiar illnesses and called to tell me he had cholera, giving me the best laugh of a tough week, I confronted him. "Cholera's usually fatal, Peter. Make sure you get to the hospital, and I'll come visit you after work."

"No, boss, you don't need to do that. It's a mild case. I'll be over it tomorrow." I hung up the phone and fired him a week later when he called in with scurvy. He retaliated by applying for unemployment compensation, and I had to spend two months fighting his claim.

My first big job as general contractor was a sweet introduction to the trade. Thomas had met a Canadian, Charles Latimer, who'd spent his adult life working in London for an English publishing firm. Charles had come to some of the Sunday brunches during Southernmost Summer and endeared himself by introducing us to Prescott's history, *The Conquest of Mexico*, the best written history I'd ever read of humanity's greatest story of civilizations colliding; and to classical music even I wasn't familiar with: Brahms' *Alto Rhapsody*, Strauss' *Vier Letzte Lieder* and the works of Rodrigo and Falla.

Charles had bought a canal-front lot with a spectacular open-water view on Key Haven, Key West's residential suburb. Thomas designed a simple house on stilts—the new code because of hurricane surges—with a widow's walk, and recommended Doug and me as electrician and builder. Determined to do it right and not embarrass Thomas, Doug and I built the house, from augering the holes for the foundation to move-in, in ninety days flat. Charles did his part, describing his role as "hardworking laborer with the checkbook."

The evening after the building department had delivered the Certificate of Occupancy, Thomas, Doug, Charles, and I stood on the widow's walk, drinking Veuve Clicquot, watching the sun set as Jessye Norman's voice singing Strauss' "Im Abendrot" poured up to us from inside.

"Thank you, all three of you," Charles said, raising his glass in a toast. Then we thanked him for the opportunity. Afterwards, on the way back out to my truck, Doug and I turned around to look back at our handiwork, tin roof turned golden by the twilight. Charles and Thomas saw us looking up and gave us a thumbs up.

"Feels good, doesn't it?" Doug said.

I was lucky again. My next big contracting job came as a referral from Jeff Hagel, who was too busy to do it: a complete renovation of a house on Key West's Riviera Canal, three doors down from Jimmy Buffet's house.

The house belonged to a New York couple, George and Alice Drescher, who wanted to gut and completely renovate it. Alice, I learned, had inherited her father's business—SESAC—a performance rights company like ASCAP and BMI, though much smaller (smaller being relative here). They flew me to New York to see their co-op at 400 Central Park West because they wanted to duplicate its kitchen in Key West. The co-op, with its tree-top view of Central Park, almost made me wish I were rich, and they had the kind of Jewish generosity that shames WASPs. Photos of Alice with Eleanor Roosevelt and Duke Ellington, among others, lined the hall, and she had been a major benefactor to one of NYC's hospitals.

George and Alice took a shine to me while I was re-doing their Key West house and on my birthday—how had they found that out?—while the work was going on, Alice showed up with a birthday card. Inside was a check for two thousand dollars, more money than I'd been able to save in a year's work in Paris. The shock must have shone on my face; I am always blind-sided by kindness.

Alice took me outside. "John, I'm a tough New York Jew. When you came to me last week to tell me the cabinet guy gave you a kickback and you brought the cash to me, it was like the Earth getting knocked off its frigging axis. That's definitely somewhere out there. Are you nuts or what? Why didn't you just keep it? You'd never survive in New York. Now, I have a proposition for you. George and I just bought a villa in Positano—Amalfi Coast—" (I nodded recognition) "and we don't speak Italian and we don't know squat about construction. We know you're a language genius, so you learn Italian and you're the construction manager, and we fly you over whenever you need to go. Deal? Come on, wipe that stupid look off your face and give me an answer. What, dumb ass, you don't want to see Italy?"

Whenever I was needed, Doug or Jeff took over my jobs and I flew first class to Rome, sometimes with George and Alice, and sometimes alone. In Rome, a driver in a black Mercedes was waiting to drive me/us to the Sireneuse Hotel in Positano, where I had the meetings with the Roman architect and Sorrento contractor and helped design and supervise an exquisite construction kiss to the planet's beauty. In our first meeting, the architect told me that his favorite building material was mud, which he'd spent three years using in building he'd done in Yemen. That made a personal connection because I told him it was also my favorite building material, and I brought him the book, *Santa Fe Style*, with the adobe architecture of the American Southwest.

On one of the flights to Italy (Swissair, overnight in the Dolder Grand in Zürich), the flight attendant rolled the appetizer trolley back to my first-class seat and asked: "More caviar, Mr. Cottrell?" I started laughing, and she apologized, thinking she had somehow offended me. I explained I had come from a background unlikely ever to have caviar, let alone *more* caviar—and she gently touched my shoulder and whispered, "Mr. Cottrell, you can have all the caviar you want."

Alice kept asking what she needed to pay me, and I kept telling her nothing. The experience itself was payment. Through them, I got to see Rome and Naples, Pompeii (a childhood dream from first sight in *National Geographic*), Capri, Paestum, and, of course, the entire Amalfi Coast.

Somehow, Alice found out that Doug and I wanted to put in a swimming pool at the Bakery but were strapped for money. A courier showed up one afternoon with a cashier's check for $25,000, a photo of the cliff-hanging swimming pool I'd designed in Positano, a thank you, and the words 'Build It.' I choked up when I called Alice in New York.

"Alice, I don't know what to say. Thank you, thank you. You know you didn't have to do that."

"Stop that sniffling, goddammit, or you'll get me started, and I have a meeting with some asshole entertainment lawyers in five minutes. Now shut up and listen." (Small wonder she and Princess-Talks-Like-A-Man hit it off immediately.) "When you made that personal contact with the architect and the builder, do you have any idea how much money you saved me? That's Southern Italy. They would've robbed me blind. But you learned Italian and made them friends, so they didn't. Stop thanking me and build your damned pool. Christ! How have you managed to survive this long? You men think you're so tough, but you're all just a bunch of grown-up babies," and she laughed. "Now tell me again that phrase in Italian you keep torturing George and me with."

"*Dovè la modanatura di soffito?* Where's the crown molding?"

She cackled. "You're a weird fuck. Love you. Gotta go. The suits are here."

Shouldn't there be a special word for the "what-if" fear a lottery winner must also feel when he finds out he's won? *What if* he hadn't stopped by the convenience store on the way home that afternoon to pick up some milk? *What if* he hadn't had the extra single in his wallet? *What if* there'd been someone buying a ticket, THE ticket, right in front of him?

What if I hadn't moved to the island? *What if* I hadn't taken Thomas' and Leigh's advice to wait just a little longer to get a job so I could stay?

Because of Alice's gift, on a late Saturday afternoon in May, Doug and I were down in the hole the backhoe had dug that was to become the swimming pool. We were using picks to square the corners and the sides to accept the concrete formwork. We were trying to save money by doing the pool ourselves and couldn't pay to have it shot-creted, which wouldn't have required precise lines or forms. It was hot down in the hole, the rock was solid, and we were ankle deep in smelly groundwater. We were not happy.

Someone yelled through the section of fence we'd taken out for the backhoe and leaned back against another section.

I yelled back at him to hold on, and climbed out of the hole. He didn't look to be more than eighteen or nineteen, tall, powerfully built, wearing the white rubber boots that was standard gear for shrimpers and fishermen. Black hair, brown eyes, and general good looks with a diagonal scar down his left cheek (broken winch cable we learned later).

"My boat left without me this morning, and I'm bad needing to make me some money. I work hard." Pronounced Southern accent.

I looked at Doug. We were both worn out. He nodded.

"OK. Ten bucks an hour. No goofing off."

"Deal." We shook hands, mine disappearing into a shovel scoop.

"I'm John. That's Doug down in the hole."

"I'm Tom Haggerty."

He took off his shirt, exposing a torso like those in exercise equipment commercials, grabbed a pick, and jumped in the hole. Doug explained what we were doing and why, while I went inside to get us water. When I came back out he was swinging twice for every one swing of Doug's. I thought he was just showing off but he kept the pace for an hour straight, except once to ask for guidance and again for a few seconds for some water.

Doug and I swapped off on the other pick, and the one not working was in charge of measuring. The backhoe hadn't cut straight so there was over ninety linear feet where the walls met the floor that needed squaring, in addition to the corners, and the rock was unforgiving.

At five o'clock I called it quits. Tom asked if he could work the next day, all day, and we agreed.

"Let me pay you for today now, though." I knew that fishermen and shrimpers lived day to day when they were ashore.

"Thanks, boss. I got to get me some food and a place to stay. All my stuff was on the boat. I don't know what I'm gonna do for clothes."

I handed him his pay, then Doug piped up: "If he's working here tomorrow anyway, why doesn't he stay here tonight? He can throw his clothes in the laundry, and I've got enough food for all of us."

"You mean it?" Tom asked.

I nodded.

"You guys are great." The Southern accent gave "great" almost three syllables. "Where can I wash up?"

I pointed to the outside shower. "Put your clothes in a pile, and we'll start a load of wash."

Doug went inside and brought out three beers—Busch, money was low—while I collected the tools and put them in the garage.

Doug sat down on the edge of the hole. "This is the hardest and dumbest thing I've ever done," he said. I agreed and we clinked cans.

"Hard to believe it's ever really going to be a pool." He grunted assent, and we both looked down into the stinky hole that, once dug, had to be finished.

Tom came walking out of the shower towards us to get his beer. "You guys got a towel somewhere?" My mind didn't register it at first—an anomaly—but then it did. Hanging between the boy's legs was the biggest dick I'd ever seen, and I'd done years of Phys. Ed. I turned away, repulsed? Horrified? Scared? How could any male compete with that freak of nature?

Doug grabbed my leg hard and whisper-pleaded: "Oh, daddy, can I keep him please, please, please?"

I shook my leg free. "Get him a towel, dammit, so he can cover up." To Tom, I said: "Follow Doug. He'll get you one and start your laundry."

I followed them inside a few minutes later and went upstairs to my room to shower, change, and make a few phone calls to customers. When I went back downstairs, Tom, wrapped in a beach towel, was sitting on one of the sofas in the great room looking at the album of photos of the renovation work. Pink Floyd was on the stereo, and Doug was in the kitchen.

"You guys did all this work yourself?"

"Most of it. We had help from Rick Bird, a contractor friend, on this part, and our employees worked on it, too. Some of the sub work, like the AC and plumbing, was by other people. It damn near killed us and broke us both. Now all that's left is the pool and decking outside, and re-building the garage. You want to see the rest of it?" He nodded.

I gave him the tour of the whole place, telling him the history of it as we went.

The renovation, deliberately understated as it was, didn't seem to impress him much, apart from when I described lifting the houses up and putting new foundations under them.

"I wish I'd been here to see that part, man. That must have been awesome!"

"Awesome and scary."

My bathroom hooked him. "I never seen me no bathroom this big. You could have you an orgy (he pronounced it with a hard "g") in here, man." I laughed, then showed him the wet bar in the closet.

He appreciated it, but then turned serious. "Hey, shouldn't we be helping (it came out "hepping") your buddy fix supper?"

"No, it's his week on," and I explained the week-on, week-off arrangement we had.

"That sounds rough."

"It's easier than it sounds."

We went back downstairs, and I set the table.

"Dinner in five minutes," Doug announced. I put Keith Jarrett's "Köln Concert" on, grabbed another beer, and went back out to look at the labor-and-money-sucking hole. Stinky ground water was rising in it because it was high tide and we were only two blocks from the ocean. Nothing I'd ever built had provided so little satisfaction during the construction for the effort it required.

Tom opened one of the doors and yelled: "Boss, supper's ready."

I walked back in and took my place at the head of the table. Doug sat to my left looking out at the yard, and Tom sat to my right. I poured the wine, a cheap California red, and Doug served us plates of pasta out of a big bowl he'd brought from the kitchen. Fragrant, familiar smell.

We clinked glasses and dug in. Tom wrapped one hand around the handle of his fork and stabbed his plate with it, then grabbed his knife with his other hand and began furiously cutting up all the noodles. Doug and I looked at one another but said nothing. Then he jammed a wad of noodles into his mouth and began chewing loudly, mouth open. Another clandestine look between Doug and me. Tom stopped, mid-chew, as the taste of the pasta registered and, with a mouth full of partially masticated linguini, said: "Man, I ain't never tasted no spaghetti this good! What is it?"

It took all the restraint I owned not to rise out of my chair and slap him: first for eating with his mouth open, which drives me completely nuts—and ranks in my books somewhere with pedophilia as unacceptable behavior—and, secondly, for the grammar. Not just a double but a triple negative! And look folks—AIN'T on top of that. Let's give the man a perfect ten for the Olympic category of bad English. Where in the hell are the parents in the lives of men who eat and speak like this?

I started to say something, but Doug caught my eye and shook his head. "It's pesto, Tom, basil pesto. You mince some garlic, pine nuts—I use walnuts instead—chop up some fresh basil leaves, add Parmesan cheese, olive oil, a little salt, and put it over noodles. We eat it once a week because it's good and easy to make. You don't have to cook anything but the pasta."

"It sure is good." Smack, smack, slurp, slurp. I gritted my teeth and kept my mouth shut. It wasn't easy. The boy had seconds. Then came the salad, which he also shredded the same way before he slurped and smacked that away. Doug cleared and brought out bowls of ice cream. 'Is it possible to eat ice cream annoyingly,' I thought to myself? Indeed it is. Much slurping, then much scraping of the bowl, as if digging through the porcelain would find you more. Doug gave him seconds, and I excused myself.

Doug whipped out a joint but I begged off. "I'm beat, guys. I'll see you tomorrow. Tom, your bedroom's the one off the kitchen. Doug'll show it to you."

Tom thanked me again. I waved acknowledgement and went upstairs.

The next morning, Sunday, was normally my favorite day of the week, except that I knew I had to be back down in the hole all day. I went downstairs to the kitchen. The coffee had already been made so I looked around for Doug. He usually slept later than me. No Doug. Then I heard something outside and saw the pick rising and falling above the edge of the hole. I walked out with my coffee.

Tom was in the pit, boots on, carving out the last of what was going to be the deep end. The pick was swinging harder and faster than I could have done even if I had wanted to show off. I yelled down to him: "Have you eaten yet?"

He stopped and looked up. "I had me some coffee, Boss, that's all. But I know you guys need this finished, so I thought I'd just do me a little pickin' before you got up." I was impressed.

"We appreciate it, Tom, but climb out of there and get some breakfast. Doug does it up right on his Sundays on."

"I'd sure enough like to finish here, Boss."

"Look, that hole's going to be there whether you eat or not. Now rinse off and get your butt inside." He climbed out and headed towards the shower.

I studied the hole for a few minutes, and when I went back inside, Doug was in the kitchen whipping something up. On his week on, Sunday was always a treat. Sometimes it would be eggs Benedict, sometimes smoked salmon and bagels, sometimes a quiche, sometimes something totally unpredictable. But each time it was with a twist: the eggs Benedict would be with Béarnaise, not hollandaise, sauce; the smoked salmon, already on the bagel, would have caviar hiding under it; the quiche would have a jalapeño bite to it, or sage.

Sunday breakfast usually included Bloody Mary's: fresh tomatoes pureed in the Cuisinart, top-shelf vodka, and lots of Worchestershire.

Thomas and Leigh joined us often. Part of the pain of working on the pool was that we had to forego the morning alcohol bump and the company, or we'd never go back to work in the hole.

We sat down to eat—a *fines herbes* omelette—with a side of hash browns that had a curry color and flavor, and a thick slice of the toasted homemade bread I tried to make every week.

"*Châpeau*, Doug! You've done it again." He acknowledged the compliment with a nod.

Tom looked up from his inappropriate cutlery use and smacking and slurping."

"What'd'ya say?"

"It's slang for congratulations in French. Doug and I both used to live in Paris, actually at the same time, though we didn't know it, but we both speak French. Every once in a while we throw it at each other to stay in practice."

"That country's way up there, ain't it?"

Doug and I were polite enough not to even look at each other at that one.

"Tom, I have a *National Geographic Atlas* on the shelf under the coffee table. After breakfast, I'll show you where we lived."

Breakfast over, while Doug did the dishes, I took Tom over to the sofas, sat down on one with him and pulled out the Atlas. The teacher in me took over. I found the Mercator projection. "This is where we are," and I traced the path down the islands from the Florida peninsula to us at the end. "See how close we are to Cuba?"

"Man, I know lots of dudes who went down there and got themselves some fine pussy."

"Tom, there's more to life than pussy, now pay attention." Did I hear a contemptuous snort from the kitchen?

"Now look. Here's the East Coast of the United States. There's Washington, there's New York City, there's Boston. Now look at the

Atlantic Ocean and over here is France. France is a country, just like we are, and Paris is the capital of the country, just like Washington, DC is the capital of our country. That's where Doug and I lived—in Paris."

He followed my fingers with his and took it all in. I realized now that he was one of those lost children the U.S. produces in abundance.

That day, with Tom's help, we finished the digging by lunchtime. Doug had sandwiches made up, which we ate quickly, then went back to work. Doug put in the main drain and stubbed it outside the hole, then started cutting and bending the re-bar and handing it to us in the hole to place and tie. Tom was faster than I was at the tying. "I used to do this in Orlando before I came down here," he told me when I complimented him.

We worked until past dark and finished the steel work. I was so happy at the progress that I offered to take the two of them to Las Palmas for dinner. When we arrived, Gail, who had an eye for hot males, shot Doug a quick, questioning look. He shook his head no. She smiled. One more for the women.

During dinner, Doug and I asked Tom about his background. It was a familiarly sad American story. Woman gets pregnant. Man reluctantly marries then abandons her before the child is born. Mother becomes alcoholic. By then, she is living in Florida, which consistently ranks at or near the bottom in every category of child protection. Tom is taken from her and moves from foster home to foster home, some decent, some abusive. Then, at eighteen, with no guidance or counseling by the state, he's kicked out into the world on his own. No money, no training, no further help.

"It's pathetic and disgusting to treat children like that," Doug said before I could.

"Hey, man, I survived. I worked me a little construction around Orlando then somebody told me I could make me good money fishing down here, so here I am. I just hope my captain hires me back after I missed the boat this last time."

The story was painful, but listening to him tell it with those table manners drove me nuts. When we got back to the house, I took Doug aside. "One of us has to teach him how to eat."

Doug agreed. "I think he'd take it better from me than you," he said. "He seems to look at you as more of an authority figure and might resist it. I'll talk to him tonight or tomorrow."

What was taken for granted was that young Tom would stay the night again since he was still helping us with the pool. Then it was just sort of understood that he would stay until his boat came back. He went overboard trying to please, working harder than either of us. We'd wake up in the morning and the coffee would be made, and he'd be washing the glass in all the French doors or mopping the floors.

He was delightfully goofy, showing off his strength by balancing a twelve-pound sledge hammer, handle end in the palm of his hand, or walking across the floor on his hands, or slipping ice cubes down Doug's or my back. He was also hilariously clumsy, able to walk across a nearly empty room and trip on a grout joint in the tile.

One day after work, Doug was using the hose to water the plants along the fence when Tom walked by, and Doug turned the hose on him. We were all giddy from having finally gotten the hole ready for the pour. Tom wrested the hose from Doug and sprayed him, then me. That began a forty-five-minute-long water fight that went from the deck to inside the house, up and down the stairs, and ended with me filling a wastebasket full of water and pouring it on their heads as they climbed towards me. A Niagara spilled down the stairs and ended the war.

We grabbed beer and went back outside and sat down, leaning against the mango tree, and looking at the soon-to-be pool. The day of the water fight changed the relationship, I think. I had thought my sense of play was intact, but when I compared myself to Tom, it was obvious that the extra years of adult life had atrophied it. He was still a kid, and the sense of play was very alive and wonderful to be around.

Watching him make the effort to change his ways was touching. Doug told me that after the night I'd taken us to Las Palmas for dinner, Tom had asked him if he could ever fit into nice places. That gave Doug the intro to explain table manners and grammar. With his acquiescence, we developed discreet sign language to remind him when he was using his cutlery wrong or chewing with his mouth open. He learned that quickly. The grammar was another story. After days of corrections and explanations, I finally adopted a series of fines: a dollar for each subject/verb not agreeing (he don't); improper tense use (I seen); and double negatives. The fine for ain't was five dollars. The money went into a pot on the coffee table to be used for a nice dinner someday. He started catching himself, and I was relentless with the fines.

"You're a real hard ass, ain't you," he complained one day after three subject-verb disagreement fines.

"Ain't. Five bucks."

"Fuck, shit, damn it to hell," he said, pulling his wallet out. "I'm never gonna have no money."

"Double negative. One dollar."

"DAMN!"

"I'll let you slide this one time if you repeat everything you did wrong, correctly, five times." We went back over the day's infractions, and he repeated the corrections.

Some of his sayings we also had to convince him not to use because of their crudeness or brutality: "stabbing pussy" was not an acceptable substitute for having sex; saying to someone in anger "I'm gonna gut you like a fish" was also not acceptable. Announcing that a girl he'd picked up had "guzzled his custard" made me want to throw up. Some I raced to write down in my journal for their colorfulness and originality, like the day he came home from helping Doug on a rush job in a gay guesthouse complaining that everybody had been "eyeball fucking" him.

The day after we poured the concrete for the pool, Tom's boat came back in. He talked to the captain and was forgiven. Two days later, he was gone.

Doug and I were good company for each other, and friends were always dropping by, but the house seemed emptier. Doug was the first to mention it one night when we were having dinner. "I miss the big goofball."

"I'm surprised, but I do too."

Three weeks later, the pool was finished. I had installed the water-line tile and the decking between the house and the pool. A friend had plastered it, and Doug had done all the plumbing and installed and connected all the electrical equipment. We'd put the hose in it the night before, and now it was full. This night was the inauguration for the hardest construction work either one of us had ever done, harder, even, than lifting the houses.

I'd bought two bottles of wine to celebrate. Dinner was over (my week on: seafood pasta, mixed greens salad with vinaigrette, and a partially successful crème brûlée), and I was doing the dishes when the intercom buzzed. Doug went to open the door, and young Tom burst into the great room a minute later, carrying Doug over his shoulder, then dropped him and ran over to me and picked me up and shook me around. "You don't know how much I missed you guys. I kept thinking about you and this place the whole time we was"—he caught himself—"*were* fishing."

"Subject and verb don't agree, one dollar," and I pointed to the pot.

He pretended to be upset and made a great display of taking out his wallet and dramatically depositing the dollar. Then he looked outside. "What did you two sissies get done on my pool while I was gone?" He walked outside. Doug hit the switch for the pool light, and Tom let out a whoop, stripped off and jumped in. I grabbed the wine and three glasses, and Doug and I joined him.

We splashed around and played silly for a while, then sat up on the edge of the pool and drank the wine, admiring our handiwork and re-living the brutal work it had involved. It is a fine, fine moment in construction work when you see what your hard work has accomplished. Few people in industrialized societies still get that satisfaction.

"How was the fishing, Tom?" Doug asked after we'd exhausted the pool stories.

"Tough. We didn't catch a lot, and I think they cheated us on the price when we landed. I didn't make but five hundred dollars for the three weeks. I cain't keep doing it if that's the pay." (I debated whether there should be a fine for "cain't" but decided not.)

There were a few minutes of silence, then Doug: "Would you ever consider working on land?"

"Yeah, if the pay was OK and it was something I could do."

I knew what was coming next. "One of my guys quit last week," Doug said. "If you want, I'll take you on as a helper. It's only eleven dollars an hour to start, but you can make more as you learn more."

Tom turned to look at him. "You ain't doing that because you feel sorry for me, are you?

"Ain't." Five dollars."

"DAMN!"

Doug looked at the kid. "No, Tom, I do need someone, and I saw you work here on the pool. It's a real offer."

Tom turned to me: "What do you think, Boss? Should I do it?"

"What have you got to lose? If you don't like it, you can always go back to the boats."

"Where would I live?"

I hadn't thought of that, but it made sense for him to live with us. I looked at Doug: "Why doesn't he stay here, pay rent and do a week on like we do?"

"Fine with me."

"You guys serious? You're not playing with me? You'd let me live here permanent?"

How many instances of betrayed trust in his childhood did that question come from?

"Shut up and put your stuff in your room, you weenie, sissy, girlie electrical helper," Doug yelled. Tom jumped up, chased and caught Doug, threw him over his shoulder again, and jumped back in the pool.

The next day at dinner—attendance or phoned excuse obligatory—we informed Tom of the rules of the house. The most important rule, we stressed, was that what happened inside the house stayed there. Doug and I shared a preference for keeping our private lives private.

Fair apportionment of maintenance tasks. Women were always amazed at walking into a bachelor pad and seeing it was clean. Once the construction was finished, there were no more beer cans thrown into a corner of the room.

The planned change to one week on, two weeks off had to be adjusted because Tom didn't know how to cook, so we gave him dishwashing duty until he learned.

Just in case he hadn't figured it out yet, Doug told Tom he was gay and asked if he had a problem with it.

"Different strokes for different folks, man. You're a good dude. That's all I care about as long as you don't try to smoke my dick. Too much there to smoke anyway," and he grinned.

The first time I took him grocery shopping with me, I told him to pick out things he thought he would like. I was looking for ground lamb for a moussaka (feeds three men twice) when he brought a package of frozen chicken nuggets to the cart and started to put it in.

"Tom, do me a favor. Turn that package over and read the ingredients." He did and looked puzzled. "Tom, even with the chemistry courses I had in college I couldn't pronounce some of that stuff, and I sure as hell don't know what it is. Do you really want to put that crap in your body? If you want some chicken nuggets, I'll show you how to make your own."

He looked at the package for a second then put it back in the freezer. Then he looked at me, studied me: "You guys really are gonna take care of me, aren't you?"

The question and look were so emotionally raw that I was taken aback and searched furiously for the right answer, a flippant one, I figured. "Of course we are, you big dummy. We like you."

He was very, very quiet.

Fourteen

Though we knew some or most of Tom's past, we didn't understand the complex ramifications of it all. Sweet as he could be, he was also capable of explosive anger, episodes that were usually triggered by a real or imagined slight. Once someone flipped him the bird in traffic and he started a car chase that ended only when he'd stopped the guy, dragged him out of the car, and given him the choice of being beaten or apologize.

After that episode, Doug and I took him aside, sat him down in the parlor (the room for serious talks) and explained to him that he couldn't behave that way for several reasons. "You risk getting hurt or killed when you confront people like that, Tom, and going to jail, and for what?"

I joined in. "Tom, a month after someone flips you the bird or yells at you, you're not even going to remember it unless you do something stupid that gets you arrested." He looked totally pissed off at being lectured, but I continued. "Doug and I care about you, but you have to think about us, too. We're both in business here. We can't have our names associated with someone who goes off like that."

He stood up. "Well, I'll just move out then if I'm such a problem." It was so obvious a ploy, I groaned, but Doug stood up and started yelling, something he never did. I was as shocked as Tom.

"Sit your dumb, cracker ass down, NOW, and listen. We're probably the only two people on this whole goddamned planet who care about you. Is it that fucking hard to change your behavior a little bit? You leave here, who out there is going to take care of you?" He waited. "Come on tough guy, answer me."

Punch Doug out or listen to him? I could see the conflict in Tom's face. They stared at one another; then Tom sat down.

"Look, Tom, John and I are your friends. But there are some things you just can't do. Reacting out of anger like that is one of them. It's an inappropriate, disproportionate response," and he explained that to him. "Now I got an idea out of the newspaper. I'm going to collect used light bulbs and put them in a box out by the pool equipment and set up a target for you. Whenever you get that angry, you come here and start slamming those light bulbs against the target. And I'm going to buy you a punching bag and hang it from the mango. Use it."

Corny as the solutions seemed, they worked. He would storm into the house sometimes and go right out to the deck and start breaking light bulbs against the wall, then head for the punching bag to terrorize it for as long as an hour before returning to normalcy.

He had another quirk that was extremely annoying to me in the beginning. I don't much like being touched, especially by another male. I don't like anyone putting their arm around my shoulder, slapping me on the back, or any other socially acceptable forms of touch. It was not pleasant for me when I lived in France to have all that hugging and brush-your-cheek kissing from everyone, and I hated it now that it had followed me across the Atlantic. For touch to have value, I allow it only from my closest friends and relatives.

I had surrendered my opposition to having TV with the invention of the VCR, which gave us access to one of my weaknesses, foreign movies. Then the usual TV creep began, and we started watching the evening news and *60 Minutes*. One night while we were watching Pasolini's *The Gospel According to Matthew*, a leg touched mine and stayed there, and a few minutes later the same leg with those size thirteen feet looped over my leg.

"What the hell are you doing?" I said the first time it happened. I knew he was straight, so I didn't get it.

Doug allowed it when he and Tom shared the sofa, but the second time he did it to me, I reacted the same way, and he jerked away. When Tom went outside for a minute, Doug took me aside. "I know how weird you are about being touched, but I think you should pay attention. You heard the story of his childhood that night at Las Palmas. It was a horror story: a foster dad holding him down and farting in his face, making him shoot his pet dog, getting him drunk when he was only eight, and all that stuff."

"Doug, come on, what's that got to do with him throwing a leg over me?'

"Think about it, John, and watch him. He doesn't have an education, so he can't think himself out of the damage done to him. He's soaking up all the attention and affection he didn't get as a child by being close to us, and especially by touching us. He's probably never had someone hold or touch him just because they loved him, and his needs are probably in the same proportion to his deprivations. He's soaking up love, caring, and everything else he lacked and needed the only way he knows, and he doesn't consciously know that that's what he's doing. He may be nineteen, but emotionally he's still a little boy. This is probably the first time in his life that he's felt protected and safe."

Mr. Psych Major made sense, so I began to observe Tom in a different way. Sure enough, he would always choose to sit on the same sofa that Doug or I was on. Then the leg would touch, followed a few minutes later by the leg being thrown over our leg. Now that I didn't protest, I noticed that he withdrew into a cat-like state of pure contentment. Doug and I would give each other a look of mutual recognition and continue our conversation or TV watching as if nothing were out of the ordinary. Doug was right: something deep and damaged in Tom needed this, and some subconscious impulse led him to what he needed.

One night, Tom started to position himself the usual way, but instead turned and lay his head in Doug's lap, his legs hanging over the end of the sofa. Our conversation stopped for a second, and Doug put his finger to his lips to keep me quiet, then looked down at Tom whose eyes were closed. We continued our conversation. A couple minutes later, Doug tentatively stroked Tom's head. Tom turned his head slightly, relaxed, and Doug continued a soft, methodical stroking.

It was one of the strangest things I had ever seen: a big, powerful, homophobic, heterosexual male resting his head in a gay man's lap to be comforted.

Doug was right, I realized. A damaged young human being was healing himself as best he could through touch. If we had confronted him with what he was doing, he would probably out of pride and heterosexual dignity have denied everything and never done it again. Yet he was aware of the ambiguous interpretation the physical contact could be given because, if the intercom buzzed, he would slowly lift himself up to a sitting position.

He loved touch, not only when we were watching TV, but everywhere. He would sling an arm around me or Doug while we were over the stove, explaining to him what we were doing, and was always trying to provoke us into a wrestling match, which he would pretend to lose. Then, when we had him pinned to the floor, Doug would tickle him to listen to the purest laughter I have ever heard, a little boy being tickled by his parents. These were delicate things that had to be protected from the world outside our doors and gates.

The change in Tom over the first few weeks of this therapy wasn't dramatic, but noticeable. He tested us less. Fewer questions like: "Hey, you guys like having me here, don't you?" which he used to ask almost every day. He was also calmer and less manic.

He was still delightfully playful: ice cubes down the back, dinner plate hidden on a chair if you happened to leave the table, bed short-sheeted (an unfortunate trick that Doug had taught him).

One night during dinner, I was talking about a customer who had accused me of overcharging her, something not in me. "I guess, in the end, what distresses me most is that she'd think I was dishonest when I'm not, and not only that, I gave the bitch lots of freebies."

"It did what?" the young giant asked.

"What do you mean?"

"That word you used ... dis ... ?"

"It distresses me?"

He burst out laughing. "That's not a word, come on."

"Of course it is. What about a 'ship in distress', smart ass?" For some reason or other, the word tickled his fancy, and it became part of his repertoire. A late dinner his week on would start off with: "I'm distressed because I put the pasta on too late." On jobsites, he would get other guys laughing with: "Oh my god, I'm so distressed. I just broke the drill bit." At home, I would walk in and it would be him, hand on his forehead pretending pain. If I fell for it and asked if he was alright, I would get: "I don't know boss, I'm a little distressed ... that girl last night didn't put out."

He was fascinated by things that had fascinated me when young, like the leavening of bread dough. I tried to bake bread every week.

It calmed me, and I liked the connection it made to the hundreds of generations of humans before me. When I explained the process to him, he was initially skeptical, then curious, then riveted, lifting the dishcloth off the bowl every few minutes to verify that I hadn't lied. He started asking if he could do the punch-down after the first rise, then checking, untrusting but fascinated, to verify that the dough came back up.

He became addicted to our routine and upset when it varied. I usually got home first, then the two of them. Whoever was on started cooking, set the table, put on the music. If I wasn't there when he got home, or Doug went out for dinner, he became restless and a little agitated. For him now, happiness and security meant the three of us at home at the same time every evening.

Things in the house became important to him. The atlas I pulled out from the shelf beneath the coffee table always had to be there so he could look something up or we could show him some place that was in the news. Once I took the atlas up to my room to study the GDP statistics for Latin America for a letter I wanted to write to the *Miami Herald*. I heard a knock on my door after dark and told him to come in.

"There it is," he said and pointed to the atlas in my lap. "I been . . ."

"Dollar!"

"*I've* been looking for it everywhere." Then in an accusatory tone: "It's supposed to be under the coffee table."

I apologized and explained what I was doing.

"What's GDP?"

"Come here, I'll explain it and show you the comparisons."

He sat down next to me on the bed, and I showed him, first the countries on the map, then the page with the statistics. After explaining what GDP was, I pointed out different things that were interesting. "Look at little Uruguay. Why is it richer per capita—had to explain per capita—than Colombia or Brazil? I'd like to know that before I make a fool of myself writing about Latin American politics."

We looked at the map of South America for a while. "You'll put it back when you're through, won't you?" he asked when he got up to leave. I promised.

One Sunday afternoon, Doug was out somewhere. Tom was still asleep from tom-catting downtown, and I was in the great room lying on one of the sofas re-reading Prescott's *Conquest of Mexico*. Tom stumbled into the room, still groggy, and sat down on one of the other sofas. We were so used to one another now that neither of us felt compelled to speak. The phone rang.

"Tom, can you get it. Cortez has just climbed the mountains and seen the Aztec capital for the first time. It gives me goose bumps every time I read it."

He got up and walked to the kitchen. It was for him. Then I gathered from his end of the conversation that it was his mother. His voice became agitated. "Momma, no, don't say that. I love you." A pause. "Momma, please don't say things like that, please," and the last entreaty was heart-breaking. He hung up and sat back down on his sofa, silent.

Then, suddenly, without a word, he got up, came over and curled up, fetal position, on top of me. His weight was crushing, and I started to protest but caught myself. I put my book down and held him, and felt tears pouring onto my chest. He lay like that for three or four minutes, and I was in agony from the discomfort. Then he got up and walked into the kitchen and started fixing himself something to eat, saying nothing. I went back to reading, silently damning parents who damaged their children like this, then put my book down. Cortez' meeting with Montezuma could wait. I was looking into the soft heart of childhood itself.

I went into the kitchen and gave him a hug.

"OK?"

"Yeah, I guess. I don't know what I'd do without you two guys."

"Well, we like you, doofus, so I guess we're all stuck with one another."

One night, he warned us he was going to fix dinner for a woman he'd met, a school-teacher on vacation, and asked if we minded disappearing after we met her. Doug and I were in the kitchen fixing ourselves plates of food to take upstairs to eat when the intercom rang and Tom escorted an attractive woman in her mid-twenties into the great room and all the introductions were made, then small talk about what she taught (Special Ed).

Tom, of course, couldn't wait to tell her that we'd both lived in Paris (made him look even better to have friends like this. . . . I could see where this was going.) We excused ourselves and went upstairs to watch a movie together. Having polished off the first bottle of wine, we decided to go downstairs for a second (and also out of curiosity).

We made a noisy descent, but it proved unnecessary. Tom had just put the food on the table (silverware properly placed, I noticed) and was opening a bottle of wine. We apologized for interrupting and put our dirty dishes in the sink, retrieved another bottle of wine and headed back out. Back in the parlor, not to our credit, we both stopped, hidden, to listen for a minute.

We heard wine being poured into glasses. "Now, Sylvia, this wine is a little young and maybe a little rough, but can you taste the hints of vanilla and raspberry?"

We held it in until we got upstairs, but once we shut the door behind us, we laughed ourselves sick, tears spurting, snot running. We'd stop for a second and all it took was for one of us to look at the other, or to say: "Hint of vanilla and raspberry" and we were off again. A man who, a few months ago, thought high-class alcohol was Budweiser instead of Busch! Doug looked at me when we finally gained control: "I think we've created a monster!"

The next morning, a well-laid (I'm surmising), sheepish-faced, Special Ed teacher joined us for breakfast. Doug and I made the kind of small talk to make her feel comfortable, but studiously avoided looking at each other to avoid igniting another laughing fit.

When Doug and I had first started living together, there were adjustments we both had had to make, most of them related to our sex lives, mostly related to *his* sex life. Tom made things even more complicated, and in ways I hadn't anticipated.

If nurture had given him a raw deal, nature had compensated. Tom was, as Doug described him, an Adonis with a big dick. His sculpted body, the slashed-face pirate smile, the killer looks, were a pussy-magnet the likes of which I had never seen. He sent out pheromones that attracted every moth in the forest. On jobsites with lots of tourists passing by, the other construction workers would push him to take his shirt off and catch and chat up gaggles of young females as they passed. To my amazement, they stopped, women snared by lines so trite they'd have sneered if anyone else had used them.

Tom shared with my friend, Jeff Hagel, the most sexual success I'd ever seen a straight man have. What seemed like hordes of young tourist women, especially teachers on vacation, passed through the Bakery. That made things edgy for me. The night I walked downstairs to grab some wine and found him with two giggling women lying on their backs on the dining room table as he slipped into one then the other, I lost it. Not then . . . I was too busy watching . . . but I lit into him the next day after work.

"For Christ's sake," I yelled, "fucking them on the table, not only on the table, but on the part where I eat. Damn, man, have some respect. And while we're at it, if you ever clip your toenails on the coffee table again, I swear I'll cut those size thirteen feet off."

He looked crushed and went to his room.

A few minutes later, Doug took me aside. "John, you over-reacted, come on. The kid was just having fun, and you know why you're reacting the way you are."

"Oh yeah, Mr. Psych Major, why?"

"Don't do this, John. You've been Mr. Alpha Straight Male ever since we bought the place, and any female on the property was yours. Now there's another male, straight male, here, and you're reacting in a normal way. Those females are supposed to be yours, but they're not. It's that simple and you know it. The whole dining room table thing was a minor part of it. Come on, my friend. You're the most intellectually honest and fairest person I've ever known. Give the kid an apology or something. You know his emotional vulnerability. He's in his room thinking he's going to get kicked out."

"Goddammit, Doug, you know I hate it when you're right, and I'm wrong."

"Doesn't happen often, big guy. Now go in there and tell the kid you forgive him."

"*Alright.*"

Doug was right, of course, so off I went. Tom was lying on his bed staring at the ceiling. I asked if I could come in.

"Yeah," he answered in a listless voice without looking at me.

"Can I sit down on your bed?"

"Yeah," and he moved over.

"Look, Tom, it doesn't matter how smart or educated a person is, everyone makes mistakes. I made a mistake yelling at you like I did."

"Doug's making you say this, ain't he?"

I let the "ain't" pass. "Tom, you know me enough by now to know that nobody can make me say anything I don't want to, not even if you pulled out my fingernails. What Doug did was show me I was wrong. So I apologize for yelling at you, though I really wish you wouldn't screw on the dining room table or clip your toenails on the coffee table. But the way I yelled at you was because of the whole alpha male thing," and then I had to explain packs, alpha and beta males. "Forgive me?"

He grabbed me and hugged me. "I thought you were gonna kick me out. I was so scared."

There was another episode a month later. I'd forgotten to restock the breakfast stuff upstairs in my room, so I was stumbling downstairs to head to M & M Laundromat for coffee and toast when I heard a loud voice in the great room. It was young Tom, yelling at Doug's latest one-week-long trick.

"You need to get the fuck outta here, dude," was what I heard when I walked into the room.

"Tom, the parlor . . . *now*!" I yelled, and he walked away. I turned to the frightened man: "Everything's OK, trust me. Be calm for a few minutes, and I'll take care of this."

I walked back into the parlor. "You stay there and don't move." Tom crossed his arms across his chest and gave me a look of injured disdain.

I climbed the stairs and knocked on Doug's door. When he opened it, I told him we had a crisis. A minute later, he came downstairs in his bathrobe, and Tom stood up and walked over to him, David and Goliath.

"I thought I was your number one man and now you got some faggot moved in with you."

I broke in. "Tom, I told you never to use that word."

"Whatever. . . ." They were standing a foot apart from each other. He looked down at Doug. "Am I your number one, or ain't I?"

I let the "ain't" pass again.

I saw Doug trying to suppress laughter. I was, too.

"Tom, you *are* my number one man, you'll *always* be my number one man. I'm just having a little affair with this guy, like you with that teacher from Cleveland last month."

"Look at me," Tom said, all injured earnestness, finger tapping on Doug's chest.

"Swear to me I'm number one man."

Doug put his arm around the kid's waist. "I swear, kid. You're my number one man. Now please apologize to my friend. He's probably in there thinking he's going to get beaten up."

Tom walked off, strode off, Alexander after Egypt. In the great room, we heard: "Sorry, dude. Everything's OK. You can stay."

Doug looked at me. "No, John, before you ask, the kid and I don't have sex, never have. That's what makes this whole episode so sweet. Anyway, you're always saying you never wanted an ordinary life. Happy?"

Thomas' acceptance of young Tom into the family showed again the nobility of his character. There were only a few signs he let slip that revealed the sexual attraction he felt, but he never pushed it, and he was an ever-patient mentor to the boy. Tom knew from our conversations the reverence we had for Thomas, and was always shy around him. But whenever he asked a question, always timidly, Thomas always accepted it and gave an answer that respected the boy's lack of education.

Leigh was mostly just amused by Tom until she was walking down Duval Street one night, and four drunken males surrounded her and weren't interested in hearing no. Leigh spotted Tom across the street and yelled for help. He ran over, and Leigh said it looked like a lion dispatching hyenas: grab, shake, throw, one after the other. They picked themselves up and ran away.

"Are you OK?"

"Thanks to you. That was scary. Can you walk me home? I'm a little shaken up."

Two weeks later, Leigh was at the Bakery for dinner. Doug was at his parents. After I'd cleared the dishes, Tom announced he was tired and was going to bed. A few minutes later, he came out of his room.

"John, will you read to me a little bit?" It was something Doug usually did.

I looked at Leigh, and she shrugged: "Why not?"

Tom yelled out when he was ready, and when we went inside his bedroom, we saw that he had set up a chair on each side of his bed. He was sitting up with the covers pulled to his waist. Leigh took one chair and I the other, then Tom handed me the copy of *The Little Prince* I'd bought him, his favorite book.

"Could you read me where the fox asks the little prince to tame him?"

I found the section and began. Tom closed his eyes, and Leigh took one of his hands and held it as I read. Slowly . . . slowly . . . a strange and powerful sensation came over me, something akin to déjà vu, but not exactly. Something outside myself was manipulating me—not in a bad way—into becoming part of . . . what? And then I looked at the nineteen-year-old man in bed and saw the four-year-old boy inside, and it hit me: I was inside a scene he had created.

I stopped reading with the lines that had captured me when I had first read it: "Good-bye," said the fox. "And now here is my secret: It is only with the heart that one can see rightly; what is essential is invisible to the eye." I put the book down. "Alright, kid, bedtime. Tomorrow's a workday."

Tom settled into the bed. I signaled Leigh to grab the other side of the covers and together we pulled them up to his chin. "Sleep tight, kid," I said.

I nodded to Leigh who got it. She leaned over and gave him a kiss on the forehead. "Sweet dreams, my little pumpkin." He closed his eyes and a look of utter peace suffused his face as he burrowed into the covers. We turned off the lights and left the room.

"Was that what I think it was?" Leigh asked. I put my finger to my lips and motioned for her to follow me to the parlor where we couldn't be heard. I fixed us drinks and sat down.

"You go first," I told her.

"He was obviously acting out the childhood scene of mom and dad reading a bedtime story, then tucking the child in."

"That's it exactly, I think. Somewhere back in his abused past he must have seen a scene like that on TV or in a movie, and he's craved it all his life. Doug's right. He really is creating the childhood he never had."

We were quiet for a while, contemplating what we'd just seen and what it said about humans when young. I became afraid, too, because I realized in full the responsibility his trust and need placed on us. It was work, constantly trying to reconcile the big, powerful adult male I saw everyday, and sometimes worked next to, with the soul and spirit of the scared and hurt little boy I knew resided inside.

Leigh shook her head at the wonderment of it. "This is special, a privilege. What would have happened to him if he hadn't met you and Doug? I don't even want to think about it. It's as strange and wonderful as one of those photos where a dog's letting an orphaned lion cub nurse on her."

Thomas and Doug had told me about Leigh's total lack of fear of social confrontation, and I had been witness to minor examples of it. We witnessed it spectacularly one night when the lioness unsheathed her claws in defense of our kid.

So many new people had moved to Key West at about the same time I did that it took awhile to sort ourselves out into the ones we wanted to know and the ones we didn't. One couple in particular had rubbed me the wrong way immediately, but in the amorphous socializing of my first couple years in Key West, I kept running into them.

Both were from somewhere in New England and both proudly WASP. Every time you met them, Emily reminded you that she was related to one of the nineteenth-century American vice presidents, and James made sure to bring up directly or indirectly that he had gone to Choate. James always made the grammatical mistake of saying "between you and I," which drives me crazy, and both chewed their food with their mouths open, she with little rabbity nibbles.

Emily had a slightly demented look to her, like she was listening to her own distant drummer, but one with a broken sense of rhythm. We eventually learned that, indeed, the blue blood coursing through her veins carried with it some multi-generational mental problems. She was socially inept and could always be counted on to come out with a remark that left people feeling like they'd walked into a spider web.

James was an odd bird: pigeon-chested, with a funny upturned nose that made him look like he was perpetually smelling something unpleasant, and a strange, duck-like walk. He affected, too, an upper-class Englishman's speech, emitting little poots of condescension through clenched teeth, relying heavily on sayings such as: "That won't wash" or "That's small beer." Doug later described him perfectly as the kind of kid in grade school who picked his nose and ate the boogers.

My first encounter with James and Emily had taken place at a dinner party Thomas gave at a house at the dead end of Amelia Lane just off Duval Street, where he was caretaker. A huge trestle table was set up outdoors and decorated with flowers, palm fronds, and candles. Thomas was giving a series of dinner parties, vetting the newcomers to see which were interesting enough to befriend. I found myself seated across from James and Emily and, by the time dinner began, was well-lubricated, dangerous in that I lose my innate Midwestern distaste for social confrontation.

To begin the meal, Thomas and Leigh spread huge banana leaves in the center of the table, placed dishes of cocktail sauce and empty saucers strategically around the table, then went inside and brought out a steaming pot of huge shrimp, Key West Pinks, which they dumped onto the banana leaves. How tropical, we all thought, as we began to shell and eat and talk.

Thomas went inside to put music on and came back out and sat down. Leigh sat next to me; then I looked up as the music started.

"Vivaldi's D-Major Concerto for Mandolins," I exclaimed. "I think the second movement is one of the most beautiful things he ever did."

James said in a totally condescending tone: "We only listen to Bach."

It was the tone of voice, probably, that set me off. If someone wanted to listen only to Bach, why not? Certainly one could do worse than listen to Johann Sebastian all one's life, but to imply a social superiority because of it set my teeth on edge. Not only that, but I was only a few years away from my life in Paris where I'd gone to over seven hundred classical music concerts, often with the world-class musicians who gave them, music as wide-ranging as a concert of *Music from the Time of Christopher Columbus* in the Conciergerie with sackbuts and crumhorns to the Fauré *Requiem* and Handel's *Messiah* in Notre Dame. Who did this idiot think he was, throwing off attitude? Arrogance enshrined on a plinth of ignorance is a statue I always have to knock over.

"You're not serious?" I asked. "Only Bach?"

"Of course," he sniffed, "nothing else."

"No Telemann?"

He shook his head.

"No Corelli?"

Another shake of the head.

"No Purcell? No Scarletti? No Boismortier?"

"No," he repeated, forcefully. By now it was obvious that I was goading him, and other people at the table started to listen.

"No Handel? No Vivaldi, no Mozart, Haydn, Schumann, Shubert, Brahms, Beethoven?"

He was getting annoyed, but I didn't care. I stopped and ate some shrimp; then, while we waited for the next course, I started up again.

"No Debussy, no Ravel, no Fauré *Requiem*? You've got to be kidding me! No Satie . . . the *Gymnopédies*? What about the operas? Don't tell me you don't listen to Puccini or Verdi. What about the "Hostias" from the Berlioz *Requiem*?"

He shook his head.

"And by Bach, do you mean only Johann Sebastian, or do you include the sons?"

I stopped only when Leigh kicked me under the table. James and Emily turned to talk to other people.

Then there was curried stir-fried chicken with slices of mango from the tree in the yard. When Thomas served ice cream afterwards, James asked Leigh about herself and soon was enthralled when he realized he was in the presence of an UR-WASP. He started asking:

"Do you know . . . " and she knew them all, and everyone else at the table was forgotten as he turned, mesmerized by her, currying favor. It was interesting to watch, and I noticed a certain ironic distance in her replies, which he didn't catch.

At the end of the dinner, when everyone else had left, and Leigh and I were helping Thomas clean up, she laughed about him. "Trust me, he'll be on the phone tonight to everyone he knows trying to place me socially. I know the type. Those scholarship boys are all alike. And notice, no follow-up Ivy college. Not smart enough, or they'd have given him another scholarship."

My dislike of the couple was cemented at another dinner party a few weeks later at Tony Falcone's house, where we were all reveling in the mystery of people from so many backgrounds having arrived in the same place at the same time. At a certain moment during the party, I was expressing my wonder and pride at the social mixing possible in the United States and was telling the party about my father's side of the family.

"Some of my uncles are still sharecroppers in the boot-heel of Missouri, still with outhouses, and one of my uncles lives in a tarpaper shack outside Pahokee near Lake Okeechobee here in Florida. He and his wife have only fourth-grade educations and, believe it or not, still refuse to believe that man landed on the moon."

Then I told them the story of trying to convince my aunt and uncle that Americans had, indeed, gone to the moon and brought backs rocks from it. My aunt's response had been: "Dat damn, I seen rocks just like that out there by Belle Glade."

Most of the table laughed, but felt the same wonder I did that people like my relatives still lived in an age where the species was exploring beyond its terrestrial home.

Most of my listeners marveled, too, at the ability American society gave you to educate and advance yourself, and I felt no social stigma for having these people as relatives, and actually admired them for their survival skills. I certainly didn't know how to slaughter a pig or gig frogs.

Emily and James were across the table from me again (to be closer to Leigh), and when I'd finished speaking, he asked: "Can we go look at them?"

The question confused me. "What do you mean 'go look at them?'"

"I'd like to see the shack and observe them for a while. I've never seen lower-class people up close."

His question made the people around him uncomfortable and shocked me.

"For Christ's sakes, James, they're not zoo animals, they're human beings. They're getting by as well as they can with what they were given."

"But I'd like to watch them," he insisted.

I turned away and talked to the other guests. Tony rolled his eyes.

Leigh found James and Emily especially tedious because from the moment James found out about Leigh's WASP background, he would sidle up to her every time they met, insinuating in everything he said that the two of them were socially superior to everyone else; made, somehow, of finer clay.

"He reminds me of all those twits from Harvard and Yale who did everything but lick my feet at the socials, as much because of my trust fund as because they were horny."

My little family met them less and less, as people began excluding them from their social circles, but we did run into them again years later at a big benefit dinner for the local hospice program. Someone must have given them the hundred-dollar tickets because they were notoriously cheap, another WASP trait. (Leigh, herself, told us the joke that there was never enough food at a WASP wedding.)

Thomas was out of town, but Leigh, Doug, young Tom, and I went. While we were standing around, drinks in hand, waiting for the dinner to start, James and Emily headed our way. Leigh, Doug, and I saw them coming and turned discreetly away, but having seen Tom with us, they introduced themselves to him.

"And what do you do, my young man?" James pooted.

"I'm an electrician's helper," Tom answered.

"Oh, really. Well, the world does need its proles, doesn't it Emily?" This from someone who now sold real estate for a living.

Tom sensed from the tone of voice that he'd been insulted, but didn't have the social skills to retaliate. The three of us had heard it, and Leigh grabbed Doug and me by the arms, hard, before we could turn around and hissed: "Not a word, you two. I will handle this. Just make sure we're across from them at dinner."

"James," she oozed as she turned around, "and Emily. So glad you're here. Please, let's sit across from one another and catch up on each others' news. It's been too long. Emily, lovely dress. Galanos?"

James, especially, glowed at the unaccustomed attention from our very own WASP princess. Doug and I led young Tom away and consoled him.

"But I didn't do anything to him. Why would he want to insult me? And what's that thing he called me?"

"Because he's a pretentious jerk," Doug explained. "And proles are working-class people, which all us construction workers are, and he's no better. Just make sure you sit next to us so you can see Leigh in action getting even for you. It will be spectacular, I bet. And, no, you can't punch him. This will be even better."

We four took our seats early, and James and Emily made sure they grabbed two directly across from us. Leigh made unctuous small talk across the table, but her face was flush.

A bell was rung, and everyone took their places. Each table seated sixteen people and, as luck would have it, a rich and annoying couple, customers of mine and Doug's, sat to my immediate left. I started throwing down the wine, the first one a very pleasant, dry, French rosé.

The head of hospice gave the obligatory speech and thanked the owners of Antonia's for donating the meal, and the wait staff for donating any tips we might want to leave, and Southern Wine Distributors for donating all the wine. Then Philip and Antonia, the owners, came out with all the cook and wait staff, and everyone stood and gave them a standing ovation for their generosity.

As soon as we were re-seated, the food and more wine started coming out. I was nervous with what I knew was coming, my stomach started to flutter, and I picked at my food.

James was homophobic, I remembered, and had always shown himself squeamish whenever the details of two men together became too graphic at a party. Chance gave Leigh her opening salvo because there was an outrageously gay Englishman we knew, and his equally outrageous American lover, seated to James' right.

"Ronald," Leigh called across the table to the Englishman. "If you're a Brit, you must be uncut. Do you and Ralph do tulip shots?"

"What's a tulip shot?" young Tom asked in all innocence, his timing as perfect as if they'd planned it. I didn't know what it was. Doug grabbed my arm and had a horrified look on his face. Ronald didn't hesitate. "That's when the guy with the foreskin makes a little cup out of it—like a tulip—and pours a drink in it for his partner to lick out. We always do it on our anniversary with Veuve Clicquot," and beamed at his partner who beamed back.

I felt like throwing up. The husband of the rich couple I knew snorted some wine up his nose and sputtered that that was hardly proper dinner conversation. Leigh leaned forward so she could look down the table at him and shot back: "This is Key West, sir, not Palm Beach," which shut him up. James had a look of extreme distaste on his face. Emily, ever the social dodo, blurted out: "James is uncircumcised, too, you know," and James' face turned bright red.

You could tell the real Key Westers at the table now, because they were the ones laughing, delighted to be getting more than their hundred dollars worth.

Leigh was quiet for a few minutes as we ate our shrimp and avocado salad with mango-papaya salsa, but I knew my girl. She was just biding her time, snake in the pit waiting for the chicken to calm down.

She went out of her way to chat with Emily until the salad plates were cleared and the entrée served: pork medallions with a Calvados and crème fraîche sauce. More wine came, a surprisingly complicated and delightful California pinot noir, and I kept on slugging it down.

"Slow down, John," Doug whispered.

"I can't, Doug," I whispered back. "You know what she's going to do." He gave me a friendly pat on the leg.

"He deserves it."

"I know, I know, but it's going to be brutal."

When Leigh addressed James next, my heart was in my mouth. God only knew what was coming. I'd rather wash a thousand mud-spattered UPS trucks than be in her cross-hairs.

"James, perhaps you can help me with a problem I have." Our end of the table turned to listen.

"Certainly, Leigh."

"I know you went to Choate, like my brother and father." His little pigeon chest swelled.

Here it comes, I thought to myself.

"The manager of my trust fund forwarded me the letter Choate sent them asking for contributions to up their endowment. They want to increase the number of scholarships they give out."

James looked a little discomfited. The word "scholarship" drew a significant social line in the sand between them.

"It is rather a worthy cause, Leigh," he pooted out.

"Well, James, my question to you is, do you really think it's a good idea to give working-class children scholarships to an elite prep school? I mean, look at you. Your father was a car salesman or some such, wasn't he, and you got a scholarship to study with people of my class. It does seem to me, though, that the only thing the poor students on scholarships get out of it is all the arrogance and none of the class."

She took a quick sip of wine and looked directly at him. "Like you."

I had never seen such a perfect and public gutting of a person. James looked as humiliated as I had ever seen anyone.

"So, James, if you don't mind, I don't think I'm going to contribute. I think class in all its definitions is worth protecting from proles like you."

James stood and pulled Emily up. "Excuse me, we have to leave."

"Leave a tip for the waiters," Leigh ordered. "And for god's sake, can't you two learn to chew your food with your mouths closed. Revolting." They ignored her and walked off.

"Impressive," Doug said. "Brilliant and frightening, Sally, but impressive."

Leigh then apologized to the table and explained to the people in earshot why she'd done what she had. "He insulted our kid here for no reason," and she tousled young Tom's hair. "Any man who saves me from a bunch of drunks on Duval Street and cries at *Madama Butterfly* is a hero of mine, isn't that right big guy?"

Tom blushed.

The evening would have been memorable enough had it ended there, but it didn't. Ronald and his lover moved into the seats vacated by James and Emily, and the cheese course, with a wonderful chèvre, arrived with a slightly rough Montepulciano.

The other end of the table pulled into themselves and left us alone.

To young Tom's right, at the end of the table, was an older couple whose last name was world famous for a fortune older, even, than the Republic. The wife seemed to be enjoying herself, and the husband looked completely toasted. I'd done minor work for them on their condo, but they didn't recognize me, for which I was grateful. I hate talking about work outside working hours with anyone other than fellow construction workers.

The wife chatted a bit with Tom, and we had taught him how to socialize at a dinner party. ("Always ask people about themselves, Tom, we'd told him. People love to talk about themselves. Ask them where they're from and what they do. Ask them why they moved to Key West and when. Ask them if they like it. Do not ask how much money they make or have, or anything close to that.")

The wife seemed to be enjoying the attention as Tom went down the list of acceptable questions, and everything was going fine until he noticed the ring she was wearing, with a diamond much bigger than the Ritz, worth probably three times the collective net worth of everyone at the table, excluding Leigh and Mr. Snorts-Wine-Through-His-Nose.

"Is that thing real?" he asked.

'Oh, god,' I thought, "please let this evening end." Doug grabbed my arm again.

"Well, yes, dear, it is. I don't believe in wearing paste and stashing the real stuff. Why have it if you can't wear it? Don't you agree?"

Leigh must have kicked him under the table and whispered the prompt to him.

"Absolutely," then a pause as the next prompt came. "A beautiful piece."

"Thank you. It was a gift from my husband," and she patted the hand of the husband, nearly comatose now, whose parents and grandparents and great-grandparents had probably never made a bed or cooked a meal.

Another prompt. "That's sweet."

"Well, it was, wasn't it?" She hesitated a minute then asked: "Did you really cry during *Madama Butterfly*?"

"Did I ever! These guys," he nodded toward us, "took me to see it at the Met in New York and told me what it was about, but it didn't hit me until the end when Cio-Cio San was giving her kid away. I'm sort of like an orphan myself, and I just couldn't help myself, I started bawling and embarrassed everybody."

She patted his hand. "What a sensitive young man you are. It's a lovely, moving piece of music, isn't it?"

He nodded agreement, and I rolled my eyes as I saw all the women within earshot going into their "Isn't he sweet" mode.

We finished the cheese course; the end was in sight.

Unfortunately, Ronald and his partner, now both as drunk as I was, seemed riveted by young Tom.

"Leigh, darling," Ronald asked, "where did you find this ravishing creature? Pray tell, is he your paramour?'

"No, he's a friend of ours," and she nodded toward Doug and me. "And he's not on your side of the fence, so quit drooling." I dreaded where this exchange might go, but Ronald just laughed and backed off gracefully.

Young Tom now had Mrs. Gotrocks talking about her house on Truman Annex, so I began to calm down.

Dessert arrived, a Charlotte anglaise, with a California Muscat that was as good as any Barsac I'd ever had, and then it was over.

The head of hospice thanked everyone again, and we were free to go.

"Goodbye, young man," the woman with the ring said to Tom when she got up. "Such nice manners, so rare now in young people." She searched in her purse for pen and paper and asked him for his phone number. "I would like to invite you to a party at our house sometime. It would be nice to have some young people around for a change."

"Thank you, ma'am. It was a pleasure meeting you."

I shook my head in disbelief. People on at least three continents would sacrifice their first-born child for entrée into the society this couple represented, and the kid had just stumbled into it totally unaware of what it represented and didn't care. One of the husband's ancestors had dined with Washington and Lafayette.

Perfunctory goodbye's to everyone else and then escape. Out on the street and down a ways from the restaurant, I yelled: "Thank god, that's over. I thought I was going to have a nervous breakdown."

"What a sissy," Leigh said. "That was fun.

"For a lioness with no fear and a love of raw meat, maybe."

"Did I do OK?" Tom asked.

"You did fine, kid," Doug answered, "though I almost had a heart attack when you asked her if the stone on her ring was real."

"She didn't seem to mind."

"That's because she misunderstood your question, Tom," Leigh said, and explained to him the practice of wearing replicas in public while the real stuff stays in the vault. "She thought you were asking about that, not if she was tacky enough to pretend to own a piece like that when she didn't."

"Weird. Hey, let's go to the Monster and celebrate that I didn't make a fool of myself, what do you say?"

Doug and Leigh seemed willing, but I protested that I'd had too much to drink.

"Come on, pops, it'll work the booze out of you," and he started walking backwards, facing us, and doing a little boogie. "You know you like to dance, old man, and you should see some of the cool new moves I been . . ."

"Dollar!"

"*I've* been practicing."

So we walked on down Duval Street to the Monster, where a line had formed to get in because it was a weekend and high season. Three places ahead of us in line, I saw Tennessee Williams with a friend. Then I saw him say something to the young kid ahead of him in line, probably a proposition, and the kid said something back and pulled away. Tennessee got up next to him and said something again, and the kid gave him a shove.

Tennessee lost his balance, probably because he was drunk, and fell, yelling out as people rushed over to help him up: "Young man, I'll ruin you socially," which caused everybody in line to break out laughing, which Tennessee joined in. Someone asked the kid: "Don't you know who that is?" and he answered, "Yeah, but I ain't that way," and headed back out to the street muttering "Weirdos."

When Tennessee thanked the man who helped him back to his feet, the man replied: "No problem, sir. Sometimes we all depend on the kindness of strangers," causing half the line to burst out laughing again and applauding, then explaining why to the other half.

Tennessee took a modest bow.

At the end of our dancing, the four of us walked back up the street to get our bikes and rode back to the Bakery, laughing and singing and flipping the bird to impatient motorists behind us on Olivia Street.

Fifteen

Only twelve years had passed since I had last shared a cheap, off-campus boarding house at the University of Missouri with racist, misogynistic, homophobic bible-thumpers. How could such a short span separate me from a culture as foreign to me now as China to Marco Polo? One of my oddest fears was that I'd be traveling across the country when nuclear war broke out, trapping me for the rest of my life in the Bible Belt, a place where the first question asked of a newcomer is "What church do you belong to?" or "Have you been saved?"

I amused myself sometimes by the imaginary introduction of one of the most prejudiced college housemates to a Key West party.

"Cecil, old buddy, glad you could come. I'll be your guide. OK, see the woman wearing jeans and hiking boots who just walked in. That's Margo, a building contractor. She's a lesbian and named her company Tongue-in-Groove Construction. Get it? Lesbian . . . tongue-in-groove? She's not in the top rank of builders on the island yet, but you gotta love her sense of humor.

"OK, now check out that husband and wife over there having an intimate conversation. The husband's real partner is the man in blue jeans and button-down shirt checking out the young man serving at the buffet table. Yep, queer as a three-dollar bill. The wife's real partner is the other woman standing next to them. They got married so he could inherit 'cause his parents would have disowned him if they thought he was a homo. Now the two lesbos and the two homos are all rich, and his parents don't have a clue. What the 'husband and wife' are talking about is probably that they all want kids. Do they do it conventional boom-boom style, or turkey baster? Whose spunk? Whose egg? Be glad you did it the old-fashioned way.

"Now see the three men over there having the conversation with the mayor? Those three men are each other's partners and have been living together for over six years. Two of them were married before, and each has two kids. Three men together! Imagine some of those arguments! Imagine the family reunions! And how do you decide top and bottom when there are three of you, and you all have a pecker? Imagine writing that will!

"Now look at those three thirty-somethings at the buffet table. That's the one none of us can figure out. How did that scruffy-looking carpenter wind up with both a hot wife, that's her on his left; and a good-looking mistress; that's her on his right. They all live together, happily we've heard, and the women take turns bringing him lunch on the jobsites, which burns our guts. All us men hate him for getting away with having two at once, and we always give him all the shit jobs, can't help ourselves. The three always form a little self-satisfied circle at the Monster. It doesn't help that he's the best dancer we've ever seen.

"Cecil, remember the time you told us you'd just proposed to your high school sweetheart, and we all got drunk in the house and all went up to you and gave you the 'we're not really touching another man' hug and clap on the back. Remember how you teared up a little bit because you were in love, and we were happy for you. Cecil, these people love each other, too.

"Look, Tennessee Williams just walked in, messed up again on alcohol, drugs, or both. Poor man hasn't been the same since his partner, Frank Merlo, died. He gave a reading the other night and was so toasted he kept turning more than one page at a time, confusing everyone, but no one laughed. At the end, everyone applauded, and married friends of his drove him home to make sure he was safe. Now watch everyone in the room watching—protecting—him. If he starts falling down, someone, anyone, in this room would help him up and take him home.

"OK, only one more. See the plain woman at the table now? She was a teacher in South Carolina somewhere and just decided she didn't like it. She did the *Bartleby the Scrivener* number: 'I prefer not to.' That's Melville . . . Melville? *Moby Dick*? Oh, that's right. I remember you saying you'd be happy to graduate from college because you'd never have to read another book. Couple of your buddies said the same thing. Anyway, Cecil, every time they put Ms. South Carolina back in the classroom, she broke down and said the equivalent of "I prefer not to." Can you believe it? They pensioned her off and she's been living here ever since. Wish I'd thought of that."

Cecil would most likely not have been amused, though I think the culture up there was changing. One of the most successful Duval Street acts was now a six foot, three-inch drag queen who stood outside Delmonicos and charged five dollars to let tourists have their picture taken with her in whatever pose they chose, and there were now TV sitcoms with gay characters.

What most of the rest of the country considered over-the-top-strange, we accepted as part of our daily lives, accepted it with pleasure because it added richness to our lives.

The strangest relationship in my Key West life wasn't the one with my Vietnam vet buddy, Jeff, or with my two close, gay friends, or with the young redneck kid under our collective wing, but mine with the rich WASP princess.

She was rich, and with certain wonderful exceptions, I don't like the rich: strike one.

She was a New England mega-WASP, a class I have great loathing for. I grant them their accomplishments but dislike their sense of entitlement because their ancestors got here first, religious bigots who poisoned the American well, probably forever, with their religion. I have contempt for their monkey see, monkey do Anglophilia. I hated their eagerness to don symbolic pith helmets after WWII and take over from the Brits as world emperor, which they thought their natural due. As rulers of the world, they lacked much, and the war in Vietnam—a WASP religious war in great part—proved that the emperor had no clothes. They were incompetent in the role and shameless in refusing to accept blame for the more than 58,000 Americans in the ground who didn't live to demand justice. At least I had lived to see Halberstam's *The Best and the Brightest* skewer them well and properly for their arrogance, ignorance, and incompetence. It reinforced for me something I had learned on my own: arrogance is always a form of blindness. Her WASP-ness: strike two.

There was never a strike three. As annoying as she could be with her own brand of arrogance, so could she be kind and humble. Her continued friendship with and protection of Thomas—we were sure she helped him financially—and her commitment of time and money to the care and counseling of abused and addicted women was admirable. Her ferocious defense of young Tom was noble.

She was a beauty, granted, but beauty alone doesn't hold a man's attention forever. Look at the world-class beauties male movie stars marry only to dump them later. As a drunk construction buddy of mine put it crudely in the Parrot one Sunday afternoon: "You see a totally beautiful, unbelievably sexy woman walking down the street, one you'd crawl across a half mile of broken glass for just to lick the finger that's been in her pussy, and guess what? There's a man somewhere who's already tired of banging her." A crude but accurate analysis of the shallowness of male sexuality.

I loved her beauty; I loved her sexiness; I loved her intelligence; I loved that we could speak French together, but it was two other things that finally brought us together. The first was that, in spite of her money, she had a sense of play. She was like the great tomboy in grade school. She loved the water fights at the Bakery, or splash games in the pool or the ocean. She loved practical jokes as much as the rest of us and actually slipped a whoopee cushion into my seat when we were at Louie's one afternoon when I'd excused myself to go to the bathroom. I've never been more embarrassed as several tables turned to check the source of the sound at the exact moment she yelped: "Really, John!" Most people laughed, and a few even applauded when I extracted the pink cushion and pointed to her.

The second was something dark that I only learned years after our first meeting. As part of her rehabilitation work with "my women" as she called them, she staged and financed a yearly fundraising fashion show at the Magdalen House she and Katie had bought for them. The fashion models were the women she'd helped and counseled over the last year. She paid thousands of dollars for dental work and whatever else it took to take women who'd looked like forty miles of bad road and transform them into credible runway models for an amateur show.

Leigh roped everyone into helping set up for the show: nailing together a plywood runway, hanging lighting, setting up chairs and make-up stations, and she was everywhere, checking every detail. The night before the show, late, when I was covering the sides of the runway with stapled-on sheets as skirts, and she was going down a checklist, I was tired enough that I finally worked up the nerve to ask her what I thought was the obvious question.

"Leigh, I admire what you're doing, but why a fashion show?"

She shot me a look that should have decapitated me, then checked herself. "John, there isn't a single woman that's going to walk down this runway tomorrow who hasn't been beaten by fathers or boyfriends or both, forced into sex by whoever was strong enough to hold her down, and had her spirit destroyed. They've internalized all that; they all think they're pieces of shit. In their minds, their pussy is the only thing of value they have, so they give it to anyone who comes along who shows them any attention.

"You're a man. Maybe you can understand it intellectually, but you can't understand emotionally the psychology of a broken woman. So tomorrow, wearing beautiful clothes that they get to keep, hair professionally done, made up like a million dollars, they can walk down this runway and have people applaud them."

I started to say something but she stopped me. "I know what you're going to say. Yes, we're making people applaud them for their looks, and how can that help? But for once people are going to pay attention to them, and they don't have to have sex to get it. And did an entire audience ever applaud you? I've gone over all the ramifications of what we're doing and its limitations, but mostly I tell them to be proud of themselves, that they can do better, that they don't have to blow some dirtbag on Stock Island to feel like they're worth something.

"Remember, too, they're not just being applauded for their looks. This is their graduation. Every woman walking down this runway tomorrow has been sober and clean for at least six months, gotten their GED, and had hundreds of hours of counseling. For a few short minutes, they get to walk in front of a crowd where people cheer them. Then we take them to a group dinner, with their kids if they have them here, give them their GED certificates and reinforce that they're worthy human beings and remind them that we're here to help them get jobs and use the "high" they got from the show to change the direction of their lives.

"Leigh, you're awesome."

"I know, John. Now get back to stapling and try to make those pleats more uniform. That last run is a little sloppy."

"Yes, ma'am."

The show was a charity event. The price of admission was twenty-five dollars and there was an open, free bar, a surefire way to get a crowd in Key West. The small auditorium started to fill up an hour before the show. Leigh was racing around, riding herd on everyone. "Amanda, spit that gum out. Not classy. Sally, quit chewing on your fingers." The hairdressers and make-up people, mostly gay and all donating their time, were swapping obscene stories with the women, and shrieks of laughter poured out from backstage.

When I walked back to see if Leigh needed any help, one of the hairdressers had just put his hands on his hips, and in answer to a question I hadn't heard, said: "Well, honey, 'cause that's where the prostate is." I rolled my eyes, and left.

Finally, the show was ready to start. Leigh tapped the microphone and explained the work that Magdalen House did, and why it was important. Then she thanked everyone for coming, all the volunteers, whom she named, and the local liquor store that had donated the bar. The lights dimmed . . . some hot disco music came up. . . .

"Now, first down the runway is Gloria in a Valentino-inspired off-the-shoulder aqua sheath with matching pumps and handbag." Leigh had taught them the runway strut and some good boogie moves. The audience applauded, whistled, and whooped as Gloria walked the runway twice.

"Next is Nancy in a dark maroon, sleeveless, round-the-neck cocktail dress with contrasting belt and clutch, and matching shoes.

"Now, for the larger woman, is Alicia in a linen dress with contrasting linen jacket, large purse, and matching belt as accessories."

The women were obviously enjoying themselves and loving the attention. Once, when one of the models came out, two young kids in the audience stood up and started yelling: "Mommy, mommy," and the whole crowd stood to applaud when she blew the kids a kiss, then strutted her stuff.

The most amazing part of the show for me was the transformation in Leigh when she was talking to the women backstage before the show and again afterwards. She spoke softly and sweetly to the women, and even when she gave an order, it was in a friendly tone we were not often used to. Her affection for these women was apparent. Each model showed four outfits, and when the show ended, I lined up to congratulate her.

"Impressive amount of work and organization. Congratulations. So you're not just a pretty face."

"You're just finding that out?" and she gave me a kiss. "Thanks for your help."

A few days later, she called and asked for a ride to the jail on Stock Island because her car had broken down. I picked her up outside her apartment building.

"Another sad case," she explained. "Drugged-out woman busted for hooking. Listen to this: her customer did her in the cemetery, then slapped her around when she asked for her money. He pushed her into the wrought-iron fence and broke her arm. There she is with a broken arm, half hanging from the fence, still trying to sell herself to guys walking past. Someone called the cops, and *she* gets busted. It'd be funny if it weren't so damned sad. Imagine the horrors of a life that would take her down that low."

I could feel the heat of Leigh's anger and wasn't sure what to say. It resonated with something in my life, too, something I don't talk about. I reached over and put a hand on her.

My stomach started growling, so I suggested lunch, as much to change the subject as anything. "Got time for Rusty Anchor?"

She looked at her watch. "Sure, I haven't been yet. Let's try it."

The Rusty Anchor was a new seafood restaurant on Stock Island across from the old dog track. Ramon, the owner, bought the fish right off the boats that moored out there now that they'd been kicked out of Old Town's harbor. Huge doors on two sides of the restaurant opened to the outdoors—no AC—and the décor was pure funk: lobster floats, fish nets, photos of commercial fishermen with their catch, all hung on cypress board walls. No tourists . . . yet.

When we walked in, there were maybe ten other people at tables, all men, all wearing white boots. We sat down at a table near the door and gave our orders to the waitress who turned out to be one of Leigh's success stories, so there was lots of face kissing and gossip.

We shared the squid rings—perfection—and then each had the pan-fried yellowtail, the best piece of fish I'd ever had in my life, fried lightly in batter one micron thick, a hint of crunch giving way to tender, delicate white flesh.

I started telling Leigh a funny construction story about the job I was doing on Southard Street for a gay man who fixed us lunch every day. Thomas and Leigh loved these stories more than the *Mullet Wrapper's Crime Reports*.

"You're not going to believe this one, Leigh. Paul, the owner, rode off on his bike somewhere after serving us lunch yesterday, so my helper collected all the dirty dishes when we were finished and took them inside. A minute later, he came running back outside and started puking in the bushes, so we all went over and asked him what was wrong. He couldn't talk for puking, just kept pointing inside, so we walked inside to the kitchen. There in the open dishwasher stood a black dildo big as a horse's dick. I almost upchucked myself. Needless to say, we won't eat lunch there anymore."

We were both still laughing when two men a couple tables away started shouting curses at one another, then stood up and started fighting. Our waitress went over and yelled at them to stop it, and I stood up, ready to help her. They ignored her and started punching each other seriously, knocking over tables and chairs. The bartender, another woman, came out from behind the bar and screamed: "I've called the cops."

The fight stopped instantly, and every man in the room jumped up, threw money on the table, and ran outside and down the street. Our waitress came back to our table laughing. "That always works. They all got warrants out on 'em for something or other."

Leigh and I were laughing again about the mass exodus from the restaurant as I drove back out to US 1. We were going along the part of Cross Street that has thickets of mangroves growing right to the street when Leigh screamed: "Stop!" I slammed on the brakes, and she jumped out of the truck and started fighting her way through the tangle of roots to where I saw a glimpse of something bright aqua. I jumped out and followed her.

Lying on top of some of the surface roots was Gloria, still in her runway dress, now pulled up above her waist. Her face was bruised, panties torn off, and there was dried blood around her vagina.

"Gloria, Gloria, can you hear me?" Leigh kept asking, bent over, listening for breathing.

"She's alive, John. Help me lift her. We have to get her to the hospital."

I pulled her dress down and lifted her by myself. "Leigh, go open the door." Stumbling and fighting my way through the inter-twined roots, and dropping her once, I made it to my truck.

At the hospital emergency room, Leigh filled out the paperwork and made the admitting clerk call the cops. While we waited for them, she paced back and forth, a caged and very angry animal, and every once in a while went to the pay phone and made a call.

When the cops showed up, she gave them all the information and every time, at even the slightest hint from them that this wasn't a big deal because it involved a homeless person, they caught the full treatment from a powerful and determined pit bull.

"I've called the sheriff, the state attorney, the mayor, and the *Key West Citizen*. You know this goes on back in those mangroves. Stop it. That's your goddamn job. Rape is rape. If some dirtbag beat you up and bent one of you boys over, that place would be cleared out in an hour. Do it."

She was completely silent the whole way back to Key West. When we got close to Old Town, she looked over. "Take me to the Bakery, OK?"

"Sure."

I fixed us both drinks when we were in my room, and she knocked hers back and asked for another. We were sitting on my sofa. When I handed her the second drink, she took a sip, then stood up and started pacing back and forth in front of me and began to speak.

"My father started molesting me when I was in kindergarten."

I stood up and started to go to her. I did not want to hear this.

"No, John, sit down. Let me finish."

"It started with a finger in me, and his penis rubbing all over me, and then, as he became more alcoholic, making me take it in my

293

mouth. All the while, he's telling me how much he loves me, and that I'm daddy's girl and special to him, and that this is our little secret. I'll never forget the sound of my bedroom door opening, waking me late at night, or the smell of cigarettes and alcohol on his breath and the musky smell of his foreskin ... and always: 'Daddy's little girl, daddy's little girl.' Then the wetness, which he wiped off with a tissue, leaving without another word.

"My mother walked in on it once, and then there was terrible tension in the house that I knew was somehow my fault. My mother never came to me to comfort me or explain to me what had been done, only to tell me that what had happened had to remain a secret. For her, the most important thing was that no one find out about it so the family image wouldn't be tarnished.

"The second time she walked in on it, there was the same terrible tension and this time, because I was older, she said: "What do you want me to do? Have your father put in jail? We'd be ruined. I've told him to stop."

"It went on for a few more years until I was old enough to stop it.

"I grew up with all the damage that does to a woman. I was angry, really angry, and I took it out on everyone, and I was rich enough and good-looking enough that people put up with it. I know you all think I'm bossy and obnoxious. You should have seen me then. I was horrible."

She paused and dropped her head for a minute, clasping her glass. Then she looked up again and continued.

"In college, I was coming out of French class one afternoon and wasn't paying attention, and bumped into a janitor, a kid about my own age, who was carrying a mop and a bucket with some water in it that spilled on my dress. I snarled at him: "'Goddammit, watch what you're doing!' Even though it was my fault."

Her voice became softer, quieter. "The boy didn't say anything, just picked up the bucket and started mopping up the water. Then he looked up at me, and I saw he was crying."

She was quiet for a minute.

"That was my 'Paul on the Road to Damascus' moment, John. That was the day I started to become a human being. I realized what an asshole I'd been and apologized, and he just nodded. Then I insisted he give me his phone number so I could take him out to dinner or something to make up for it. "You don't have to do that," he said in a soft and gentle voice I can still hear.

"But I want to," and he gave in.

"The next night I met him at a small place near the campus. His name was Andrew, Andy. He'd cried so easily because his mother had died the week before. I felt like a total piece of shit and couldn't stop apologizing.

"Andy was putting himself through school, a community college, working as a janitor at Radcliffe. We started an affair the next night. He was a gentle, kind man, gay as it turned out, and when he admitted it to himself, finally, and to me, we stopped having sex but became each other's best friend. For some reason or other, knowing he was gay let me open up to him about what my parents had done. He was intelligent, Andy, and wise . . . I'm looking for another word here . . . sort of like you and Thomas . . . you hear or see or read something and see right to the heart of it and grab its import.

"Sexually abused women often become either frigid or whores or something equally screwed up. I didn't because of Andrew, talking me through it all, relieving me of the burden that most abused women carry—that somehow they are responsible for what happened to them. That's why I try to help these women. They don't have the money or education, or intelligence I do, and they don't have an

Andrew in their lives. I try to lift the unfair burden of guilt off them, just like Andrew had done for me."

She stood up and walked out on the front balcony, and I followed her. Across the street, parents were playing with their children at the little playground for the now completed Navy Housing.

"Do you still talk to Andy?"

She didn't answer for a minute, then said: "He was killed during Tet in Vietnam, and I've never stopped missing him," and she started crying.

I pulled her to me and held her. 'With family and country as enemies,' I thought, 'who needs others?'

When she'd gained control of herself, we went back inside, and she continued the story.

"My father stole my childhood from me, and one of the damnable things about the whole business is that I feel sorry for *him*. How twisted is that? He's a sick man. He's never been up to playing the role that's expected of him: big time investment banker. He's not good at it, he's a failure, and he knows it, and he's married to a cold-hearted bitch, my mother, who's got an adding machine for a heart.

"You men just don't know the damage you can do to women. Anyway, the day I found out Andy had been killed, I swore I would live my life entirely on my own terms, by my own standards, and to hell what the world thinks. Fortunately, I have the money to get away with being pushy and bossy and kicking assholes out of my way.

"Spring break my last year of grad school, I drove to Miami, which bored me, then drove down here on a whim. My first night, I went to a gallery opening and met Thomas. When I graduated, I moved down here, and the rest is history, magical history, emphasis on magic."

We went back out on the balcony and I pulled her to me and put my arm around her again, kissing her on the top of her head and debating whether or not to tell her my own story. I decided against it. A single day should only bear a certain weight of sadness.

She pulled in tight to me. "You and Andy are the only people I've told that to."

"I'm honored you'd trust me that much, Leigh," and kissed her again.

"You know, it sounds funny, but I feel safe with you," and she put her head on my chest.

We slept together sexless that night, the pleasure being two people cuddling together for comfort.

I got crazy busy after that afternoon and spoke to Leigh only once the whole week, and had to cancel a dinner out with her and Thomas. She called me on Saturday. "John, are you avoiding me now because of what I told you? I'm damaged goods?"

"Christ, Leigh, of course not. I've been busy on that house I'm building on Truman Annex. Look, Doug's having dinner out with an affairette tonight, and Tom's got a date with another teacher. Come over for dinner. I made that onion tart you like."

Doug had already left when Leigh showed up, and Tom was on his way out.

"Come here, kid," she told him. "Turn around." She straightened his collar. He gave her a kiss, and then she swatted him on the butt: "Go knock 'em dead, cowboy, but wear a rubber." He blushed.

I poured us wine and started dinner while she leaned on the kitchen island and kept me company. I hadn't had time to read the paper that morning, so I hadn't read the story she started telling me.

"They were digging on Higg's Beach three days ago for those new beach pavilions and dug up some skeletons. The sheriff came over and decided the bones were too old to be a recent crime scene. You didn't hear anything about this?" I shook my head. "Well, there were so many skeletons, they figured it had to have been some kind of cemetery, but no one knew of one ever being there. Someone got the bright idea of going to the library and asking Tom Hambright.

"Tom looked at all the old newspapers, and it turns out that the U.S. Navy captured three slave ships off Cuba after importing slaves was illegal and brought the poor bastards to Key West, fourteen hundred of them. They made a camp for them there on what's Higg's Beach now, and the Conchs fed them and gave them clothes. Almost three hundred of them died and were buried there, and the rest were taken back to Africa. The horrible thing is that they came from the Congo and were taken back to Liberia. Sensitive move on the part of the government, don't you think? What fascinates me is that you never know on this island how much history is beneath your feet. Incredible."

As taken as I was by the story, I was preoccupied with the debate going on within me. Finally, I made the decision.

We made small talk for a while, then, at the end of the meal, I told her I'd like her to come upstairs with me after dinner. "There's something I have to tell you."

"Oh hell, John, you're not going to tell me you're gay, are you? That'd be just my luck to have another horse shot out from under me."

"Don't be ridiculous. But it's important. Let me clean up here first." She sat on a sofa, pensive, nursing her wine, while I did the dishes.

Upstairs, it was my turn to pace and hers to listen.

"Leigh, I almost told you this the other day when you told me about your father, but I thought it might seem like some kind of sick competition, and you deserved better. But I never want you to believe I think less of you because of what your father did to you. We come from way different backgrounds but with similar stories. I'm going to tell you things no one else has ever heard, but you have to swear to keep it to yourself. Promise?"

She nodded.

"My dad came from rural Missouri from a huge family—fifteen kids—so poor that the kids went hungry, the kind of misery that doesn't allow any of the softer emotions. He grew up malnourished and psychologically damaged. World War II and the Navy were his escape. He met my mother when he was in training at the Navy boot camp in Chicago.

"My mother's father sexually abused her until she was six or seven, then completely abandoned the family." Leigh started shaking her head side to side and covered her ears. I gently pulled them away. "Leigh, if we're ever going to be real partners, you have to listen."

I continued.

"It was the Depression. Trying to support my mom was too much for her mother, who became alcoholic. One day when my mother came home from school—she was eight or nine—the neighbors met her and told her that her mother had just killed herself."

"Oh hell, oh hell, John, your poor mother," Leigh said and came over to me. We held each other for a minute, then I told her I wanted to finish, and she sat back down.

"For the rest of her life until she met dad, my mother was shunted from one unloving, impoverished relative to another. It created an insecurity in her that can never, will never, be healed.

"She'd just graduated from high school when she and a girlfriend went to an amusement park in Chicago, and a hot-looking sailor and a pretty "sweater girl" met, and two terribly crippled people who should never have married, did. She was seventeen, he was nineteen. I was born nine months later while my dad was at sea during the war.

"When the war ended, my father left the Navy and moved back in with his parents with six of their kids still at home, and now the three of us, all in a four-room tarpaper shack with no indoor plumbing. It was a bitter, ugly time, my mother told me. My father was unhappy, his parents were unhappy, and my mother was extremely unhappy.

"My father was emotionally frozen, so my mother began turning to me for all her emotional needs. The family nicknamed me the judge because her neurotic attention turned me from cheerful to always serious. How could you not be when you're being burdened with things you can't understand, let alone control, and from infancy on. That was my childhood.

"Dad solved the family's money problems by re-enlisting in the Navy. By the time I was in school, my mother added to my burden by demanding academic excellence, no exceptions, no excuses, not even the dislocation of moving every two years. As I got older, I learned that the easiest way to be left alone was to do everything the adults around me—my parents, my teachers—wanted. I was intelligent enough to know that things around me weren't "right," but not knowledgeable enough to know what that meant.

"I was in fourth grade the first time I walked in on my father sexually abusing my little sister who was in first grade then."

"No," Leigh screamed and ran outside to the balcony. I followed her and held her for a few minutes as she sobbed on my chest. When she'd calmed down, we went back inside.

"What happened to your sister? Tell me she's OK."

"I told her the next day while we were waiting for the school bus that I'd seen her and dad, and that she needed to tell mom. Leigh, I can never forget the trusting look that little girl gave me as I told her what to do and hugged her. I was her big brother, I was her hero. I was going to save her."

I had to stop for a minute, and Leigh came and hugged me. I gained control of myself.

"OK, sit back down. Rest of the story.

"Laura, my sister, told my mother, who then had a nervous breakdown. She screamed at my father and at my sister, and then came to me—a fourth-grader, remember—and poured out the story of how she'd been sexually abused herself and about her mother's suicide, then closed herself off in a bedroom for over a month. It was at that point in my life that I shut down, closed myself off to all adults. I would do what they told me to do, but I would never let them know what I was thinking or ask questions except when absolutely necessary. If I wanted to know something, I would try to find it out in books. I hid myself in books.

"I felt sorry for my mother with what I now knew about her past, and I tried to protect my sister, trying to be in the way every time my dad was home, but I was just a kid. How old are you in fourth grade? Nine? What could I do?

"The Navy started sending dad out on nine-month-long cruises on his aircraft carrier, and the emotional tension eased until it came time for him to come back. On one of his trips back, while mom was at her part-time job, I walked in on my father and sister again. He was trying to force it in her mouth and yelled at me to get out but didn't stop. When I talked to my sister the next day, she was crying and scared. I told my mother myself this time.

"She screamed at my father again, and put my sister and me in the car and drove off with us. After half an hour of driving in total silence, she pulled over to the side of the road, shut off the engine, and broke down, sobbing in a way I hope never to hear from any human being again. 'I don't know what to do, I don't know what to do,' she kept crying, head on the steering wheel, and we tried to console her. Can you believe it, the young abused kids trying to console the parent?

"Dad moved out for a while, and my mother took refuge in returning to the Catholic Church, dragging my sister and me with her. We had to switch to parochial schools, and I had to become an altar boy. In one of those sick twists life loves to throw up, one of the priests tried to molest me, but I was clever enough to resist it and knew I couldn't tell my mother or anyone else.

"My mother was a broken woman, barely able to cope with the outside world's demands. Her own childhood had crippled her enough that she simply couldn't deal with what had happened except to somehow deny its import. She had no skills. Out of economic and emotional necessity, she let dad move back in, and we lived years of horrible tension, relieved only when dad was sent back out to sea.

"I walked in on my father trying to molest my sister one more time, and she was resisting. This time I yelled at him to stop it and screamed I'd call the police if he ever did it again. That, and the talk I had with my sister the next day, stopped it. My father treated me with complete contempt from that day on.

"Then my father had an affair with a neighbor, and my mother swallowed pills when she found out. They pumped her stomach, and she survived. As much as I felt sorry for her, I began to resent her for her cowardice and weakness in not leaving the man or forcing him to get help. He was obviously sick.

"It was somewhere around there that I had some kind of a breakdown. I still don't know what it was, but I think it was related to reaching puberty with all those extra complications. You must know what it's like coming into your own sexuality after you've seen all that. You must have gone through it, too. For almost ten days, I felt completely enclosed in an impenetrable capsule. People would talk to me, and I could answer them, but I refused all other communication. My mother and my teachers kept asking me if I was alright, and I would answer with a simple 'yes' and nothing more. I felt totally isolated from all feeling. All I wanted to do was be left alone or sleep. Then it lifted. I've never understood it.

"For a long time, I wasn't the same after that. I could be talking to a teacher and then just disconnect from all that and connect to the dirt on the window, the fly buzzing in the office, the spindles in her chair. Listening to someone talking, I would disconnect from their speech and notice the asymmetry of their face, or how light illuminated the blood vessels in their ears, stuff like that.

"And I was emotionally frozen. I understand now that it was because I was afraid to feel. As soon as I felt anyone, a teacher, a classmate, a priest, getting close to breaking through the protective membrane, I pushed them away, often cruelly.

"When my mother pushed me to become a priest, I grabbed at the chance to leave home. I was thirteen the day I got on the Greyhound bus to leave for the seminary, and I felt so much guilt climbing into that bus, looking back at my mother and sister crying at the abandonment, that I had to run to the toilet at the back of the bus and throw up.

"It was a minor seminary—high school—and for three years I hid the fact that I had no religious feelings or belief at all. I resisted sexual molestation one more time, by one of the religious brothers.

"Ironically, those years in the seminary were my salvation. Silence was enforced almost everywhere outside the classroom, and they had a good library, so I continued to piece myself together through what I read and then thought about in the hours of meditation. Leigh, I'm not religious, you know that, but I will be eternally grateful to those priests for giving me a top-notch education and instilling in me a lack of materialism. You've seen I don't care about things or money other than making sure I have enough to live on, though I'm really attached to this house now.

"The seminary gave me maybe the best gift of my life, a joy in the life of the mind. I can let my mind wander for hours, literally hours and, along with reading, it's my favorite entertainment. Those hours of silence in the seminary gave me that.

"Anyway, I left the seminary and had one last horrible year in a public high school before college, and you've heard how hard I had to work to put myself through that, but I wasn't bitter about it. At least I was getting to do it and was getting to read and hear more things that helped the recovery from my childhood. Then, just as I was hitting my stride, developing a social side and coming into my own, I had to face what to do about Vietnam, and went into exile.

"That first night in Paris, though, when I walked out of the Gare du Nord and saw that city, Leigh, that was redemption, those lights, those smells. I put my backpack down and memorized the scene, and I said to myself that no matter what life had given me up until then, we were now even for this, for what I saw spread out in front of me. Sometimes I think my life, my real life, began that moment.

"So that's my tale. Do you understand why I didn't want to tell you the other day?"

Leigh got up and came over to me and put her arms around me. "You poor man. I had no idea. You come across as the Rock of Gibraltar. No one would ever guess."

"Leigh, I'm like you. I never tell people the story because I don't want my social persona to be that I'm an object of pity. I rose above all that. My life is very much something else."

"How's your sister?"

"She's like me. She survived it all, understands it all, and is doing fine. She married a good man and has three great kids. She's happy and we're close. She told me once that being able to talk about it later in life did save her."

"What about your mom and dad?"

"Dad died . . . Alzheimer's. He apologized to my sister before he got sick but would never see a counselor. Mom is alive and finally happy, very involved with the Church."

We were quiet for a few minutes, a silence which she broke first. "I love you, John. I wasn't lying the other day when I told you I feel safe with you. Now I know why."

"I love you, too, Leigh. You're the only one I've ever told all that to, the *only* one," and I turned her to face me, "but Leigh, I'm serious. I couldn't stand to have you thinking I cared less for you because of what you told me. That would break my heart. If anyone is damaged goods, it's me with all my mental quirks, strange man who cobbled himself together out of things he read in books, lines from movies, overheard conversations, college lectures. I'm strange, I know that."

"Sweet strange, John, sweet."

We were quiet for a while. She spoke first.

"Isn't it funny how Thomas with his screwed up childhood, you with yours, me with mine, and young Tom with his all wound up together? Do you think we somehow sensed it about each other?"

"I don't know. How would you explain Doug? He had a normal childhood."

"Well, let's start torturing the little shit to make up for it," she said, and we both laughed, grateful for a bit of levity.

"My childhood is why I never want to have children," she said a minute later. "Is that why you don't want them?"

"I don't know, Leigh. I just never felt the need to have kids, and I hate the idea of nature manipulating me into it. I want to spend my time alive living and examining my own life, not creating others."

We got into bed, which led to the gentlest sex we'd ever had. When it was over, she turned on her side, and I cuddled up to her back, one arm under her pillow, the other over her holding a breast, our usual position. Before she fell asleep, she turned her head back to me. "Do you think we wound up in Key West to have the childhood we got screwed out of?"

I thought about it. "Don't know, Leigh. I'm just amazed we all survived with a sense of play at all. I mean, look at young Tom and his sense of play. I would've thought that children from abusive families would be warped a different way. Maybe it's the play that heals us, I don't know, but I've come to love that in a person more than almost anything else."

She snuggled in deeper and fell quickly asleep. I slowly pulled my arm out from under her and lay on my back looking at the night sky through the gable-end windows, re-playing the exchange of confidences. Unwelcome and repressed images began flooding my brain.

I got up quietly and went to the bathroom, kneeling and retching as quietly as I could. She heard me and walked in, knelt next to me, crying, arms around me, stroking my back.

Far beyond my modest talents and insights to explain love, along with joy the most inexplicable of emotions. Like most attractive and even semi-attractive males on the island, I'd had more sex than we'd ever imagined possible in our puberty. At a certain point, though, there was for me a decreasing pleasure in the conquests. How many times can you repeat picking up a beauty at the Monster, charm them with a description of life on the island, take them back to their hotel room for wild, animal sex, before the repetition, itself, begins to diminish the pleasure? When do you begin to feel like the tour guide who's worn out his love for the wonder he's describing? What's left is the porno-addict's search for preferred examples of certain body parts. It was a voyage I had already decided diminished a person.

In my first years on the island, Leigh had been gone a lot, up in New York taking fund managers to task about her trust fund, then taking over its management herself when she reached the stated age, then dealing with her father's death. We had been hit-and-miss lovers, always happy to see each other again, always jealous—but hiding it—when we saw the other out in public with someone else, always comfortable in bed together after the first jealous scraping-away of possible fun-in-absence.

The exchange of confidences about our damaged pasts changed us both. Leigh became gentler and less bossy; I stopped playing macho male to compete. Looks across a table now carried personal information, now totally personal.

Falling in love usually precedes being in love. We'd put the cart before the horse.

I had loved her as a friend and happy sex partner for years, but now I fell in love. Did her making herself that vulnerable make that happen? Did common, shared damage make it possible?

I had to recognize, too, that something profound had changed in me since my arrival on the island. Academic excellence, high intelligence, a certain appreciation of culture: the standards I had once judged people by and which I thought were the lanterns to lead me out of my personal darkness, were joined now by what? Kindness? Generosity? Playfulness?

For the second time in my life, I was in love. I analyzed it from every angle because I didn't want to be hurt again. Didn't do any good to analyze it, which may be the ultimate mystery about the emotion. I was in love, in love with a rich woman.

The big head said this was a recipe for disaster: Mr. Sackcloth-and-Ashes in love with a plutocratic princess.

The heart said two damaged people had found each other and deserved the happiness from the discovery.

Little head had succumbed that first night together.

Love, strange emotion in a strange animal, giving even simple actions moment, gilding even the most banal shared experiences.

Leigh began spending most weekends at the Bakery, and the boys loved it, being teased and teasing in return. On Friday night, if I knew I didn't have to work the next day, I would bike to the motel where she worked 'til nine as desk clerk and wait for her to get off. We would go somewhere on the water for a couple drinks, then bike back to the Bakery together.

With her asleep next to me, I would watch the night sky until I heard the downstairs door open and hear a woman's voice—Tom was home with a date—then the door again, Doug was home, too. The world was out there now, and we were in here. I would slide one arm back under her pillow, throw the other one over her and settle into my own sleep.

Sixteen

A month after the exchange of confidences with Leigh, after work one day, I was lying in my hammock on the balcony off the back of my bedroom, drinking in the beauty of the transition from summer to winter. The sunlight on the island changes in November to the kind of distilled and pure light of the American Southwest, scouring out the texture of wood siding, tree trunk scars, the mason's strokes in stucco. The sudden withdrawal of summer's heat and humidity gives you new, clean breath and energy.

There was a knock on my bedroom door. It was young Tom. He often came up to my bedroom to talk. I think it pleased or comforted him to know he had this kind of close, personal access that other employees—Doug and I now had ten—didn't. He plopped down in a chair on the porch, but was silent, the usual prelude to a favor I wouldn't approve of: a small loan until payday, or for me to pick up his week on so he could cavort with yet another tourist.

"What's up, kid?"

Silence.

"Come on, kid, what's up?"

Like that first visit from Thomas and Leigh, where Thomas had spoken words that had changed my life's direction, I was only seconds away from words that changed it again.

"John, will you be my dad? You don't have to adopt me or anything like that," words rushing over each other, "just be my dad and let me call you daddy."

I put down McCullough's *Path Between the Seas* that I had been planning to read. Coati-mundis, orchids, and my very own case of malaria in Panama were childhood memories. I was looking forward to this history of the Canal.

"Give me a minute here, Tom. That's a life-changing thing to be asking someone."

He looked hurt. "If you don't wanna do it, just tell me," and he started to get up. "I know you're a big brain and everything, and you probably don't want a dummy like me for a kid."

"Tom, sit back down."

Addressing that statement, saturated with hurt and insecurity bought me time. "Tom, I never think of you as a dummy, and your intelligence or education has nothing to do with my feelings for you. You know I care about you, love you in fact, just like I love Doug. You must know that by now, don't you?"

"Yeah, I know all that, John, but I need me a daddy."

"Alright, let me ask you a few questions. I'm honored by you asking, but why me instead of Doug?"

"Doug and I are more like buddies or brothers. We goof around, and I know he loves me, but you're the dad type, serious and always telling me what's right and wrong and correcting me."

"Let me ask you another question. Why do you want someone to be your dad in the first place?"

"John, you know I never met me my dad. The whole time I was growing up I'd be looking at faces in crowds wondering if one was his. When the other kids got met by their dads at school, or when their dads would be there watching them at ballgames, I almost couldn't stand it, and my heart liked to have died inside me, John. Sometimes I even made me up a dad I could talk about with the other kids." The pain in his voice was palpable.

"Tom, this is a big thing you're asking. If I agreed to it, it would change our whole relationship."

"How?"

"If I were your father, I'd feel responsible for all your behavior. I'd have to be able to tell you sometimes you can't do things. I think you go out partying too often, and you drink too much, for example, but most of the time I don't say anything because we're just friends, and as long as it doesn't affect me, I figure it's mostly your business. If I were your father and you didn't listen to me, I'd have to punish you somehow, do you understand that?"

"Sure, that's what dads are supposed to do, and I know I need it."

"Tom, you say that, but what if I told you to do something, or not do something, and you didn't want to listen to me? I'd be upset. I might even be distressed."

He grinned at the word that had become our personal joke. "Well, we might have an argument, maybe, but I'd have to listen to you because you'd be my dad. Please be my daddy, John, please."

"Tom do you *really* understand how serious this is? If I agreed to accept you as my son," his face lit up at the word, "it would mean a lifetime commitment for me. I couldn't do something like this half-assed, or just whenever it felt good. And if I did it, I'd expect the same commitment from you. Do you understand that?" He nodded.

"Are you sure you understand? It would have to be a two-way street. If something happened to me, you'd have to help me because you'd be my son, not just a friend."

"If you was . . ."

"Dollar! Subject-verb disagreement."

"See, who else takes the trouble to correct me all the time? If you *were* my dad, I'd take care of you no matter what."

"Tom, this would mean a change to my whole life. You have to give me some time to think about it."

He looked disappointed. "How much time?"

"Look, let's talk again tomorrow night. But whatever I decide, it won't change how I feel about you."

"I know you love me, John, but I need me a daddy. Please."

"Tom, don't pressure me. This is too important to be decided in a few minutes. You know me a little bit now. If I agree to something this important, it's a lifetime thing," I repeated. "I need time to think about it."

"You're going to think about it, though? Seriously? Promise?"

"I promise." He got up and turned to leave, then turned back.

"What?"

"Can I say something else?"

"Of course, kid. This is too important to keep anything back."

"You asked me why I want you to be my dad. John, I feel safe here with you, and it feels real good."

I hid the shock I felt and stood up and took his hands. "Tom, look at me," and he did. "Kid, I know what it's like not to feel safe, and you telling me that is a great compliment," and I gave him a hug. "I have to think about this, though. This is big."

He left. The digging of the Panama Canal would have to wait.

I felt unanchored by his request, even more so by the statement that he felt safe with me. How could Leigh and he have said the same thing? More to the point, how could anyone feel safe with someone who had never felt it himself? Even at the most tranquil moments in my life, safety had always felt provisional. You walked in on your father trying to fuck your sister, or the bill you couldn't pay arrived, or a farewell note from a lover was left on your table, or "Greetings from the President" or a clever immigration agent saw that your documents were false. There was no safety.

My mind cast wider nets as I watched the sun paint the fronds of the coconut palm next door. I loved this nuanced autumn light now even more than the summer sun's exuberance.

What is the obligation of one with more intelligence to one with less, the one with some money to one with none? Given that I had risen from near the bottom, did I have an obligation to anyone else from there?

What obligations did an education, however achieved, impose on a person? Were the treasured dinner conversations I had on the island and in Europe the ultimate reward for years of studying? Or were there obligations that came with all that work—mine and the teachers'—to drag a human brain out of the cave and put me at those tables? Did that put me in debt to people less educated and, if so, how much debt? I was being tested.

I had always asked as I passed through my personal moltings that there be the reward of a life not ordinary. Dangerous request. Life on the island had been more richly textured and satisfying than anything I could have imagined. Would this intersection of two such unlike souls have happened anywhere else?

At a certain moment in my meanderings, I realized that what mattered most in his request was the simple word: "dad." When he'd posed the question, that word had pulled emotions out of me I had deliberately buried. Damaged and shown no love by my own father, I could understand the power of "dad." I could only imagine the comfort of a child being able to approach a father and ask for help, or get a hug or an arm around the shoulder. I'd never had it.

Entering a territory for which I had no map or guide, I knew I shouldn't make the decision without outside perspective. I called Leigh and Thomas to schedule a Louie's meeting, and the next morning grabbed Doug on his way out and extended the same invitation.

Tom came upstairs again the next night after work. We talked as I showered. I'd been under a house where the cat shit was abundant.

"Have you thought about it?"

"Yeah, but can I have my shower first?"

"Sure. I'll wait for you in your bedroom. Got any beers in your fridge?"

"I think so. Crack one open for me, too."

I wrapped a towel around my waist when I finished, and then it was time to talk. I sat on the bed, Tom on the sofa. "Tom, this is the most difficult thing anyone has ever asked me." He looked down.

"Tom, you're asking me to be your father, your dad. Think about it. Who are the closest people in a human's life: mother, father, brothers and sisters, wife and children. I want to do it for you . . ." I couldn't finish the sentence because he'd jumped on the bed, hugging me. I made him sit back on the sofa and listen to me.

"If you're going to be my son, Tom, there'd have to be some changes. Don't drink so much. Get your GED. Learn the stuff that Doug and I are teaching you."

"But I'm a dummy."

"Stop saying that, and do what I ask. It will make your life better, and you have to do it if you're really going to be part of the family. You also have to be more serious about money and quit spending everything you make."

"You just tell me what to do, and I'll do it."

"Tom, this is serious. If I agree to be your dad, you'd damn well better listen to me."

"I promise I will. Can I call you dad now?"

"No. I have to talk to Thomas and Doug and Leigh first, and see what they think. This is a biggy, kid; I need advice. We're meeting at Louie's on Sunday."

"If you're talking to them, you must be thinking you're gonna do it."

"I'm thinking. Do you have any idea how big this is for someone like me to take on a kid? I never wanted kids. Now get out of here. I have paperwork to do."

"Alright. When you gonna let me know?"

"In a week. Go! One of us has a business to run."

It was a week of intense thought. How could any sentient human reject this naked a request? If my existence could give this pleasure to a wonderful kid, how could I say no? There were no guidelines here. Dad, daddy . . . of all the roles I'd been asked to play by all my teachers, lovers, and friends, this was the most unexpected and potentially life-changing.

Doug and I arrived at Louie's first and took our favorite table and ordered our usual Bloody Mary's from Marvin.

"What are you two queens up to these days?" he asked when he delivered the drinks, ducking just in time to avoid the sea-grape branch.

"Need I remind you once again that that would be one queen and one king to you, sir," I retorted.

"Don't get your panties in a wad, bitch, or I'll spit in your soup. How many people in your party today, Sir King?"

"Four, and we want royal service."

"Tip me enough, and I'll give you whatever you like, you bon-bons" and walked off just as Thomas and Leigh arrived. The two of them could have been models for a yachting magazine: Leigh in white pants again and tight-fitting, sleeveless lime-colored top; Thomas, deeply tanned, in khaki pants, an aqua-colored Polo shirt, and Ray-Bans.

Marvin, back to take their drink order and to confirm that we wanted our usual appetizer, conch fritters, belted out: "Jesus. Now we got more royalty than a coronation in Westminster Abbey."

"Our drinks, please, peasant," Leigh ordered.

"Yes, your Majestyness."

Our brunches had developed small, endearing traditions: the joking with Marvin, the game with the fifth conch fritter and lately, instead of shared hilarity over a crime report in the *Mullet Wrapper*, Doug or I would recount a tale of things gone wrong on a job. In construction work, I'd learned, things often go wrong, and when they do, they usually go magnificently, monumentally wrong.

Leigh tasted her Bloody Mary then looked up. So before we hear what mystery is important enough for you to pay for brunch, does either of you have a goody for us?"

Doug had a big grin on his face. "Oh, do I ever! It's so good, though, that I think you need to pay something for it."

Leigh looked at him. "Doodle-head, John's already paying for the meal, so tell us or I'm going to spread the rumor around town that you have herpes."

"Alright, alright . . ." and he began the story. "I'm wiring the second-story addition to an expensive house on Casa Marina Court. The owner is mean, stingy, and arrogant. Rick, the contractor, had to tear off the existing roof to form tie beams on top of the existing concrete block walls to support the second story. Of course, that exposes the entire first floor to the elements where the owner has left all his furniture and—can you believe the stupidity?—has just installed *white* wall-to-wall carpeting. Then he and his wife left town after warning Rick it's his ass if anything got damaged.

"Poor Rick is having a nervous breakdown spreading acres of tarps at the first sign of a cloud and supporting them from underneath to spill any rain off the house. They get the formwork and steel installed with zero damage to the house, a miracle really, and they're ready to pour the beams. I feel sorry for him, so I stay to help him. It's hot, it's Friday afternoon, and all we want is to finish and hit the Parrot. The concrete pump arrives, and the first concrete truck comes rolling down the street." Doug looked over at me. "Remember how nervous that made us when we did the pool?"

"Finish the story," Thomas ordered. "I'm about to piss my pants because I think I know what's coming."

"Well, Rick stayed down by the pump to relay orders from us on top, and we started pumping, filling the formwork for the perimeter beams first. Rick's crew had entombed the entire downstairs, wall-to-wall, with extra tarps, but it was still nerve-wracking as we balanced on top of the forms and shifted those heavy hoses around making sure we didn't overfill a form, or drop the hose.

"It took over an hour to fill the outside forms. Now there was just the form on top of the wall running down the middle of the house. We moved the hoses and started pumping, and the form began to fill up, but very, very slowly."

"Oh hell, I do know what's coming next."

Doug nodded.

"We pumped and pumped, but the form wouldn't fill above a certain point. Rick yelled up asking how high the concrete was in the form, and when the foreman told him, he screamed 'STOP!' to us and the pump operator. Once the pump stopped, we saw the concrete slowly subsiding in the form. We all jumped down and followed Rick to the front door, which wouldn't open. We ran to the back door and opened it, and lifted up the tarps. Inside, like tongues of lava, concrete had spread across the floor, soaking the carpet and wrapping itself around the legs of all the furniture."

"We traced the lava flow back to the laundry room, which had a dropped ceiling, or used to have a dropped ceiling, and above that ceiling, hidden from view, they'd punched an AC duct through the concrete block wall on top of which we were pouring the beam."

Leigh looked puzzled. "I don't understand."

"Leigh, the formwork we were pouring concrete into sat on top of the concrete block wall, and concrete blocks are hollow. The wet concrete went down those voids, crushed the AC ductwork, and started pouring out the hole. In the laundry room, it collapsed the dropped ceiling and filled the washer because its lid was up, and poured on out into the living room."

Thomas was already laughing, but Leigh was open-mouthed. "That poor man, what did he do?"

"What could you do? We tore out the rest of the ductwork, and some of his guys sealed the hole with plywood. Then we all shoveled concrete into buckets and wheelbarrows before it could set up and bucket-brigaded it back up into the form. When that was finished, we cleaned up as best we could, and all went to the Parrot and got drunk. I haven't heard what's happened since. Imagine making that phone call to the owner."

We all laughed and shook our heads. Then it was my turn.

"You all know Jeff Nablo, Gail's boyfriend?" They nodded that they did. We'd all met him at Las Palmas, Gail's restaurant, and he was the one who got a Beetle Cat first.

"Jeff headed up the renovation for this rich couple from South Africa or Australia, I forget which, and I can't distinguish the accents. Jeff's a perfectionist and drove us all crazy, but we all respect him, and we felt sorry for him on this job because the wife is a real nut case. Anyway, fast forward to the end of the job. Jeff finished it just short of having a nervous breakdown. Two weeks after he turned the house over, the wife called him. You're not going to believe this. She complained to Jeff that the showerhead in the master bathroom was too high because the water wasn't hot enough by the time it hit her head!"

They all laughed, and Leigh stated the obvious: "Didn't he tell her to turn up the hot water?"

"He told her that, and she answered in a very exasperated voice that, of course she'd tried that, and it didn't work. The water was still too cold when it reached her. Jeff paid the plumber to lower the showerhead four inches, and the wife called Jeff, triumphant . . . 'I told you it was the showerhead.'"

Thomas looked at me in disbelief. "You made that up, John. No one on the planet's that stupid."

"Thomas, trust me, I'm not imaginative enough to think up something like that."

Thomas told us about a job he might have coming up, and then Doug turned to me. "OK, John, I know why you've invited us, but let's hear it."

I explained Tom's request and my answer. Thomas and Leigh didn't react immediately.

Doug started. "He told me he'd asked you and asked me to lobby you."

"What did you tell him?"

"That it was a heavy thing to ask another person, and that the decision had to be yours."

"Doug, does it bother you that he asked John and not you?" Leigh asked.

I jumped in before Doug could answer. "That was my first concern, Doug."

"It doesn't bother me at all, and I don't think it could affect my relationship with him or my feelings for him. If I had to define it, I guess I look at him as a younger brother. I love him that way, and he knows it."

"That's how he describes it."

Thomas looked at me. "Have you already made a decision?"

"No. It's one I don't want to make without advice from you guys and without giving it more thought."

Thomas looked away for a few seconds, then turned back to me. "So if you haven't made a decision yet, that must mean you're considering doing it, is that correct?" I nodded.

"It seems to me, then, that you have to decide, number one, if you really want to do it, and number two, that you should base the choice on whether it'd be a good thing for both of you. Only you can decide if you really want to do it, so I think what we should discuss is would it be a good thing for both parties. Leigh, what do you think?"

"The easy half of the question is would it be good for Tom, and we probably all agree that it would." Everyone nodded. "He's made it obvious his need for a father figure, just look at how he's bonded to the two of you," and she looked at Doug and me "and now he's told John directly about the hole not having a father left in his childhood.

"And we've all seen that strange, wonderful way he's building a happy childhood for himself—now—to substitute for the brutal one he actually had. I'll never forget that night I was there when John read him a bedtime story. You could see the deep, healing pleasure he took from it. So, yes, I think it would be good for him, with some reservations I'll come back to. Your turn, Doug."

"I think it would be fantastic for him. I think it would be another part of the recovery from that grotesque childhood. And John," and he stared straight at me, "I think you'd be perfect for the job, or damned close to it. I've gotten to know you from working and living together at the Bakery, and I can see you're everything he needs: intelligent and serious, a natural mentor, and once you get through that protective barrier of yours, a real softy in a geeky sort of way."

They all laughed at the last part, which helped me cover how touched I was.

"Before you get the big head, though, I have a few reservations, too, just like Leigh."

"Let me see if I can guess them," Thomas offered. "John in the 'father' role becomes too strict on the young lad, trying to mold him into something resembling himself."

Leigh and Doug nodded agreement, and Doug explained: "You're always fair, John, and honest, but you're hard on people . . . on yourself, too, I know, but I'm not sure that that would be the best approach to take with Tom." He stopped, then added, "Mr. Gravitas," and grinned.

Thomas agreed. "I've heard you explain how difficult it is trying to reconcile the big adult male Tom is with the underdeveloped kid inside, so I think you'd have to soften your usual light touch," and he grinned, too.

"Well, I'd never even consider doing it if I didn't have the three of you as my own family now. I'd depend on you to correct me if you thought I was being too harsh."

"Trying to correct you, my love, is *always* a thankless task," Leigh shot back, and they all laughed.

"Come on, guys, I'm not that bad, am I?"

"I'd rather have two root canals," Doug said.

"Six," Leigh added, but gave me a sweet smile.

"Come on, you're exaggerating." All three rolled their eyes.

The usual five fritters arrived, and I didn't even make my usual complaint. Leigh speared the fifth, cut it in two and handed one piece to me. "Special day for you, so I'll be nice."

We ordered a second round of drinks and our usual entrées—eggs Benedict—and Thomas started the discussion of the second part of the issue: would doing it be good for me.

Leigh led again. "I know how seriously you'll take it. If you become his father, it will limit your freedom. Some of the time you spend reading now, you'll have to spend teaching him, what? Almost everything. And what do you do about traveling? If he's your kid, you have to take him along with you, at least sometimes, for it to be a real father-son relationship. I think you'd be great at it, with the reservations I mentioned, and I think it could be good for you. It might further humanize Monsieur Le Professeur we all know and love. But are you ready to be father to an uneducated, uncultured man, no matter how sweet or funny he is? There are serious cultural differences here. You're the most intellectual of our little family, and he's the least. He's never going to become you, John. Can you accept his limitations? That's a biggie, John; don't underestimate it. Let me repeat it: he's never going to be a younger version of you."

Doug, the psych major, took his turn. "What do you do, too, if you decide you don't like it? Do you tell him the deal's off, and what would that do to him? Also, part of your job is going to be to change some of the things about him we love most. Now we love his silly playfulness and irresponsibility. He's like a wonderful puppy dog. But he has to grow up, sad but true, and you'd have to force that to happen.

"Something else you'll probably have to accept is that he'll probably never return as much as you give. Kids as damaged as he is suck in all the emotional energy around them and rarely heal themselves enough to reciprocate fully. They do the easy stuff, like telling you they love you, but unselfish actions, giving of any kind, is tough for them. The hardest thing about that is when you're in pain or in need yourself. Instead of commiserating or helping, they often get angry or distant or resentful because you represent their security, and you're never supposed to be weak or vulnerable. Do you think you're ready for all that, big believer that you are in fairness? I saw all that working with abused kids when I was doing my MA in psych. They're sometimes delightful in ways we could never be, but they're still damaged, and they're usually incapable of the full range of emotions."

"I don't know, Doug, I honestly don't know. But, believe it or not, when he asked me, I felt twinges of something, paternal tenderness? Did he sense feelings in me I didn't even know I had?"

"I think animals in need sense which human they can go to," Thomas said. "And I agree with Leigh that it will probably be good for you, too, though there aren't any guarantees. At the very least, he'd have a better father than any of us had."

Doug nodded agreement. "John, in a lot of ways he already sees you as his father. I've never brought it up before, but I've watched him when we're all on a job together and there's a real conflict, pissed off customer, whatever. If he feels threatened by it, he looks around for you and slowly works his way as close to you as he can get, just like when little children feel threatened and back up to their parents' legs. It triggers an automatic response in the parents where they reach down and put their arms on the child. He feels safe if you're there."

By now we'd finished our meal and were ready to order our traditional port—Ten–year Taylor Fladgate—when Marvin showed up with four glasses of it. "On me, folks. It's not often I get to wait on three queens and a royal. . ." he looked at me and pretended to think . . . "pain in the ass! Don't forget to tip. This girl needs a vacation," and he started to walk away, then turned back and looked at Leigh. "Ain't it high time for someone to make an honest woman out of you, girl?"

"Why would I want to do that when it's so much more fun this way?"

We applauded.

"OK, it's vote time," Doug said. "Everyone who thinks John should become Tom's dad, raise their hand."

Three hands rose.

Thomas proposed our traditional toast: "To the family we've made and the island we live on." We clinked glasses, and when we'd finished the port and I'd paid, Leigh made her traditional remark as we were getting up: "Bet we had the most interesting conversation here today."

As we separated outside, Thomas hesitated, then turned around to catch me. "Listen. I just had an idea. If you agree to do this, why not put a probationary period on it, say a year, so if either one of you isn't happy doing it, you have a pre-determined way to get out."

"Good idea. Thanks."

The week I had given myself to make the decision was not conducive to deep thought. I came home angry several nights from pitched battles with a rich customer who got a perfect ten on the asshole scale, and only a couple stiff drinks and a dip in the pool calmed me down. Tom kept giving me questioning, expectant looks all week, but I was determined to give myself the full week.

I had come from an unbroken but dysfunctional family that had damaged me greatly; then was further damaged, though educated, by the Catholic Church. Leigh knew all the stories, Thomas and Doug some. I had survived it all, triumphed over it I believed, and mostly on my own, but my entire childhood had been marked by mistrust of all adults. How much faster would I have healed had I been willing to expose my damaged soul to someone worthy? Tom deserved enormous credit for doing that with me.

I have depended on writers for knowledge and wisdom, and I now remembered Mailer's observation, something to the effect that the most important things about life concealed themselves. The feelings pulled out of me by this young and damaged man had been hidden even from me.

Doug, Thomas, and Leigh each spoke to me a couple times during the week, checking to see if I had decided yet, or to see if I wanted to bounce any other ideas off them. Leigh was especially sweet. "I think it's wonderful that you would even consider it, John, and I know why now. You're such a softy under that cold, intellectual mask. He's a great kid, and you'd be great at it, but just make sure you want to do it. It's a big responsibility."

By Friday I had made my decision and let everyone but Tom know, and swore them to secrecy. Leigh, Thomas, and Doug hid upstairs in Doug's room after work. I waited for Tom downstairs in the great room, sitting on a sofa reading. I heard the front door open, and a minute later he walked past me on the way to his room.

"Could you bring me a beer from the fridge, son?"

"OK." One second, two seconds, three seconds, then it hit him, and he turned around. I stood up. He looked at me, and I nodded.

"You're gonna to do it? For real, for real?"

"For real, for real."

He let out a whoop and ran over to me, picked me off the floor, hugging and kissing me. "Dad, dad, dad . . . I got me a daddy."

Leigh was carrying a cake when the three of them came downstairs. "We heard the yelling, so we guessed it was alright to show ourselves." She put the cake on the table and took Tom over to look at it. Spelled out in big letters on the top was: "LIKE FATHER LIKE SON," and then: "JOHN AND TOM."

Doug put on Copland's *Fanfare for the Common Man*. "Come on, this merits it."

Tom started crying, and everyone started hugging him, and it turned into the kind of emotional moment that embarrasses me. Doug filled glasses of champagne for all of us. Leigh made the toast: "To Father and Son." We clinked, and then I went over and looked Tom in the eye and toasted: "To my son."

"To my dad," and the other three applauded.

I waited for a second of quiet.

"Tom . . . son . . . I went looking for a quote I remembered from college and found it in one of my old college textbooks. It's Schiller, a German writer. 'It is not flesh and blood, but heart, which makes fathers and sons.' It's my heart, kid, that makes me your dad. Now finish your drink, and let me take us out to dinner. Hurry up and shower and change your clothes."

"Yes, dad," he answered, dragging "dad" out in such a perfect imitation of an exasperated child tired of obeying orders that we all started laughing again.

Dinner was at Las Palmas. As we drank and laughed and celebrated, how could I not think back to that night years before, and my fear about the wisdom of my decision to move to Key West? At a certain moment, Leigh and Thomas put their hands on mine. "Remember?"

The laughter and obvious love at our table, the jokes swapped back and forth with Gail and the waiters, were a comfort and affirmation. What if I hadn't done it, moved here? What if I hadn't bought the ticket with the left-over single?

At a certain moment while they were talking and teasing and laughing, the perfect clarity of what I'd agreed to hit me, like the focused vision that hits when you first get stoned, and the sunset you're looking at becomes SUNSET. I looked across the table at the young man whose shirt Leigh had just dropped an ice cube into, and he caught my eye and gave me a thumbs up. This was the least ordinary thing I had ever done in my life, and I felt . . . too many things to describe.

We all biked back to the Bakery for cake and more champagne. When Thomas and Leigh had left, I asked Tom to come to my room.

"Tom, this was a big decision for both of us. Thomas suggested we have a one-year trial period so if you or I decide we don't like it, we can back out. I think that's a good idea. What do you think?"

"I know I won't change my mind, and I hope you won't, dad, but OK, if you think it's best, dad," and he grinned. "I can't believe it, I just can't believe it, I got me a dad!"

"Yes, you do, son," and he grinned ear to ear at the word, "and this dad is telling you to get to bed. We're all working tomorrow."

He bear-hugged me. "Thanks, dad. I promise I'll never let you down, or if I do, you just take the belt to me." The image of me trying to spank someone as big and strong as he was made me laugh.

In bed, looking again at the moon shining through the gable-end window, I gave thanks for the sanctuary that our house, our *home*, had become, and marveled at the power of two simple three-letter words, "dad" and "son."

I had thought Tom would prefer to keep our relationship private because of its unconventional nature. Two days later I was on a job that Doug and he were wiring for me. I was there to do a material take-off for the siding we were going to replace and was in a hurry. Tom was drilling through some studs for the wiring, and I watched him for a minute.

"Tom, you're getting sloppy. Drill those holes closer to the center of the studs, or we'll have to put protector plates on all of them. Use the right-angle drill and a shorter bit if you have to."

I was headed out of the house when I heard one of the plumber's helpers ask him: "Who's the hard ass?"

"That's my dad," Tom answered. "You think he's a hard-ass here, you oughtta see him at home. He fines me five dollars every time I say 'ain't.' Can you fuckin' believe it? Five bucks!"

Seventeen

In Paris, I had watched out my window as they tore down the pavilions where the central market, Zola's "the stomach of Paris," had fed the city for over a hundred years. Along with the demolition of the beautiful cast-iron buildings, an entire way of life was being destroyed. The café-restaurant life where the top and bottom of Parisian society had mixed in mutual fascination was gone forever. Men in white tie or even opera capes and women in evening gowns had gone there after the theater or opera or cabaret for onion soup, seated at tables in the same rooms where butchers in their bloody aprons, *putes* (the prostitutes, who serviced the workers), and the poor stood eating and drinking at the zinc bars only inches away. All gone.

An authentic human commerce had been surrendered to industrial efficiency. The liveliest neighborhood in the world's most beautiful city died, right outside my door. The glorious clamor of night-long activity and singing in the streets was replaced with a sad silence. France was surrendering to the modern world to get all that traffic out of the city. It broke my heart. When the demolition notice was posted on the entrance to my sub-standard apartment building, I resigned my job and left. My drunken, night-long goodbye walk through humankind's greatest artwork, Paris, ended on the Pont

Neuf. I looked towards the Place Dauphine, and tears of both gratitude and sadness fell into the Seine. How could I not feel grateful for having had this? How could I not feel sad?

I had never expected to fall in love again—too strange a person— or to live in as wonderful a place again, but fate had been twice kind.

Girding up every morning to go to work on the old wooden houses on an island I had come to love, I gave thanks; thanks for the feeling of inclusion I got with my Cuban coffee at the M & M Laundromat and hanging out at the Parrot with my fellow construction workers, thanks for being able to earn my living from something that I loved, and thanks for my little family.

I had never expected to bear witness a second time to the destruction of a magical way of life.

Four years after I moved to the island, *The New York Times Travel* section deigned to notice us. One Sunday it announced to the world that we were a quirky tropical island, gay and artist friendly, with decent restaurants, and in the United States (so your money's safe, was understood), and real estate was "dirt cheap."

Planeloads of New Yorkers started arriving the next week, and the week after, and the week after. A feeding frenzy began with prices on everything from mansions to shacks jumping every month, a gold rush electricity in the air. Realtors became the new royalty.

The edgy New York energy we now had to deal with sometimes struck false notes. You'd meet one at the airport and be bombarded with: "What bar's hot? Any new restaurants? Is Pacific Light Orchestra playing anywhere? Any good deals on real estate? Can you score me some drugs?" . . . and that was the first five seconds.

The real estate frenzy fed on itself, as one person bought something they thought was ridiculously cheap, then invited their friends down to see it, and then the friends bought, pushing prices ever higher. People from other, more boring parts of the country, whiffed it and starting buying.

The tragic dimensions to Key West having now been officially discovered began to reveal themselves. As more houses were bought and went up in price, rents went up and wages did not. People who'd lived a long time on the island, people we knew and who gave meaning to our lives, began to leave. Before, working-class people—waiters, carpenters, plumbers—could afford to own a home in Old Town. Now, it was impossible unless both halves of a couple worked two jobs.

The women left first, unable or unwilling to keep up with the exploding costs: Shelley, Thomas' friend with the degree in medieval studies (there were three churches in the Middle Ages with the Holy Foreskin); Wendy, the wife of a shrimper with a straight-A son we all mentored, Wendy who had endeared herself to everyone at dinner one night with her financial naiveté ("I'm so tired of being poor. I just read in the newspaper that a bond trader in New York can make $5 million a year, so I'm going to learn how and just do it for two weeks 'cause that's all the money I'll ever need"); Joan Lewis, a gentle Miami Jewess who'd fallen in love with a Key West fisherman, Lou. Both always lived close to the edge. At dinner one night, Joan bemoaned they were out of money again. Lou, sitting next to her at the table, put his arm around her—man obviously in love—"Joan, don't worry. We're OK. I still got five dollars in my pocket."

How could you not want to wrap your arms around these people? How could you not miss them at parties, dancing with them, affirmation that we were wonderfully different?

Gone, all gone, and dozens more like them.

Apartments that had rented for a hundred sixty to three hundred dollars per month, often with utilities included, jumped to twelve hundred dollars per month, utilities not included. People who had worked twenty-forty hours a week to lead a wonderful, communal life with like-minded people, now had to hold down two or three low-paying jobs to stay in the same apartment or house.

Waiters and bartenders who'd nodded agreement in the past when tourists commented on how laid-back the island was—because it was—were replaced now by dead-tired waiters and bartenders who agreed with tourists when they commented how laid-back the island was because that's what they were trained to say, Key West now being branded as a laid-back Caribbean island. The reality was that it was neither Caribbean (wrong sea), nor laid-back now because of the escalation in house and rent prices.

What was being lost was something that can't be priced, and something Americans didn't seem to care about: authenticity. A cigar-worker's cottage was a working-man's house, usually shotgun-style, whose beauty resided in its simplicity. It housed a working-class family in a way that provided for all their needs, but minimally. The families that grew up in them—we met them on the island all the time—had warm memories of their childhoods in them. When these simple cottages began selling for up to half a million dollars, then got fitted with $100,000 kitchens and $80,000 swimming pools in their small backyards, it seemed as sad to me as those advertisements on TV where an admired actor was now selling larcenous insurance policies.

Those of us who'd arrived before the *New York Times* article were faced with a dilemma. Old Town was our neighborhood, but if we sold what we had, we could buy something cheaper in New Town and finally have a little money to put away, a comfort because we all lived paycheck to paycheck. In reality, we didn't have a choice. As adjacent properties were improved, the assessment went up on the whole neighborhood, leading to higher taxes and insurance. Everyone was pushed farther and farther out of Old Town. To go out at night now required a choice: to bike it, more dangerous because of having to take more heavily traveled streets, or get a car, which meant restraints on drinking. Getting together with friends and acquaintances now started taking place in each others' homes, still wonderful, but the public, communal social life that had been even more wonderful and so much fun, began to die.

What made the trend most disheartening was that this latest wave of arrivals bought these old houses as vacation homes. As we exited Old Town, it went back to being vacant again for most of the year but now, instead of the vacant houses seeming to whisper the secrets of their past as we biked past them, they seemed to taunt us with: "You can't afford us." Within two years of the *Times* article, Bill and Tony from Fast Buck Freddie's and Leigh were the only people I knew who still lived in Old Town. Tony complained that nine of the ten houses around him were empty nine months a year, a spooky neighborhood of million dollar homes that had once been a neighborhood of full-time residents, all of whom he had known.

The publicity and gouts of money then attracted one of capitalism's least attractive animals: developers. On the south end of Simonton Street, a developer from up there tore down the single-story funky restaurant with tables on the beach where we used to dine barefoot and watch sunset-lit clouds sail majestically above us. A four-story hotel complex rose in its place with mediocre dining inside, a space that could have been anywhere in the country. The restaurant was named after a sitting city commissioner who'd voted to approve the project.

Other developers came. An explosion of building left us with a concrete wall of ugly buildings nearly circling the island: condos, time-shares, and hotels that blocked the ocean views and breezes. Our protests at city commission meetings gained us nothing as rich outsiders made deals with corrupt or unsophisticated locals.

I squirmed through one cocktail party where a man with millions, who'd built one of the worst condos, held forth on the superiority of the Soviet Union's political system as he rested his barefoot, toenail-fungus-deformed feet on a coffee table of Argentinian onyx worth at least fifteen thousand dollars.

Then the Navy decided to surplus several acres it had confiscated from the city during WWII. It was valuable land on the sunset side of the island. A war began over who would buy and develop it. The most bizarre and ultimately successful bidder was a French-Canadian American with demonic blue eyes (his wife's description) and serious body odor who wore a turban (claimed to be Sikh, later Buddhist). He flew most of the city commissioners up to his projects in New England and won the rights to develop the property.

"This project will be an integral part of Old Town, with artist studios and children's playgrounds," he promised the town. Halfway through the construction, a wall went up and Key West, possibly the most democratic town in the country, had yet another gated community, its largest, and the rich fell over themselves buying into it. Nice to live in a raffish town where you can keep the "raff" out after they've waited on your table. There were to be no studios for artists or playgrounds for children.

Why were these rich coming to an island with funky infrastructure and crappy beaches? Why, we asked, ourselves, over and over, were they attracted to a place that celebrated a kind of eccentricity they wouldn't allow in their own lives up there and then seal themselves off against it behind gates?

Why didn't they go away and leave us alone? was the question we most wanted answered.

A short column in the *Mullet Wrapper* one morning mentioned that a cruise ship was coming to the island, a new event. We made our way down to Mallory Square to witness the cruise ship's arrival, imagining the romance of a *Normandie* or the *QE*.

From afar, it was exotic, a big, white ship headed our way. As it got closer to the harbor, Thomas was the first to speak: "My god, it looks like a container ship the way they've stacked those cabins." An oddly proportioned leviathan, taller than the tallest building on the island, snailed its way into the harbor towards us, blowing silt off the bottom that turned the entire harbor milky white as it made its awkward way to the dock.

I was the first to be outraged. "I spent two grand for mitigation and turbidity curtains to keep silt out of the water when I built a seawall on Key Haven last year and look what they've just done. How much sea life have they just killed? This isn't fair."

We drank rum and OJ from our stash and sat on the edge of the dock to watch the whole anchoring, mooring activity. Suddenly three hatches popped open on one side, and people on the dock maneuvered the gangways to them. Once secured, an employee on the boat said something, and hundreds and hundreds of people poured out onto *our* dock and headed towards Duval Street. Watching the disgorgement of humanity required a suspension of disbelief: surely that many people weren't pouring out of one ship. It had to be one of those operatic processions where the same actors raced behind scenes to stride again across the stage to give the illusion of hordes, masses, whatever.

This was no illusion. We threaded our way through it all, past the sites of our fun and went home. We learned later that the city got a disembarkation fee for each disgorged person. We also learned that the slut of a city government accepted a fee less than half of what the Caribbean islands charged.

Like an addict shooting a new drug, the city now went after all the cruise ships. Within months, there were days when four would arrive, more than the docks could handle, and some would have to lighter their passengers in.

Mass tourism is a blight, and in a small place is spectacularly destructive. The disease, a wave of humanity sometimes five thousand or more people at a time, would hit Duval Street, our Duval Street, and this human tsunami flooded up the street seeking souvenir T-shirts and a piece of Key Lime pie, and killed everything original for ten blocks. The Monster, Delmonicos, the hippie leather store, the funky local bars, the craftsman jewelry stores, El Cacique restaurant, Shorty's Diner, all disappeared within two years, replaced by T-shirt shops selling shirts that said: "FARTING IS MY WAY OF SAYING I LOVE YOU" or "SIT ON MY FACE AND LET ME GUESS YOUR WEIGHT." They made a fortune and pushed out everything in its way as Duval Street rents soared. The fast-food restaurants that infected the rest of the country started popping up downtown so tourists wouldn't have to feel like they'd left home. No *picadillo* or *palomilla* steak for these hordes; they wanted Big Macs and fries.

Duval Street, our tribal stomping grounds, the place where we'd all met and reinforced the uniqueness of what we'd done and what we were living, turned into a foreign country, unfamiliar and unfriendly.

One and a quarter million people a year began arriving on the cruise ships, in a town with a population of twenty-eight thousand. There were times now when the downtown sidewalks of Old Town were more crowded than those of New York City. The blown-up silt from the cruise ships fanned out and settled on the coral reef (they denied their impact and scientists fought back and forth over it). The reality was that those glorious underwater forests were under stress already, bleached and blackened, and to snorkel or dive them after the arrival of the cruise ships was another sad proof of man's inhumanity to his home, Mother Earth. Our trips to Simonton Beach with our swims out to the channel marker ended. No one wanted to swim through water turned dirty by the cruise ships.

Then the truly rich arrived, having sniffed god-knows-what money pheromone, people not just millionaires, but multi-millionaires, then two Forbes-list billionaires.

These were not the rich I had known in Paris and London. They were, with few exceptions, a Balzacian mix of incredible wealth and lack of culture, and they arrived in a tiny town where throwing that kind of money around got them all but one thing: inclusion into our little society, which they didn't care about anyway. We were marginalized, we who had created the magical way of life that had attracted attention in the first place. At one cocktail party of rich newcomers, I gave what I thought was a brilliant disquisition on how wonderful our communal life on the island had been, and one man listening said: "How quaint," and I was ignored the rest of the evening.

Thomas suggested at an alcohol-fueled brunch at Louie's that we start telling any visitors to the island how awful things were to try and stem the tide. "Let's tell them about getting stung by scorpions in your shoes, or waking up in the middle of the night with a cockroach as big as your thumb trying to crawl in your mouth, or what about the ants that eat the electrical connections in your stereo or refrigerator and ruin it." We made up a hilarious list, but we were pissing upwind in a hurricane.

A few of the newcomers, the new writers like Annie Dillard, Jean Carper, and Rosalind Brackenbury got the wonderful stew that Key West society was, but they were the exceptions. My family and tribe pulled even further back from public socializing into our homes and backyard gardens.

Several incidents put into focus for me the change to the island's character.

I was helping Doug do the electrical work on a house on White Street that a couple in their late fifties had bought. The husband's brother had been the U.S. ambassador to some Asian country; the wife looked the perfect Washington hostess type. The house they had bought had belonged to two seriously outrageous queens who'd owned a store downtown, and one of their contributions to the house had been to install kissing penises gingerbread trim on it. On three corners of the house, a penis climbed from the wall to meet one dropping from above, and fretwork at the base of each formed the balls. It was unexpected and not immediately obvious because of the fretwork. One day, one of the laborers joked with the wife about the gingerbread, and she froze when she looked at it and the image came into focus. We arrived the next morning to find sheets covering all three pieces, and she ordered the gingerbread removed and destroyed.

Only a few years before, an owner would have laughed and kept the gingerbread or, if they had it taken down, would have displayed a piece inside the house as a humorous piece of the house's history. The same woman sent the town into hysterics a few months later by suggesting at a meeting to address the increasing number of homeless people that the city buy them designer luggage to replace their grocery carts. "That way tourists won't think they're homeless," she said, and was greatly offended when the room burst into laughter.

I was contractor on another job on Southard Street and had to drive the wife one afternoon to a store to choose the tile for the kitchen. The woman, icy and detached, had already suffered a Key West shock the previous week when she'd made the mistake of attending a local artist's wedding. She had shown up overdressed at a ceremony where the bride and groom were barefoot, and the rings exchanged were made of each other's pubic hair.

On the way to the tile store a friend of mine, Lupe Flores, who had the only Mexican restaurant in town, recognized my van and flagged me down. "My car broke down. Can you give me a lift to the restaurant?"

I asked my customer if she minded; it was on the way. She said she didn't. Lupe climbed in and sat on a toolbox behind my seat.

We'd only gone another three blocks when Lupe yelled: "Stop!" I slammed on the brakes, and he jumped out and yelled: "Roadkill" to a man on the sidewalk dressed in jean shorts, combat boots, pink tank-top, and motorcycle jacket. Lupe asked me to wait and ran over to the man, and they talked for a few minutes. When he got back in the van, Lupe was laughing, happy. "I can't believe Roadkill's back in town. Best sex I've ever had." My customer went rigid and went out of her way that afternoon and for the rest of the job to keep as much distance between us as possible. As soon as her house was finished, she sold it and scurried to the safety of turban-head's gated community.

A few weeks later, I was invited to another party at a house I'd done work on. The owners were a tight-fisted, middle-aged couple from Greenwich, Connecticut, but had always been fair. I understood and was amused by these American plutocrats when their prep-school son and a classmate showed up on the job one morning during spring break holding the *Wall Street Journal* and looking for the father. When they found him, I heard the son ask: "Father, can you explain the ladder strategy for bonds to James and me again?" I remembered Thomas telling me about Leigh's description of WASPs and laughed to myself.

When the job was finished, the couple invited me to have drinks one night with friends of theirs. I arrived with a small gift for them, the before-and-after photos of the work we'd done.

There were fifteen or so people seated or leaning against the back porch railing. After introductions had been made and the normal chit-chat, the husband asked me if Key West had really been as wild in the past as they'd heard.

"I don't know what you've heard, but yes, it was pretty wild."

"Why don't you tell us all something about back then? It would be interesting."

I racked my brain for a "good old days" story.

"Alright," I began, "in the old days, the bars in Key West closed at 4 a.m. It was a city ordinance. But Stock Island is in the county with different ordinances, so bars there could stay open all night. People who didn't want to stop partying at 4 a.m. went to the most notorious one out there, the Boca Chica Bar.

"It was pretty rough, lots of fishermen, and there were knife fights, so the owners finally put in a metal detector you had to pass through to get inside. A chain-link fence protected the band. All my friends kept telling me I had to go see the place because it was so wild, but it didn't start hopping until four in the morning. I'm not a night person and I have to be at work early, so I never went, but my friends kept nagging me to see it. So, I decided to do it. I went to bed early Friday night after setting my alarm for three-thirty.

"I was dazed when the alarm went off. Did I really want to do this? I dragged myself out of bed and drove to Stock Island. I passed through the metal detector and went to sit at the bar. The customers were the kind of mix I was expecting: a few tourists on the slum, lots of fishermen, a few coke whores, several gay men out for "seafood" (their name for fishermen or sailors), and lots of trips to the bathroom followed by lots of sniffing and nose-wiping.

"I ordered a drink. Then the man on the stool next to me ordered something from the bartender who said something back that I didn't catch. "What that man needs," the man next to me muttered, "is a long de-rationalization of all his senses." The bartender ignored him, but the synapses in my brain started firing left and right. I have a degree in French lit. That was the French poet, Rimbaud.

"I turned to the man: 'That's Rimbaud.'

"'No shit,' he spat out.

"We were obviously not going to have a deep, literary conversation, but something about the man seemed familiar. It was Phil Caputo, Pulitzer Prize-winning author of *A Rumor of War*.

"I turned away just as another fisherman in white boots walked in with a fairly attractive woman in tow and sat at the end of the bar. Then the fisherman turned to one of the tables occupied by some fisherman buddies. 'Hey, guys, ain't my lady hot?'

"His date smiled and his buddies agreed.

"A few minutes later, the man asked the same question: 'Ain't my lady hot? And she can suck a golf ball through a straw.' The woman tensed up at that, but the men at the table nodded and laughed and agreed again.

"(By this time in my story I'd expected a few chuckles from my listeners on the porch, but they were quiet. I thought maybe I was taking too long to tell the story. Too late, I thought, I have to finish it.)

"A few minutes later the same question. Now the men at the table were irritated, and one of them said: 'Yeah, she's hot, but she's got really big feet.' The woman froze.

"Then another of the men at the table said: 'She's got big hands, too, dude.'

"A third pitched in: 'That ain't no lady. That's a dude, dude.'

"The entire bar tensed up, expecting violence, but the woman, upon closer inspection indeed a man, stood up, put her hands on her hips and looked at the table: 'You assholes wouldn't know a real woman if you saw one,' and sashayed out of the bar, followed a few seconds later by her date. Everyone in the bar was laughing.

"I'd seen enough, so a few minutes later when I'd finished my drink, I left. Outside in the parking lot, the woman was on her knees proving her oral skills. The problem for me was that her date was leaning back against my truck. I cleared my throat to let them know I was there. The 'woman' looked over at me: 'Give me a minute, honey, I'll do you next.'

'Thank you, sweetheart, I appreciate the offer, but I have to leave and that's my truck.' Without missing a stroke, she scooted her boyfriend sideways so I could leave."

When I finished the story, I had expected laughter. Instead, there was an embarrassed and embarrassing silence, and most of the guests looked away from me. I was horrified, humiliated, and excused myself from the party as soon as possible.

On my way home, I realized that among other things, none of my listeners knew who Rimbaud or Caputo was.

In the past at a dinner party, nearly everyone was interesting and had an interesting history to share. I'd listened to a man, now a carpenter, tell the story of his trip through the Panama Canal in a rowboat with a hilarious description of his fight with the Canal Authority bureaucracy for permission; a man, now a painter, describe walking across Alligator Alley in South Florida during a pitch-black night because no one would give him a ride and stepping on the tail of a fourteen-foot alligator that almost out-raced him; a woman, now a waitress, who'd lived a year in dung huts with an African tribe; a man, now a waiter, who'd dived newly discovered antiquities just off Alexandria; a Dutch woman who'd sailed a Dutch river barge across the Atlantic, sold it in New York City, then used the money to buy the house Leigh lived in; a man who'd been on Ken Kesey's bus and described how scared they'd all been at Cassady's drunken and drugged-out, but perfect, threading of a mountain highway. I got to talk to a man who had talked to Kerouac and Cassady!

We were all more than what we did to make a living, and everyone at the table would have known who Caputo and Rimbaud, Kerouac and Cassady were, or would have wanted to know.

Now the conversations with the new arrivals were about real estate, making money, real estate and making more money. Doug and I had more business than we could have imagined, but we counted the money sadly.

Key West had now become KEY WEST, a destination to be marketed. Disney, which had driven a stake through the liquid heart of Central Florida, now had a KEY WEST pavilion. The bridges to our island had been re-built at a cost of hundreds of millions of dollars, so day-trippers from Miami and elsewhere didn't have to worry about dying on Seven-Mile-Bridge.

The airlines discovered the island. Air Sunshine, known by us all as Air Sometime, was gone forever, along with those beautiful planes. Now we had airlines that the rest of the country had. Jets shattered the sky with their noise, landing over two thousand people every day in an airport where, on a good day, fifty people had landed when I first moved to the island.

Working for the newly arrived rich was almost always ugly. I had studied renovations in trips to Charleston, Savannah, and Santa Fe, and my chest had puffed up when I saw that we were better craftsmen. The houses we worked on were in worse shape, and the building codes we had to adhere to were stricter. We were proud, those of us who carried these buildings forward for future generations, but the people buying these buildings began sapping away the pleasure we took in our skills.

Jeff Hagel was recognized by everyone in the trades as an excellent craftsman. He accomplished something epic one afternoon that put paint to canvas on the changes in the customers we now had to work for.

A very rich couple was building a very big house in turban-head's gated community, and in the guest wing there was to be a spiral staircase, wooden and custom-made. The manufacturer kept delaying delivery, and the owner, an attorney from New York, took out his impatience and anger on Jeff because he wanted the guest wing finished *now*. Jeff kept explaining that the staircase had to go in first because it came in one single piece.

"I don't give a fuck," the man snarled one afternoon. "That's your problem. Build the goddamned wing, or you're not going to get paid," and flew back to New York on his Gulfstream.

The next day, Jeff came to the job with a tiny, perfectly scaled balsa-wood sculpture of the guest wing and a tiny perfectly scaled balsa-wood sculpture of the spiral staircase. Together, he and his carpenters worked at corkscrewing the model staircase into the model building, trying first one way, then another, and then they got it and practiced it over and over.

They built the guest wing, and the staircase arrived late one day on a semi, all encased in layers of plastic. I was working with Doug wiring the house, but we all stayed to help, but really to watch. Jeff explained to each person exactly what he was to do, where to stop, when to begin. "If anyone has a question, ask it now. This will only work if everyone knows exactly what he's doing. Remember, we only have two inches of clearance."

It took ten men—five of them unpaid volunteers—two hours: slowly sliding the very heavy staircase through the doors, and then ever so precisely turning it up and corkscrewing it in with guys upstairs pulling it with ropes, inches at a time. Then, one last little turn and it was in, without even a scratch to the walls! We yelled and applauded and back-slapped Jeff and went off to the Parrot to celebrate.

A week later I went up to the owner and his wife and gave them the scale models Jeff had given me and told them the story. "You should display these somewhere in the house when it's finished as part of the house's history. It was an amazing feat" and I described it.

The owner took the models from me and looked at them like I'd handed him a dog turd. I found them the next day smashed up on the trash pile.

Jeff, at even his most exasperated moments, always seemed to manage to keep it in perspective. War's only gift? In the Parrot, one afternoon, we swapped horror stories of rich customers. I told him what Thomas had said to me after watching one multi-millionaire flick cigarette butt after cigarette butt with their non-biodegradable filters into the ocean. "'Their egos reminded him,' he said, 'of those sea animals who vomit out their stomach to envelop their prey.'"

Jeff told me he'd just come back from a trip to Boston where he'd seen a thirteenth-century Japanese scroll painting depicting one tale of the Heiji War. In the painting, richly dressed people crowded around the gate to their palace. Beneath the scroll was the explanation: "Confused nobles reach the palace to find that the gate has been locked. Unable to enter, they mill around helplessly." We both burst out laughing and spent the rest of the afternoon imagining particular rich customers milling helplessly in front of toilets that wouldn't flush, doors that stuck, dimmers that didn't work.

Doug wired the total renovation of a house on the corner of William and Southard Streets for two old queens from somewhere out West who had just bought the place for over a million dollars. Their arrogance was surpassed only by their ugliness, he told me, (one had an inappropriate wig), and it quickly turned into one of the construction nightmares we were all beginning to live through. I got the story over dinner one night.

"Listen to this, John," Doug started after dessert. "It's only the first week of work, and we're still doing the demo. I'm on the second floor. Tom, here, is on the first floor where the two queens are circling him like bees around honeysuckle."

"I didn't punch 'em or say anything, did I? You taught me that."

"No, Tom, you didn't, and we're both proud of you for that."

He gave us two thumbs up.

"Anyway, to continue the story, they never stopped bitching about how much it was costing while adding more and more work to be done. And, of course, every money draw is late, or short, or both. I hate that."

Doug and I high-fived on that.

"Seriously, where else in the world can you order 30 percent more of something and think you don't have to pay for it?"

"Preaching to the choir, my friend," I said, then had to explain the expression to Tom.

"So, we're working there another day, and Adonis here has his shirt off because he's just crawled through a shit-load of fiberglass in the attic, and they make a sex-for-money proposition to him. Our kid here is a genius. He yelled downstairs to me, loud enough for all the plumbers and carpenters and AC guys on the job to hear: 'Doug, the owners just offered me a hundred dollars to suck my dick. Can I take a half-hour break? I'll buy us all lunch.'"

I got up and clapped Tom on the back and shook his hand.

"Two-and-a-half floors of construction workers roared. The two owners scurried out of there like cockroaches out of a kitchen when the light goes on, and they never came back. They hired a construction manager to tell us what to do and the two of them come in to look at the progress at night when we're gone for the day. And, of course, to get even, they're contesting the final bill."

If we had had any doubts about the island now attracting poison, they were permanently erased by the arrival on vacation of one of the most evil men the country had ever birthed: Roy Cohn, McCarthy's pit bull during the witch hunts of the 1950s. His destruction of great diplomats, closeted homosexuals (he was one, himself), and people chosen seemingly at random was an evil that had led to an irrational China policy, which had contributed in part to the Vietnam war.

Doug and I were called to do an electrical service call at a house in a compound on the corner of Varela and Catherine Streets. The AC kept tripping the breaker, and the person renting the house for two weeks, Roy Cohn, was pissed off and threatened to sue. Doug and I both recognized the name, and both agreed we didn't want to meet him.

He was walking out as we walked in.

"Who the fuck are you?"

"We're here to fix the AC," Doug told him.

"Well fix the fucking thing, or I'll sue you. You lazy, island assholes don't know who you're dealing with," and he left.

Doug looked at me. "Are you OK?"

I was in shock, but not from the words. "Did you see his eyes?"

He nodded.

"Those are the most evil eyes I have ever seen in my life."

The house smelled like shit. We were tracing the problem through all the possibilities: bad wire, bad appliance, bad breaker . . . electricity is pure logic . . . to a defective circuit breaker, when the maid arrived. The face said Central America. She came out of the bathroom crying, and I asked her in Spanish what was wrong. She pointed to the bathroom. The toilet seat was covered with shit; the bowl was filled with shit.

"Come look at his bed," she told us. The sheets had shit stains all over them, and there were turds on the bed. "I don't understand," the woman said in Spanish, crying again. "It's like this every day." I held her and told her the man was a sick monster.

We replaced the breaker. A man who had shat on an entire country's body politic was a "scat queen", Doug explained. "Pays guys to shit on him. Matches his soul. Let's get out of here."

Why were these people coming to Key West?

Eighteen

I didn't know when the first powder arrived on the island, or who the delivery man was, but an 800-pound gorilla was in town and taking over. I remember the first time I saw it brought out at a party: the powder on the mirror, the razor blade chops, the straws and rolled up dollar bills, the snorting and nose wiping. I declined the honor, and it was a real honor, coke being more expensive ounce for ounce back then than pure gold.

Coke was a sharp ax chop to our way of life.

My research and personal preferences convinced me to take a pass on it. I was in a small minority (Doug and Leigh passed, too). The arrival of coke at a party stopped all else as people lined up in a bedroom or outside a bathroom for their turn at the mirror. The silly fun of being stoned as joints went around a room gave way to something edgier. The person you were talking to seemed like the same person as before, but I often felt like I was talking to a collection of quivering opiate receptors instead of to a human being as the pure clarity of a coke high kicked in and gave my interlocutor a perfect vision: that he needed to get back in line.

I was often pressured at parties to use it. I always refused, trying to do so in a way perceived as non-judgmental. Every possible reason was offered, the most common one being: "Man, you've never experienced sex until you've had it on coke." Much as I liked sex, I didn't see any need to improve on the pleasure. When they said that to me, my first thought was that they didn't know how to do it right.

My education helped me, too. My favorite writer, Baudelaire, had gone through an opium/hashish phase and had come out on the other side against devoting a life to it, but saying that he doubted mankind could ever live without "artificial paradises," given the brutality of life for most. Our lives were not brutal. We were the most spoiled humans ever to have inhabited the planet. How could you complain about having to work hard for forty hours a week when it gave you every food available, air conditioning or heat when you wanted it, immunity to almost all the diseases that had ever plagued the species? Our shit disappeared with the single push of a handle. I had little sympathy for people I knew who "needed" coke or heroin.

I observed and studied, and didn't see a single person whose life, understanding, or personality improved through coke use. On the contrary, I did begin to see the degradation in lots of lives and personalities and then, as prices for the drug dropped and purity increased, the first addictions. Money began pouring out of the island (and the whole U.S.), going south to Colombia to enrich some of the most evil men on earth and quickly changing, for the worse, every place in Latin America I had visited.

Cocaine changed the social life of Key West. Coke use became a criterion for who was and who wasn't invited to parties. The wonderful small 'd' democracy of Key West socialization took another hit, already under assault by the arrival of the rich.

Some of my fellow construction workers, Parrot buddies, who spent a whole week doing physically difficult work under arduous circumstances, now blew a week's pay for one night's coke blow-out.

Families began to suffer, especially when husband and wife began using. Men began losing their jobs because of coke addiction, and some lost their businesses and entire life savings, yet the drug still maintained its chic. The Full Moon Saloon on Simonton Street got nicknamed The Full Spoon Saloon, and The Chart Room at the Pier House began selling cases of Cristal and Perrier-Jouët to the dealers who hung out there.

Early on, Doug and I had a long talk with young Tom about cocaine and emphasized that its use was not acceptable to us.

Coke fucked up our lives anyway.

Thomas Szuter, the most vulnerable of us all, who already had problems with alcohol, fell hard. In addition to the occasional alcohol-induced disasters we were used to rescuing him from, there were now coke catastrophes. His already strange financial management became totally self-destructive.

Thomas had received a ten thousand dollar commission for a job he'd done up the Keys for the couple who had insulted young Tom at the hospice benefit dinner, James and Emily. Bored and boring, they liked to use Thomas as the court jester because he could be brilliantly funny, even when fucked up. They plied him with alcohol and coke—and the two of them loved coke—to fire him up enough to entertain them.

James paid Thomas the final three thousand dollars of the commission in cash. Three days later, Leigh was on her way back from the jail when she saw Thomas climbing out from under the bridge between Key West and Stock Island, filthy, bruised and bloody, sick and filled with self-disgust. She put him in her car and took him back to her place where she cleaned him up, dressed his wounds, tried to feed him, and put him to bed.

He told Leigh later, that he had started doing coke at James and Emily's; then drunk, too, drove to Key West and started doing more coke and drinking more. Finally, overwhelmed with self-loathing and guilt for what he had done and was doing, he sought out the bridge where he gave away all that remained of his commission to the homeless people living under it. They, in return, supplied him with more alcohol until one of them, under some alcohol-induced delusion, accused him of being a cop and beat him up.

We were distraught. The most talented and intelligent among us, the most original person I'd ever known, was fatally flawed. His addictions were proportionate to his talents and intelligence, and he and we were overwhelmed.

Doug, Leigh, and I met with Thomas at Leigh's apartment a couple days later. He seemed totally ashamed and humiliated. I spoke first.

"Thomas, everyone here in this room loves you, loves you a lot and admires you, but we don't know what to do to help you, yet we have to help you. We can't let you kill yourself this way, you're too much a part of our lives." At that Thomas started crying, and Leigh went over and sat next to him on the bed and put his head on her breast and stroked it as he began sobbing. Doug sat down on his other side and put his arm around him.

When he had calmed down, I looked at Thomas and asked him what we could do. "Thomas, we can't just stand by and watch this. You need help."

"I'm so ashamed of myself."

"Thomas, I don't think that's a helpful reaction. You have addiction problems, and assholes like James and Emily encourage it for their amusement. You have to start by avoiding people like them, and you have to do rehab of some kind or other."

He dropped his head to his chest for a minute, then whispered: "I'm so tired. Can I just sleep for a little bit?" Leigh tucked him in and kissed him, then turned out the light. We left the room and closed the door.

Out in her living room, Leigh fixed us coffee, and we discussed what to do.

"I think he definitely has to go into a rehab program," Doug said, "and probably not here. Can we find a good one in Miami somewhere?"

Leigh offered to do the research, and we agreed to share the expense.

Leigh called me two days later and said she'd found one, and Thomas had agreed to try it. "It's expensive," she said, "six thousand dollars for two weeks, but it's supposed to be effective." Doug and I chipped in two thousand each, a stretch at that time. I found out later it had cost twelve thousand, and that Leigh had made up the difference.

We drove Thomas to the facility together. He looked thin and shaky on the trip up the Keys, but the eyes never stopped. At a hokey pink store in a strip mall in Florida City—"YOUR TRASH IS OUR ANTIQUES"—he asked us to stop. We rolled our eyes as we walked through aisles of worthless shit: old dinette sets with damaged plastic chair seats, nylon-webbed aluminum lawn chairs, and the like. Mr. X-ray eyes scoured everything, then pounced. It was a block of wood, one foot square, two inches thick and impossibly heavy for its size.

We asked Thomas what it was, and he put his finger to his lips to signal us to be quiet. The owner gave it to him for five dollars.

Outside, he showed it to us and let us hold it. "It's an original cigar-worker's cutting block. Look at this," and he turned it to show us the end-grain. There was no visible end grain. "It's lignum vitae. Has to have been cut from a two-hundred-year-old tree. It's native to the Keys but almost extinct now. It grows so slowly that the wood it produces is so tight-grained and heavy that it sinks in water, and it's so dense, they even used it in place of metal for ball bearings during the war. Give this to Eleanor for her cigar factory when you get back. She'll love it."

Back in the car, Thomas kept toying with his find to keep his mind off what was next.

We found the facility in a Miami suburb. It was on beautiful grounds, attractive in an institutional way, and we went through the bureaucratic drudgery of check-in. We each gave him a hug and final words of encouragement and left him looking bereft and crying.

As we headed down Card Sound Road, the pleasant and safer alternative to the dangerous eighteen-mile stretch of US 1 into Key Largo, Leigh asked if we wanted to stop at Alabama Jack's, an open-air, country-western bar at the foot of the tall toll bridge. "I need a drink."

When the drinks arrived, we toasted Thomas: "To Szuter, good friend and artist. May you heal yourself." We ignored the clog dancing that started, watching instead the changing light on the mangroves across the canal next to us, all of us strangely quiet.

Two weeks later, Leigh picked up a chastened, sober, somber but healthy-looking Thomas and drove him back to Key West. We kept him near us as much as possible and he seemed better. It looked like he had conquered one demon completely, cocaine, and the alcohol binges, when they occurred now, seemed to be no worse than when we'd been together for Southernmost Summer.

Leigh knew Thomas' ex-partner, John Hopkins, the man he'd built the house for in Roatan, and let him know what had happened. John, spooked by the politics in Honduras, had been exploring land to build a house on in Costa Rica to escape London winters. The timing was perfect. Thomas flew down to look at a site John liked above

Lake Arenal and came back filled with enthusiasm. We took him out to dinner the night he got back.

"It's more beautiful than you can imagine. The land John bought sits above the lake with a perfect view of Arenal Volcano and these beautiful windmills on the hills on the other side of the lake. He wants me to design a house for him."

A week later, Thomas asked me if I would fly down with him and interview local contractors and choose one to build the house. John's Spanish was good but he didn't know construction; Thomas knew construction but didn't speak Spanish.

It was, after the Bakery and Positano, the most satisfying building I'd ever been part of. For a year, I flew down whenever there was a hitch in the building, or Thomas just wanted company (John stayed away in London during the whole process), and it was humbling to watch Thomas' talent and the contractor's skills pull the building out of the ground. Doug came down twice to guide the electrician who was hardworking, but whose skills were not quite up to ours.

On one trip, I found out from the contractor that cladding the building in stone was no more expensive than a stucco finish. When I told Thomas, his eyes lit up. I suggested we do the whole building.

"I don't think so, John. That always seems too 'busy' to me, or even makes it look like that fake stone siding. Let's do this," and he led me over to the contractor's scaffolding. "Look at these scaffold planks." They were six inches wide and four inches thick. "This is a really dense, local wood. Let's do a band of it above and below the windows all around the house and put stone up to it from below and down to it from above and stucco in between." The contrast in textures was stunning.

When it was time to install porch posts, the contractor trucked in whole *pilon* trees that had been de-barked but still had their largest branches sticking out a foot or so from the trunk. I caught Thomas studying them, and when the contractor showed up with a chain saw to trim the trunks, Thomas asked me to tell him not to. The man looked puzzled, then really puzzled when Thomas asked him to install the tree/porch posts as is. Trees with branches holding up the porch roof was as brilliant a bit of design as anything I'd ever seen him do.

The house as finished product was so beautiful that the contractor, who'd been skeptical, copied it for the house he was building for his own family.

On my last night there, with the house finished, Thomas fixed dinner, and then we sat on the porch and watched the last rays of the sunset walk down the side of the volcano, then silhouette the windmills across the lake.

We went inside when it was dark, and Thomas lit a fire in the living room fireplace, and we sat, listening to music. At a certain moment, he turned to me. "John, why can't this be enough for me? Books, music, a beautiful house on a piece of planetary paradise, a good friend to talk to? Why isn't this enough?"

It was a plea I felt helpless to answer.

We were quiet for a few minutes, and then he told me about his last trip, one to Manaus and the Amazon rainforest. "I've always liked visiting former boom towns like Manaus and Mérida. There's something about that faded architectural elegance that appeals to me. That's one of the first things I liked about Key West. What I remember most about the trip to the rainforest was the silence, and then the guide's explanation of it all. 'The vegetation from the trees decays faster there than any place else on Earth,' he told us, 'and any immature trees are in a desperate race to join the canopy and reach sunlight.' But he told us that a few trees make the race up there and burst on through the canopy and stand above the carpet of treetops below them. Those trees are 'the emergent layer.' Don't you love that term, John? Isn't that us . . . you, me, Doug, Tom, Leigh, the struggle we all had clawing through that early darkness to get up there, then bursting through, creating our own emergent layer, nodding to each other when the wind blows?"

How could I not care for this man?

When he dropped me off at the airport in Liberia the next day, and we hugged our goodbyes, I had the feeling I was abandoning a friend in need. I worried, but I knew John was arriving from London in a few days to see the house and hire a family as caretakers.

One night, a few days after my return, there was a knock on my door. It was Doug. "We have to talk, John." Has any news ever been good that starts with that sentence?

"OK, shoot."

"I found out three days ago that Tom's been doing coke."

I sat down, gut-shot, all emotion flushed out of me, prelude to a tsunami, followed by a flood of explosive anger, and started scream-ing. "How could he do that to us after all we've done for him? Tell him to get his ass out of here, now!"

Doug slowly calmed me down. "John, I was as much afraid of let-ting you know as I am of confronting him. Let's approach this ratio-nally and present a united front."

"I don't have time for this, Doug."

"We don't have the luxury of doing nothing, so let's think this through."

Together, we/he came up with a plan. I mostly listened. We went downstairs. Tom was outside by the pool, and we asked him to come inside and sit down. He looked scared.

I started. "Tom, I'm going to ask you a question, and ask it only one time. If you lie, you're going to have to move out tomorrow morning."

He looked shocked and started to say something. I help up my hand to stop him. "Tom, have you been doing coke?"

Now he looked really scared.

"Answer me, now. Yes or no."

He dropped his head.

"ANSWER ME!"

"Yes," he whispered. "I'm sorry, guys."

I was as angry as I'd ever been. I left it to Doug to announce the new rules: no going out at night unless accompanied by one of us; no visitors to the house except in the public spaces and only when one of us was home; and random piss tests to make sure he wasn't still doing it. Doug told him also that he couldn't work for either of us until he'd pissed clean for six months. Tom was shocked.

"Why can't I still work with you guys?"

"You hid from us that you were doing coke, Tom, and spending money on it; all the while, we're giving you a cheap place to stay. How do we know you weren't stealing from us or from the jobsites?"

Tom jumped up, furious. "I'd never do that, goddammit, and you know it."

"Yeah, and you promised us you'd never do coke, too."

Tom got a job working with Mel Fisher's crew, diving for the treasure from the *Atocha* and the *Santa Marguerita*. In lieu of a paycheck one month, he accepted a chipped emerald, which he loved showing to people. He'd put it on top of his mag flashlight to let its color awe them. Whenever Leigh was over, she asked him to show it to her because she knew it gave him pleasure to show it off and also because she loved emeralds.

Some of the treasure salvors were legendary party animals, so Doug and I feared Tom would fall again. At dinner one night, Doug asked him to come back to work for him. Tom jumped up from the table and gave Doug a big hug. "I'm sorry, guys. I know I let you down."

It was still not easy. Making the mortgage, tax, and insurance payments on the Bakery was a struggle, which made the surveillance of the kid even more of a burden. If he came back too late from the store, had he been meeting someone to make a deal? The opportunities to fall back were endless; Doug and I worried constantly. He always pissed clean, but there was always a tiny doubt that maybe he'd found a way to cheat. Any mood change in him and our first suspicion was that he was back on it. It was wearing us out. Then an "only in Key West" solution presented itself.

Katie, the twice-divorced Southern heiress to the liquor fortune with the "goat-eats-decal" story, asked Doug bluntly one day when he was working at her house if he knew anyone who could screw all night. She said she was desperate. "I don't care who he is as long as he's clean, honest, and horny. I'll pay him whatever he was making working and pay all the bills. Know anyone, sugar? I'm tired of sleeping alone, I'm tired of being horny, and I'm tired of complicated relationships. You're queer. You gotta understand."

Doug thought a minute, but it was obvious. "As a matter of fact, I do know someone. I'll have to talk it over with him and see if he wants to do it. If he does, you have to promise me you'd never be mean to him. He's simple but intelligent, very damaged by his childhood, and special to me and my friends. I'll let you know in a few days, but promise me you'd never be mean to him, or humiliate him, and that you'll advance his education, and I don't mean school. You hurt him, and we'd all hate you."

"I promise, and if he's that special, sugar, I might adopt him."

Doug talked it over with me. I didn't see a problem with it. She got something good out of it—good shagging and a humorous and protective companion—and he got something good out of it: introduction to a larger world we were too busy to show him, and where he could see that the language and manners we were trying to teach him were important.

Tom lived and worked with men, all construction workers, and our common denominator was usually crudeness. Nothing polished a straight man like a woman, and Tom needed polishing.

Something this important required a family meeting, at Louie's of course. Doug and I wrote it off as a business lunch. Marvin was off that day, so we had no tit-for-tat insulting to interrupt us.

Doug and I arrived first and ordered Bloody Mary's. Thomas and Leigh arrived together and stopped to chat with Tennessee and his friend for a minute, then joined us.

When their drinks came, I opened the discussion. "You know why we're here today . . . Katie's offer."

"Wait," Thomas said, holding up his hand. "What about our tradition? Does either of you have a construction story for us?"

Doug and I grinned, and he said: "I've got the best one yet, but let's save it to enjoy with the port." They agreed.

"OK," I began, "the question before us is should Tom do it or not? Before we start, am I correct in saying no one here has any moral objections to it?" They all chuckled at that. "Leigh, you know Katie best from your work with her on your non-profit? Would she be kind to him?"

"Yes, I think she would. Underneath all that Southern drama, Katie's a decent person, a tough businesswoman, but she's got the proverbial heart of gold. She's the biggest contributor every year to my non-profit, and it's always anonymously."

"OK, let's assume she will be," Thomas said. "Would this be a good thing for the kid? And would he be hurt when it ended, and we know it would eventually? John, you're his father now. Do you think he'd get hurt?"

The conch fritters arrived with each of us taking one, and Leigh cut the fifth in half, gave one piece to Thomas, popped the other in her mouth, and flipped me the bird.

"Well, Thomas, there're no guarantees, but I don't think he'd get hurt. I've watched him, and sex doesn't make him fall in love or get emotionally involved yet. To him, it's still just a game. Emotional maturity is still years away for him. I think it would just be a grand adventure. But I want a meeting with Katie and us before I make the final decision. Doug, what do you think?"

"I think he should do it, or I wouldn't have conveyed the offer. I think Tom's hit a plateau in learning manners, language, everything. He's too comfortable with the status quo, and I think he needs to be pushed outside the nest for a little while, knowing it's there for him whenever he needs it."

I turned to Leigh. "Can you set up a lunch, on me, with Katie next weekend?" She said she would. Thomas said he was going to be in Arenal again to spend some time alone there, then prompted Doug again for his construction story when the lunch was over and the port had arrived. I'd heard it already, but it stood listening to again.

"OK, I'm doing the electrical work in a top-floor condo that's a total gut and re-do. The floors of the condo are pre-stressed concrete slabs. The owners of the unit are re-configuring the master bath, which means new holes for the drain lines have to be drilled through the floor slabs for the toilet, the sink, and the shower."

Thomas understood construction, but I wanted to make sure Leigh followed the story, so I turned to her. "Leigh, the drain lines for each unit hang from the underside of that unit's floor slab and above the dropped ceiling of the unit below. So changing around the bathroom fixtures means taking out those drain lines, drilling holes for the new ones, and installing the new drain lines." She nodded that she followed me.

Doug continued. "The bathrooms in that building stack above each other: one unit's bathroom is above the bathroom of the unit below. It would be a lot easier to do the job if you had direct access to the drain lines from the unit below, so the contractor knocked on the door of the unit below where we're working. A woman answered, an entitled trophy wife who'd already shown herself to be a real bitch, complaining about everything.

"Bob, the contractor, explained what they had to do, and that it would be a lot faster and easier if he could take down the ceiling in her bathroom. He explained that they'd protect everything in the bathroom, replace the ceiling at his expense, and give the woman and her husband five thousand dollars to compensate them for the inconvenience. She told him no, under no circumstances, and further ordered him to tell all his men and all the sub-contractors that when she got on the elevator, we had to get off. 'I'm not going to share an elevator with a bunch of construction workers.' Now this is the same woman who tells . . . tells, not asks . . . us to carry her groceries upstairs.

"When we all heard the order about the elevator, we started giving her filthy looks. Didn't help relations when she came upstairs one day just as Colin was telling one of his rapid-fire jokes. Colin's back was to the door so he didn't see her and catch our signals to shut up. Joke was: "What's the difference between a condom and a condominium?

A condom can hold only one dickhead at a time." Rich bitch turned on her heel and complained later to the contractor.

"Alright. Fast forward to the day the plumber comes in with the core borer to cut the holes in the slab."

I looked over at Leigh and explained. "A core borer looks like a big jackhammer but has a diamond-tipped hole saw where the bit on a jackhammer would be. It's loud and noisy, and has a hose hooked to it to keep the bit cool and reduce friction as it cuts." She nodded that she understood, and Doug continued.

"OK, we're all standing around when the plumber's ready to start because this is heavy-duty stuff, and we want to see it. They've already drilled a tiny pilot hole through the slab to get the exact thickness, then made a mark on the first hole-saw bit a little short of that depth and start drilling. Two of the plumber's helpers have wet vacs sucking up the water as the drilling goes on so it doesn't go into the unit below, and they're also watching for the hole saw to sink in up to the mark they made. When it does, they pull the machine out, drill two Tapcons into the concrete plug they're taking out, and attach wires to them, which they hold on to. Then the plumber uses a small, regular masonry bit on a regular drill and finishes the job by drilling hole after hole around the entire circular cut until the plug is free. It doesn't drop through the ceiling below because the helpers have hold of it by the wires. When they pulled that first plug out, we all applauded. Masterful work."

"I bet I can guess what happens next," Thomas said. Doug put his finger to his lips to keep him quiet.

"That was the drain for the sink. They repeated the process for the shower drain, same hole size. Then they changed hole-saws to drill the big hole for the toilet. Now we're to the fun part. They either made the mark a little too high, or the slab was a little thinner, because the core borer went all the way through the slab, and a six-inch-diameter plug of concrete, six inches thick, went crashing through the ceiling of the bathroom below.

Leigh was open-mouthed and Thomas laughing.

"It gets better, oh it gets much better. Trophy wife was sitting on her toilet, completely naked, when the plug came through the ceiling and crashed into and shattered her tub. She jumps up screaming, then sees a man looking down at her through the hole in her ceiling and screams even more. Five minutes later, she's upstairs hissing and spitting at the contractor, threatening lawsuits, getting angrier and angrier because the rest of us are standing together in the corner and can't stop laughing."

"Things like that make me love this business," Doug ended.

"Yeah, as long as we're not the ones getting sued," I countered.

Leigh made the traditional toast with the port: "To our island and our little family."

The following weekend, Leigh and Katie scheduled a business meeting at Louie's for their non-profit so they were already there, working, when Doug and I arrived. Marvin put his finger to his lips to keep us quiet, then led us to the door to the outside deck and pointed to Leigh and Katie's table where they sat tapping their pens on the yellow legal pads in front of them. Marvin stopped us before we walked out and whispered: "How'd you like to be a hundred dollar bill trying to sneak past those two?" and the three of us laughed.

"What's so funny?" Leigh asked when Doug and I joined them.

"Marvin told us a dirty joke you don't want me to repeat."

Introductions were made, and I reminded Katie of the dinner party where I'd met her.

"It's a shame Robert's left town. His parties were always fun."

We ordered drinks and appetizers. Leigh shot me a look when the *five* conch fritters arrived, speared the fifth one before I could and shared it with Katie, discreetly shooting me the bird by drawing the finger across the side of her head when no one was looking, and grinned.

Now that we were all together, I felt a little awkward given the unconventional nature of the business at hand. Katie broke the ice.

"John, Leigh told me about your arrangement with the kid, that you're kind of his dad, and that Doug is like his brother. That's sweet. You know, the longer I'm here on the island, the more I wish I'd moved here earlier. You people have way too much fun." I told her I felt the same way about wishing I'd moved here earlier.

We ordered entrées, and when Marvin brought them, I asked him why Leigh hadn't asked for the table with the low branch above it.

"Ha! When I saw Her Majestyness' name in the reservation book, I took the first customers of the day to that table so you guys couldn't torture this tired old queen with another concussion."

When we were through with the main course and Marvin had cleared the plates, Leigh called the meeting to order.

I started. "Katie, the only concern I have is that my son not be hurt or humiliated. He's a special person, or we wouldn't all love him. I think the experience would be good for him. He's rough around the edges, and living and working with construction workers isn't going to polish him up like being with a good woman will. As far as I can tell, too, just like I told these guys last week, I think Tom is still too emotionally immature for a sexual relationship to cause him to fall in love. Are you prepared for it to be just fun and nothing more?"

Katie snorted. "Sugar, after two rotten marriages and a couple worse non-marital relationships, I definitely do not want any emotional depth beyond a friendship. And come on, the kid's twenty years younger than I am. So if this happens, I'm going into it with low expectations and eyes wide open."

"Leigh's already told you he had a problem with coke but has licked it?" She nodded. "That doesn't bother you?"

"Both my kids got addicted to the shit, but they've licked it, too. I'll take your word that he's OK now."

Doug put his hand on Katie's. "I think you're a good woman. You deserve to have some fun. But please, please, just never be unkind to our kid. He's had too much of that in his life already. If he gets on your nerves, or you just have to end it, call us and do it kindly, promise?

"Promise."

"OK, as dad, I guess it's up to me to talk to him. I'll get him aside this week, and Leigh will get in touch with you."

"Doug and John, I don't mean to be rude, but Katie and I still have some more business to take care of. Can we skip the dessert and port today so she and I can go back to work?"

"No problem." Kisses all around and Doug and I left.

After dinner the next night, I asked Tom if he could come to my room.

"I haven't done anything wrong, have I?"

"No, I just want to discuss something with you."

Up in my room, he was completely silent when I finished explaining the offer. I was afraid I'd offended him.

"Dad, you guys aren't trying to get rid of me, are you?" How could I not have known that might be his first take on it, given his childhood?

I got up off the bed and sat next to him on the sofa and put my arm around him. "Kid, you're my son, and I love you, and you'll always be my son. There's no way we're trying to get rid of you. You have a home with Doug and me as long as we're alive, even if we ever moved somewhere else, which I hope we never do. You also don't have to do this.

It's entirely up to you. Say no if that's what you want."

"Do you think I should do it, dad?"

"Only if you want to. I think it might be fun for you for a while. Doug and I are strapped down here trying to pay the bills every month, so we can't do the kind of traveling with you we'd like to right now. With her, you'll probably get some hot sex, get to travel, and learn better manners than you would with us. Then when either one of you has had enough, it's over. Shake hands, give each other a kiss and remain good friends.

"Don't answer now. Think about it, but remember two things. You don't have to do it, number one. And number two, this is your home, and it will be here waiting for you when you finish if you decide to do it. It's a big decision, so take your time. Now give me a hug, and let me do some of this never-fucking-ending paperwork."

Tom talked about it with Doug and said he might try it, but wanted to meet Katie first. We made reservations for everyone at Dim Sum, an Asian restaurant that had just opened near the bus station just off Duval Street. Doug had done the electrical work and liked the owner, so we decided to give it a chance.

I went to the restaurant straight from a meeting with a customer and got there twenty-five minutes early. I sat at the bar and ordered a drink. Right after I sat down, a tall black woman in a beautiful dress and long, straightened hair sat down on my left, and I looked over and nodded, then went back to checking out the details in the restaurant. Above the bar, wide pieces of canvas with lights above, hung, hammock-like, from the ceiling, bathing everything in a soft glow. It was a nice touch. One of the seated diners looked familiar, and I realized it was Senator Moynihan, another poor boy raised up by a good education.

"Did that ear infection of yours clear up?"

I jerked my head to the left.

"*What?*"

"That swimmer's ear problem you had?" I stared at the woman next to me, and a familiar face emerged from the mask of wig and make-up.

"Dr. Abernathy?"

She/he laughed. "Got you good, didn't I?"

"Christ almighty, I thought I was in the frigging twilight zone for a minute. I didn't know you were a drag queen. Not that I care," I added quickly.

"I prefer the term cross-dresser, sweetie. And you may call me Tammy when I'm dressed."

"Whatever. You scared the hell out of me." At that minute, Doug, Leigh, Tom, and Katie walked in, saw me and came over. I introduced everyone around. Leigh already knew him/her, it turned out.

Our table was ready, so everyone headed that way. I paid for my drink. When I got off my stool, I turned to my bar-mate. "So, Dr. Abernathy, Tammy, give me some guidance here. Handshake? Cheek kiss? European double cheek kiss?"

"Oh, honey, don't say 'double cheeks' or I'll get so excited I just might levitate off this stool."

"Stop it, or I'll pull your wig off." I gave him a quick peck on the cheek with a whispered warning: "If you ever check my prostate, it's with a finger, understood?"

Tammy started laughing. "You are just too funny and too sweet. Now go join your friends."

"I need a stiff drink," I said when I sat down. "My new family doctor is a drag queen?" and I explained how Frank/Tammy had scared me.

"You mean that woman is a man and a *doctor*?" Tom asked, shocked.

Leigh patted his hand. "Yes, both, and a good doctor. Most people don't know it, but he's a specialist in tropical diseases: malaria,

Chagas disease, dengue fever, all that stuff. He does a lot of charity work in Haiti and the Dominican Republic every year. Anyway, let's order. Everything's supposed to be good here."

While we were studying the menus, I noticed that Katie was discreetly checking Tom out. When she caught my eye, she did a quick 'hand-fanning-the-cheek' gesture and mouthed: "He's hot." She was no slouch, herself, slim and trim, wearing a dress that, like Leigh's, probably cost as much as I made in two months. In all my years of studying eyes, I had never arrived at an explanation of why the French, Italians, and Argentinians had eyes so alive and most Americans' eyes so dull, even Americans whose minds were as lively as anyone's. Her eyes were the exception: they shot fire.

Tom seemed a little overwhelmed at first by the situation and the setting, but each person at the table went out of their way, subtly, to include him in everything and make him feel comfortable. Katie was unusually demure (knowing she was being examined, I guess). In spite of all the undercurrents, the dinner was fun. Leigh had the table laughing about the trip to Miami to dress the kid, with "all the women and gay men leaving a slime trail behind him." Tom blushed.

To keep the conversation light, Doug and I talked about some of the jobs we had and that let Tom join in.

"Do you like construction work?" Katie asked him.

"Yeah, I do, especially with these guys. We work hard and bust our . . ." he started to say asses but changed it to "backsides" and Katie laughed. "Honey, you don't have to pretend with me. I bust my ass all the time trying to keep those liquor distributors in line. I'm with you there."

That broke the ice, and we all settled in to have a good time at a dinner whose purpose was to give my non-biological son over to sexual servitude.

Doug started the story on Tom about a job we had done for two gay guys on Love Lane next to the library.

"Doug," Tom protested, "don't tell her that."

"Sorry, kid, it's too funny, and it's sweet, too." He continued. "We couldn't park in the lane, so we parked on Fleming Street in front of the library, and I sent Tom on to the house with some of the tools. He was back in a couple minutes and threw his tool pouch into my van and told me he quit. I asked him what had happened."

Leigh started laughing because she'd heard the story before, but reached over and put her hand on Tom's.

"He told me the front door of the house was open, and when he'd arrived one guy was on top of another on the sofa, and they were kissing and calling each other things like 'sweetheart.' 'That's disgusting,' he said. I calmed him down and explained to him that they had just as much right to do that as anyone and reminded him I was gay. He went back to work.

"Now here's the part of the story that shows how great the kid is. Two months later, we were working on a house that this old, fat, outrageous queen owned. Poor guy was going out of his mind every time he looked at the kid; and then he started walking around in a thong—not a pretty sight. I was busy wiring the under-cabinet lights in the kitchen one afternoon when Tom came out of the bedroom and said he had a question and came over to me and whispered: 'The dude has this machine next to his bed called an Accu-Jack. I figured out what it's for, sort of like a milking machine for dudes. Do we need a separate circuit for it?' Totally serious, totally non-judgmental. I burst out laughing and gave him a hug."

We all laughed, including Tom.

Near the end of the meal, Katie brought up that she was planning a trip to Greece in a month, and that she might like a companion. To give Tom a chance to take in the information, Doug stepped in. "One of my first customers here sold everything and moved to one of the Greek islands, Hydra. If you go to Greece, go there. It's only an hour-and-a-half hydrofoil ride from Piraeus. You'll love it. No cars. Everything, I mean *everything*, arrives by boat and gets hauled around the island by donkeys. Sophia Loren and Ponti have a place there, it's so beautiful. I'll give you Alex's address and phone number."

We headed out of the restaurant, and I caught Tom and Katie giving each other a last check-each-other-out look.

Two nights later, La Yndia Bakery was short one inhabitant.

Doug found an excuse to work at Katie's house the next day even though it was something that could have waited. Shortly before noon, she came out and took Doug over to a corner.

Doug asked the obvious: "How'd it go?"

"Sugar, that boy lit up my pussy like a pinball machine." (I raced to put that one in the journal.) "Mother Nature was good to that boy. Have you seen the size of that dick? And do you know he brought me coffee in bed. None of the jerks I married or screwed ever did that. Come on in and chew the fat."

Doug walked inside. Seated at the breakfast table was a silk-bath-robe-enshrouded young Tom with a "cat that ate the canary grin" on his face.

"I'm going to Greece, Doug," he said, strutting the information. Then, "I'll be OK there, won't I?"

"You're going to love it. But we need to get you a passport."

He spent alternating nights with Katie and us. We'd told him "gentlemen don't tell" so we didn't hear any of the sexual details, at least I didn't. When his passport arrived in its Manila envelope, he opened it with wonder and looked at every page, as I had done with my first one. He took it to work with him to show the guys: "Hey, I got me a passport."

For four weeks, every night he spent at the Bakery, he'd pull the atlas out from the shelf under the coffee table and trace the route: Miami . . . London . . . Athens.

"Athens is a long ways away, isn't it dad?"

"A long way. It's almost to Asia."

"I'll be OK there, won't I?"

"You'll be OK."

"What if something happens? How can I get back here? It's across an ocean."

"Son, if I had to walk on water all the way across the ocean to come get you, I would."

That made him laugh. "You can't walk on water, you silly."

The day they left for Greece, Doug, Leigh, and I drove them to the airport. Tom was all but dancing around the building, he was so excited to be going to another country for the first time. When it was time to board, though, the shock of it all hit him: he was leaving us and his home and going a long way away. He became very subdued (and scared, we knew). We reassured him his home would always be waiting for him, and I slipped him a hundred bucks and told him he had to call us twice a week at least, or I'd kick his butt. I learned on the way back into town that Doug and Leigh had slipped him money, too.

"And don't forget the time difference and wake us up," I said. Explaining time zones and currency differences had not been easy lessons.

"And take her out to dinner once a week and pay for it." That was Leigh.

"And have fun and remember your manners." That was Doug.

Katie took his hand, and they walked out to the plane.

He called almost every day, and three weeks later asked if we'd pick him up at the airport on his return. Katie was staying on in London for a while. When he saw us, he ran over and almost knocked us over in his excitement, bear hugs all around.

At dinner, he couldn't get the words out fast enough. "London, man, what a cool city. Stuff's going on all night long. Did you know that the Germans bombed it in WWII? How weird is that? Why would you want to bomb London? I seen. . ."

"Dollar! Subject-verb disagreement."

"Damn! I *saw* the Parthenon in Athens. Did you know democracy started there? And the Venetians—they're from Italy—blew it up, and it had to be pieced back together."

Doug asked him how he liked Hydra.

"Man, that is one cool island. I walked way up the hill to the monastery one afternoon and could see the whole island. You were right: no cars, only donkeys, but I liked it. Your buddy, Alex, was eyeball-fucking me the whole time, but I know how to deal with that now, just ignore it like you taught me."

Leigh left us, and Tom spent some time with Doug, then came up to my room and jumped on the bed with me.

"I have two questions for you, son. Are you glad you did it and was she good to you?"

"Dad, I'm really glad I got to see all that, and she was always good to me. She's a good person, but I kinda feel sorry for her. Her husbands were mean to her, and I think from stuff I heard when she was on the phone that her kids are after her all the time for money."

I put my arm around him. "You still my kid?"

"Dad, I'll always be your kid, you know that, you silly. Being with you is the only time I feel safe, I already told you that. When the police stopped our car in Athens because the driver was speeding, the first thing I thought of was: 'Where's dad?'"

"OK, go to bed. Some of us aren't spoiled, lazy, world travelers and have to work for a living."

For six months Tom traveled and expanded his knowledge of the world. Katie kept her promise: his language and manners improved. One day I almost wept at the first, perfect, present perfect tense: "*I've had* a lot of fun on these trips."

We'd get postcards:

From Buenos Aires: Man, you wouldn't believe these steaks! And you two were right. The water in the sink drains out in the opposite direction from up there. I looked.

From Barcelona: Dudes, you ain't—Ha! Ha! Dad, can't fine me here!—able to imagine some of the buildings here. There's a church that looks like it was built out of wet, drippy sand. I ate octopus for the first time. It was creepy.

From Amsterdam: Did you know there was a sea battle where the airport is today? They pumped all that water out. Can you believe it? And there's a whole section of town where the prostitutes sit right in the windows of their houses. Some of them are hot, but I pretended not to notice.

Eight months after the dinner at Dim Sum, it was over, and nicely so. Katie told Leigh: "What am I going to do? Spend the rest of my life with someone the hoteliers keep calling 'my son' when they're not snickering behind my back? Fall in love with a twenty-year-old boy? My children, my doting heirs, are already hiring lawyers. I have to give him up. I kept my promise to be kind to him, and I want to settle some money on him, but I don't want him to know about it. You take care of it for him until he grows up," and she paused here, "and it has to happen, I guess, but what a shame, huh? There's something wonderfully pure about the kid. I can see why you all love him, and he's lucky to have all of you."

Young Tom moved back in, and it was as if he'd never left, apart from a first few days of insecurity: "You're still my dad? I'm still #1 man? Who's on this week?"

Katie and Tom stayed in touch, even after she moved back to Texas to be closer to her business. Listening to Tom laughing on the phone with her, I believed that it had been a good thing for both of them.

Leigh told Doug and me that Katie had given her twenty-five thousand dollars for Tom, but asked that he not know about it until we all thought he could handle money on his own. "I'll invest it for him," Leigh added, "because the two of you would do something stupid with the money like go 'long corn' or something," and she laughed like that was really funny.

When Tom was back on the jobs and his buddies asked him where he'd been, he remained a gentleman and always answered: "I was traveling with a friend."

Nineteen

Gay men formed a high percentage of the people who had moved to the island in the late '60s and early '70s. A small community of gays had already been there for a long time, some famous like Tennessee Williams, leading a discreet, quiet life that pre-1960 had included the ninety-mile trips across the Florida Straits to the fleshpots of Havana. Others, like Henry Faulkner and Johnny Knight had not been discreet, but so outrageous that the town accepted them, a town that appreciated outrageous.

The new gay arrivals were different. They were a younger generation and had no interest in being closeted or discreet. Gay bars and restaurants started opening up, the boards started coming down from the storefronts on Duval Street, and some of the big houses in Old Town were converted to B&Bs catering to a gay clientele.

As the new people settled in, bridges were slowly built between the new people and the locals. A gay man would start a business and hire a local who then became more familiar with him and the community in general. Gay men started charities or helped the existing ones, and more bonds were forged.

Gay women followed the gay men to Key West, first as visitors and later as residents, and added to the store of funny stories. One morning, the page two headline of the *Mullet Wrapper* read: "Two Women Argue Over Ownership Of Designer Dildo." The story followed: Two women had checked into a gay guesthouse for the weekend. Things had gone well until the last few hours when one packed into her suitcase the dildo belonging to the other. It was apparently an expensive, custom-made dildo with extra features, so a fight ensued with black eyes and bloody noses. The police were called and both women arrested.

Radio stations picked up the *Mullet Wrapper* report and spread it around the entire country. Our phones started ringing with out-of-town friends asking: "Did that really happen?"

What the entire island really wanted to know, what the subject of discussion in every office, on every jobsite, and at every dinner party that night was: what designer features? Sadly, the question remained as unanswered as "Where is Bum Farto?" But we all suspected that one of the cops now had a very satisfied girlfriend.

That gays had earned a permanent place in the local community was proven forever the night the Copa burned down.

When the Monster disco closed, the people who had the Copa in Ft. Lauderdale opened a Copa disco on Duval Street. It was enclosed and cavernous, in the theater that had once screened *Deep Throat,* seemingly forever. It wasn't as wonderful as the Monster had been, but still a good place to dance, and where gays and straights still mixed easily. The Copa had a stage and began putting on drag shows, some by out-of-town performers but more often by local drag queens.

Firemen, all Conchs, were notoriously homophobic in Key West, but then the son of a fireman was diagnosed with a rare and usually fatal disease, and the family was being ruined by the medical bills. One of the local drag queens heard about it and came up with the idea of doing a benefit show for the family. They advertised it heavily, gave free tickets to the skittish firemen and their wives, and the show sold out.

The mayor, all the city commissioners, *le tout* Key West was there.

By five minutes into the show, nearly everyone—including the firemen's wives—was roaring with laughter at the predictable jokes about pumps and hoses accompanied by outrageous and ribald skits. At one point four drag queens were riding a fire hose they'd gotten from god knows where. Ten minutes into it, the firemen themselves were laughing. Ten thousand dollars was raised for the family.

At the very end, Lola L'Amour, the drag queen who'd organized the benefit, walked to the front of the stage, took off her wig, waited for the room to fall silent, then looked down at the audience and said: "Remember that it doesn't matter who or how you love, but that you love, and when a neighbor is in need, we are all in need." The audience exploded with applause.

In the dancing that followed, the rumor is true that firemen danced with drag queens as their wives looked on, laughing their asses off and taking photos that their children would use to embarrass their fathers later in life. Leigh, Doug, Thomas, young Tom and I were part of the crowd that night. For Doug, I saw that it was redemption, too, to see his fellow Conchs dancing there and acknowledging him with nods and smiles.

A year later, someone set fire to the building adjacent to the Copa late at night, and it caught fire and burned, too. Outside on Duval Street, as we sadly watched it burn, drag queens, some in costume with mascara running, were screaming: "Oh my god, all my dresses are in there, all my make-up, what are we going to do? Where can we go? That's our home" and were seen sobbing on the shoulders of firemen who put a shy arm around them. "You'll come back, girls. You'll come back. You girls are tough."

A few years after my arrival, Key West elected the first openly gay mayor in the country. Richard Heymann's victory was only possible because of thousands of votes from straight people, Conchs and outsiders alike, and the town stood prouder the next day and a short time later adopted as its official motto: One Human Family.

Then a sick mathematician came up with the equation: Sex = Death that killed Richard and over a thousand others.

It was a bad science fiction movie: humans push too far into a tropical rain forest in Cameroon and kill and eat the green monkeys living there. The monkeys avenge themselves: they harbor a virus for which the naked ape has no immunity. The virus leaps, human to human, country to country, jumps an ocean and makes its way to a tiny island a hundred and twenty miles out to sea and into the bodies of hundreds of the island's inhabitants.

Like humans everywhere on the planet, we didn't know at first what caused the strange illness or illnesses that struck and quickly killed so many on the island. It started in Key West, as in most places in the United States, in the gay population. Local doctors were as confused and horrified as the rest of us.

Dr. Abernathy, my black drag-queen doctor and specialist in tropical diseases, all business now, arranged for the CDC to send a man down to tell the town what was and wasn't known about the disease. Leigh called me and told me about it. "Look, this could be really important. You tell Doug and young Tom to get their butts there, and I'll tell Szuter."

We sat together that night listening to something that simply could not be true. It looked like it could be sexually transmitted, the CDC doctor said. It looked like blood might carry it, so mosquitoes might or might not be dangerous again. "But the disease," the man said, "whatever the causative agent, has a 100 percent morbidity rate. It kills everyone infected. Everyone." A shock wave went through the crowd, followed by stunned silence, then a buzz of conversation.

Weren't fatal, plague-like infectious diseases a thing of the past, like silent movies? This was the late twentieth century; we'd conquered them, hadn't we? The Black Death that had killed a third of Europe, reduced to a few cases a year in the Southwest, easily treatable. Leprosy/antibiotics. TB/antibiotics. Syphillis/antibiotics. Our communal mind had made no room for this scenario; it simply couldn't be happening to us.

What we didn't know as we sat there at Lighthouse Court, in an open courtyard, fragrant breeze blowing, surrounded by friends and neighbors—Bill and Tony from Fast Buck's, Fred Troxel, the barefoot dentist, and dozens of others—listening to this B-movie script, was that it was already too late for over fifty of the men there that night, and for one of my little family. The virus was already swimming in their blood. Nature, indifferent to the wonderful life we had created for ourselves on a beautiful island, had already pronounced the death sentences. The tumbrels were rolling our way.

Unlike most places in the country where gay people were marginalized even more because of the disease, and those infected condemned to horribly stigmatized deaths, this little island proved again that magic lived here. The gay community was reeling and stunned by the first wave of deaths and the frightening, spreading infections. When the American population shamefully used the disease to further demonize gays across the country, often in the name of religion, the straight community in Key West jumped into the traces with their gay friends and neighbors and together took the bit in their teeth and ran with it. This at a time when the *New York Times,* the beacon of enlightened journalism, shamefully, wouldn't even run a ten-line story on an inside page about the fund-raising gay circus for AIDS victims in that city.

Community leaders here demanded money from the Feds and the state to help the sick and the dying; married couples took their emaciated, dying friends into their homes and eased their deaths at a time when it wasn't yet known if they themselves could be infected by helping. AIDS HELP was founded to help the sick, many now bankrupt as well as dying. At every benefit, the straight community rose up and emptied their wallets and purses. Men with Karposi lesions on their faces and emaciated bodies were still invited to all the parties, and everyone pretended not to notice unless they, themselves, mentioned it.

Almost daily the obituaries included the name of someone we'd danced with, or worked with, or whose restaurant we'd eaten at. Before, a group of people in dark clothes on one of the beaches in the afternoon was assumed to be there for a wedding; now it was to spread another victim's ashes in the sea.

Doug asked me one day if I could help him do a charity job. Two friends of his, already very sick, needed air conditioning. Someone had donated a new unit, but it required running a new circuit. I agreed, as long as it could be done after work.

We showed up at a small house on Newton Street. Doug knocked on the door and I tried not to express the shock I felt when a man who looked like one of the concentration camp prisoners in WWII answered the door.

"Thanks for coming, Doug," the man whispered and invited us in. The place was stifling and had a strange and unpleasant smell. Doug gave the man a hug and a cheek kiss and introduced me. "Alex, John. John, Alex." We started to shake hands, when the most horrible sound I'd ever heard in my life came from a room somewhere inside, the sound of an animal trying loudly and desperately to breathe and not succeeding.

Alex ran towards the sound, and there was some commotion, a blood-curdling scream of pain, and then quiet. Doug and I waited in silence for a few minutes until Alex returned. "I'm sorry, Steve has pneumocystis and can't breathe sometimes. I had to give him an injection and the oxygen. He's so thin the injections hurt him a lot. He's breathing again. You can go in there now."

Going in there was the last thing I wanted to do, but that's apparently where we had to work.

The bedroom was horribly hot and smelled of shit. I had read that one of the ways AIDS killed you was that you literally shit your body out of you, which explained the emaciation. Lying on the bed was a stick figure breathing oxygen, a figure too skinny to be a human being, naked and uncovered because of the heat and polka-dotted with purplish-red lesions. I fought hard to keep from throwing up.

"Steve," Alex addressed the figure, "this is Doug and John. They're here to install the AC." A feeble nod.

Doug and I went to work. I enlarged the opening in the wall, and we lifted the new AC unit into place and framed it in. Then we went outside and ran conduit down the wall to the unit, drilled through the wall and set a box. When we walked to the truck to get the wire to pull into the conduit, Doug looked at me. "You OK?"

"How in the hell could you be OK after seeing that?"

"I know, John. And it's happening all over town. These two guys have it really bad because their families disowned them and refuse to see them. Won't help them or even call. Some kind of evangelical Christians. They believe this is just punishment for their sons' "lifestyle.""

"Doug, that's totally fucked up. You're going to let your son die a horrible death ostracized from his family. The parents deserve to get it from a blood transfusion."

We pulled the wire, Doug outside feeding it and I inside pulling. Alex was sitting next to the bed, alternately fanning and caressing the head of this "thing" that had once been—still was—a human being and I heard him whispering "I love you, I love you," knowing he was next on the taxi-way. I had never been witness to such love or courage, but I also wanted out of there. It was too raw, too sad; Death's foul breath too close.

Doug and I switched places. I wired the circuit into the panel, and he installed the new outlet. When I came in and told him it was ready, he plugged the AC in and chilled air started pouring out.

"Steve and I don't have much left," Alex said as we were packing up, "but let me give you something."

"On the house, my little cupcake," Doug answered, trying to keep it light.

"Thanks." He gave Doug a kiss and started to shake my hand. I hesitated a second, which he caught, then I gave him a hug instead. No flesh: bones prominent under a cheap hotel sheet.

On the way home in the truck, Doug started to say something, stopped, then said: "Everyone I know who's dying is doing it with a courage and dignity I would never have expected." He paused. "I don't know that I could do that."

Three weeks later both men were dead.

Leigh called me one day after work, six months after the meeting we'd gone to at Lighthouse Court. It was that time in late summer when a faintly pink, high haze hangs over the island for a couple days, dust from the Sahara, blown all the way across the Atlantic. For whatever reason, it always puts me on edge, and I'd already had a bad week with a rich customer who didn't think he should have to pay for two hundred dollars worth of light bulbs—at my cost—when the bid clearly stated that materials weren't included.

"What?" I snapped, when I picked up the phone. She was crying. "Leigh, what's wrong?" She started sobbing, uncontrolled animal pain. "Leigh, what's wrong? Tell me. Are you alright?"

She gained partial control but, still crying, said: "Thomas has it."

There was no need at this point in the island's history to explain what "it" was.

"No, god, Leigh, please tell me no."

"He found two lesions last week, and the doctors confirmed it."

I screamed: "Not him, Leigh, NO, not HIM."

Michael and Ursula Keating, who owned The Mermaid and the Alligator guest house on Truman, took Thomas in so he would have someone to look in on him all day. We all visited often and took him out to dinner when he was able. Courage isn't a strong enough word to describe his descent into death. He would joke about his lesions: "As an artist I've always disliked the color red. Isn't it ironic that something red" and he pointed to the Karposi lesions on his face and body "is killing me?" And then that famous Szuter laugh.

One night—early morning—the phone rang, and Doug and I picked it up at almost the same time. It was Thomas, crying. "I'm scared. Can one of you come over? I'm sorry."

"We'll be there in a minute. Hold on, kid." Doug and I threw clothes on and raced to the guesthouse and let ourselves in the side door of the room he was staying in. A table lamp was on, illuminating a now familiar horror: a rail-thin man spotted with lesions and slicked with another of the disease's nastier tricks, the night sweats.

"Hey, guy, we're here," Doug said. "What can we do?"

With great effort, Thomas pulled the sheet up over his lower body, hiding what must have been a diaper.

"Can you just sit with me awhile? I'm OK most nights, but sometimes the death terror hits me. It's bad tonight."

"No problem, kiddo. We're your friends, remember? Call any time."

Doug took charge. "John, can you get a towel from the bathroom and wet it . . . lukewarm, not cold." I did as told and gave it to Doug, who climbed in bed with Thomas and started wiping him down, giving me the towel to rinse and re-soak as needed. He pulled the sheet off Thomas to wipe down his legs, exposing the diaper. Then there came a smell that announced incontinence of the worst sort. Thomas closed his eyes and turned his head, crying. "I'm so ashamed."

"Nothing to be ashamed of, Thomas," Doug said. "Let's just clean you up." I admired many things about Doug, perhaps most his strength and ability to act like all was normal in these horribly abnormal situations. What I wanted to do first was throw up, then flee from something so awful and frightening.

"John, get another one, will you?" Doug asked when Thomas told him where the diapers were kept. "Then go outside while I change him, will you? I know how squeamish you are."

Ashamed, I did as told. Outside on the porch, a warm breeze carried the now familiar tropical smells, and a full moon painted rustling palm fronds silver, nature carrying on unconcerned that the most extraordinary friend I'd ever had was dying a horrible death. I wanted to believe in God so I could pull Him screaming from the heavens to rub His fucking nose in what Doug was cleaning up.

Doug called me back inside when the clean-up was finished. Thomas was lying quietly now, eyes closed. Doug got in the bed with him and lifted his head to put it on his chest. I pulled a chair up to the bed and held Thomas' hand in mine and stroked it slowly.

Tired and sleepy in that special consciousness that comes in the middle of the night, I looked at the hand I was holding and wondered how many times it had been put to canvas or wood, giving life

386

to things as wonderful as the collage that hung in my bedroom and was the first thing I woke to every day. I could not grasp the thought of these Etruscan eyes, this hand informed by a consciousness that fascinated me, leaving me, but one look at the now sleeping body revealed the inescapable: he was dying. How could that be possible? The arrogance of my own existence demanded he stay and teach me more. Of the billions of human units walking around the globe, this one had touched and educated me as none other.

Sitting with him that last night in Arenal, on the porch of a house that touched Frank Lloyd Wright genius, listening to that plea, I had felt the entire human condition, in all its glory and anguish, crawl close enough to touch me.

We stayed like this until dawn, when Thomas woke up, and Michael and Ursula checked in on him, thanked us and took over.

We didn't speak on the way back to the Bakery, and each of us went to our rooms to get ready for the workday. I caught Doug just as he was about to leave. "Doug, can you come here for a second?"

"I'm in a hurry. What's up?"

I walked over to him and gave him a big hug. "You are a remarkable person."

He hugged me back and thanked me, then pulled away. "Gotta go and make the world safe for rich people."

Remarkably, Thomas rallied for a short while and had time enough for one more show. The opening was in a store on Duval Street that a friend had bought and hadn't opened yet. Key West showed up in unheard-of numbers to look at beautifully detailed photos of the doors of colonial Mérida and textile sculptures, with the color red predominant. Thomas, emaciated and disfigured, too weak to stand, sat in the middle of the space and greeted everyone, and every once in a while let loose that wild, wonderful laugh.

The show sold out, half because the things were wonderful, half to give him money. I worked my way to him and congratulated him. He thanked me in a whisper, then asked: "Do you still have that collage you bought from the show I had when you first came to Key West?" I was amazed that he remembered. "Thomas, I'll have that with me the rest of my life." I gave him a long hug and a kiss on the cheek. He was tiring fast, but the eyes, those indescribable all-seeing eyes had not diminished. He was leaving life seeing it all.

Leigh came up. "Thomas, you look tired. You want us to take you back?"

"Thanks. I think I'm OK for a little more. Michael and Ursula are here. They'll take me back."

Leigh and I left a few minutes later, neither of us speaking in the truck on the way back to the Bakery. When we pulled up in front, I asked her if she wanted to come in.

"I don't think so. I need to be alone, I think." We kissed, and I got out. She rode off on her bike.

A month later, I was in Positano visiting George and Alice at their villa. I was alone on the terrace with a glass of wine, looking down at the town, one of the most beautiful accomplishments of Man, when the housekeeper came out and told me I had a phone call.

It was young Tom. "Thomas died last night, dad."

I started crying.

"Dad, are you gonna be OK?"

I couldn't answer. I had known it was going to happen, and soon, but the animal brain couldn't accept mortality.

I got control. "Yeah, I'll be alright, kid. Thanks for calling me. How are Leigh and Doug taking it?"

"I think they're both having a tough time, especially Leigh."

"How are you doing?" If your child has done the wrong drugs, you always worry.

He knew what I was asking about. "I'm fine, dad. Love you."

"Love you, too, son. I'll be back day after tomorrow. Pick me up at the airport, OK?"

I walked over to the edge of the terrace and tried to understand the incomprehensible. Out of the swirl of emotions I was feeling, the strongest surprised me: I felt sorrier for myself than for Thomas. I wouldn't even be standing where I was, looking down at one of the most beautiful views on the planet—the hand of Man well placed—if he hadn't reached out and touched my eyes. And now he had left me, us. Thomas deserved better than to die, and I deserved to have his brilliant observations next to me as we biked, walked, talked, and sailed through our rich island life together. I was bitter.

The memorial service was held at a house on Washington Street where Thomas had designed the renovation and introduced a Caribbean roofline to the island for the first time. An acquaintance who owned the house called me with the information and begged me to come. "I know you were important in his life."

I wasn't going to go. I wanted to grieve privately, my style, but Leigh told me I had to go. "His sister is going to be there from Cleveland. You may need to speak."

"Leigh, you know I can't do that. I'll start crying."

"So what, tough guy. You think anyone's going to hold that against you?"

It was Sunday afternoon, cloudless sky, soft breeze. We parked down the street and got out. I was a mess. Leigh put her arm around me, and we walked towards the house. As we got almost to the entrance to the property, I saw Stewart Andrews, a fireman and fellow construction worker, coming from the other direction, tears pouring down his face. That's all it took. I started, crying, too. Leigh let go of me, and Stewart and I, arms around each others' shoulders, walked inside, held each other for a while then split up. I walked over to Leigh's side again.

Inside, was gathered for probably the last time, Key West as it was when I moved there: a few modest, rich people for whom Thomas had designed houses; Paulie, the Cuban plumber; Gail from the restaurant where I'd had the first dinner with Leigh and Thomas; Stewart the fireman; Jeff, the contractor; Tony from Fast Buck's (who was soon to lose Bill, his partner to the disease); and carpenters, roofers, Fred, 'our barefoot dentist from Big Pine Key'—an entire community. A few minutes were spent greeting each other and catching up on each other's news, all of us sobered by what was happening around us on the island.

A writer friend of Thomas', David Kaufelt, began to speak and said what had to be said: that Thomas was special and that his death left a hole in the fabric of the community that could not be repaired. Then he introduced Thomas' sister, Geraldine, who spoke.

"My family and I had no idea that my brother was so loved by this town and that gives us great comfort. When I first learned that Tom had AIDS, I was shocked and saddened. But the great burden was that it fell on me to tell our mother because Tom was mother's special love." (I remembered the wonderful old woman who had cleaned the baseboards at Southernmost House on her hands and knees with a toothbrush.)

"Our mother is eighty-three now, and I feared the effect the news would have on her. I pondered for days the best way to tell her and decided finally that there was no one way better than another. After Sunday dinner, I said 'Mama, there's something I have to tell you,' and then took her into the parlor. We sat down and I said: 'Mama, Tom has AIDS.' My mother looked at me for a minute, then asked: 'He's going to die, isn't he?' I answered yes, and she began to cry."

Having said that, Geraldine began to cry. David came over and put his arm around her. The image of the old mother hearing her son's death sentence set nearly everyone else to crying, too.

After a couple of minutes, Geraldine composed herself and said: "Again, I would like to say how comforting it is to know my brother was loved so much. It makes the loss a little easier to bear. Thank you all."

The writer, David, stepped back up and asked if anyone had anything they would like to say and, wonderfully, no one stepped forward with kitschy or bragging tales about how special they were to Thomas. David acknowledged the significance of that and said nothing more. People began to go up to the sister and introduce themselves and express their condolences. When Leigh and I introduced ourselves, she looked over at David who nodded. "They're the ones."

Geraldine looked at us. "Tom asked you to decide where to spread his ashes." She went inside the house and brought out an urn and handed it to me. It was surprisingly heavy, and I wasn't ready for this, which Leigh recognized immediately.

"How much longer are you going to be here?" Leigh asked the sister, taking the urn.

"I have to leave tomorrow."

"I'll write you and tell you what we decided and when we do it, OK?"

"Thank you so much." We all hugged and kissed, and Leigh and I left.

"Could you drive, Leigh?"

She took the keys and drove me home and came in for a drink. I set the urn on the coffee table and tried to understand the inexplicable: that inside that container resided all that was left of one of the kindest and most original human beings I'd ever known.

We sat there for a while, not saying anything, and then Doug and Tom came in from work, a rush job that had to be finished that day. We described the memorial service and told them about the ashes and asked their opinion about where to spread them.

It was Leigh, finally, who came up with the best idea. "He loved his little Beetle Cat, and he loved Channel Key. Let's go there, get Gail and Jeff to go in their Beetle Cat, too." I liked the idea. So did Doug. Leigh called Gail and set it up for the following Sunday.

Sunday's weather was perfect again: a few wispy clouds in a deep blue sky and a southeasterly breeze. We decided not to take young Tom. He was still too vulnerable to see all the adults in his life in uncontrollable grief.

Leigh picked Doug and me up in Thomas' last car, a Studebaker sedan with a bad clutch, and we met Gail and Jeff at Jeff's parents' house on Key Haven where the boats were docked. We walked through the yard to the boats in back, released them from the dock and hoisted the sails, Jeff and Gail in one boat, Leigh, Doug, and I in the other.

The wind filled the sails, and the southeast breeze took us out the channel where we began tacking eastward towards Channel Key. The slap of water against the hull, the sight of the two sails chasing one another was calming. Halfway to Channel Key, a pod of dolphins picked us up and played with us for a while, surfacing first on one side of the boats, then the other. No words except for Leigh's "Coming about," warning Doug and me to duck our heads as the boom swung to the other side.

Both boats struck sail at the entrance to the channel.

"I've brought wine and glasses," Gail said. "Does anyone want any?"

I was ready, but Jeff suggested we wait until we were spreading the ashes.

"OK, let's go," Leigh said. Doug turned on the tape player to the "Sanctus" from the Fauré *Requiem,* a piece that had always calmed Thomas after one of his episodes; then we pulled ourselves into the channel, and Jeff and Gail followed us.

We reached the pool as the "Sanctus" ended and Doug shut the player off. The nesting pair of Great White Herons lifted off again as we entered. A school of small snappers raced through, off to feed somewhere or being pursued by something we couldn't see. For a couple minutes, none of us said a word as the utter beauty of the place settled into us. The great irony, the fatal and damnable irony, was that the only thing missing to make the scene perfect was Thomas, the man with God's eyes, Thomas, who would have immediately noticed something we hadn't and pointed it out to us, not Thomas the "thing" inside the urn.

There was a sudden slap of a fish surfacing, then silence again.

Jeff opened two bottles of wine and handed us glasses and poured. We drank a glass each and then another. I picked up the urn and opened it. I was surprised to see that the ashes were inside a plastic bag inside it. I did not want to do this. I pulled the bag out and held it against me for a minute. What desperate folly to think we can comfort or resurrect the dead, but I couldn't help myself. "Thomas, don't be dead, please don't be dead," I pleaded, and we all started crying.

I looked at the others. "I don't know how we're supposed to do this." I had always thought you just dumped the ashes out, but that seemed too brutal, like dumping trash.

It was Leigh who knew. "We each reach our hands into the bag and scatter a handful until they're all gone." That seemed kinder to me, but oh . . . the finality. She took the bag from me and reached inside, grabbed a handful and spread it across the water. Jeff, then Gail, then Doug, then me. Gray ash with bits of white bone. I grabbed a handful and threw them on the water. "Goodbye, good friend." Two turns emptied the bag and Leigh took it, leaned over the gunwales and rinsed it out.

Ten handfuls, one life.

Gail opened the last bottle of wine and poured it into the water for Thomas. Doug, securing an oar, knocked the tape player into the water, and we all looked at one another and started laughing/crying. Thomas had always loved it when things went wrong, believing to the end that chaos and accident were the norm, not order.

Doug gave voice to what I was thinking when we had made our way back out to open water: "I know it's not rational, but I just don't want him to be scared and lonely there all by himself tonight. How dumb is that?" and he started crying again. I told him I was thinking the same thing. Leigh was quiet, pulled into herself.

Two sails—the hand of Man lightly placed on the seascape— made their way back to Key Haven. We struck the sails, coiled the lines, lashed the boats to the dock, and made our way back to Key West, a lonelier and now more ordinary place.

Two months later, a Costa Rican lawyer called to tell me I had inherited the house in Arenal. John had moved permanently to London and had given the house to Thomas who had left it to me.

Twenty

Thomas' death sucked music out of my world and made me bitter, an emotion I had always rejected whenever it had courted me. Bitter people need a kind of absolution they can't find, and spit poison on the world around them. I refused to do or be that, but that is what I felt pushed toward.

The changes taking place on the island added fuel to my anger, but I was not alone. Our little island went to war against the city, the state and federal bureaucrats that year, proudly proving we were not the sheep the rest of the country seemed on the way to becoming, that we were something quite "other" that we were willing to fight for.

The fight with the state began one morning when people started arriving at M & M Laundromat for their café con leche only to find it shuttered. "CLOSED BY ORDER OF THE STATE HEALTH DEPARTMENT."

One of the Mexicans from Mérida, Juan, who now ran the shop, explained to those of us milling around that the health officer shut them down because the cooking area wasn't screened in. What! A state that consistently failed children in foster care and old people in assisted living facilities was worried about our coffee and Cuban toast! What!

The coffee shop part of the laundromat was the size of a small walk-in closet, with a service window facing the sidewalk and another facing the laudromat itself. With customers ordering and picking up coffee and food every minute of every day, putting a screen on the windows would be ridiculous. The cooking area had fans, and all the food was refrigerated until it was ready for cooking anyway. We were being picked on because we were a small town. Miami had hundreds of these Cuban hole-in-the-wall eateries, but the state health department didn't tackle them because there were hundreds of thousands of Cubans in Miami now, and they voted consistently and as a bloc. Cuban coffee got Key West going in the morning. The social mixing that took place at M & M Laundromat and others like it was an important piece of island magic.

Word of the shut-down spread quickly from construction site to construction site—construction workers, not women, are the biggest gossips—and individual anger became collective anger. We decided we weren't going to stand for it. Instead of showing up on our jobsites the next morning, we protested back and forth in front of the laundromat with signs saying: "NO COFFEE, NO WORKEE" and: "NO FUEL, NO ROCKETS." The resident *Miami Herald* reporter photographed and interviewed us, and our protest made the front page.

The governor of Florida, on a fishing trip up the Keys, was famous for his common touch and had done walking tours of the state to win votes. Someone told him about our protests, and he drove down to see for himself. He talked to some of us protesting, and I explained to him the social importance of the place as well as the obvious need it filled. He seemed amused. I pointed out Juan, the manager, to the governor.

The governor asked Juan to open the shutters on the windows and take him inside the kitchen. When they came back out, the governor went to his car and used the car phone, then went up to the sidewalk window and said: "Juan, can I get a café con leche, *por favor*? Cheering and applause, and we all lined up to thank the governor and shake his hand.

The next battle got the national TV cameras back to the island. The United States Border Patrol, claiming a need to stop illegal immigrants and drug smugglers from using the Keys as a gateway to the United States—what were we, a foreign country?—set up a roadblock in Florida City. Everyone leaving the islands by land was stopped and had to prove citizenship, and there were searches of vehicles. The traffic jams at the checkpoint were sometimes seventeen miles long. As word spread, tourists stayed away, and commerce started drying up once again. Deliveries of food, gasoline, and other commodities were now erratic.

One week of this, and the town had had enough. The mayor protested to the Feds and took them to court to get an injunction. Injunction denied. Outside on the courthouse steps, the mayor announced that if we were going to be treated as a foreign country, we had the right to our independence, and Key West was going to secede from the United States in two days.

The Feds did not take lightly to the idea of a piece of the South seceding again. Dozens of men in suits with cuff mikes and flesh-colored earpieces arrived in town.

Standing on a flatbed truck in front of the old customs house, surrounded by TV cameras and over a thousand people, the mayor read the statement of grievances and declared that we were seceding from the United States: the Conch Republic was born. There was lots of cheering, but then some booing when Old Glory was lowered and the Conch Republic flag run up the pole. The flag was blue and had a conch shell centered in a large sun with the motto beneath:

WE SECEDED WHERE OTHERS FAILED. The men in suits all started talking into their cuff mikes.

Members of the new nation's cabinet, using loaves of stale Cuban bread, attacked men dressed in U.S. Army uniforms, who were laughing. Old Glory was run back up the pole with our flag beneath it, and the mayor "surrendered" to the Feds and requested $1 billion in foreign aid. Peter Anderson, the secretary of the new republic, proclaimed we were now "a sovereign state of mind," and the crowd applauded and howled with laughter.

When my little tribe left the square, Leigh bent over the cuff of one of the "suits" and yelled: "We really do want to secede." The man was startled, then told her to fuck off.

"What's wrong, Mr. Fed, your sense of humor get caught in your zipper this morning? We really would like to secede." The man was shocked, then angry, and we pulled her away before it turned ugly.

Up the street, Doug asked the obvious question. "Leigh, why do you *always* have to rub people's noses in it?"

"OK, boys, you want to know my opinion? I wish we really could secede. Imagine this: we're independent and become an offshore banking haven like Grand Cayman. Now all the taxes are paid by rich people who don't live here. All motor vehicle traffic has to stop at Stock Island, and we're now an island without cars like Hydra." She looked at Tom: "Was that cool or not?"

"Super cool, Leigh."

"Now we live in a beautiful place with no cars and no taxes, and we limit cruise ships to the high-end ones carrying no more than five hundred people."

Comparing that vision of the island to what we had now—we were threading our way through crowds of cruise ship passengers, walking past one tacky T-shirt shop after another on our way up Duval Street to retrieve our bikes—made us all quiet.

A few days later, the Feds quietly dismantled their checkpoint.

A month later, the *Key West Citizen* announced one morning that a group of developers and the city were about to make a deal that would give the developers Simonton Beach to build a hotel on in exchange for buying the city a piece of land elsewhere.

The city and the developers had misjudged the anger boiling in many of the city's residents, Conchs and outsiders alike, at the transformations taking place on the island, and there was an explosion of outrage that surprised even us, the outraged. Simonton Beach had been our sunset and summertime swimming venue. Riding down Simonton Street and seeing the blue water of the harbor at the end had been a piece of island magic that had help confirm I had made the right decision to move here. We couldn't swim there anymore because of what the cruise ships stirred up from the harbor bottom every day, but we still had that view, the last piece on that end of the island that hadn't had a blocking concrete wall built on it.

A carpenter I knew from the Parrot roped me in, and we organized the protest. I called the governor's office and told the man who answered the phone how much we'd loved the governor's intervention at the coffee shop, but that we needed his help even more now.

The next night, late, the phone rang, and it was a surprisingly friendly aide to the governor. I asked the aide to thank the governor again for his help with keeping the M & M coffee shop open.

"Mr. Cottrell, I wish all our battles were that easy and made that many people happy. By the way, you folks down there have got the whole staff up here addicted to Cuban coffee."

"Rocket fuel."

He laughed: "You've got that right." A pause. "OK, Mr. Cottrell, can you explain your present problem?"

I asked him to call me John, then I explained the new battle and why that particular piece of land was special. There was silence for a minute on his end; the man sounded tired.

"Mr. Cottrell, sorry, John, land issues in this state are the biggest pain in our collective behinds. I'll be frank. The developers in this state have a lot of power, especially in the legislature. They'd pave the whole state to make a buck, but if you tell anyone I said that I'll embargo all shipments of Cuban coffee to the Keys." We both laughed. "Let me talk to the Big Guy tomorrow, and I'll get back to you."

I was touched by the fact that the man had actually called me, and even more touched by his frankness.

He called me back the next evening. "OK, John, here's the deal. You arrange a community input meeting in three to seven days, and we'll send down the cabinet member in charge of land issues. He's very much pro-conservation, but please don't make that known. He has to appear completely neutral."

I thanked the man, then thanked him again for trusting my discretion.

"John, the governor can play the 'good ol' country boy' to perfection, but I've never known anyone who can size up a person's worth faster or more accurately. He liked your description of why the coffee shop was important to the community, and that you weren't whiney when you asked for help."

I was touched again. "You guys got two cases of Bustelo coffee headed your way." He gave me a phone number to call when we were ready.

The Waterfront Theatre lent us the building for the meeting, which we advertised heavily. The man from the governor's cabinet, Jason, flew in the day before the meeting and called me from his hotel. Leigh, Doug, and I took him to Louie's for lunch, giving Marvin a "lips zipped shut" signal.

I felt immediately sorry for the man. He was slight, had something wrong with one eye, and I could imagine the hell of his life going up against the "scratch your balls, spit, and fuck the alligators and birds" mentality of the developers in Florida. He ordered iced tea, so we did, too, though it seemed a sacrilege.

I explained the issue, and Doug and Leigh added details. His questions revealed a personal intelligence, but also a focus not narrow enough for island issues. There weren't acres involved here, but a piece of land smaller than most house lots on the mainland. We were beginning to worry that he wasn't getting it, but then our brilliant princess proved her brilliance.

"Jason, can you ride a bicycle?"

He looked surprised by the question, but said yes.

"OK, let's pay and go. We'll show you why this tiny piece of land is important." Jason insisted on paying for his own lunch.

I gave Jason my bike and borrowed Marvin's. I was a little nervous, worried that Jason might be a little bicycle rusty, but he told us he rode often up in Tallahassee.

We mounted up and rode over to Whitehead Street, yelling over tour guide info: place where the undersea telegraph cable from Havana had come ashore; building where Pan Am airlines had started; house where Robert Frost had spent several winters; place where Hemingway had punched out Wallace Stevens; then we crossed over to Simonton Street at Fleming and stopped. I looked over at the man, who was obviously having fun, and I gave him both barrels.

"Jason, we're powerless here, in state terms. There are only twenty-eight thousand of us on the island. But it's a tiny, magical place that's being destroyed by developers. I came here sad and lost, and one of the things that made me realize I had found a home was the bike ride we're about to make. You lead and look down to the end of the street after the next block."

We mounted up again, rode through the overhanging tunnel of mahoganies, and there it was: blue water harbor—and we got lucky again—a sailboat under sail. We rode to water's edge.

"Jason, this is the last view like it on this end of the island, the only little piece they haven't done *that* to," and I pointed to the buildings on either side. Help us if you can."

"I'll try."

I think the simple act of riding a bike on a pretty island gave him the same rush it had me.

The meeting at Waterfront Theatre was raucous, democracy at work. Jason stood on the stage, disinterested listener, as speaker after speaker railed against one more desecration of a special place. One man, representing the developers, made the case, against constant booing, for the land swap, and Jason asked the crowd to let the man present his case.

The meeting ended with Jason telling the audience that he would consult with the governor about having the state purchase the land and get back to us within sixty days. People in the audience booed at that, but I felt sorry for the man and went up to him and thanked him, and drove him back to the airport the next morning. Right before he boarded his flight, he leaned towards me and whispered: "I'll do everything I can to help you, and thank you for your passion."

Two months before the protest meeting, I'd had a message on my answering machine asking me to look at a small job. I hadn't recognized the man's name, but when I showed up the next day at the address he gave me at the corner of Southard and William Streets, I realized it was the family compound of the Delacortes who, along with the Spottswood and Ramos families, were the economic rulers of the island. The man who had called me, Roger Talbot, was married to Simone Delacorte. I looked at the job, replacing rotten tongue-and-groove decking on the downstairs porches, and gave him a price. Two days later he called me again and asked me to do it. It was a messy but fairly simple job, the most difficult part being trying to keep Roger and Simone's children off the new deck once we'd painted it.

After I'd gotten the go-ahead for the job, I asked Doug at dinner one night if he had any idea why an old Conch family like the Delacortes would use me instead of someone they knew. He thought about it for a few minutes after he'd served Tom and me, his week on: roast beef, scalloped potatoes, and braised leeks.

"You say it was Simone's husband who called and dealt with you?" I nodded. "Then they're letting him manage the compound, and he wants to get away from using the same old people, just to keep everyone honest. The quality of your work's probably better, too. And if the people they usually use get pissed off, they're pissed off at Roger, an outsider."

The compound was a triple lot. In addition to Roger and Simone's house, with its small swimming pool, there was a single-story shuttered building, a large garage, and then the main house where Simone's brother, Robert, and their mother lived, according to Doug. I'd seen Robert a couple of times while we were working as he stopped over to talk to his sister and brother-in-law. He was a little overweight, handsome in that "gray fox" way women seem to like, but very reserved. Except for a subdued "Good morning" or "Good Afternoon," he never spoke to me or my men.

The main house was a two-story, white wooden beauty sitting far back on the property. Gingerbread-embellished porches wrapped around the front and two sides. Black shutters framed classic two-over-two sash windows. The entire compound was heavily planted, especially around the perimeter, giving the yard complete privacy from its neighbors and the street. It was as good as it gets for life in Old Town Key West.

Two days after Jason's visit and the protest meeting at Waterfront Theatre, I had a message on my machine from Robert Delacorte, himself, inviting me to dinner with him and his mother, which I thought strange. Doug had already told me that Robert was gay and very closeted, which made me nervous.

"The only thing I can tell you about him apart from that is that there's a rumor he paid a young guy a hundred dollars once just to dance with him at his house."

"That's kind of sad."

"John, you have no idea what life was like for gay Conchs in his generation. 'Closets' is way too weak a description. Vaults would be more like it."

We both puzzled over the invitation, which I reluctantly accepted. It might lead to more work.

I was dreading the evening when I pulled up in front of the gate to the main house, an impressive solid wood affair hung between two cut stone columns. I pushed the button on the intercom on the left column, and a few seconds later heard the buzz of the gate release. The walkway to the house was lined with the most delicate palms I had ever seen. A slight breeze caused their fronds to sway, revealing a beautifully silvered underside.

I climbed the stairs to the porch and, just as I reached the door, it opened. It was Robert, dressed in dark pants and an immaculately white guayabera. We exchanged greetings, and he invited me in.

"Follow me," he said, "we'll have a drink before dinner, if you don't mind. Mother's not quite ready."

We walked past the stairway (Dade County pine, white spindles, unpainted Dade County pine railing), down the hallway past dozens of photos, including three of a man, his father, I assumed, with three presidents of the United States. We walked beneath two large, crystal chandeliers whose pendants hung from the tiniest of gold wires, then passed through a sitting room onto one of the side porches, which had a wet bar and several wicker chairs. Two ceiling fans provided a breeze. I gave him the flowers I had brought, and he disappeared inside.

I steeled myself for a boring evening. Provincial aristocracy holds little interest for me. Their power is almost always disproportionate to their accomplishments, and they usually wed arrogance and dullness in deadly combinations.

When Robert returned, he went behind the bar. "What would you like?"

"Would it be too much trouble to have a Pernod?" I had seen the bottle while he was inside.

"Not at all." He put ice in a glass, and poured the pastis. "I'll let you do the water," and handed me a small pitcher. I filled the glass and took a sip.

"Memories of France?" he said and laughed at my surprised look.

"Robert, I'm not even going to ask how you know that about me." He grinned and we sat down.

He caught me looking back towards his sister's house.

"I'd like to thank you personally for the work you and your men did back there. Beautifully done and for a fair price." I thanked him for the compliment; then small talk ensued. He asked how much work I had, and we discussed the history of one of the houses I was working on. Then his mother appeared.

I don't know exactly what I had been expecting (a rotund, grandmotherly type, perhaps?), but Robert introduced me to a trim, aristocratic-looking woman in her mid to late sixties, I guessed. She was beautifully coiffed (full head of hair professionally colored), intelligent blue eyes, beautiful skin unlined except for laugh lines at the eyes. She was dressed in a tailored white blouse and a pleated navy skirt, and wore no jewelry but a simple strand of pearls and a plain wedding band.

"Mother, this is Mr. Cottrell; Mr. Cottrell, my mother, Claudine." I shook her hand and made a slight bow with my head. She smiled, having caught, I think, my surprise.

"Thank you for the flowers, Mr. Cottrell. Birds of Paradise are among my favorites. Please come and sit down, you two. Forgive us the informality, but we're dining on the other porch rather than inside. It's such a lovely evening, I hope you don't mind."

"Not at all," I answered, knowing the real reason was more likely the awkwardness of three people dining at the table for twelve I'd seen in a room as we walked down the hall.

She led us back across the hall, through what was obviously the living room to the porch on the other side of the house. Wall sconces and candles lit a small table that sparkled with cut crystal, expensive china, and silver of surprisingly modern design. My flowers were now in a beautiful, multi-colored (Murano?) vase on the center of the table. I realized with pleasure that I was now a guest at a truly formal dinner with people with elegant manners. I adjusted my manners and language to match.

Robert seated his mother, then the two of us took our places. A white-haired, Cuban man named Juan I had seen when I was working on Simone and Roger's house, dressed now in black pants and starched white shirt, looked to Claudine, who nodded. He disappeared inside and returned with three small plates. "*Paté de foie truffé*," she announced. Real *petits cornichons* and a *baguette* accompanied the small, fragrant slabs.

"You're spoiling me, Mrs. Delacorte."

"Claudine, please. I noticed she pronounced it the French way with the "au" a long "o.""

"Please call me John, then."

She smiled and nodded to Juan. He poured a small amount of a dark gold wine from a half bottle, first into Robert's glass, who did the obligatory tasting and nodded, then filled Claudine's halfway, then mine, then Robert's. Robert lifted his glass: "Welcome to our home." We toasted and I tasted. There is only one wine I can identify without failure, eyes closed. That explosion of flavor was familiar. I looked at Robert and Claudine.

"d'Yquem?"

Claudine laughed, pleased, I think. "Very good, John. I hope you don't mind a sweet wine with the *paté*, but it was once a traditional pairing." I liked her manners and the slightly formal language, and the very clipped, precise way she spoke. She was obviously used to giving orders.

"Not only do I not mind, I am honored." They both smiled.

We began eating. A formal dinner party with strangers is often hard slogging, trying to prevent those painful silences that can easily occur. I asked about the chandeliers I had admired in the hall. "Czech?"

Claudine confirmed my guess. "My father bought them in Havana. That was the closest place to buy fine things, to buy anything really. Back then, Miami was just a backward village."

"Instead of the backward city it is today," I added. We all laughed.

"Havana was wonderful, back then," Claudine continued, "cosmopolitan, lovely people from everywhere; opera, ballet, great parties, and dances. Corrupt, too, alas, but the corruption wasn't what it became when the Mafia moved in. And then that animal took over and turned it into a prison camp." There was real anger in her voice.

I asked what they thought would happen to Key West when Castro fell or died, a source of endless speculation here on the island, with some people expecting dire consequences, others an explosion of activity as the two historically related islands, only ninety miles apart, re-connected.

Robert stopped eating and began talking in an almost pedagogical tone of voice. He had obviously, as one of the economic leaders on our island, given the topic a lot of thought. "Key West and Havana have a natural connection. Look at the past when Flagler sent boxcars to Cuba, and Cubans and Key Westers moved back and forth all the time. There used to be travel agencies on Duval Street where you could buy plane or boat tickets for Cuba and rent your hotel rooms in Havana or book tours in advance."

He became animated. "Imagine being able to drive to the airport here and thirty minutes later be in a wonderful, beautiful cosmopolitan city in another country that's the most beautiful island in the Caribbean. The projections are that all the marinas in south Florida combined won't be able to handle the boat traffic to and from Cuba. Key West will become a working place again, not just a tourist destination."

Claudine interrupted. "Robert is so involved in this, I'm afraid he might bore you and the entrée will get cold."

He smiled at his mother and agreed. "I'm passionate about the subject, it's true. I just hope to live to see a free Cuba." He lifted his glass and toasted: "Cuba Libre!" We clinked glasses.

Juan had already cleared for the next course and brought it in. I rudely sniffed the dish, and the fragrance gave me goose bumps.

"A pork tenderloin, John, cooked Cuban style, but done *aux pruneaux*."

"I think I've died and gone to heaven, Claudine."

"Wait, my young friend." She looked at Robert, and they exchanged a conspiratorial glance. She turned and said something to Juan, and he went to the bar and took a napkin and wrapped it around the bottle of wine he was about to serve so I couldn't see the label.

"We want you to guess this one, Mr. Francophile." How did they know that about me?

Robert tasted first again, then Juan poured. I tasted. Obviously French . . . another sip . . . Bordeaux not Burgundy, though I had been tricked once before by a Romanée Conti. I tasted again. Obviously Premier Grand Cru, obviously one of the planet's finest wines.

"I can't say exactly. French. Bordeaux, of course. If I had to guess, I would say Pétrus or a really old Sainte Estèphe."

They both laughed. "Wrong, wrong, wrong," Claudine said with pleasure. "Juan, show him the bottle."

Juan came to my side and removed the napkin. Vega-Sicilia 1968. Spanish!? I was shocked. "I concede defeat." They looked at each other and laughed again. In their mutual pleasure at my surprise, I began to see that there was real companionship and love between mother and son.

I have always been good at playing the imp that doesn't respect social conventions, knowing just how far to push without actually disrespecting them.

"Alright, I have been tricked twice tonight," I used a semi-serious tone of voice, and they both went neutral-faced. Was I really angry?

"First," I began in my best injured tone, "I was led to believe that I was to have dinner with Robert and his mother, a woman I assumed to be elderly and quite kind, only to find she's a great beauty with devastating wit. Then I am tricked again with one of the finest wines I've ever had, and it's not French. I'm afraid of what's next."

Real laughter. One can always tell when a dinner party starts to go well or, god save us, bad. This had just tipped to good. I tasted the wine again. "OK, you win. You have to tell me about this wine."

"Spanish, you know now that you've seen the label. A group of Spanish vintners swore to match the Grands Crus from Bordeaux. They worked hard at it, and if your reaction is correct, they succeeded. Unfortunately," Claudine lamented, "like all good things, it's been discovered and fetches similar prices."

I tasted the pork *aux pruneaux*. "Claudine, I think I may be in love." Again pushing the social envelope, but the art of flirting, even pretend, is fun.

"Ah, you men are too easy. You think only with your stomachs and your anatomy."

"Mother!" Was it real shock or pretend?

"Well, it's true, gentlemen. Men are much simpler and more dangerous creatures than women."

"Well, madame," I said reverting to formality, "I would have to differ. Think, for example, of the expression 'Dear John letter.' There is no expression 'Dear Jane letter.' So it must be that women are far crueler to the human heart than men."

"Hogwash, my friend. I suspect a trail of broken hearts lies behind your charming sweet talk. Why else would someone of your stature still be unmarried?"

"And behind you a trail even longer, I suspect," I retorted. She smiled and took the compliment.

I laughed and looked at Robert, who looked a little uncomfortable. "Your mother is a worthy adversary."

There was a pause in the talk as we focused on the pork and the wine. Perhaps I had gone too far, and any talk of men and women together, I realized, probably pained them because of Robert's orientation. Time to switch topics. The lights in the yard came on, discreetly lighting plantings from underneath, including one striking Bismarkia palm.

"What are those palms you have lining the walk out front?" I asked. "They're beautiful, and I don't know them at all."

"You have now definitely won my mother's heart," Robert said.

"The common name is Keys Silver Thatch Palms," she explained, "but there are two palms with that name, the *Thrinax Morissii*, also beautiful, and these, *Cocothrinax Argentata*."

"Why haven't I seen them before?"

"They only grow inland above flood level. You can see them on the Marquesas and in the middle of Big Pine Key. They're very difficult to transplant and only grow a foot every ten years, so they almost became extinct. Poor Robert here had to help dig these up years ago up the Keys when they were small enough to get the entire root ball. I think they're the most delicate of all our natives."

"Can you buy them anywhere? I'd like to plant one in my yard."

"I don't think so, John. They grow so slowly I don't think it would pay a nursery to carry them."

Juan served the salad. I appreciated the European order of salad after entrée.

Claudine was the first to pick up the conversation again. "Why did you move to Paris and why did you leave?" We were back to formal conversation. I debated whether to ask them how they knew that about me but decided not to. I told them the story of my first arrival in Paris, and what it had meant to me, and my vow to live there someday.

Claudine reached over and put her hand on top of Robert's and let it rest there. "I wanted something like that for my son so much" she said and she looked at him with great tenderness, "but he had to take on the family burdens far too soon." She stroked his hand for a second. Then Claudine asked again why I had left Paris.

"I had a very stressful job working for the national oil company. I had the American work ethic, and none of the people working for me did—American or French—yet I was responsible. It wore me down. Plus the French government had decided to demolish the buildings in my neighborhood, and my apartment building was one of them. The combination of things made me ready to leave."

"Why are the French so rude, even to Americans with French surnames like us?" Claudine asked.

"Well, it's not the French as a whole, but mostly the Parisians, and not just to Americans but to everyone, even each other. I speak fluent French, and it made no difference. You'd be waiting in line to buy cheese and reach the counter and be insulted by the clerk just because he was in a bad mood. It's part of their culture. I remember my last month in Paris," and I launched into one of my favorite "Paris" tales.

"My boss at the oil company was a French aristocrat who pretended to have the common touch. He lived in the 16th Arrondissement, the chicest part of the city. His speech was so formal that we Americans would count the number of subjunctives, which is very formal, that he would use in a departmental meeting. When I gave in my resignation, he invited me to his flat for a cocktail party. Now remember that the French never invite you into their homes. You meet in a café or a restaurant, so this was a great honor in gratitude for my having worked like an animal and because the students I taught liked me. Also, more importantly, he knew that because I was leaving, he would never have to repeat the invitation.

"I arrived at this elegant apartment building and made my way upstairs in one of those quaint, wrought-iron and brass elevators. I was the only employee at the party. All the other guests were friends of the same social status as my boss. His wife greeted me with minimally acceptable manners and left me on my own.

"On the far side of the room was a large buffet table that I walked to. Wonderful pâtés, smoked salmon, cheeses ripened to perfection, and the like. Two uniformed servants, with white gloves, stood behind the table to serve. A woman of a certain age, as the French describe middle-aged, came up next to me and remarked at the color of the salmon. I glanced at her: elegantly clad, discreet jewelry, perfect coiffure, understated make-up, perfectly French. I explained to her that we were very lucky to get this salmon because the company's drillers brought it back every week when they returned from the rigs in the North Sea.

"Now remember," I said, looking at Claudine and Robert, "that I am by now totally fed up with Parisian rudeness, and one of the things I hated was that they would always ask what your father did because they couldn't class you by your foreign-accented French."

"'How do you know, Monsieur Bouiller?' the woman asked. I explained that he was my boss at Total, the company I worked for. The next question was what I did there. Then came the question I was expecting."

"'What does your father do?' she asked.

"I stared straight into her eyes and said as belligerently as possible: He raises pigs, Madame.

"'I can see that,' she shot back without even a nanosecond's hesitation and turned on her heel and walked away."

Robert and Claudine gasped.

"I think that was the funniest thing that ever happened to me in Paris. The Parisians have trained for centuries to do this. It's in their blood. I laughed when she walked away, knowing she'd given me a story I'd use the rest of my life."

When we finished the salad, Claudine stood. "If you don't mind, I'll have Juan serve you dessert in the bar. I have to excuse myself and wrap some birthday presents for my grandson's birthday tomorrow."

I thanked her for the meal, and we stood and left the porch.

Juan served flan, then glasses of port. I knew there had to be a reason for the dinner invitation, and I expected to find out why now, but Robert just talked about the history of their house and asked me about my project renovating the Bakery. I explained about the problem Doug and I were having getting the permit to re-build the garage because of the encroachment on the right-of-way and he sympathized.

"It sometimes seems they go out of their way to stop the people doing good work and let the other work sail through. It didn't always used to be this way."

He walked me to the door when we were through and thanked me for coming. "It does my mother good to see new faces. We'll do it again."

When the gate had closed behind me, and I was on the street again, I looked back and realized what a sanctuary their property was. I knew I had been honored, but I also knew I had been studied closely and couldn't stop wondering what they wanted. People of their position in town didn't invite carpenters to dinner, and certainly not dinners of that quality.

The next day, I got a call from the building department asking me to pick up the permit for the garage. When I went downtown to pick it up, the same obstructionist bitch who had given me reason after reason for *not* issuing the permit, handed it to me after I'd paid the fee and said: "You have good friends." I refused to acknowledge the remark.

Two days later I came home to find a four-foot tall *Cocothrinax Argentata* sitting on the porch in a pot with a card attached explaining how to plant and care for it.

Now I was intrigued.

Doug and I discussed the dinner party, the permit, and the palm. "They want something," he told me after he thought about it.

"Why haven't I heard anything, then?"

"They're waiting to hear if you've told anyone about the dinner or the palm, or gone around bragging about his influence with the building department. I'm guessing that they want to know that you keep your mouth shut."

I sent a thank-you note for the dinner and the palm.

Twenty-One

A week later, the phone rang and it was Robert again, inviting me to dinner again.

"It will be just the two of us this time, I'm afraid. Mother had to go to Charleston because her sister's ill." Now I was *really* intrigued.

I arrived at the gate at the same time as before and was buzzed in. Robert met me at the door, dressed this time in jeans, a Polo shirt, and moccasins. We went directly to the bar.

"I hope you don't mind eating out here at the bar tonight since it's just the two of us."

"Not at all." I asked about his aunt and heard that she had had a heart attack. I commiserated.

He served me a Pernod without my asking, and I could see that he was either distracted or nervous, or maybe the intimacy caused by the absence of a third party made him ill at ease. We talked about the weather and the recent airplane hijacking, where a man who'd hijacked a plane to get from Cuba to Key West had now hijacked a plane to get back to Cuba. We both laughed at the interview with Larry Formica, owner of a local gay guesthouse and restaurant, who was wringing his hands on national TV. "What am I going to do?" he wailed. "The croissants for tomorrow's breakfast were on that plane."

Juan served again. Gazpacho, done to perfection, served with a glass of Sancerre, then the best *picadillo* I'd ever had on the island. This was accompanied by a Spanish red I hadn't heard of; not the Vega-Sicilia of the last visit, this one a little rough, but a good partner.

Robert spoke little and always about inconsequential things: the latest, hours-long power outage, or the change in airlines serving the island, but in a disconnected way. I wondered why he'd invited me.

There was salad again, but then he asked if I minded if we skipped dessert. "Not at all. The *picadillo* was good enough to be dessert." He smiled in an obligatory way at the compliment. Juan cleared.

"Thank you, Juan, that will be all." Juan nodded and left us. Robert asked if I'd like some port (of course), poured two glasses, and sat back down. For a painfully long time, probably only a couple of minutes, he said nothing, just looked away and absently turned his glass round and round. Then, a decision having obviously been made, he looked at me and spoke.

"I think we may have a common interest in something and can help each other." They did want something from me. I wasn't surprised, but it made me nervous.

"OK, Robert, shoot."

"How passionate are you about stopping the development on Simonton Beach?"

"Robert, very passionate. Building there would destroy one of the last little pieces of magic on the island. Land meets ocean . . . pure nature . . . free magic, a wonder we all get to have, regardless of how little money we have. You can see the sunset from there without putting up with the carnival that sunset has turned into on Mallory Square. It's ours, dammit, and we'll fight to keep it."

He smiled, probably amused at an outsider professing such an attachment to a piece of land on an island where his family had lived for three generations. I was prepared for some condescending remark. I was not prepared for what came next.

"I can help you," he said, "but you have to help me." He started to go on, but then stopped himself. "Let me make sure Juan is gone," and got up and went inside.

When he came back, he poured us more port and sat down. "How much do you know about me?" he asked. Now I was on the spot. Did I mention *that*?

"I know your family is rich and powerful here. How else did I get that permit the other day?" He laughed, then shrugged, like the favor was too small even to bring up.

"No, John, what do you know about me?" I squirmed a little. "Do you know about my condition?" and he looked away when he pronounced the last word.

I thought, 'What the hell, what have I got to lose by being honest?'

"Do you mean do I know you're gay?" There was an almost imperceptible jerk when he heard the word.

"That's what I was referring to."

"Robert, it's not a condition," and I emphasized the strange choice of words but then softened my voice. "If you're gay, you're born that way." It seemed strange at this point in history and in this particular place to be having this conversation. If gay men glowed, Key West would be visible from space. I subdued my initial impatience by reminding myself of what Doug had told me: that if you were a Conch, Key West was a redneck town, and also that Robert had grown up in a different age.

He looked away for a moment, then started speaking. "When I was twenty-nine, I ran for sheriff of the county. My family expected it of me. My father had been sheriff, then state representative, and I was supposed to follow in his footsteps." His eyes became distant, and he began to turn his glass slowly in circles, tapping it with one finger at the end of each revolution.

"I was uncomfortable being that exposed to the public. You see how I grew up," and he nodded toward the tall fences surrounding the property. "But I felt it was my duty. My parents had provided me with a good education and a privileged life. My grandparents were still alive then and were strong believers in 'dynasty,' and getting and keeping power."

He paused and took a drink, then went back to turning his glass, quarter turn, quarter turn, quarter turn, another, then a little tap to the rim.

"The campaigning was pretty much routine: posters, big Cuban pig roasts here on the property, speeches to the chamber of commerce and in Bayview Park on the 4th of July. My family had been generous, a lot of people owed us favors, and my opponent was a crude man from the projects who'd always been a bully in school and later. My election was guaranteed."

He got up and brought the bottle of port back to the table. Rather than sitting back down, he walked over to the edge of the porch, looking back toward Simone's house. When he began to speak again, it was in a different voice: slower, sadder, and he kept his face turned from me. I had to strain to hear him.

"I'd given a speech in Marathon one day. I'd driven up there with my friend, Carlos."

He emphasized "friend" in a way I assumed he meant lover.

"We were both happy. The speech had gone well. It was a beautiful, cool, sunny day. October 28th. I was ahead in the polls, and the election was the following week."

He turned back around. "Carlos and I were drinking rum on the way back to Key West. Back then at that time of year you'd be lucky to see ten other cars on the road the whole way down. We were a little drunk by the time we got to Key West. The top was down on the car.

"When we hit Duval Street, one of those little squall lines came ashore, one of those island rainstorms barely a quarter of a mile wide. It hit us, but then we realized that by speeding up or slowing down, we could keep the leading edge of the rain just on the trunk of the car. Down Duval Street we went, speeding and slowing, leading the rain along, misjudging once in a while and getting wet. We could look straight up and see clear sky and the edge of the squall both. It was so spontaneous and magical that we couldn't stop laughing." A long pause and then, in almost a pleading tone of voice: "We were happy. At one point, out of the pure joy of the moment, Carlos leaned over and gave me a quick kiss on the cheek."

His voice darkened. "Two days later, flyers started showing up on car windshields, telephone poles, and in mailboxes. It was a picture, a drawing actually, of Carlos kissing me with the caption, in big letters: 'QUEER FOR SHERIFF?'

"There'd been rumors about me before. Why hadn't I married yet? Why wasn't I dating anyone? But I'd always been careful, as much to protect my family as myself."

He turned around. "It ruined my life, and my family was never the same again after the humiliation of it. My grandfather never spoke to me from then on, and he and my grandmother died shortly after. My father blamed me, and from then until his own death, his only words to me were related to running our businesses.

"I lost the election, of course, but my family lost much more. I was a dirty little secret exposed. I felt sorriest for my mother." He hesitated, then put down his drink. "Follow me."

We walked through the house to the other side and across the yard to the shuttered wooden building I'd seen on the property. He opened the shutters over a set of French doors, entered and flipped some switches. I was stunned at what I saw: a ballroom, an honest-to-god ballroom, with polished wooden floors, crystal wall sconces and chandeliers, and brilliantly-painted frescoes on the ceiling depicting episodes from Key West history: the wrecking industry, sponging, cigar-making, and the arrival of Flagler's railroad.

"Robert, it's magnificent. This has to be the most beautiful space on the island." He accepted the compliment without speaking, walked across the room to check a lock on a door, then walked back.

"This was the social center of the island when I was young. The dances and parties in this room gave my mother more pleasure than anything else in her life apart from her family. When Simone and I were young, we were allowed—if we behaved ourselves—to watch for an hour or so. It was wonderful to see my mother, so beautiful, so young, so alive, dancing and enjoying herself. We were so proud of her, and seeing the pleasure she took in it all made us impatient to become adults. Ernest and Pauline Hemingway danced here. President Truman and Bess and their daughter, Margaret, came once."

He started to say something else, then turned away, and I thought I heard a choked-back sob. When he turned back to me, he was in full control of himself, and anger had replaced sadness. "After the flyers and my lost election, there was never another party or dance in this room. It has been shuttered and unused ever since. The loss to my mother, who never, ever reproached me, made me hate myself and hate the man behind it all, my opponent in that election. Now let's talk business."

He closed the door we'd entered through, then the shutters, and we walked back to our drinks.

"My opponent in that election was Luis Aguilar." The name slapped me in the face. He was the city commissioner pushing hardest for the Simonton Beach deal. Robert was all business now. He checked again that Juan was nowhere near, sat down, and poured us more port.

"Carlos, my friend, a sweet, gentle man, killed himself a month after the posters showed up. He couldn't bear the shame of being exposed, and the remarks people made to his family about it. I wanted to die, too, but I couldn't do that to my mother, but I swore that before I died I would get even with Luis, ruin him, destroy him like he destroyed everything I loved, no matter how long it took." He looked straight at me. "That time has come. I want you to help me, and I will help you."

I was hooked. "How, Robert?"

He lowered his voice enough that I had to strain to hear him. "Luis has enough votes on the city commission to make the swap. What people don't know is that Luis is also part of the development group that's going to buy it. They're going to give him part ownership for rounding up the votes when it passes, but he still has to come up with $200,000 cash of his own to seal the deal. He doesn't have the money, but he's going to get it real soon. And they won't or can't do the deal without his money."

"How is he going to get it?"

"Luis deals coke, not big time, but enough to allow him to live well. He gets it in—I'm not sure yet how but I'll find out—and then sells it, so far only to people out of town. He FedEx's it to his customers. I know your part in fighting the sale of the beach, and I know your feelings about cocaine, which I share, by the way."

He took a sip of his drink, started turning and tapping his glass again and continued. "I know the state has already told you it will try to help you, but they may not be fast enough. I've already arranged through friends I have in the legislature in Tallahassee to secure the purchase by the state, but we have to stop or postpone the deal long enough.

"Sometime soon, Luis is bringing in a lot of coke, which is how he's going to get his $200,000. I want him exposed for doing it, his coke confiscated as publicly as possible, publicly, dammit, just like what he did to me. I want him ruined financially and busted. I want to destroy the man who destroyed my life, and that will stop the deal and save your beach. Interested?"

Of course, I was interested, but I told Robert I had to give it some thought.

"We don't have a lot of time, remember."

"I need a week to decide on something this big." He agreed, reluctantly.

I spent most of the next two days trying to sort Robert's offer into its elements.

I hated cocaine and what it had done to Thomas and other friends, so I was pre-disposed to accept Robert's proposal on those grounds alone. I was tempted to do an end run, though, call the DEA anonymously with the tip, then claim ignorance when and if they made the bust, but I didn't know when the coke was going to arrive. I needed Robert's information, and he wasn't going to give it to me unless we made Aguilar's downfall public and dramatic to exact revenge.

As important as getting Aguilar's coke confiscated was the other issue: the developers needed to lose a round, and they needed to lose this round in particular. If you lived on a beautiful island, how would you know it on a daily basis if concrete warrens for rich rabbits blocked every view of the ocean? They'd won every fight to date. We were determined to give it our best shot on this one, and I now had an inside track to stop it.

There were two other issues related to the offer: How to do it? And, how dangerous was it? There were several possible ways to do it, but I didn't have to decide that yet. The issue of the danger involved was serious. Taking down a powerful Conch could get you killed. The popular T-shirts that asked: "WHERE IS BUM FARTO?" were funny, but there was a Conch somewhere on the island who knew the answer, and all bets said that Farto was permanently under water or dirt. I was an outsider. Push come to shove, I was completely expendable. Conchs were as tough a breed as existed on the continent. If I did this, I might be endangering not only myself, but my family. There had been three cocaine-related murders on the island already. I needed Doug's advice.

I gave young Tom the excuse that Doug and I had to have a business dinner with a new customer and took Doug to the Hukilau, a faux-Polynesian restaurant on North Roosevelt with seats where private conversation was possible. I owed him a nice dinner anyway for throwing me a good job.

When we'd been seated, Doug looked over at me: "Do I want to know what you're about to ask advice on? Tell me you're not screwing one of Leigh's friends behind her back, and you need the gay insight into infidelity."

"Doug, it's more serious than that." Whispering the details in between food delivery, I gave him the whole story. He shook his head back and forth through it all.

"John, give me a few minutes here. This is major. I can't believe he told you all that, and I can't believe he asked you to help him."

We tore into the pu'pu' platter when it arrived, making fatuous remarks about each appetizer, both knowing we were delaying the obvious. I sensed that Doug was not pleased with me, for only the second time. The first time had been when I'd intervened and kicked one of his tricks—with whom he was infatuated—out of the house when I'd found him in our office. Doug had been angry, then apologetic two weeks later when the trick had been arrested for beating another gay man into a coma.

"John, I know you want to save the beach. So do I. But do you have any idea what you're going up against? Aguilar is as dirty and connected as it gets here. You go up against him, and you've made a powerful enemy in a very small town."

"Doug, I understand that, but I'm sorry, I'm getting tired of all that Bubba Conch corruption. Look what it's done to your own home town. You and I both lived in Paris. What if someone corrupt got permission to build condos in the Tuileries Gardens?"

"John, this is dangerous. Are you willing to accept that?"

"I am, Doug, at least I think I am, but that tiny piece of land with that view deserves as much protection as the Grand Canyon."

We argued the issue back and forth, the danger versus the chance I'd been given to stop a corrupt land deal. At the end of the dinner, Doug proved again why he was as close to me as anyone in my life.

"John, whatever you decide, I'll back you up, but don't do anything without running it past me first. I may be able to find things out that help you . . . us. I'm in this with you now, but we really have to be careful."

"Thank you."

"No problem. Let's talk again tomorrow after work."

As I raced around town the next day dealing with all the problems of two large renovation jobs, I began to feel something familiar creeping into my subconscious, but I didn't have time to examine it. Stopped at a traffic light on the way to the lumberyard, it bubbled right out. It was dread again, the same, familiar dread I'd felt as the decision about what to do when I was drafted approached.

Doug and I talked again that night after work, up in his bedroom. Did we let Leigh know? Tom? How could we best accomplish the

public humiliation Robert required? We came up with some inge-
nious ideas . . . flyers all over town offering free coke with Aguilar's
address was one . . . and some outrageous ones that actually had us
laughing. I was glad I had taken him into my confidence.

Robert called the next night after work and asked me to come
over. We sat outside at the bar again. He checked again that Juan
wasn't around.

"It's coming in this week," he said, "by boat. They're going to store
it here in town somewhere until men from Miami come down, test
it and take delivery. I don't know exactly which day it's arriving or
where they're going to store it yet, but I think I'll be able to find out.
Luis is clever, I'll give that to him. He has a layer of people between
him and the load, and uses a courier to take messages back and forth.
It may be tough tying him directly to the load. I'll let you know more
when I know it."

Assuming Robert could get the needed information, I still faced
the issues of danger and whether to let Leigh and Tom in on what I,
and now Doug, were planning. Doug and I decided to tell Leigh but
not Tom, because of his past problem with the drug.

I was nervous climbing the stairs to Leigh's apartment the night
I planned to give her the news, because facing a displeased Leigh is
something even a Navy SEAL, who could kill with his bare hands,
would cringe in front of.

We ordered pizza (even mediocre pizza was better than her cooking), and then I started with the words no one likes to hear: "There's
something I have to tell you."

She shot me an unhappy look: "I've had a bad day. This better not
be that you're having an affair, or you want to end ours."

"Don't be silly. How could I even look at another woman after
I've had you?"

She gave a contemptuous snort. "OK, spit it out."

She made no comments as I told her everything, including that Doug was with me on it. She drummed her fingers on the table for a few seconds when I'd finished, then said: "Good for you. Do you know how much damage coke has done to my women? And look at what it did to Thomas. And you know I'm just as passionate about stopping the building on that beach."

Relief! "Leigh, you know there's danger involved."

"Well, we're not wimps, any of us. Count me in."

Robert called me the day after Leigh signed on. I met him at his house again right after lunch.

"It's here. Street value, $2 million. It's in a house on William Street," and he gave me the address. "Two men and a dog are in the house, guarding it twenty-four hours a day. It's time. What are you going to do?"

Driving back to the Bakery, looking at people in silly costumes starting to celebrate Fantasy Fest already with the parade still two days away, I had it.

I called the DEA and told them I needed to speak to an agent immediately.

Walking into the Federal Building on Simonton Street where they had their offices, I admired the WPA sculptures and murals. If the Feds had to stimulate an economy, how sweet was doing it this way? I gave a mental thank you to FDR and Julius Stone.

The DEA is on the second floor. I was escorted directly into an office. I told the agent, Phillip, what I had.

"So, give me the address, and we'll be there in fifteen minutes."

"It can't happen like that, Phillip. It has to wait until Fantasy Fest night, unless they start to move it before then."

"So you're telling me that you have knowledge of the whereabouts of $2 million worth of cocaine and won't tell a federal officer? That could make you an accomplice."

"Phillip, it will all be set up for you to make the bust that night so you get the main man at the same time as the drugs. Trust me. I'll call you right before you need to be there and tell you where to station your men, but please be ready."

He conceded.

I called Robert and told him I was ready to go, but he had to help. "Robert, you have to make sure the stuff is still in the house Saturday night. If they start to move it before then, call me. Have someone you trust watch the house twenty-four hours a day. For this to go down the way you want, the stuff *must* still be in the house. If they try to move it, make something happen that spooks them enough they stop. This will get you revenge beyond your wildest dreams."

On one of my jobsites was a big, old, wooden two-wheeled cart. I waited until everyone was gone from the jobsite, then Doug and I pulled it back to the house, taking backstreets and waving to any curious observers. Fantasy Fest was close enough that people were used to anything.

I called Tony Falcone and asked him where the floats were going to stage and what the route was going to be. I desperately wanted to tell him what we needed, but I couldn't endanger him, so I said I wanted the info because some out-of-town friends wanted to be at the beginning of the parade.

"Well, it's a little nutsy, but we're going to line all the floats up behind the jail and then start from there, turn the corner on Olivia and head down Duval and go past the judging bleachers at the corner of Duval and Front. Our float's named "A HURRICANE NAMED DESIRE." That year's theme was a tribute to Tennessee Williams.

"Thanks."

I realized now that we had to involve young Tom or enlist one more person. I took Tom aside and told him what we were planning and told him it might be dangerous.

"Let's do it, dad."

Leigh flew to Miami to a costume store and flew back. Doug, Tom, and I built a plywood altar on the cart. I stapled skirts to the side of the cart and glued tons of glitter to them and, in contrasting glitter, spelled out: "BITE OF THE IGUANA." Lame, but it was the best I could do on short notice.

Doug, Tom, Leigh, and I cleaned out every grocery store's inventory of flour and spent most of the night filling two hundred Ziploc bags with it. Leigh stayed over, but we didn't get much sleep. The next morning we all went to M & M Laundromat for coffee and Cuban toast and juggling Jim starting rhyming: "Things going down, town blown around, people on the ground..." and it freaked me out. Leigh told me to calm down, that it was just a coincidence.

"Oh yeah, sweetheart, look who just drove up."

Commissioner Aguilar got out of an obscenely large truck and walked to the window where they take the orders, pushing two people out of the way, then demanding his coffee and cheese toast, telling the Mexicans inside to hurry. Once he put in his order, he turned around and started digging at his teeth with a toothpick, then spit. I shot him a sideways glance, afraid my eyes would reveal my thoughts, but one glance at those little self-satisfied pig eyes stiffened my spine. This man deserved what he was about to get, but I was shaking.

He got his coffee and cheese toast and brushed me on his way back to his truck.

We talked and rehearsed the rest of the morning. After lunch, we prepared the cart. The bags of flour were stacked in alternating directions for stability on top of the altar. Using stencils, I painted signs on both sides of the altar. Then we spread a tarp over the flour bags and altar that Leigh was going to lie on, masked and dressed in virginal white, being bitten over and over by a shirt-less Tom wearing a lizard mask and head-dress. Doug and I, costumed like Tom, would be pulling the cart. I rode downtown on my bike and slowly tracked the whole parade route and found a pay phone just off Duval Street, one block from the reviewing stand, and tested it to make sure it worked. I hung an "Out of Order" sign on it. We were ready.

That afternoon, waiting for the time to roll the cart over to the staging point, was long—very, very long. I paced, I jumped in the pool, I paced more, and the others were the same. We even caught ourselves whispering to one another out of fear and anticipation.

Sunset. It was time. Tom and I started pulling the cart with our bikes on it. Doug and Leigh rode their bikes to the corner of Front and Duval and locked them up. It took Tom and me the better part of an hour to get to the staging point where Fast Buck Freddie's crew was testing their float with its airboat fan and water soaking everyone, causing everyone to laugh like kids playing with a garden hose. We parked the cart near their float and left Doug and Leigh to guard it while Tom and I took our bikes down to Front and Duval, then walked back.

Doug and Leigh kept looking at me, used to my quirky stomach. "John, if you're going to get sick, go over there behind the building and get it over with."

"I'm OK."

Then the signal came for the floats to start moving, and I ran behind the building.

"I'm OK, I'm fine now," I said, wiping my mouth when I got back. "Let's do it."

The parade marshal started the floats off. When we rolled into place behind Fast Buck's, he looked puzzled. "I don't see you on the list."

"We're Wilde's Guesthouse. Why don't you have us?" Leigh asked, in her most officious voice.

"Doesn't matter," the man said. "Go."

Doug and I started pulling the cart. It was stop and start, speed up and slow down, and we were getting some wet blow-back from the Fast Buck's float, the star of the show judging by the applause. Leigh, lying on top of the altar, screamed convincingly as Tom, the iguana, bit her over and over.

We made our way down Duval Street, slowly. As we got closer and closer to the reviewing stand, my stomach started knotting and I was glad I'd already emptied it.

Seated on the reviewing stand that year as judges were the mayor and all the commissioners, including Aguilar, a representative from the Navy, the head of the chamber of commerce, a state senator, and Tennessee Williams, himself.

When we got to Greene Street, I signaled to Tom to come down and take over my shaft of the cart. I raced to the phone and called Phillip. "Fifteen minutes. Assemble at the northwest corner of William and Southard Streets but stay hidden. We'll get there on our bikes." He acknowledged the message, and I took over from Tom who climbed back up on the cart.

Fast Buck's float approached the reviewer's stand, and I looked back at Tom and Leigh.

"One more bite when we're in front, then run."

We pulled the cart in front of the judges and stopped. I looked back at Tom and Leigh and yelled "NOW!!" They climbed off the cart and started running as Doug and I grabbed the edges of the tarp and pulled it off, dropped it, then started running, too. On top of the altar sat hundreds of bags of what looked like cocaine, and on all sides of the altar in big letters was a painted sign that said:

"COMMISSIONER AGUILAR'S COKE. HELP YOURSELF."

We heard later that there was a moment of stunned silence, then chaos as people in the crowd started grabbing the bags of "coke," and on the reviewing stand, a moment of incomprehension as people turned to look at our buddy. Once he read the sign, he jumped up and ran towards where the VIPs had parked their cars.

The four of us raced on our bikes to the rendezvous with the Feds. I told Doug, Leigh, and Tom to stand hidden across the street from the stash house and went up to Phillip. "He'll probably be here in a minute. Keep everyone hidden but ready."

Phillip had just finished giving the orders when we heard a car tear around the corner, race up, and park half on the sidewalk and half off. Aguilar looked around, then went inside the house. Two trucks disgorged men all dressed in black, with masks, automatic weapons, and flak jackets with big, white lettering on the back: DEA. They spaced themselves around the front door, some lying down, all with guns aimed at the door. I thought Phillip would order them in, but he waited.

A few minutes later, Aguilar and two other men came running out carrying two duffel bags. Huge lights clicked on, and six men with guns walked up to them and forced them to drop the bags and raise their hands.

Phillip walked over. "Gentlemen, you are under arrest for the possession of cocaine with intent to distribute," and read them their Miranda rights, as a photographer took the shot. They put the three men in two unmarked black cars and drove off. Crime photographers headed in, and then the agents started hauling out the rest of the coke and putting it in evidence bags. Phillip thanked me.

Back at the Bakery, we fixed ourselves drinks and high-fived each other, but the adrenaline was drained out of us, and we all went to bed.

I was first up the next morning and rode over to M & M to buy four coffees and four copies of the *Key West Citizen*, where a photo of Aguilar being arrested was on the front page with the story that mentioned the puzzle of the false coke at the parade and the real coke at the house. We'd done it. I phoned Robert. "Go get the *Citizen*. You're going to love it, I promise."

"Got it already. Bravo. Let me call you right back. I want to go to another phone."

The phone rang three minutes later. "Yes, John, bravo, bravo and thank you. Brilliant, exactly what I needed. And I have good news for you. Senator Pinder is staying here at the house for a few days. He was in the judges' stand and described what happened. Brilliant, just brilliant. The senator's an old friend of the family and head of the Appropriations Committee in Tallahassee. He's confirmed that the state will buy Simonton Beach when the deal falls through and preserve it."

'Good old boy network,' I thought to myself, 'but whatever it took.'

"Thank you, Robert. I'm happy we took that piece of shit down, but I'm happier we saved that beach. My friends and I are going down there at sunset to celebrate. Why don't you join us and bring the Senator? And Claudine?"

"Well, you know, we just may do that. I'll mention it to both of them."

We rung off.

Twenty-Two

At the next city commission meeting—one member notably absent—the mayor announced that the developers had withdrawn their offer for Simonton Beach, then read the letter from the state announcing that it was buying it to preserve it. The audience burst into applause. We had done it.

What we didn't know was that Aguilar had made bail.

On a Friday night, ten days after the commission meeting, Tom and I had just biked back from dinner at Antonia's, a now weekly father-son event. A car was parked across and slightly down the street. We didn't pay attention because people looking for a dark, private place to have sex parked there sometimes. We locked our bikes up on the porch.

Tom walked in ahead of me and on into the great room. I dropped my keys and was bending over to pick them up when the shotgun blast came through the louvers, and I felt the tiny hot penetrations into my skin. Tom came running, and I screamed at him to hit the floor. A second blast came through the door, both of us on the floor, then silence, followed seconds later by the screech of tires outside. I crawled to a window to look outside, then crawled back toward Tom, still on the floor between the two rooms.

"Dad, are you OK?"

"I've been hit but I think I'm OK. Turn all the lights out, and let's sneak out to the garage. You have to drive me to the hospital."

My reward for all the dad installments I'd paid came back "paid in full" at that moment. The kid raced out to the garage to open the door to my truck, then came back and helped me out and drove me to the hospital. It was only when he turned me over to the emergency room nurses that he broke down and started crying. "This is my daddy. Please don't let him die." They pushed him away, put me on a gurney and rolled me into an X-ray room.

There were twelve shotgun pellets total: in my right arm, my butt, my upper back, and under my scalp low on the back of my head, none deep. The metal louvers on the door and bending over to pick up my keys had saved my life. They gave me local injections and used a scalpel to extract the pellets. I wanted to go home when they were finished, but they insisted I stay in the hospital for twenty-four hours for observation and explained also that all gunshot wounds had to be reported to the police.

Someone had just tried to murder me. For the first time in my life, I took a sleeping pill.

Leigh, Doug, and Tom all showed up in my room the next morning, and our conversation—in whispers because of a roommate recovering from prostate surgery—was composed mostly of speculation: it had to have been Aguilar, but how had he found out it was me/us? My main concern was more to protect them than me, but before we could discuss that, a police investigator arrived and asked them to leave.

The man was a stereotype, a buzz-cut, no-nonsense type in civilian clothes. He asked about my injuries, and if I was in good enough shape to walk out into the hall. I got up, grabbed shut the back of the stupid hospital gown and followed him.

"Mr. Cottrell, tell me how you came to have a gunshot wound."

I gave him only the bare facts of it.

"Do you have any idea who might have wanted to shoot you?"

I told him I did. He asked me for a name.

"No disrespect to you, sir, but I don't want to say anything more unless Phillip from the DEA is present. I was working with them on a case. Then you'll get to hear it all." He acted surprised. I gave him Phillip's phone number.

"I'll get back in touch with you," he told me, and we shook hands after I gave him my phone number.

The hospital released me, and Doug and Tom picked me up. We drove past the Bakery looking for strange cars before we pulled into the garage. We shut the door and slipped into the house.

"I have to call Robert right away. I'll be back down after I talk to him."

When Robert picked up and heard it was me, his first question was loaded with serious concern: "Are you alright?" The coconut telegraph had already wired him the news.

"I'm OK," and described what had happened. "But, Robert, if I hadn't dropped my keys, or if the louvers weren't metal, I'd probably be dead and maybe Tom, too. It has to have been Aguilar, but how did he find out? You, me, and the DEA are the only ones who knew. I know my family wasn't the leak. It would have threatened their lives and they know it. I doubt the DEA would do it since it gave them a huge bust, but you can't rule them out. What about your end? Could anyone have overheard anything?" I phrased the question to allow him to save face, but I had a suspect in mind.

"I don't think so, John. I was always careful to make sure no one was around when we talked about it. Can I call you back? Someone just came in who might know something."

I went back downstairs. Leigh had arrived. Tom was making a mushroom macaroni and cheese, with Parmesan and shiitake mushrooms. I had a real fondness for our simple routine of dinner and conversation every night. Now, feeling fear at the sound of every car passing destroyed any possibility of routine joy. We even caught ourselves whispering.

Dinner was good, and the kid's chest swelled from the compliments. Then the phone rang and it was Robert.

"John, your life *is* in danger. You need to leave town immediately until I can take care of things, and I promise you I will. Come over here now so we can discuss it all. Tell your friends to be careful until I can get word out you're gone."

Leigh drove me to the Delacorte compound and dropped me off. "I'll pick you back up when you're ready. Just call me."

I pushed the button on the intercom, and the gate and front door opened. Robert pulled me inside, and we went out to the bar where he poured me a Pernod over ice and handed me a small pitcher of water. "Aguilar wants revenge, John. He may suspect or even know I had something to do with it, but he's a Conch, too, and knows he can't come after me or my family because he knows the power we have now and knows we'd crush his family. He knows your part in it. I don't know how yet, but I will find out, and he will kill you or have you killed if he thinks he can get away with it. You have to leave right away, go someplace comfortable until I tell you it's safe to come back."

"I can't do that, Robert. I have to work and pay my share of the bills on the Bakery."

"John, my family'll take care of all that for you until you come back. Wait here." He walked inside, and then I heard his steps on the stairs. I heard a sound behind me and jerked around to see Juan enter. He looked shocked to see me there, or to see me there alone, and turned and left immediately.

Robert returned and handed me a fatly filled, legal-sized shipping envelope. "Here's ten thousand dollars in cash to help you when you leave. I'll give you more when you need it, and I'll arrange with your roommates to pay your share of the household bills, but you have to leave for a while."

"Robert, you're forgetting something. How do I keep Leigh and Doug and Tom safe? That's more important than protecting me."

"I'll get word out that it was just you and some hired people. They'll be safe."

I finished my Pernod and had him call Leigh. He walked me to the gate.

"John, I can't tell you how sorry I am. You evened a score that redeemed years of pain for me and my family. I'll make this right, I promise you."

Leigh pulled up and drove me back to the Bakery. I protested when she said she was spending the night. "Leigh, this isn't a TV show. Someone tried to kill me and might try again. Go home."

"No way. You think I'm a coward or something? Don't forget who the wussy was at the coral spawning. Besides, I'm feeling romantic tonight. Lead the way."

We parked on the side street and walked to the door looking everywhere for danger. This was sickening and not at all what I wanted my life to be about.

We said good-night to Doug and Tom and went upstairs and deliberately avoided talking about "it." We showered together, had a drink, went to bed. I pulled my arm out from under her after she'd fallen asleep, and my mind slammed into overdrive.

I had to protect these people above all else. Next, I didn't want to get killed by a corrupt sub-human. How could I accomplish both things?

When I woke up the next morning, I knew what I had to do. After a somber breakfast, after Leigh had left and Tom and Doug had headed off to work, I made another phone call.

My friend, Rudy, was now living in one of the projects (subsidized housing for poor people). A quarter of the people in the projects were scamming the system, which was obvious every night when the uncommitted, deadbeat fathers parked on the streets along-side and went back in to plant more seed in the women they wouldn't marry or support.

Rudy and I had grown apart when cocaine hit the island. He had not only indulged but had become a small-time dealer, caught and jailed once, and knew my strong feelings about the drug. Rumor had it that he had graduated to dealing big time.

His girlfriend answered the door and said she'd get him.

"*Amigo*, *mi hermano*, how are you? Come in." The open, joyous face from our days at the restaurant had turned guarded, suspicious.

Inside, I saw a little girl clinging to the woman who'd answered the door.

"Juan, this is my woman, Isabel, and that little jewel there is our daughter, Christina."

"*Con mucho gusto*," I told Isabel, and then stroked the head of the little girl who gave me a shy smile.

"Isabel, bring us a couple beers outside, OK?"

We stepped back outside, and when Isabel brought the beers and went back in, Rudy led me a little ways away.

I told him what I'd done and what had happened, but lied about who had helped me, telling him I'd hired tourists who hadn't known what we were doing.

"Rudy, you told me years ago if I ever needed something, you'd help me. I need help now. Aguilar must know it was me. That's why someone tried to kill me. I need someone to tell him I'm leaving the country—I'm moving back to France. I'm leaving tomorrow. What I *really* need is for someone to tell him that the men living in my house had nothing to do with it. I would never get them involved in something like this."

Rudy put his arm around me and walked me further from his door. "Juan, *amigo*, why did you do this very stupid thing? Luis is *un hombre muy malo*, a very bad man and sometimes sick in the head." I noticed the use of the first name, so I had guessed right: Rudy did know him.

"Rudy, I'm sorry I have to ask you this, but I need to keep my friends safe."

"Juan, John, I promised you when you helped me get my mother and brother out of Cuba that I would help you whenever you needed it. I will speak with Luis and tell him what you've told me. I think it is smart to leave Key West. He will never forget or forgive this. I will make sure your friends stay safe."

I hugged and thanked him, then asked if I could say goodbye to Isabel and the daughter.

"*Por favor*, I know your heart is in the right place, but it's better if you didn't."

"*Adios, amigo.*"

"*Adios.*"

Leigh was with us for dinner that night. I told them what Robert and I had talked about, and what I had asked from Rudy.

When I was finished, Leigh spoke first. "You're leaving?"

"Leigh, I don't have a choice. It's the only way I save my life and protect the three of you. I told Robert and Rudy I was going back to France to throw everyone off the scent, but I'm going to the house in Costa Rica."

"When?" Doug asked.

"Tomorrow morning. I'm renting a car and driving to Miami. The flight to Costa Rica is at one in the afternoon. Carlos, the caretaker of the property, is going to meet me at the airport in Liberia. I should be at the house by five or six, and I'll call you. Tell anyone who asks that I've gone back to Paris."

Leigh and Doug looked shocked; Tom looked stricken. "You're moving out and leaving us? When are you coming back?"

"Tom, I don't know, not until Robert, or Rudy, tells me it's safe." He jumped up and ran outside.

"John, you need to go out there," Doug said. "You know his abandonment issues." Leigh agreed.

I walked out and went over to him and put my arm around him, which triggered what I had hoped it wouldn't: he began crying.

"Dad, please don't leave me," he begged. I held him and let him cry. When he stopped I asked him to look at me.

"Tom, son, I'm not leaving you forever. I'll give you a ticket to come down and visit once I'm settled. But listen to me. Remember when you asked me to be your dad and I told you it had to be a two-way street, and that you had to help me if I ever needed it." He nodded. "Tom, those two in there are going to need you, and you have to be there for them, OK? Leigh thinks she's tougher than she is, but since Thomas died she's been fragile, and I don't even want to think what Doug would do without you. So you've got to be tough for your dad and take care of those two for me until I can come back. Will you do that for me?"

"I'll try, dad."

It was a horrible night. I couldn't sleep, Leigh couldn't sleep, and we finally decided to give up. We went downstairs and started drinking rum. Tom stumbled out of his room in the Betty Boop pajamas Leigh had given him. "What are you doing?"

"We're going to get drunk and dance, so get your butt upstairs and tell Doug to come join us."

When Doug came into the great room, Leigh told them to fix themselves a drink and turn on the music. We danced together like the old days at the Monster, and when we wore ourselves out, we jumped in the pool.

Back inside, Leigh asked for a slow song. She and I clung together as we danced. Tom lifted Doug onto his feet like a parent dancing with its child. How could I leave this?

The song ended. "Let's go watch sunrise," Doug yelled. "I'll go get coffee and toast from M & M and meet you across from the airport." He left.

I checked the street, then the three of us piled into my van in the garage and drove to the beach. The sun was just breaching when Doug showed up.

Silence before the miracle of light's gilded birth. When the star had cleared the water, Leigh yelled: "All things good to us. Death to assholes!"

Back at the Bakery, it was time. Leigh left first. "John, I'll fly down next week or as soon as I can. Don't be too sad."

"Leigh, don't you be too sad. You're not as tough as you used to be. Watch these two for me, and let them watch you, OK?"

"OK," and she walked out, looking both ways before crossing the street.

I packed clothes and toiletries in the smaller bag, then went downstairs with the big bag and stood before the bookcase. It was like the cocktail party question of what do you want with you if you're going to be stranded on a desert island. Baudelaire, Flaubert, Vargas Llosa, Prescott, Erskine Lane, all of Amado, Durrell, Kerouac, Orwell's essays, two Stegners, Valladares' condemnation of dictatorship . . .

one more, who? Rawling's *Cross Creek*? Why not? Sensitive description of arrival in an exotic place that became home.

I lifted the bag: seriously overweight with writing, like my life.

Tom and Doug loaded me into Doug's van and drove me to the car rental lot on North Roosevelt.

They rolled my bags to just outside the office door. Doug and I hugged first. "Take care of the kid for me, Doug, and watch Leigh, too, OK. And take care of yourself. Let Tom take care of you a little bit, too. He needs to feel important. This is temporary. We'll all be back together again. Robert will call you and make the arrangements to pay my share of the house bills. Jeff Hagel is taking over my jobs but may need help from you."

Tom came over to me, and we hugged for a long time. I whispered to him: "You know how much I love you, you know you're my kid, but I need you to be strong for me now. Promise me you'll protect Doug and Leigh."

The appeal struck the chord in him I knew was there. "I'll take care of them, I promise, dad."

"I'll fly you down as soon as I get settled. I promise."

They drove off, and I drove up the Keys. Gut-wrenching sadness when I got to Big Pine Key and remembered the rainstorm and the demented Citroën bouncing down the road.

Carlos, the caretaker, was waiting for me when I cleared Customs and Immigration at the airport in Costa Rica. Two hours later, I was in the house . . . MY house . . . though claiming ownership seemed strange. I called back to Key West, and they took turns talking to me. The displacement jet travel makes possible is wonderful and awful. They were here . . . there . . . but not here.

I hung up and spent another first night's lonely sleep in exile.

I woke up in a beautiful bedroom with a gable-end window,

stumbled out to the kitchen and made coffee. When it was ready, I took it out on the porch. Before me lay the Garden of Eden.

As the lake turned blue, the parrots chattered across the valley, the oropendolas burbled in the trees below me, and the volcano vented Earth's hot breath upwards. I held my own breath, afraid to break the spell of Nature displaying when it thinks we're not looking.

But I was alone.

Three weeks later, Leigh kept her promise to fly down and brought me a surprise, the kid. Their trip had started awkwardly, they told me, because the "bitter old woman trapped in a fat man's body" was on the flight with them from Key West, and then from Miami to Liberia. He was off to the Pacific Coast, they'd overheard, where Americans were busily Californicating one of the last unspoiled places on the planet.

We laughed off the coincidence over a nice lunch in Liberia, then bought groceries and headed to the house. I was busy playing tour guide and explaining everything, but what I was feeling was . . . whisper it . . . never trust those road signs . . . happiness. Leigh kept reaching over to stroke the back of my head, and Tom was bouncing all over the backseat. "Dad, did you know Costa Rica has a higher GDP than Peru or Ecuador?" I had to smile at that one. Then: "When do I get to see monkeys? Where's the volcano? Can I see it erupt, for real? I want to see a poisonous snake. Do you think I could catch one and put the skin on my hat?" The only question lacking was, Are we there yet?

When we passed through Tilaran and climbed the last hill holding in the lake, I pointed out the windmills and told them the outline of a children's story I had in mind to write about them. We crested the hill, and I pulled over. The sky above the lake was clear. "Hop out, guys. Now look down to the other end of the lake. That's a real volcano. See the steam coming out the top?"

It was a magical week. Tom connected with the wilderness in a way not expected and ran off with Carlos everyday in search of monkeys, snakes, birds, everything in the book of Costa Rican wildlife. Carlos helped him catch a *terciopelo,* a fer-de-lance, one of the most venomous snakes on the planet, and he brought the corpse back, totally manic with happiness when Carlos showed him how to skin it. He became friends with the howler monkey tribe in the forest behind me and learned to call them up so he could watch them. I had never seen the kid so happy.

Leigh and I that week were like those wonderful old couples you sometimes see in restaurants, still reaching across the table to touch the partner's hand after all that history.

We agreed to skirt the subject of what had brought me here and just enjoy our time together.

One day we made the trek to the Monteverde Cloud Forest across the lake from me, hoping to see one of the few remaining quetzals on the planet, birds with impossibly colored plumage and trailing tail feathers that made me shake my head in disbelief when I looked at the drawing in the guidebook.

The guide led us into the preserve, then whispered: "I hear one. Follow me, but be quiet." We tiptoed behind him, then he pointed up. There was quetzal, in all his/her multi-colored excellence, grooming itself.

We walked on, then the guide motioned to us to be quiet again. He cocked his ear and looked up. Then there was an explosion of color and sound as two male quetzals (had to be) flew at one another and tangled, falling to within ten feet of our heads, then separated and flew away. A single feather floated down from their fight and when I saw it, I yelled at Leigh to grab it, luminescent green turning royal blue when you turned it.

The weather cooperated the last day, and I told Tom and Leigh I had a surprise. "Bring your bathing suits and be ready to leave right after lunch." I wouldn't tell them where we were going.

We drove on through Arenal and headed down along the lake, past enormous stands of bamboo and patches of impenetrable jungle. I pointed out the penstocks in the lake as we drove slowly across the dam and then on towards La Fortuna. I turned off the road and we started climbing.

When I stopped, Tom asked me where we were. I made the "lips sealed" gesture and had them follow me.

You can hear it before you see it and then, at one turn in the climb down, you see it, water falling through dense tropical vegetation.

We walked the rest of the way down, and there it was . . . my Panama and Trinidad childhood summed up: water falling two hundred feet through a tropical jungle into a clear pool, parrots flying overhead.

Even Tom was stunned into momentary silence. Then we jumped in and splashed around, and Tom tried to swim under the waterfall, but the force of those falling tons made it impossible. Leigh and I got out and sat on the rocks surrounding the pool and watched him.

Tom climbed out of the water. "That waterfall kicks ass. I couldn't get closer than ten feet to where it hits the water."

"Alright, next surprise. Dry off, put your clothes back on, and prepare yourself for that climb back up."

The sun was getting lower as I drove back toward the lake, looking for an entrance, then found it and turned off the road.

"Where're we going now?" they both asked.

I made the "lips sealed" gesture again, and we twisted and climbed up a gravel road and arrived at a parking lot where the attendant asked me to back in. When they got out, I pointed. There, in all its primordial majesty loomed the volcano, active, unbelievably close. They were both shocked.

"Is this safe?" Leigh asked.

"Probably not. That's why they have you back in to park, to give you a couple extra seconds to flee."

"Dad, are you kidding us?"

"I swear not. You're about to have dinner at the base of one of the world's most active volcanoes. You sissies going to join me or not?" I looked at Leigh. "Remember the taunts at the coral spawning?" I led them into a large tent-like structure, twenty feet high, with tables underneath. I asked for the tables closest to the view and ordered wine.

"Dad, are you sure we're OK here?"

"I already told you, probably not, but can't beat the view. Look at that." Tropical vegetation rolled away from us to the base, and then one third of the way up the cone. Above that was cinder-gray to the top.

The sun set while we were drinking the first glass of wine. Then, just as the waiter was serving the Caprese salad, there was a loud rumble, and we all turned to watch a cascade of incandescent boulders roll down our side of the volcano. Tom flinched and the waiter laughed. "You're OK, *amigo*. It's only when you feel the ground shake you need to say your prayers and run."

I looked at Leigh looking at the volcano, looked at my kid, and couldn't bear the thought that this time tomorrow, they'd be back in Key West together, and I'd be alone again. My cheer through the rest of the dinner was manufactured.

Tom was bouncing around again when we left the restaurant. "Man, I seen me . ."

"Dollar, or 510 colones. Wrong use of past tense."

"Shit, even down here?"

"Even down here."

"OK, I saw a waterfall and a volcano erupting all in one day. That was awesome. Why can't we all live down here? It's sure prettier than Key West."

"Alright, let me concentrate on driving now. I've come close to hitting deer, men on horses, and animals I can't even name on this road at night."

There was mostly silence in the car all the way back. I sensed Leigh's same separation anxiety.

There's sex without love, sex with some affection, and sex with real love. I had never felt closer to her than that night. We clung to one another afterwards, watching the fire die down in the bedroom fireplace.

"John, we have to do something. I don't want to live without you."

"Leigh, I feel the same way. But what am I supposed to do? Fly back and get us all killed? He'd do it. Robert and Rudy both said he'd do it."

She turned over, and I curled up against her back.

The next morning, she and I were all business, and it was only Tom who voiced his feelings. "Dad, why can't I stay here with you? I don't like living back there if you're not there."

"Tom, I told you, you have to take care of Doug for me until I come back. Imagine how lonely he is right now."

Liberia's airport was Key West in the old days: roofed sheds open to the elements; was my personal history on a loop?

Leigh found a small, velvet-lined, wooden box of laminated exotic woods in the gift shop and gave it to me. When I opened it, the quetzal feather lay brilliant against the black. "Belongs on the coffee table in the house, John."

We hugged, we kissed, and then they left me. I drove back to the house, feeling as lonely as my first night in Toronto. I fell into bed, drunk.

Ten days later, Doug flew down. Facial recognition happiness as I saw him exit the plane. He walked into the Customs and Immigration shed, saw me and waved.

We re-played Leigh and Tom's trip because they'd told him all about it: waterfall, volcano, cloud forest. No quetzals that day but he marveled at the feather in the box on the coffee table. The delight of his visit for me were the dinners at the house. I had always envied the long-term friendships of people who had gone through years of school together. I had something similar, even better with him.

Together, we'd completed one of the most difficult renovations in Key West under tremendous financial pressure. Together, we'd taken a damaged child in and begun the healing process for him. Together, whenever necessary, we'd coaxed each other out of what the French call a *cafard*, a funk. He was my brother, my friend, my soul mate.

We got toasted most nights during his visit and laughed at shared stories and watched the fire in the living room fireplace. It was surprising how chilly it got at this altitude, even at this latitude. The fireplaces were another gift from Thomas.

Doug's last night together, he broached the subject we'd avoided all week. "What are you going to do, John? What are *we* going to do? I'm worried about Leigh. She lost Thomas, and now she's sort of lost you, and I think she's starting to flounder. At dinner, I catch her staring off in the distance, disconnected, and the kid is going nuts without you there. I go looking for him in the house sometimes, and he's upstairs sleeping in your bed."

That upset me so much that I got up and walked out on the porch. Doug followed me and put his arm around me. Strange man who once hated being touched, now took comfort from it.

"John, you told me once I was more important to your life than your own family, and I was shocked that someone would say that, but I'm the same way now. You, Leigh, the kid, are more important to me than my own family, and I love my family. We have to figure something out."

The next morning was a repeat of Leigh and Tom's departure: all business getting breakfast together, then the drive to Liberia and the airport. Heartfelt hugs . . . "Love you . . . love you back" and then I drove back alone. This was tearing me apart.

I met all three of them two different times later for a long weekend in Miami. When it was over, and they dropped me off at the airport and drove off together back to Key West, that departure hurt me even more than when they'd left me in Costa Rica.

Twenty-Three

One morning two and a half months into my new exile, I was drinking my morning coffee on the front porch. Steam was spewing from the volcano at the other end of the lake. Powerful winds caught and rolled it down the south side of the cone. Backlit by the rising sun, it resembled thick tongues of San Francisco fog, here licking through Edenic valleys.

A flock of small, green parrots chattered their morning passage across the valley in front of me. Butterflies sipped on the blue porterweed near the porch. The broken fan-belt call of toucans came from the forest to one side of me and the roar of howler monkeys from the forest behind. There were times in this part of Costa Rica, sitting quietly, when a person could still believe that the world belonged to the plants and animals, and we were only guests. Man's hand touched the planet lightly here.

The phone rang. I got up and walked inside.

It was Doug. "Robert had a stroke yesterday, John. He died this morning." He paused. "Claudine wants you to be a pallbearer. She told me she knows everything and promises you'll be safe now.

I was quiet for a moment, shocked. Why was so much death coming at me so early in my life?

"John, it's time to come back. We miss you."

"I miss you guys, too, Doug, you know that. I get drunk, put music on at night, and dance on the balcony, looking at the lake and the volcano, but it's lonely. "Remembered pleasure is not an acceptable dance partner." He recognized the Thomas Szuter quote and was quiet for a few seconds.

There was another pause in the conversation with lots of static. Costa Rica got a lot of things right but the telephone system wasn't one of them. "We're lonely, too, John. It's not the same without you. Please come back."

I traced out a pattern in the carpet with my toe as I re-lived the incident that had forced me here.

"The funeral's on Monday, John. Come back."

We rang off, and I poured myself another cup of coffee and walked back out on the porch. The winds down the lake had died, allowing the steam from the cone to shoot straight up into a lightening sky. The lake itself had changed color from sunrise gray to daytime blue. A donkey brayed somewhere and I could hear the caretaker's rooster crowing down the hill. A couple of horses clip-clopped past on the road below, carrying their riders to work.

I had been hunted twice now: once, for eight years by the FBI, and now by the man whose reputation, plans, and fortune Robert and I had destroyed. I prided myself on the battles I'd fought, but these months in Costa Rica had shown me the long-term psychological price: I carry in me a constant, low-grade feeling of dread and fear, the subconscious equivalent of the universal human nightmare of being pursued but unable to flee, a tumpline's phantom pull on the forehead after the load has been dropped. These months in Arenal doing only things I loved—reading, writing, thinking—had whittled that paranoia down to kindling.

Just the day before, I had been lying on the sofa re-reading Baudelaire's *Les Fleurs du Mal*, a bottle of wine and my college French dictionary in reach. Yo Yo Ma was on the stereo playing a Bach Cello Sonata and a sound outside distracted me. I turned my head to see a howler monkey looking in my window from a tree nearby, behind him a blue lake with clouds weaving between lines of hills—Chinese brush print—and in the distance the volcano steaming away. I had thought in the '60s that this kind of solitude with my books and beautiful surroundings was all I needed to be happy, but life had taught me since that I needed the love of friends just as much.

This second exile had had an unintended consequence: I had fallen in love with this place where Nature sketched bold. Active and beautiful weather was daily entertainment: the volcano end of the lake got 180 inches of rain a year and my end 120 inches. Huge storms could churn down the lake while sun shot through only drippy clouds above me. Once, on the drive back from town, I had seen a fog-mist sunset as beautiful as a Big Sur sea-spray sunset. At least once a month thunder rumbled as the volcano spit out incandescent, bus-sized boulders, and every once in a while the earth shook and rolled, reminding you that the land you sat on was in movement, sliding towards Japan two inches every year.

In the blur of activity that is being a builder, I had mostly not felt the passage of time. I was now free to contemplate it, and it gave me a sense of urgency. In the last several years, I had revisited my past: Canton, Ohio, where I had spent three years studying for the priesthood; Columbia, Missouri, where my college education had begun; Toronto, where my education had continued during my political exile; and Paris, where my view of all human activity had been transformed.

The seminary in Ohio and all its buildings had been sold and turned into a golf club. The chapel where I had spent hours every week in silent meditation or chanting plainsong was filled now with the clicking of shoe cleats and the laughter of rich people eating and drinking.

The off-campus house I'd lived in at the University of Missouri had been torn down for a parking lot.

The house I had lived in in Toronto, where I had hidden under covers at night when the sadness of my exile overwhelmed me, had been torn down for a thirty-story apartment building.

My apartment building in the First Arrondissement and the entire neighborhood I had lived in in Paris had been torn down and replaced with something so banal that it embarrassed even the French.

Seeing all that, then living through the plague years in Key West fueled the urgency I now felt. A predator was following me, gaining even, destroying everything behind me in its pursuit. Whatever else I wanted to do in life, I felt I needed to do now. The leisurely contemplation of what came next was over.

The flight from San José to Miami passes over Cuba, Key West's sister island, and I looked down on that island prison and remembered the shouting matches I'd had with intellectuals on three continents. Why should Latin America be condemned to a metronome of dictatorship hell: right then left, then right, then left again? Was there something in Latin American genes that should condemn them to live without a democratic voice? How could educated people justify torture, summary executions, and the suppression of free thought?

I had no illusions about my country's mostly shameful role in Cuban history, but how could Garcia Marquez and Sartre, writers I loved, be apologists for Castro when he had condemned other writers, Valladares and Arenas to name two, to hideous imprisonments unmatched since the Nazis or the Soviet Gulag? They (we) wouldn't accept it for ourselves; wasn't it patronizing in the worst way to think that was the best they could do or have? Was Vargas Llosa the only Latin American writer brave and honest enough and still alive to argue for basic human freedoms? The chant "Libertad, Libertad, Libertad" we'd heard from the 125,000 refugees arriving in Key West on overcrowded boats during the Mariel boatlift proved my point. Those people were not all just seekers of a better economic life. It would take Beethoven's *Fidelio* to do justice to the scenes we had seen when those boats landed in Key West.

Writers were my heroes, the men and women who had led me out of my personal, childhood darkness. How could anyone justify imprisoning and torturing—TORTURING—someone for what they wrote? If the admiration and love I felt for writers could cut bars, all the ones on the island below me would be free.

In ten minutes, the plane crosses the island and flies above the Florida Straits. The seabed below is carpeted with the bodies of people trying to escape Cuba who did not succeed. A building on Stock Island, the *Hogar de Transito*, is the first stop of the refugees who do make it, giving them information about the legal steps necessary to work and live in the U.S. From waist level to head height, four walls of a large room are tightly covered with photos of men, women, and children assumed not to have made it, with notes below each posted by relatives or friends. "Mother and three children left Havana three weeks ago. No news. Please call . . ." and then a Miami phone number.

I had read about the building, and what the photos meant, so I thought I was prepared. Nothing could have prepared me for the number. Thousands of faces looked at me, all now presumed dead in their attempt to escape. I looked at as many as I could to give what—validity? recognition?—to their lives? A few escape boats were displayed around Key West as tourist attractions, boats so pathetically small that I could barely look at them after my trip to the *Hogar de Transito*.

Somewhere on the seabed just below me also lay the remains of Hart Crane, who slipped over the side of the ship he was on and gave up on life, one of his last poems titled "Key West." Why do so many voices with the most to say mute themselves when we want/need to hear more?

On the bottom of the sea below me also slept Rudy's friend, Alfonso, who'd slipped off the truck inner tubes to die.

Ahead, the Keys were now visible, from this height patches of floating sea-grass joined by tiny threads—Flagler's bridges—then the Everglades, then Miami.

Abundance—over-abundance—blasts you in the face when you arrive in the U.S. from rural Latin America. Planes, cars, more cars, highways, ads, people, noise, things, STUFF . . . the eyes and ears can't escape it: there is something everywhere demanding, needing, selling, trying to grab your attention. I had to shift gears.

I walked the concourses to my gate, reading the screens as I do in every airport. When I had landed in Miami the first time in 1975, there had been only four flights a week to Europe: three to London and one to Paris. Now there were four flights a day just to the UK, and daily flights to Paris, Milan, Madrid, Amsterdam, and Frankfurt.

I took the escalator down to D-35, the sub-standard waiting room that fed American's feeder flights, and sat down. Forty or so people were waiting for the Key West flight—in summer!—and they all looked so clean-cut and Yuppy-ish it proved that Key West, the island I'd moved to in 1976 and whose location I'd had to describe, was now KEY WEST. It made me angry that the predator behind me was winning another one. What would these people think if I

458

stood up and started to tell them of the first time I'd flown to Key West with a drag queen and three shrimpers? Experience had already taught me that most would turn away in embarrassment.

Today's flight was called, and a shuttle bus took us to a 727 I couldn't imagine landing on Key West's short runway. Forty-five minutes after take-off, it turned over Christmas Tree and Tank Island (and a tiny undeveloped beach at the end of Simonton Street), and there below me lay the mosaic of shiny tin roofs and treetops I had first seen how many years ago?

After we'd been escorted to the now-enclosed and air-conditioned terminal, I got my bags, walked outside, and grabbed a taxi, painted pink, Key West pretending to be Bermuda. The driver tried to strike up a conversation, but I was angered again by what I was seeing on my way into town. Seaward, the first mile was the same: two shades of blue-green water with the hand of man lightly placed on it: a sailboat in the distance, two shrimp boats closer in with outriggers extended. The landward view, before a wilderness of mangrove-lined salt ponds, was now a nearly solid wall of condos and hotels, all unimaginatively designed or outright butt ugly.

Then a right turn off Roosevelt Boulevard, a left onto Atlantic Blvd., and greed's subjugation of the land was complete: seaward was now a mile-long wall of concrete, Orlando-ugly condos, all built since I had moved here and blocking the sea breezes to the rest of the island. Greed, as ugly as it was to deal with, was something I could accept more than building something ugly on a piece of paradise.

Butterflies in my stomach, I anticipated the turn off White Street, then the dog-leg, then the Bakery. "Didn't even know this place was here," the driver admitted. I paid the fare and got out. He drove off. I stood across the street for a minute and looked at my and Doug's handiwork then walked to the door, noticed that the louvers had been replaced, and let myself in.

Strung across the parlor was a crudely painted banner: "WEL-COME HOME." I was moved. I called out but no one answered. Tom and Doug were still at work.

Memory's brush-strokes paint imperfect pictures, but not this time.

I had touched every board in this house, and they had touched me, this sanctuary for so many of the most special moments in my life. The laughter of my little family had varnished these walls; our tears had washed these floors.

On the way up to my room I had a strange feeling that I would find me already there, a younger innocent me to comfort the older and sadder one climbing the stairs, but, of course, the room was empty.

I put down my bags, took a shower, then poured myself a glass of wine from a bottle that Tom and Doug had left on the wet bar in my room with a big "Welcome Back" note attached. I paced for a few minutes, then lay down on the bed, looked out the gable-end windows at clouds passing "and my precious memories . . . heavier than rocks" pulled me down and back in time.

An hour later, the door to my bedroom burst open, and two men tumbled on top of me, hugging, play-boxing, and tickling me. The three of us got out of the bed and went downstairs to the great room and popped open some beers. "It was weird not having you here, dad," Tom said. "For a while after you left, I'd forget you were gone and expect you to be here when I got home. I'd even go up to your room and look to see if you were there. And I wanted to pack you in my bag and bring you back with me that time I visited you down there."

"Weird for me, too. I never stopped missing you guys."

"I'm sorry," Tom said.

"Why?"

"I know that you did what you did because of me and what I did with cocaine."

"Tom, I hated what cocaine did to you and the town, but I did it more because of what they were going to do to Simonton Beach. "

"Hey, enough of the heavy stuff," Doug said. "Let's go swimming." The three of went outside and jumped in the pool.

I looked over at Tom. "This is where it all started, remember?"

"Doesn't it seem like a long, long time ago, dad?" he asked and I nodded. Then he went underwater and grabbed me by the legs and pulled me under, and the horseplay started. This was what I needed to keep the nostalgia at bay.

Doug went inside and started to get dinner ready. Then a vision of loveliness appeared from inside the house: a beautiful blonde in a navy blue sheath and matching flats. "Yum, yum, one of my favorite things: hot men in bathing suits."

I jumped out of the pool and went over to hug her.

"Don't get the threads wet."

I dried off and we hugged. "I missed you," she whispered.

"I missed you, too. A lot."

"Well, now that we've got that out of the way, fix me a drink. And put some clothes on, or I'll start to do you right here." Tom laughed.

Dinner, lobster Alfredo, Doug's week on, was the best version of old friends back together. We dredged up stories that embarrassed each of us in turn, and when Leigh and I finally left the table to head up to my room, Tom and Doug yelled to me on the way out: "Hey, if you need any pointers on what to do, old guy, just ask us, OK?"

The death of a rich Conch is a state affair, Doug explained to me, the next morning. "It will be a mob scene. People who would never get inside the Delacortes' compound normally, will make it in tonight because of the family's social obligation of receiving condolences."

"There's an element of currying favor with the rich and powerful. There you are, a little guy expressing heartfelt condolences, and maybe the recipient family member will remember the gesture some-day when he can help you. Claudine will be under a lot of stress.

"The church won't hold all the people at the funeral, there'll be so many. Three-quarters of the police and the firemen will be escorting the hearse. Your presence will be noted and talked about because outsiders don't belong there, so be prepared to have everyone, and I mean everyone, looking and wondering."

I called Claudine, and Simone answered and went off to get her mother. When Claudine came to the phone, I expressed my condolences. She sounded tired.

"Thank you for coming back, John. It means a lot to me. We need to talk before the services. Can you come by later tonight after we've received the public?"

"Of course. And Claudine, if there's anything I can do for you or your family, I don't care what it is, please let me know. You know I'll do it."

"Thank you."

Police were waving cars down side streets because there was no parking anywhere near the house. I managed to find a space four blocks away on Eaton Street and walked back. Roger, Simone's husband, was at the gate greeting and probably vetting people. He shook my hand and led me inside. There was still a line of people making their slow way towards the back of the house where Simone and Claudine stood accepting the condolences. The house was filled to excess with flowers, and the combination of the heat from so many people and the smell of the flowers was overpowering the air conditioning.

Roger led me through the crowds to the study. "There are more people than we expected so it's taking longer. Claudine asked if you'd wait in here until it's over."

"Of course."

"Juan will bring you a drink, if you like," so I asked for a rum and orange juice. He left, closing the door behind him.

A few minutes later, the door opened, and Juan came in with the drink. He said nothing and made no eye contact. He, or someone from the DEA, got my vote for who had given Commissioner Aguilar my name. It was unlikely I would ever know which one.

I pulled a book from the shelves, Les Standiford's *Last Train to Paradise,* a masterful description of Flagler's building of the railroad from the mainland to Key West, and started reading it to pass the time. It was almost an hour before the door opened again and Claudine came in. I stood up and gave her a long hug, then stood back. "I'm sorry, Claudine. I know there's nothing I can say to make it better, just I'm sorry."

She sat down and kicked her shoes off. Juan showed up a minute later—again avoiding even looking at me—and we both ordered drinks, she a double martini. "God, do I need it."

She rubbed her feet for a few minutes until Juan brought the drinks. She told him to close the door when he left. She took two long, thirsty sips and I noticed that she now looked old. The mental dam holding back old age had given way with Robert's death.

When she'd relaxed a little, she started talking. "Robert told me what you did to get Luis. I kept asking him where you were and why you weren't available for dinners, and he was evasive until finally I told him to tell me, period. I'd had enough bullshit, pardon my French. When he told me what you'd done, and what had happened, I was furious, and we had a huge argument about why he hadn't protected you better. He finally convinced me that what you and he both did after it happened was the best thing, but I was still upset. You can't know my feelings about what you did for my son," and her voice got soft and she stopped for a minute.

"You made my son happy, John, in a way I never could have. Do you know your friend, Doug, convinced Robert to open the ballroom and have a dance there after you left? Near the end of the night, Robert even danced with his friend, and nobody, not even the Conchs, made fun. Do you know what it means to a mother to see her perpetually sad child made happy?"

She finished her drink and set the glass down. "Anyway, here's what's going on. I would like you to give one of the eulogies tomorrow at St. Mary's."

"Claudine, I'll do anything else you ask, but I can't give a eulogy. I have a phobia about public speaking. I'm sorry."

"That's alright. I hate it, too. Anyway, there'll be enough others as everyone tries to show how important they are to the family."

Then she looked over her shoulder to make sure the door was still closed, then looked back at me. "You did my son—this family—a favor by punishing the man who ruined my son's life. You shouldn't have to fear for your own life because of it. Listen carefully and never repeat any of this, please," and she looked over her shoulder again, then back.

"Aguilar has gone away and will never be back, and his family and partners have been given proof that if they ever threaten or endanger you or your friends again, something very bad will happen to them because anything they do to you will be like doing it to us. It's been made abundantly clear, trust me. You don't need to know more than that, and I know it sounds all Godfather-ish, and it is, but that's the way we do things here, and you may not like it but that's the way it is. So you're safe, and I'm sorry for what you went through."

I was dying of curiosity to know what they'd done, but knew she'd never tell me and this wasn't the time anyway.

"Thank you, Claudine, now let's talk about you. Are you OK, can I do anything for you?"

"Yes, you can, young man. Take care of your friends. Life is shorter than you think."

She gave me the times and details of the funeral the next day then stood up. "John, I'd love to spend more time with you, but I'm so tired I need to go to bed."

"Claudine, you know you don't have to apologize. Get some sleep, I'll see you tomorrow." We kissed, and I left the house with the very strong feeling that this woman and her son had had a man killed to protect first, themselves, and then, me, as an after-thought, or maybe they were more noble than that. I had learned in my years on the island that Conchs did whatever was necessary to survive, laws be damned.

The next afternoon, I showed up at St. Mary's on Truman Avenue and met and nodded to the other pallbearers, all Conchs: the present and one former mayor, two sons from the other ruling families, the U.S. Representative to Congress from our district, and me. They talked among themselves and ignored me.

The hearse arrived, escorted by nearly every police car in town. A funeral home employee directed us to the gurney he set up behind the hearse, and as the casket was pulled out of the hearse we set it on the gurney and walked it to the front of the church. I took my seat in the Delacorte pew, and a ritual familiar to me from my youth began, the Requiem Mass, now in English, not the Latin of my childhood.

I didn't belong here and just wanted it to end. I no longer believed in the ritual and hated the hypocrisy of a church full of people paying their respects to a man they'd shunned in life for a sexuality he had been born with as surely as they'd been born with theirs.

After the placement of the body in the family vault, in the cemetery I had visited on my first trip to the island with Vera, I managed a moment alone with Claudine.

"Are you OK? Is there anything I can do?"

"Thanks, John. Yes, I'm OK. Roger and Simone are going to take over the family business and move into the big house. I'm moving to New York to be with my friend."

I grinned. "I knew you had one. Good for you. Don't lose touch because Leigh and I fly up a lot. We'll have fun together."

Twenty-Four

I went back to work with Jeff Hagel, history looping back on itself again. I didn't want to jump into a general contracting job right away until I knew for sure I wouldn't have to leave overnight again, and he'd been kind enough to take over my jobs when I fled. He'd also visited me for a week in Costa Rica and bought property near mine.

It was sometimes strange putting my Key West public persona back on after months of not wearing it. Some days I felt like one of those photos where you stick your head through a hole in a cardboard cut-out figure and there you are—your face on a mermaid's or Superman's body. After a few months of being a reader, a writer, a thinker, I was again slotted by everyone I knew as a "construction worker."

There were awkward moments at home, too, where I felt excluded by a tale of something they'd done together while I'd been gone. Doug called me into his room one night because he'd sensed it.

"John, cut yourself some slack. You went into exile during the Vietnam War, you almost got killed here, then had to flee all alone. Coming back has to be strange. We all see the stress in your face. But we're a family, tribe, whatever. A few months of unshared history doesn't change that. And don't underestimate how sad it was for us not to have you here. Do you have any idea how many times I wanted to walk across that hall and knock on your door and have you throw an arm around me after a bad day?"

"Thank you for that, Doug. It just feels weird sometimes, like I've just woken up from a coma. But there's something else, too. Ever since I got back, I've had the nagging feeling that something's being hidden from me."

He looked away for a minute, then looked back. "You're a clever fuck, you know that?"

"So you are hiding something."

"It's this house, John, the money to keep it. The bastards have raised the taxes to thirty thousand a year and the insurance to thirty-five thousand because we improved it."

I was shocked. "You're not serious. That's over ten times what it was when we bought it. That's not fair. We saved a piece of the island's history."

"John, we appealed it and they rejected it. With the mortgage, taxes, insurance and utilities, it costs over $100,000 a year now, and the insurance and taxes go up every year. We were going to wait to tell you until you'd been back a while longer."

I felt sick and sat down.

"What do we do now?" he asked. "This is home, and I know it's the only place the kid has ever felt was home."

"For me, too, Doug."

We talked a while longer, and then I walked across the hall to my bedroom. I was over forty now, not thirty, and my reservoir of energy for coping with major changes was seriously depleted.

The new financial reality on top of having been away for a few months put new lenses on my eyes. I biked down to sunset on Mallory Square alone one afternoon after work. Over a thousand people swarmed around, watching a man with a performing cat seeking money, jugglers with tip baskets in front, a man walking a high wire with donations accepted. The spot where Rex and Tennessee had been having a barbecue the first time I walked here was now occupied by a man playing a shell game. Noise and loud music everywhere. Over a quarter of the people on the dock had their backs turned to the sunset, watching the performers instead.

I rode over to 'our' beach, the one we'd saved from Aguilar and development. During my absence, the city had installed public toilets—totally ugly design, of course. I looked out at the channel marker we had swum to and climbed to watch those incomparable sunsets. A dozen homeless people milled around me now, looking for handouts. I gave the saddest looking one five bucks and left. This was an imperfect victory. At least we'd saved the view.

What to do? It was obvious: sell the house, but anything on the island that could accommodate the three of us in such privacy and give Doug and me office space would cost even more than what we were on the hook for now. Living with Doug and Tom, and some-times Leigh, was an integral part of me now. Strange as it sometimes felt to be back, being around them completely eliminated the loneli-ness I had felt in Costa Rica and so much of my life. The personal history I'd shared with them was the only loneliness-killing conversa-tion in my life.

The French have an expression—*déformation de métier*—that means how what you do for a living, your profession, molds your per-sonality. The months in Costa Rica, with the burden of work lifted from me, let me see how my profession in Key West had begun to *de*form me. Because of the time and money pressures in the construc-tion industry, forty-hour weeks had become, routinely, fifty- and sixty-hour weeks on the job. The paperwork and interaction with four layers of bureaucracy was crushing.

Good at what I did, I had paid the price, but now saw how it had been shaping me. My natural rhythm, which was slow, had been forced into over-drive. I didn't read as much as I once did, and was impatient now when I did. I had begun skimming passages, even in books I loved, silently yelling, *Get to the point!* This was a *déformation* that was not an improvement to my life.

One night when Leigh stayed over, I explained the dilemma. We were lying in bed, after.

She was quiet for a minute. "What if I moved in with you and then contributed?"

That one surprised me. "I thought you always wanted to live in your own space."

"Oh, guess we're headed into the heavy stuff." She sat up, and the jiggle hit the reptilian brain as always. I reached over and grabbed one. She pushed my hand away. "Let's get serious for a minute," and pulled the sheet up over her.

"Alright, John, don't let this go to your head, but I realized something while you were gone. I discovered that not only do I love you, but I really love you, and I don't want to live apart anymore, not even here. Being together all day everyday down there was sweet, and I want that now."

I started to say something, but she stopped me. "Let me finish. I'll move in here with you guys, and then I'll be contributing, too. What about that, big boy?"

I was quiet for a minute.

"Got you this time, didn't I?"

"Yes and no. Yes, I think it's time we lived together, too, but I'm trying to do the math in my head."

"We won't live long enough for that. Give me the figures and let me do it."

I told her what Doug had told me, and it shocked her. "That much in taxes and insurance! The bastards. OK, how much rent does the kid pay?" I told her. "So you and Doug split the rest down the middle?"

"Yes."

"Alright, let's take the total expenses and subtract Tom's rent, which is low, by the way, but it's sweet you guys do that. Now we divide the remainder by three, not two, and we come up with . . . thirty thousand a year, each, more or less."

I was shocked at how high the figure was, even divided by three.

"What's wrong?" she asked when I didn't say anything.

"Leigh, do you have any idea how much construction work we have to do to clear thirty grand each just for house expenses? Overhead in construction is astronomical: liability insurance, workman's comp insurance, trucks, truck maintenance, truck payments, truck insurance, construction licenses, occupational licenses, payroll taxes on employees, payroll taxes on us—which we have to match—tools, tool repairs, gas, permit fees, and most of that goes up every year.

"For Doug and I to have thirty thousand dollars free, after feeding ourselves and paying all those bills, we'd each have to do over $250,000 a year in work, minimum, year-in, year-out, and usually for people we despise. Leigh, that's all we'd be doing: working, including most weekends, and forget vacations and putting anything aside for retirement. What kind of a life is that? And for what? To feed the city and make asshole insurance companies rich? I don't mind working hard, you know that, but I'm not going to over-work the rest of my life to feed parasites who weren't here helping during the eighty-hour weeks Doug and I put in to save this place. Fuck them."

She didn't say anything. The figures and my anger had shocked her. This was not the island either of us had moved to. We were both quiet for a few minutes, and I was marveling in how much pleasure it gave me just to be sitting next to her, skin touching skin. I never wanted to be without this again.

"What if I took money out of my trust fund and paid this place off? Then you wouldn't have mortgage payments, and you wouldn't have to carry insurance."

For a second, the idea of those burdens being lifted from us gave me a rush as great as the lifting of the Feds' indictment. Then I checked myself.

"Leigh, I love you, and I love that you would offer that, but I can't let you do that." She pulled away from me.

"Why do you have to be so goddamn weird about my money?"

"Leigh, let me repeat myself: you're smarter about money than we are. Grant me the recognition that I'm smarter about how it can change relationships. If you paid this house off, then we'd all feel indebted to you, even if you didn't remind us of it. Look at how silly we can all be together, ragging you just like we do each other, in spite of your money. Very subtly, those interactions would change. If we sensed you didn't like something, we would begin to defer to you, and you probably wouldn't even notice it at first. What the four of us have is wonderful, and I don't want that to change." She wasn't happy. I paused. "Actually, there is one change I want to make."

"What?"

"I thought about what we talked about in Costa Rica and I agree. We need to get married. Remember, you're supposed to tell me when." That distracted and softened the old girl.

Three weeks later, Leigh took all of us to a Louie's brunch. When I told Doug on the way out of the house that I couldn't wait to swap insults with Marvin and watch him pretend to bang his head on the sea-grape branch, there was the silence that is prologue to bad news.

"What now?"

"Marvin died while you were gone, John, heart attack. We didn't want to tell you while you were down there because you were already sad. They had the memorial service at Louie's."

Before I could say anything, Leigh said: "Tell him the good part, Doug."

"The day after the memorial service, there was a bad storm with high winds, and it broke that sea-grape branch completely off."

"You're making that up."

"I swear. No one could believe it."

I didn't know whether to laugh or cry.

When the four of us walked in, a hostess I didn't know passed us off to someone else I didn't know, who seated us and asked: "Is this your first time here?" Leigh grabbed my hand to shut me up and made nice.

They began ribbing Tom about his latest teacher-on-vacation conquest.

"The National Education Association needs to give you a plaque for making the nation's teachers happy," Leigh teased, and he blushed. "I've heard they're taking up a collection to do a bronze replica of your pecker to hang in their headquarters."

"*Leigh*!" He looked around to see if anyone had heard.

"It's OK, kid," Doug kicked in. "Your secret's safe with us." Then he did a pretend 'raise-the-voice': "Yeah, the fact that you've got the biggest dick east of the Mississippi is safe with us, I swear." Tom turned beet red, and we all started laughing. This was what I needed.

We ordered our traditional port at the end of the meal. When it arrived, Leigh's extravagance at paying for the brunch, always suspect, was shown to have a motive.

"Let's talk," she started. I knew from the tone of voice that I was about to be strongly "advised", like the night on the seawall when she'd convinced Doug and me to move into Southernmost House for the summer.

"The problem we have before us is that you can't afford the Bakery anymore and have to sell it." Hearing the truth, bluntly put, hurt.

Tom looked stricken. "You mean sell it and go somewhere else?"

"I'm afraid so. But calm down, kid. You guys sell the place—the market's hot now—and now you have money."

Tom stopped her. "They have money, Leigh, but what's gonna happen to me? I don't have nothing."

"Dollar, dammit." No laughter and no protest. Instead, an eyes not meeting eyes moment of silence.

"What?"

"Well, Tom, you do have some money," Leigh said.

"What are you talking about?"

"Katie gave you some money, but didn't want you to know about it. She gave it to me to take care of for you."

Tom jumped up. "You guys hid this from me? Where is it?"

Leigh gave him a hard look. "Young man, sit back down, now. John and Doug, go down to the bar for a few minutes. Tom and I need to talk."

Leigh's wrath was something no man had balls big enough to face. We left gladly as Tom sat back down.

Five minutes later, Leigh waved to us to come back and ordered a second round of port.

"I've just explained to Tom that Katie gave me twenty-five thousand dollars for him, and he wasn't supposed to know about it, and that I was supposed to take care of it for him. I put it in zero coupon bonds when interest rates were high, then when interest rates went down, the value of the bonds went up, you know, the inverse relationship." She shook her head at our incomprehension. "OK, dumb asses, why do I bother? Anyway, the kid has a portfolio of fifty thousand now, actually $49,679 as of Friday's close. I doubled his money. He will now apologize to all of us." She looked over at him.

He stood up. "I apologize. Leigh's right. If I'd had the money, I'd have frittered it away or spent it on that shit."

"Thank you, Tom, now sit back down, and let's get back to business. You guys sell the Bakery, and you all have money. Then we all move to John's house in Costa Rica."

Stunned silence.

"Listen to me. You know I'm better at this stuff than you. The house down there is paid for, and the utilities, taxes, and insurance are less than a thousand dollars a year." She looked at me for confirmation, and I nodded.

"So this is what we do. We all move down there. Three bedrooms and three bathrooms, so we all have privacy. Doug and Tom can build a place for themselves on the property to start, and the three of you start designing and building houses for the gringos moving there after we've settled in and you decide you need to go back to work. You have more skills and better taste than anything else I saw going on down there. Tom maybe falls in love with a Costa Rican beauty and gets married and builds a house for them on the property and makes a few babies for us to spoil." She looked at him. "It's probably time you stopped screwing around, kid. You're special and need to find a good woman to make happy and settle down."

She turned to Doug. "You, too. I've heard those Costa Rican gay boys are lots sweeter and more innocent than the boys up here. It's time you got a partner we can all spoil. Then the two of you are on the property and we have our own compound: Tom and family, Doug and partner, and John and I. How sweet is that?

"Plus, John's always threatening to start writing, so now he's free to do it. That sweet children's story about the windmill angels on the lake was a good warm-up.

"The icing on the cake is that I have always wanted to do my own line of designer clothes, and that's what I'll do. I found out that the wife of the Minister of Culture is also a Cliffie"—she explained that to Tom—"and she's going to get me through all that god-awful Latin American bureaucracy. I want to start a little factory and employ a lot of poor, young women. We'll make clothes so awesome that New York, Paris, and Milan will all beg to have them on their runways. So, what do you think? Am I brilliant, or what? And remember, we can always come back here or go somewhere else if we decide we don't like it."

More stunned silence. How could I not love this woman who always tried to heal my pain, praised me when I rose to be my better self, went on attack to protect the kid, was beautiful, nailed the French subjunctive in every tense, and was a great lay?

The next two weeks were unsettling as we talked the idea back and forth, and then individually and jointly decided to do it. The decision was hardest on Doug because, born and raised on the island, it was his home in every sense. The decision was easiest on Tom, because he'd lived in Key West the least time and, for him, it was special mostly because he'd found us, a surrogate family.

Leigh, though I knew the idea had to be painful for her, too, acted all business-like. WASPs, for all their faults, are as tough as you get.

I was torn. I'd finally found a place that felt home and didn't want to leave it. Chance gave me the sign that it was time.

An architect called Doug to do a pre-bid walk-through on a job and I accompanied him. When he turned the truck onto Peacon Lane, I had a horrible premonition, which proved itself out when he stopped in front of Henry Faulkner's old house, my first construction job in Key West. Doug sensed something was wrong and asked me about it.

"I'll tell you later."

In the building industry, architects are the most arrogant and least respected members of the trades. The 'cover-my-butt and throw-the-contractor-under-the-bus' language of the standard AIA contract is something anyone else in the trades would be ashamed to ask another man to sign. Most architects had no shame, and nearly all of them held unearned pretensions to Frank Lloyd Wright or Phillip Johnson talent. Only two architects on the island could draw stairs that could be built as drawn. We saved their asses over and over again.

The architect waiting on the porch to lead us through the house was the worst on the island. He wedded Ivy League arrogance to the least knowledge of the trades and was notorious for blaming contractors and subcontractors for his own mistakes, then refusing to authorize payment for correcting them. On one job, he had watched as men began shooting concrete onto the walls of a free-form pool he'd designed, then yelled at them to stop, accusing them of having dug the hole too wide. The contractor ordered his men to continue shooting with the architect yelling that he was going to make them jack-hammer all the concrete out. The contractor got out the plans, pointed to the drawn dimensions, then had two of his men measure the hole, wall to wall. Dead on.

"I don't care what I put on the plans," the architect screamed. "That's not what I meant," causing the nine men building the pool to burst out laughing.

'Try putting that line in Yale's architectural curriculum,' I had thought.

Now, that same Mr. 'That's not what I meant' passed out plans to those of us on the porch and briefly explained what the new owners wanted to do, then led us indoors. The first and most striking element inside was the Szuter-designed structural bookcase, which the architect made fun of. "The first thing I want demolished," he said, "is this silly bookcase so we can put up a proper wall." The other men there for the walk-through snickered agreement, courtiers praising a king's fart. Only Doug spoke up that he thought it was cool, even though he didn't know Thomas was its author.

I told Doug I'd wait for him outside. When he rejoined me, I told him the history. "Doug, that's my sign. Thomas is telling me it's time to leave."

It hurt when the realtor's sign went up on the front of the Bakery. How do you sell a piece of your heart, a piece of your soul, a piece of your history? One day, back for lunch, listening to the realtor describe square footage, wall and floor finishes to a prospective buyer, I had to run upstairs and pay homage to white porcelain. This wasn't a 'property': it was a home, and a real piece of the island's history.

An offer came in. Two men from the Carolinas who appreciated our work made us an offer, which we countered, and in ten days it was done. I would have $209,000, Doug would have $209,000, Tom had $51,997 at yesterday's close. Part of the deal included leaving most of the furniture in return for a closing delayed long enough for the things we wanted to ship to Costa Rica to arrive there.

We ordered a container and loaded it one morning, then watched as the truck driver drove off with our entire history towards Miami and an ocean freighter. Strange, I thought, as I watched the truck turn left at the end of the street and disappear.

Doug and I started finishing up his jobs. I said goodbye to Hagel, who promised he'd come down and build something, and then I flew down to Costa Rica when the container was coming to the house. I emptied it, put everything away, then flew back.

Two days later, it was time to say goodbye. Leigh asked Doug to go to the airport with Tom to give me and her time alone to say our own goodbyes.

We called a taxi and walked out of the Bakery for the last time. I couldn't look back. She held my hand.

In the cab, I explained to the driver we needed to make two stops before he took us to the airport and understood the meter would keep running.

"Simonton Beach," Leigh said. It was a quiet ride downtown. When we got to the end of Simonton Street, we got out of the car and walked to the edge of the water. The city had now paved most of the land to the water's edge and installed parking meters in addition to the toilet building I'd already seen. Homeless people were camped out next to the building and in the trees that separated the property from the hotels on both sides.

Leigh and I held hands and walked out on the short pier and looked across to the channel marker. A Coast Guard cutter made its way through the now cloudy water of the harbor, and some of the men on deck waved and we waved back. We stood on the dock for a while, both silent, both mourning a shared past. On the way back to the taxi, a woman approached us for a handout. Leigh gave her twenty dollars and a card with Magdalen House's phone number. "Call them and go there, sweetheart. They'll help you get back on your feet."

"White Street Pier next, please," I told the cabbie. When we got to the end of White Street and got out, Leigh and I put our arms around each other and walked to the AIDS Memorial: black granite slabs cut into the paved approach to the pier, with the names of the victims engraved, over a thousand names. We walked slowly along the recumbent tombstones and picked out aloud all the ones we'd known and danced with . . . Conkle, Formica, Andrews, Bond, Leavesley, McArthur, MacIlheeny, Meyers, Fleming, and then, *that* one—Thomas Szuter—and Leigh started crying.

Two young kids walked past, headed out on the pier with fishing rods. Two seagulls squawked overhead.

On the way back to the cab, a tourist couple came up to us. "Are you guys from here?"

Leigh told them we were.

"Can you tell us where Jimmy Buffett's house is?"

"Jimmy doesn't live here anymore," she told them. "He lives in Palm Beach now."

They walked away, shaking their heads, disappointed or not sure whether to believe her.

"Airport," I told the cabbie. We met Tom and Doug in the waiting room.

Half an hour later, the roar of engines . . . then up over Stock Island, across Key Haven and Charles' house, and Channel Key where we had scattered Thomas' ashes. . . .

We had three hours in Miami, so I took everyone to the restaurant at the top of the Airport Hotel. We took a table near the windows so we could watch the planes. Leigh, Doug, and I were subdued, but Tom was goofy and excited.

"Dad, can I have a motorcycle down there? It's not the United States. Besides, I got my own money now so I can buy one if I want." He strutted the words out, testing the waters.

"Oh, you think so. You think we raised you this far to let you wrap yourself around a Costa Rican telephone pole. Forget it. No way. This requires a family vote. Motorcycle for young Tom? Let's see the hands." His was the only one raised.

"Look, we'll get you a horse, instead." He registered disappointment for a second, then "horse" registered.

"Serious? I can have a horse?"

"Why not? There's ten acres for it and everybody rides them down there. There's even a three-day horse race around the lake every year.

Just don't break your neck falling off it."

"Oh, man, I'm gonna have a horse! I don't believe it." He looked at me skeptically. "You're not playing one of your jokes now? A real horse."

"A real horse you have to take care of."

"A horse. Serious now, dad? You're not fucking with me? My own horse?"

"Of course. Who else will it belong to?"

"Can I pick it out?"

"With Leigh's help. I'm sure she's been to the Saratoga auctions."

Leigh stuck her tongue out—of course she had—Doug laughed, and Tom bounced around in his seat like a kid getting his first car.

"Hey, what about a dog? Can I have a dog, too?"

"Don't push your luck."

Leigh butt in. "I don't care how early it is, I need a drink."

"Me, too," Doug said.

Two Bloody Mary's later, I felt better, and then it was time to leave.

Again, a roar of engines. We lifted off, turned west out across the Everglades, Florida Bay, and then below us the little chain of islands and, at the end of the little chain, Key West.

"It looks so tiny and fragile from up here," Leigh whispered. "One burp from the ocean, and it would all be gone. Hard to believe that little rock created so much magic." She put her fingers to her lips, then touched the window. "Goodbye, Thomas; goodbye little island—and thank you." She looked back at me. "OK?"

"Overwhelmed, but OK I guess. Bittersweet moment—sad and happy." She pointed across the aisle where Tom had just put something down Doug's back. Tom looked over at us, and in time with some music on his headphones pretended to be holding reins and galloping on a horse and gave us a thumbs up.

She went back to looking out the window as we passed over Cuba and, while she looked down, I looked at her. She turned back from the window. "What?"

"If I told you, you'd make fun."

"Tell me."

"I was just thinking of how much I love you. Now make fun of that."

"Well, that brings me to some business we have to take care of."

"What business?"

She took my hand, looked me in the eyes, and in an uncharacteristically soft voice said: "John, it's time."

"Time for what?"

"Time for THAT."

"That what?"

"Time for you to propose, dummy, but we have to do pre-nups."

"Pre-nups? What pre-nups?"

She reached under her seat for her purse and got out paper and pen. She drew a line down the middle of the paper and headed one half John, one half Leigh.

"Alright, one for one. I go first." In her column, she wrote: "Always and forever my own separate bathroom" and she underlined separate. She handed me the paper. "Your turn." In my mind, I quickly designed a second bathroom off the master bedroom in the house we were headed to.

My turn. "You let us cook anything more complicated than oatmeal." She snorted at that.

"With pleasure." She took the pad back. "You stop offering to pick up the whole tab every time we eat out with other people."

I took the pad. "You stop dividing the bill to the penny. Split it equally even if someone has more than their share." She didn't like that one, but agreed.

"You tell me honestly and immediately if you ever stop loving me," was her next.

I looked her straight in the eye. "I promise to love you to my dying breath. I'm never going to love another woman." She stared for a moment. I think WASP princess almost started to cry.

I wrote: "You never have sex with another man." She shrugged like that was easy and took the paper back.

Her turn. "If we fly the Atlantic, it's always in first class."

Damn! Damn! Damn! I suppose every human being can be corrupted. Once you've turned left boarding a 747 for the flight across the pond, it's not easy to board right again. She had a big grin on her face. I conceded, and a WASP disguised as a camel's nose entered the tent.

My turn. "You tell me how big your trust fund is." She didn't like that one *at all*. She sat for a few minutes looking out the window, tapping pen on the pad, debating with herself, then turned back to me.

"How did I know you were going to ask that? Why do you need to know?"

"Because I want to know how big a dowry to ask for."

"Always the jokester. Let me ask you again. Why do you need to know that, Mr. Dumb-Ass About Money?"

"OK, let's get serious here for a minute. You obviously have a big chunk of money, and we get married. What if something happens to you before me, god forbid."

Her expression changed.

"Ha! You hadn't thought about that, had you? Do I inherit if we're married. I don't want the money or need it. Where does it go? You need to cut me in on what's there and what you want done with it."

She looked out the window for almost a full minute, then turned back. "Alright, I'll tell you, but only on the wedding night and only if you never tell anyone else."

"Sweetheart, that better be the wedding night of all wedding nights, memorable, twelve on a scale of one to ten. The earth better shake and that volcano spit fire. You rich girls are experts at the old 'bait and switch.'"

"It will be memorable, I promise."

"How memorable?"

"*Memorable*, memorable. So do it."

"Do what?"

"Propose . . . and on bended knee." A familiar tone of voice, a command, but she was grinning. "I want a proper proposal if I'm going to be respectable. And I want a ring. I can't believe I'm going to marry into the peasantry. My ancestors must be rolling over in their graves."

"I don't have a ring."

"Pathetic. You always let us know how smart you are. Get one."

An idea came to me. I got up and went to the galley where the attendants were loading the drink cart. I told them what I needed and why, and they immediately pitched in. Who doesn't love romance? I got two different-colored garbage bag ties and wrapped them together into a ring. On my way back up the aisle, one of the attendants got on the intercom: "Ladies and gentlemen, the drinks will be a little late because 20E is about to propose marriage to 20F." Everyone started looking around and some stood up. Doug and Tom figured out it was us and were standing up with big grins on their faces when I walked back.

"Is this for real?" Doug asked.

"For real." I showed him the ring.

"No, wait. Tom has something he was going to give to Leigh. Use it." He turned to Tom who dug out his wallet and pulled something out and handed it to me. It was a gold band with his chipped *Atocha* emerald mounted and held in place by tiny gold filaments.

"Tom, I can't take this. I know what it means to you."

"Dad, it means less than what you and Leigh mean to me. It was going to be a birthday present for Leigh anyway. Use it."

I took it, then turned to Leigh. She stood up, and before I went down on one knee, I held her and whispered in her ear, the entire cabin quiet and watching. "Leigh, this is serious now. Swear to me you love me, promise me this will last forever, and that it will never be ordinary."

She whispered back: "I love you, John, it will last forever, and nothing that begins this way or has anything to do with you and me is ever going to be ordinary. Now on your knees."

I knelt. "Leigh Farley Dickinson, will you marry me and be my wife?"

"I would be honored and happy to be your wife, John Wesley Cottrell." I opened my hand with the ring in it, and when she recognized the emerald she shot Tom a look. "I'll deal with you later, young man." He grinned as I slipped on her finger a ring whose stone had been on the ocean floor below us for three hundred years. I stood up to kiss her and the cabin broke into applause. Tom and Doug slapped me on the back and gave Leigh big hugs and kisses.

When we sat back down, the flight attendants gave the four of us non-stop champagne from first class. As we began our slow descent over the volcanoes in Lake Nicaragua towards the airport in Costa Rica, Leigh and I squeezed hands, and she rested her head on my shoulder.

The plane landed, and the pilots and flight attendants congratulated the two of us on our way out. We cleared customs and immigration and walked outside and were greeted by Carlos, who loaded us into the car and drove us off.

An hour and a half later, we climbed the hill to my house and unloaded. I fixed us drinks, put Keith Jarrett on the stereo and lit a fire. We all walked outside to look at the volcano, lake, and windmills. Tom and Doug went back inside. Doug sat down on the sofa. Tom checked that the atlas was on the shelf under the coffee table and plopped down on the sofa, head in Doug's lap.

Leigh and I put our arms around each other. Their conversation and laughter came through the windows and open door: "Doug, you get a horse, too, and we can ride all over the place together. And you need to help me talk the old man into letting me have a dog, OK?"

Leigh and I laughed, then stood looking at the earthly beauty before us.

"I love you, John," she whispered, and pulled tighter into me.

"I love you, too," I whispered back.

"Thomas is here. I feel it."

"I know. He's how we got here, I think. How sweet is it that we wound up in one of his best houses?"

Then Tom, country boy at heart, put on a country-rock song, and they came back out on the porch. "Come on, guys, I'm so happy. Let's dance."

Moonlight sparkling on lake, volcano steaming away . . . brother, son, and love of my life dancing and laughing together, I declared personal victory. A life's voyage I had imperfectly plotted, but whose every leg I had examined closely, had led me to a destination I could never have guessed at, here, with these three people, and the joy I felt was reward. Grace had been granted me again.

We laughed and danced as life's elusive meaning danced through us. I was happy.

A week later, as Carlos led them on an exploration of the forest behind the house, I sat down at my desk, feeling panic before the tyranny of the first blank page. I paused, then looked above my desk at a torn-paper collage of a plant in bloom, a photo of me sitting in a rowboat in the middle of a swimming pool, and a sign that said "TRANQUILO, TRANQUILO".

"Once upon a time," I began, "shortly after I turned thirty, I moved to a tiny tropical island far out to sea . . ."

Acknowledgements

I could not have written the book without the encouragement of many. To my test readers: Max and Mary Rendall, Carol Stroud, Gail Chambers, Lynn Kaufelt, John and Merrilee Dickinson, John and Cathy Nicholas, Dolores Sizemore, Elaine London and Wayson Choy, I extend my enduring gratitude.

May Sandra and Lee McMannis, who gave me a beautiful and quiet place to write, have many happy years on the island.

Many thanks to my fellow islander and fellow Francophile, Rosalind Brackenbury, for her insightful comments on the manuscript.

Gratitude and thanks to all my construction buddies on the island—my tribe—for the camaraderie and friendship throughout the years. It is true that we work harder but have more fun than anyone else.

Above all others, I would like to thank Tomas Kozel for running the business while I wrote, and Angela Fina, whose constant encouragement and a lifetime of conversation make her midwife.

This is a novel in the form of a memoir, a work of fiction that weaves real and invented characters into both real and invented events. John Cottrell, Leigh, Doug, Rudy, Maria, Dolores, young Tom, the entire

Delacorte clan, Katie Fritzlen, Steve and Alice, James and Emily, Mrs. Thompson, the police chief, Phillip (the DEA agent), and Luis Aguilar are all fictional characters and any resemblance to anyone living or dead is coincidental and unintentional.

The preservation of Simonton Beach did come from the outrage of the island's citizens, but this version of it, involving a drug deal, is fictional.

My apologies to my Key West readers who will recognize events I have displaced in time to help me construct a manageable narrative.

The island floating in its beautiful waters is real.